PRAISE FOR FILTER THIS

'Ali is one of the best flawed heroines in Irish commercial fiction since Rachel Walsh in Marian Keyes' ground-breaking *Rachel's Holiday*' *The Sunday Times*

'Hyper current ... hugely relevant' *Irish Independent*

'Hilarious. Like Sophie Kinsella for the Instagram world' *Irish Examiner*

'Shades of Marian Keyes in this highly entertaining satire' *Sunday Independent*

'Witty and wonderful – I devoured this in a single sitting' *Image*

'A cracking read' *Woman's Way*

'Modern and witty'
Emer McLysaght, co-author of the Aisling books

'So sweet, so funny – I loved it' Marian Keyes

'Fresh, current and thoroughly enjoyable' Eithne Shortall

'Written with heart and humour, *Filter This* peels back the social-media mask so many wear as a disguise and reveals the real people beneath' Cecelia Ahern

Sophie White writes regularly for the *Sunday Independent*, *Irish Independent*, *IMAGE* and *Irish Tatler*, and has been nominated three times for Journalist of the Year at the Irish Magazine Awards. She is co-host of the chart-topping podcasts: *Mother Of Pod* (comedy), *The Creep Dive* (comedy) and *The Vulture Club* (pop culture and commentary). She also co-founded *Rogue Collective*, an online space for creative non-fiction, long-form journalism and multimedia works.

She lives in Dublin with her husband and three sons. *Unfiltered* is her second novel.

Instagram: @SophWhiteWhoop
Twitter: @SophWhiteWhoop
www.sophiewhite.info

Also by Sophie White
FICTION
Filter This

NON-FICTION
Recipes for a Nervous Breakdown

Sophie White

Unfiltered

HACHETTE
BOOKS
IRELAND

First published in Ireland in 2020 by HACHETTE BOOKS IRELAND

1

Cataloguing in Publication Data is available from the British Library

Trade paperback ISBN 9781529343427
Ebook ISBN 9781529343410
Audio ISBN 9781529331394

Typeset in AGaramond by Bookends Publishing Services, Dublin
Printed and bound in Great Britain by Clays Ltd, Elcograf, S.p.A

Hachette Books Ireland policy is to use papers that are natural, renewable and
recyclable products and made from wood grown in sustainable forests. The logging
and manufacturing processes are expected to conform to the environmental
regulations of the country of origin.

Hachette Books Ireland
8 Castlecourt Centre
Castleknock
Dublin 15, Ireland

A division of Hachette UK Ltd
Carmelite House, 50 Victoria Embankment, EC4Y 0DZ

www.hachettebooksireland.ie

For our dads, Kevin Linehan and David White –
funny, kind, unfailingly generous, the ultimate mensches

Chapter 1

Ali woke up in her childhood bed on the morning of her dad's funeral with a song in her head. 'God Only Knows' by the Beach Boys. Memories of long-gone Saturday mornings when Miles would sing the Beach Boys as he ambled down the creaking stairs of their ramshackle three-storey Georgian villa by the sea to make rasher sandwiches drifted through her head.

Ali closed her eyes and felt a loss so vast it was like falling. What will I be without you? Even though her dad had been drifting away from them for years, his Alzheimer's advancing at a glacial pace, in the past two years it seemed that as fast as he'd forgotten her, she'd forgotten him. Or at least she'd forgotten the Miles she'd grown up with – who he was before the vacant stare and food-stained pyjamas.

She rolled over, burying her face in the pillow, and was hit unexpectedly by a glimpse of Miles from her teens, trying to get her up for school. A wet facecloth to the face was his main method. Truly evil. She smiled into the damp pillow.

What'll I be without you … ?

And what will I be with you? She poked her belly and sighed. Very hard to believe there was a blueberry-sized Sam–Ali mash-up cruising around in there. And, according to the pregnancy calculator she and her best friend Liv had consulted five days before, she was already almost eleven weeks along. And Sam, the father and her former, sort-of boyfriend still didn't know. Even worse, she was pretty sure he never wanted to see her again.

Her phone buzzed under her pillow. A calendar reminder to share a #spon post about a pregnancy supplement. Awkward. She cancelled the reminder, opened the calendar and scrolled through the endless scheduled sponcon leading all the way to September and her fictional due date. Fucking hell, who has a fictional due date? Then she spotted the email notification and felt a swell of sickening anxiety. She had been ignoring all notifications in the five days since she'd been exposed as a pregnancy faker – there was a tsunami of hatred in her inbox just poised to hit her should she wish to read any of it – but this email address caught her eye: dholmes@rte.ie. The subject line read: *Prime Time Investigates.* She gingerly tapped the message to expand it.

Ms. Jones,

David Holmes here. I am a researcher on Prime Time *and was hoping to speak to you about participating in a special episode focusing on public shaming. We are keen to work with you to get your side of the story heard. To provide balance, we are also approaching some of the victims of your scheme and the creator of the below video. I know it may be a daunting prospect for you but please don't worry, we will endeavour to present you as fairly as possible...*

Ali glanced at the linked YouTube video at the bottom of the email and threw the phone to the bottom of the bed. *Why the Internet Hates Ali Jones (The Full Story with Receipts!!!!)* UGH. Ali groaned. She'd been staying as far from the internet as possible to avoid exactly this kind of thing.

She stared at the pale-green, glow-in-the-dark stars stuck to the ceiling above her, mandatory in all teenage girls' rooms. *I am not watching it. I'm not, I'm not,* even as she sat up and searched through the duvet for the phone.

It's self-harm, Ali. Do not watch that crap.

She retrieved the phone. *I'll just skim-watch it. I need to know what they're saying.* She loaded the video. Gleeful voiceover narrated the screenshots of her Instagram account before finally settling on the picture of her in an unflattering dress that sparked an immense outpouring of congratulations about her being pregnant when she was most certainly not.

'Ali Jones was just your average insta-nobody until she was announced as a wild card nomination at the 2019 Glossie Influencer Awards. On the day her nomination was announced, it seemed Jones had even more exciting revelations to come. An Instagram post appeared to be breadcrumbing a pregnancy reveal and when host Blake Jordan welcomed her to the stage, she made it official.'

'That is not what happened,' Ali hissed as footage of Blake Jordan on the stage at the Glossies WildCard launch appeared. He was holding the envelope that contained her name and keeping the audience in suspense. 'Phew, sorry for that *pregnant* pause there! Though our next nominee knows all about that... Please welcome Ali Jones and her "little surprise" to the stage!' he crowed.

Ali clearly remembered panicking as she struggled through the crowd to the stage. She had just come from her dad's nursing home, she recalled. It had been a very bleak day. She watched herself scrambling up on stage, helped by two waiters. After she was installed on the third plinth beside the other nominees, Blake had tried to get some banter out of her but it was clear from the video she was utterly paralysed by his announcement of her supposed pregnancy.

If I could just go back to that moment… Ali knew regrets were futile but it was surreal watching the exact point when her life went into a tailspin. Of course, at the time, she was so obsessed with getting big on Instagram and trying anything – drinking, outfits of the day, getting her lips plumped – to distract herself from her dad's horrendous decline that she didn't immediately correct Blake. *Why didn't I just explain?*

She watched as Blake clicked his fingers in front of her face to try and snap her out of her reverie.

'You dilating, hun?!'

Here it was, Ali held her breath as the Ali on screen finally spoke, unwittingly setting in motion the events that would ultimately lead to her downfall and this very fucking real baby she was now carrying:

'Sorry! I was just saying I'm going to double in size, LOL.'

Ugh. Ali X'd out of the video and buried her face back in her pillow.

The last few months of faking pregnancy symptoms on her Instagram to gain followers – she'd gained over 100,000 in the end – felt like a deranged fever dream. If only it had been. And now she was pregnant for real.

What on earth had she been thinking, telling everyone she was pregnant for a few followers and a shot at being named influencer of the year? Of course if it had just been strangers online that would've been one thing but she'd dragged Sam down with her. Every time she thought of Sam, who she had allowed to believe was the father of her fake baby, she felt a despair so profound it scared her.

God, how did it all get so fucked? A squirm of sickness in her tummy seemed to be answering her.

'It was a rhetorical question,' she muttered to her stomach. It was mad how utterly blindsided she'd felt when she saw the positive pregnancy test and then how quickly she'd come around to the idea. The baby was like a little beacon of promise and hope amid the dreariness of planning her dad's funeral, being cast out by the Insta world and being publicly shamed online.

'It must be a biological quirk.' Liv had laughed grimly in a voicenote the night before, when Ali mentioned her growing optimism. 'There's no way you should be buzzing over this baby. You don't know anything about babies. My sister says parenthood is hellish. And *she's* got a husband. How're you going to raise it?'

'We'll raise it together!' Ali'd mugged, to Liv's annoyance. 'Or we'll convince Sam to move in with us and we can be sister wives while he does the night feeds.'

Despite her joking, Ali knew that telling Sam was not going to be easy. She hadn't heard from him since he'd found out that the baby that she'd claimed to be expecting with him was an elaborate Insta-sham. And he'd found out in the worst possible way, stumbling across the thesis on Instagram that Liv had been working on for her master's. Page after page had detailed Ali's Insta-insanity. Then her dad had died just hours later, and the world had dropped out of orbit.

In the past five days, in between disbelief at her father's death and planning the funeral, she'd sent lengthy texts and voicenotes pleading with Sam to talk to her. And nothing. He'd blue-ticked every single one but not a word back – torture, 2019-style. Sometimes in the elaborate showdowns she waged in her head at night, she wanted to retaliate. 'I didn't *tell* you the baby was yours. You just assumed after the timing fit our botched Tinder date. And *you* insisted you wanted to be part of it,' she'd go, on the defensive, then she'd hear how she sounded. Completely batshit.

Of course, everyone online thought she was completely batshit too. Screengrabs of the fateful pic she'd drunkenly posted after Blake Jordan's announcement at the Glossies showing a positive pregnancy test had trended online in the last few days. There were even memes of it going around, the haphazard caption 'So excited to officially announce my *pegnancy*' had been ripe for mockery.

'TFW you're fake pregnant but too stupid to spell it right' read one meme. Someone had even added the word 'pegnant' to Urban Dictionary. The definition read: 'A dumb whore who lies about being pregnant for attention.'

Sighing, she pulled up her inbox again, deleting the one from *Prime Time* and scanning the hundreds of other emails. She hadn't opened any but the subject lines were vitriolic. 'You deserve to die' and 'Women like you are why victims of abuse are not believed'. The deluge of hate had been relentless. Still, coinciding, as it did, with the death of her father had given Ali a sharp shock of perspective. Her whole Insta-scheme was mortifying but, let's face it, trivial when compared with the stark brutality of death.

On the less demented end of the inbox spectrum were countless riffs on 'Termination of contract' and 'Ambassadorship revoked' from the many brands she'd worked with during her brief spell as Ireland's hottest up-and-coming mumfluencer. At least there was no need to email any of the PRs with some cobbled-together excuse – the one upside of cataclysmic public disgrace.

I'm clutching at straws, she thought as she dragged herself out of the bed and began trawling through her bag for something to wear.

Ali'd spent the last five days locked in some bizarre alternate funeral dimension, sitting around the kitchen in her mum's house with a constantly rotating cast of family and friends drinking tea and boozing at odd hours of the day and night, fortified with endless rounds of boiled ham and gross mayonnaisey salads. At this stage, all she wanted to do was go home to the house she shared with Liv.

Her mum, Mini, had entered a strange phase of grief that involved becoming bizarrely fixated on tiny details like the socks Miles was to be cremated in and ignoring massively important decisions such as where to even have the funeral. Mini had hired and fired several priests (Ali hadn't even known you could do that) before deciding that an actor friend of Miles's would 'MC' the funeral.

'That's not a thing,' Ali had tried to protest but gave in when she realised that she had far more important things to talk Mini out of, such as the six pallbearers wearing chef whites in honour of Miles's career as a restaurateur.

'Fine, fine, you want him to have a boring "normal" funeral. Fine, the boys can wear suits. But we're keeping Eric on MC duties. He's already finalised the soliloquy.'

'You mean … eulogy?' Ali was iffy.

'I mean soliloquy.' Mini was steely, holding Ali's gaze.

While Mini focused on the more esoteric aspects of the funeral, Ali had become the production manager of the entire affair, traipsing around pricing horrific, carb-heavy buffets in bland hotels that Miles would have detested.

Ali was relieved that it was all going to be over in a matter of hours and the Mini madness would hopefully end. Then it would be on to the far more complicated task of sorting out her life. She knew people baby-proofed their home ahead of a new baby's arrival. She'd need to baby-proof her whole bloody life. She flashed on the shambolic state of her room in the house she shared with Liv. Before, she'd like to think her discarded half-eaten takeaways and empty booze bottles stashed everywhere said 'insouciant wild child' but, aesthetically, the vibe was probably a bit more 'cry for help'. How on earth would a baby fit into that picture?

She shook the question from her head. First things first, get Miles sorted. Then tell Mini about the baby. Then tell Sam. Then get on with figuring out how to *work* a baby and pretending everything was fine.

My speciality, she thought ruefully.

Now among the posters and relics of her teens, Ali pulled off her pyjamas and slipped on her dad's old Velvet Underground tee-shirt that she'd cut into a crop top. She zipped up the simple black pinafore dress she'd chosen. It was definitely weird, she decided, having eight different Harry Styles watching you get dressed for your father's funeral.

'Liv's here, Ali!' she heard Mini call from downstairs.

Thank God. Ali pulled on her Docs, headed out the door and down to the kitchen. Not the kitchen of her childhood, they'd had it redone. Now it was a kind of glass-box-style extension – practically a mandatory addition to affluent Dublin homes during the boom years. Its sleek lines and stark atmosphere jarred with the rest of the house, which was still all sagging sofas and warm wood panelling, the shelves stooped under the weight of books and records.

Liv was backed up against the concrete-topped island, a plate of boiled ham already in hand, being booze-bullied into wine by Ali's aunt Eleanor.

'Is it even 10 a.m. yet?' Liv murmured helplessly as Eleanor thrust the enormous glass of white into her hand.

'This is how the Irish do funerals,' one of Mini and Eleanor's distant cousins told her, apparently not realising that Liv, her dark skin and brown eyes courtesy of Meera, her Indian mother, was Irish. He was part of the American contingent, who had arrived late last night and played the piano till 3 a.m. Ali'd met each of them about a million times, but they had all coalesced into a freckly mass of middle-aged, Irish American man meat.

Ali drew Liv away to the farthest corner of the kitchen, where they could avoid the funeral chat in which the main topic of conversation seemed to be who else had recently died.

'I'm counting down the hours till we can go home,' Ali whispered to Liv. 'At least *you* can drink through this misery.'

'Yeah, it's definitely taking the edge off the mourning,' Liv agreed. 'How are you doing?'

'I don't really know. I feel really numb about Dad. I just can't keep it straight in my head that all this has happened. Any of it. I feel like the last months weren't even real. I *wish* they weren't real. I keep thinking of all the times I sat up in his room at the nursing home just reading the internet until it was time to go. Some days, I'd barely look at him, Liv.' Ali stared at the picture of Miles on the wall above them. Miles on his wedding day, squinting into the sun with confetti in his shaggy blond hair and a flower in the lapel of his grey jacket. 'He's my age there.'

'You look so like him, it's crazy.'

'That's not how he looked at the end.' Ali had a flash of his cracked lips and blank eyes. This grief pain was something new and horrible. She wanted to cry and scream but felt paralysed.

'Try not to think of him like that.' Liv took her hand and Ali wished it helped.

'Why not? It's what he was at the end. And I did nothing. Nothing. I just keep thinking of the times when he needed me, and I couldn't even bring myself to kiss him because I was so ...' she searched for the word '… so afraid. God, I'm a monster. There's literally no other word for me. I'm a monster. Who ignores their dad when he's so goddamn helpless? Running around pretending to be pregnant and loving life on the 'gram?'

'Ali, please don't do this to yourself … you did everything you could … you were up there all the time …'

She doesn't understand. Ali stared down at their hands, gripped in her lap. She doesn't realise.

'You don't get it, Liv. I deserve to feel like shit. I am shit. All these people are right.' Ali waved her phone.

'Ali. They are internet trolls. You can't read this stuff – it's self-harm. I will take that phone away right now,' she threatened.

'I should be reading it. It's the truth. They're not trolls, all the stuff they're saying is true.' Ali flicked open her inbox. 'I am a "selfish, lying cunt". I am. The way I treated my dad … That's just *fact*, Liv.' Ali wasn't sure why she was getting ratty but at least feeling angry was feeling something. Better than this frightening, fathomless ache. She stood abruptly. 'I need to get the pamphlets from the printer before the funeral car comes. Will you come with me? We've got a couple of hours.'

'Anything you want, pal.' Liv took out her phone. 'Do you wanna do a to-do list? Always makes me feel better.'

Ali managed a grin. Liv's devotion to to-do lists was verging on pathological.

'Yep, sounds comforting. I think I'm going to need several. One for the funeral, one for the public shaming and one for the unplanned pregnancy.' Ali laughed grimly. 'I'll dictate on the way to the printer.'

They slipped through the uncles, some of whom were now singing 'The Banks of My Own Lovely Lee', while two others were having what looked to be a middle-aged attempt at a fist fight. Ali's cousin Lily looked bored as she weakly tried to pull them apart.

'John-John brought up the Christmas Turkey Debacle of '76,' she explained, rolling her eyes.

The funeral sesh was hardcore, so much daytime booze and feelings. They headed for the door just as Mini began calling her from upstairs.

'Jesus, keep going,' Ali muttered to Liv, jogging down the front steps into the misty April day and jumping into Mini's car. Liv hastily buckled her seatbelt as Ali slammed into gear and lurched forward, up the narrow road and away from the house.

Indicating right, Ali started towards the cluster of shops in the nearby village. 'Look, let's to-do list me. It'll take my mind off things.'

Liv opened her PimpMyList app and created three new lists.

Funeral

Public Shaming

Pregnancy

'Let's go from least to most complicated,' Liv suggested, while Ali scouted for a spot to park near the printer's. 'Funeral. Let's put printer's on here so we can tick it off – that always feels good. Outfit?'

'I'm wearing it.' Ali backed into a spot outside the off-licence. *Parallel parking while making a funeral to-do list is an advanced level of adulting*, she mused.

'Is moody Lou Reed smoking a spliff appropriate funeral attire?'

'I'm one of the chief mourners. I could wear a black mankini and people would have to put up with it.'

They headed into the printer's and joined the queue for collections.

'So, I suppose "public shaming" and "pregnancy" kind of intersect,' Liv said cautiously. 'People today are going to have *heard* about Fake BumpGate, Ali.'

Liv was right, of course. In the last few days, Ali had mainly been around the North American branch of the family but, in just a few hours, she'd be facing down a huge crowd – most of whom had surely heard some version of the story by now.

They stepped forward to the desk.

'I'm collecting for Jones,' Ali said and took the hefty envelope proffered. She hugged it to her chest to protect it from the light drizzle as they went back outside.

'I should've included a formal statement in the funeral pamphlet.' Ali sighed. 'Something like "Ali recently changed her medication, prompting her to have a mild psychotic break … all over Instagram".'

'Well. You definitely weren't in your right mind. Could you maybe reference it during the eulogy? Get it said and out of the way?'

Ali laughed. 'Just a quick sidebar? "I'd like to pause in the fond reminiscing and grieving for a moment to clarify that I was drinking and Instagramming heavily during recent months and I am deeply sorry for any of the harm I caused with my actions. Oh, and BTW, I'm pregs for real now!"'

Liv winced. 'It's jarring, you're right. Maybe you don't have to say anything at all about it to anyone today? Who's going to grill the daughter of the dead man?'

The words 'dead man' momentarily winded Ali as she sat in behind the steering wheel. Her dad was a dead man now.

On the drive back to the house, she said little. She tightened her grip on the steering wheel and made the turn to her parents' terrace. It was nearly time to go.

'I haven't even written the eulogy.' Ali stared out to sea after she'd parked in front of her parents' dove-grey house at the end of the row. 'I've sat down a million times to do it but there's nothing coming. It's a bad idea to just wing it, right?'

'Yes.' Liv was firm. She rooted for a pen in the glove compartment and extracted a pamphlet from the printer's package. Ali watched her decisively scribble across the back of it and hand it over. 'Just say this.'

My dad was the most wonderful father to me. I love him so much and I can't believe he's not here anymore. Thank you to everyone who came today to remember him as he was. I'll never stop missing him. We're all better for having had him in our lives.

Ali swallowed hard to push back the tears. Crying didn't help. If anything, she felt worse afterwards – raw and wrung out. This is grief, Ali was realising, there was no relief. You couldn't just cry it out and feel better. How long was it going to be like this?

Liv was on her phone, pulling up PimpMyList again. She added 'Eulogy' to the Funeral list and passed it to Ali. 'Here, tick it off. It'll help.'

Ali pressed the screen to strike off the eulogy.

It *was* oddly satisfying. She imagined wading through her myriad swirling problems and anxieties, striking off each one. She X'd out of the Funeral list, selected the Pregnancy list and added three items:

Go to doctor.

Tell Mini.

Tell Sam.

She added a question mark.

Tell Sam ...?

❖

Ali sat nervously in the front row of the Victorian chapel where Miles's distinctly showbiz funeral was underway. She swallowed repeatedly but couldn't seem to calm the swelling angst. Her throat felt tight and her breathing was constricted. Projected onto the wall in front of her

13

was a scrolling slideshow of Miles's life. Young, blond Miles looking rakish in a panama hat and flares in an impossibly sunny Stephen's Green. Miles in a Breton tee squinting into the sunshine. Miles and Mini tanned and relaxed in a village in northern Spain.

Baby Ali began appearing as the shoulder pads and bleached perms gave way to the grungier look of the early '90s, the nostalgia-tinged Polaroids to the harsher, red-eye-strewn snaps of the pre-smartphone age. The slideshow was beautiful – she'd stayed up late hunched over her laptop lost in the old holidays and raucous house parties of her childhood putting it together. Between her and the projected scrolling feed, the coffin squatted heavy and dreadful.

She snuck a look over her shoulder. It was terrible to be on show like this, in front of hundreds of people. She pulled in another laboured breath. She couldn't quite get her lungs full enough. She was about to be called up. She'd folded and refolded Liv's eulogy so much it was fraying at the creases. She flattened it down and scanned the words again.

My dad was the most wonderful father to me. I love him so much and I can't believe he's not here anymore. Thank you to everyone who came today to remember him as he was. I'll never stop missing him. We're all better for having had him in our lives.

It just feels so flaccid, she frowned, so bland and generic. There's nothing of him in it or of what he did for all of us. What he did for me. She heaved in more useless oxygen and her lungs contracted weakly. This moment was lasting for ever. She looked up to check how the speaker ahead of her was going. It was Sean De Burca, an old theatre friend of Miles's, who was taking up quite a lot of his allotted time with plugging his forthcoming play and name-checking the prestigious awards he'd won during his four decades in the business.

'Of course, as you probably all remember, that was the year that we took the show to Albany and the late, great critic Harold Carthieu himself sat in the front row. I remember texting Miles about it. Carthieu was a bore, but his review was quite complimentary.' Sean paused to fumble among his pages.

'Christ, he's brought the review with him.' Mini's voice was hot on Ali's ear. 'I never should've asked him. He's trying to get funding for his new play, and this is as bald an attempt at a pitch as any I've ever heard. He's practically reciting his CV.'

Ali glanced around at the bored crowd apparently untouched by the moving tale of one 'criminally underrated Irish theatre director's trials and triumphs'.

'He's really losing them,' Ali whispered back, indicating a snoozing Marcus, her dad's old business partner, a few rows down, whose head was lolling on Liv's shoulder as she tried to shrug him off.

'So we plan to begin workshopping in mid-May, ahead of this year's Dublin Theatre Festival, and I know Miles, always such a supportive patron of the arts, would have wanted any who feel they have the means to dig deep here today.'

My God, I have to stop this! Ali pushed herself up to standing, feeling shaky and unmoored, and began to make her way to the podium, trying not to look at the coffin as she passed. Sean looked shocked at her muscling him gently out of the way but reluctantly relinquished the mic and backed off.

'My father,' Ali began, 'would have wanted me to shut down that shameless hard sell, Sean!' She threw a look over to Sean, who shuffled awkwardly. Ali gazed down the chapel and felt a pang at the size of the congregation. God, the things her dad would never see. This huge crowd of people who loved him, Mini sitting ramrod straight at the head of them all, staring unblinking at the coffin. Then

Ali glanced down at herself. Inside her right now was a soon-to-be person, who would contain some tiny element of her dad. If the baby had her brown eyes, then it would have Miles's brown eyes.

'I wanted to prepare some words to say today but when I went to write them down, nothing came. In the end, my friend, Liv, wrote something for me but I guess it's just that words don't come close to … I guess I just never believed this would happen. I can't believe he's gone. He deserved to live. He deserved to live to see this, to see how much all of you loved him. This disease is so cruel – it robs the person of their memories and it robs *us* of *them*. I can't believe I'll never hear him singing in the car or arguing about who did the best *Krapp's Last Tape*.'

Ali looked at the coffin and tried to imagine Miles inside. This was the last time she'd be near his body and she couldn't even kiss his cheek with the little sandpapery stubble and his Miles smell. 'I wish I could tell you what an amazing father you were to me.' Ali could feel her throat clogging with tears. 'I wish I could tell you how much you mean to me and that I'll miss you … every … day.' The words were catching but she had to get them out. 'I want you to know how much I love you. I want you to know I'm going to name this baby after you … And I'm going to be a mother you could be proud of. I swear to you.'

When 400 people jolt with surprise and gasp in unison, it's pretty loud. It wrenched Ali from her daze.

Fuck. What did I just say?

❖

After the funeral service, the line of mourners seemed to be unending. Ali was pinned into an alcove in the church feeling hounded by sympathy and shaken by her own insanely cavalier baby announcement.

16

Jaysus, forget Mercury, this baby is in retrograde: conceived during a social media hoax, the pregnancy test taken in a funeral home and now announced at the emotional climax of a eulogy. Poor baby Miles. Or baby Millie?

Mini had raised a single terrifying eyebrow in the tense seconds after Ali'd announced her forthcoming loinfruit from the altar. When Ali'd returned to her seat, numb from the shock of what she'd just done, Mini's eyes remained fixed on the coffin as she muttered, 'I don't even know where to begin with that, Alessandra. I guess we'll discuss it when we're not about to cremate your father.'

Fair, Ali'd thought.

'Ali, such a beautiful speech.' Maura Lane, an eminent theatre actress, gripped her shoulders. 'It had everything, pathos, vulnerability and then the payoff of the baby character. Your father would be so proud, you really *produced* this whole incredible … homage to him.'

Oh God, they all think I timed that on purpose. With the guts of her parents' friends being artists and theatre luvvies, really was it any wonder she wound up a fantasist on Instagram?

'Em, thanks …' Ali was pulled into a vice-like hug and swore she could feel her bones clicking. Over the black velvet shoulder of Maura Lane, Ali could see her friend Kate looking awkward in the solemn condolence line. They were mates, though during Ali's Insta-rise things had become strained between them. Kate had been trying to make the influencer thing happen for herself for ages and was understandably jealous of Ali's sudden success. After Ali's lies had unravelled, Kate'd texted a couple of times, but Ali hadn't been able to string a response together.

Maura disengaged from the hug. 'Ali, I must go. The director of the Abbey is over there,' she murmured, a determined networking grit having entered her voice. She adjusted her hair and smoothed her cape. *A bold energy, wearing a cape to the funeral of an acquaintance,* thought Ali watching Maura go as Kate stepped up and limply hugged her.

'So now you *are* pregnant?' She peered at Ali through the tangle of lashes. Her Insta-face looked particularly garish in the context of a funeral. Ali felt bad. She'd sat around talking about the 'pregnancy' with Kate, knowing full well that Kate was madly jealous of her growing following. Ali'd no idea how Kate's own bid for Insta-fame with her account, @ShreddingForTheWedding, was even going. She'd been too wrapped up in herself.

'I'm sorry, Kate, I really am.'

'But, like, which is it? Are you pregnant? Were you this whole time? What is going on?' Kate looked quietly seething, though she kept glancing around, conscious she was supposed to be offering her sympathies. 'Like, I'm really sorry about your dad and all, but seriously, you know what they're saying online, right? *Prime Time* approached me about taking part in a panel to discuss the "Ali's Baba Scandal". Everyone is talking about this' – she leaned in and hissed – 'and now you're here still lying about it, at your dad's funeral.'

'I'm not lying. Not anymore. Look, I am pregnant. I just found out a few days ago. Ask Liv, she knows. And I don't know what I'm going to do but please, please don't go on *Prime Time*. I can't take that on top of everything.'

Kate drew back, appearing to consider this, when Marcus slipped in front of her and gathered Ali into his arms.

'Ally Pally! You did wonderfully. Miles would've been so proud of you.'

Ally Pally had been her dad's name for her. She narrowed her eyes –

clearly, he was trying to get in with her so he could get on with boning her mother. Mini and Marcus had been on the verge of going on a date just a couple of months before, though with all her Insta-bullshit, she hadn't even asked Mini what happened, she realised guiltily.

'Yeah, yeah.' Ali extracted herself. 'Excuse me, I need to get some air.'

Where was Liv? She needed a buffer from all these funeral people. She couldn't get two paces without being sucked into vortex after vortex of people emoting. Though now, after the baby bombshell, the mood had taken a turn for the better.

'Ali! You're glowing. What a wonderful, joyful thing to have to look forward to!'

'Devastating about Miles but wonderful news about the baba. Mini must be thrilled!'

Everyone seemed much better equipped to deal with the bizarre baby news than the dead man in the box.

❖

Ali finally broke free of the chapel, squeezing through a side door to the graveyard outside. She was about to ring Liv when she spotted her gesturing wildly at a very tall and ornate monument – an angel crouched on a large engraved plinth.

'Li-iv!' She jogged towards her. 'What are you—?'

As she neared the monument, she clamped her mouth shut and screeched to a halt, realising Liv was not alone but in full, wild, ranting flow with Tinder Sam. Shite! Ali'd never dreamed Sam would be there. She reversed abruptly and hid behind the angel's plinth, grateful that neither of them had noticed her – they were too engrossed in what sounded like an extremely tense exchange.

'I can't believe I let you convince me to come. You said she was sorry, you said she was *suffering*. That little spectacle in there didn't look like remorse. It looked distinctly like she is still out there lying to everyone and refusing to face up to what she did.'

'Sam,' Liv sounded anguished. 'Please, you have to talk to Ali about this. It's not what you think. Please just wait and give her a chance to explain.'

'I'm done with you both to be honest. You're not much better than her, you know. The amount of times that we all hung out watching TV and I'd be chatting about baby names. And you just sat there, Liv. Making little notes for your precious thesis – mining *my* life for your career, never stopping to think that maybe I deserved to know the truth. You're no different to Ali, ya know. You're both completely unhinged. Did you never think about what you two were doing to me? I thought this would be my chance to have a family? I was so stupidly happy that Ali and I were going to have a baby. And then, I pick up your thesis and realise I've been going along living in some messed up *Truman Show* experiment she'd concocted and you were exploiting.'

Ali cringed remembering his face when she came home to find him holding the thesis, open at a picture of them both taken at an Insta event.

'This is sick, Ali,' he'd said. 'You're sick.' She swallowed hard. He wasn't wrong.

'Sam, I know what you're saying,' Liv sounded pleading. 'And believe me, we never meant for you to find out like that. And, I know I should have told you but I just felt protective of Ali. You don't know what she's been through the last two years. Miles and Ali were so so close before he got sick and I've just watched her crumble under the grief of losing him over such a long time—'

'It's not an excuse, Liv. Everyone has hard stuff in their lives.

I'm not listening to anymore of this—' Sam suddenly marched out from behind the monument and nearly collided with Ali. His face instantly clouded over with abject disgust at the sight of her. It did not feel good.

'SAM—' Liv was following after him but stopped dead upon seeing Ali.

For a moment no one spoke. Then all three tried for an opener at once.

'Liv made me come but I was just leaving,' Sam began, looking completely furious.

'He was trying to run off,' was Liv's contribution.

'I'm ... having a baby, a real one,' said Ali stupidly.

An awkward silence reigned and then Liv started to creep away, pausing by Ali's side to whisper, 'I let him know the funeral arrangements. I did NOT think he'd come. I also did NOT think you'd be filling everyone in on your little situation from the pulpit.' She clumsily rubbed Ali's upper arm. 'I'll be by the hearse. Good luck.'

Ali stared at the ground, listening to Liv's footsteps fade. Sam remained silent and eventually Ali chanced a look in his direction. His face was twisted with rage and Ali crumpled into tears.

'Please, Sam—'

'Yes? Please what?' His words were clipped and sharp.

'Please ...' Ali didn't know where to go frankly. Please don't be mad? Please can it be the way it was? 'Please don't hate me,' she tried.

'Ali. What the hell just happened in there? Are you the girl who cried "pregnant!"? This is the second time you've told a roomful of people you're pregnant before telling me you're pregnant. Are you sick in the head? Or just desperate for attention?'

The internet was already awash with this very debate but hearing Sam say these words was too much. A crushing hopelessness invaded Ali, and any will to try to convince him to forgive her ebbed away.

'I am pregnant, Sam. It looks like I'm maybe eleven weeks, but I need to go to the doctor to confirm it.' At this, Sam crossed his arms, a sneering eyebrow cocked sceptically, and Ali continued, 'I'll piss on the wee stick in front of you, if you want. I honestly don't know what happened in there.' She gestured to the chapel. 'It was weird. I felt really overwhelmed.' She swallowed with difficulty, the same feeling rising up again. 'I just wanted to tell my dad, I guess. I didn't know you were there.'

'Right.' Sam looked deeply exasperated. 'Look, I'm not the person to play the dead dad card with, Ali.' Sam had lost his mum when he was little. Ali bit her lip as he continued. 'To be honest, I was fairly certain I'd never have to see you again and that's how I needed it to be. I was in love with you. You knew that, right? Of course you did. And still every single day you lied to me. Every minute of every hour. You sat through every conversation about names and where we would live and what our life would be like.'

'I know and I'm so sorry, Sam. It started by accident. Some people took it up wrongly and then, before I knew it, it was everywhere. I never meant to get you involved.'

'Uh huh.' Sam was withering. 'But ya did. And then you lied your balls off about it for two months. I can't even watch *Special Victims Unit* anymore because of this.'

It was their show. This sounded like a joke but one look at Sam's face told Ali they would not be laughing about this anytime soon.

'Well, I have to go to the rest of my dad's funeral. If you want to come to the doctor with me, you can.' Ali began to move off.

'I can? Can I? Has it occurred to you that maybe you're unfit? That maybe I'd have a pretty good case to have sole custody of this child? If it definitely exists.'

Ali rolled her eyes.

'It exists and good luck getting custody while it's inside me. You can be a part of this baby's life but I'm not going to beg you to be a father to your child. I can do this on my own. Now, if you'll excuse me, I have a carbtastic hotel buffet to attend.' With that, she marched back to the crowd milling at the front of the church.

Her womb felt like it was staging a mutiny. Google said it was stretching pains. It was mad how last Thursday she'd had no idea she was harbouring a tiny stowaway and now, even with her life in shambles and the internet and Sam hating her, the thought of anything happening to this little thing trumped everything. How could you care so much about something so small? It was a bloblet with miniscule fingers and toes, but Ali knew it was now the most important thing in the world.

Liv was being berated by several uncles when Ali rounded the front of the chapel and she quickly swooped to rescue her, not that Liv ever required such a thing.

'No man yet, Liv? What's going on with that?'

'Too much peen for my tastes,' Liv said casually, silencing them. In slow motion, understanding dawned on each of them in turn as they gave each other meaningful looks. Ali laughed, which felt good until one of the uncles turned to her to deliver the ultimate funeral small talk clanger, 'And this one, of course, has had too much peen.'

'Oh God,' Liv muttered. 'Right, we'd better be saddling up. I'll see you at the hotel.' She hugged Ali and headed to the car park.

As Ali neared the family funeral car back at the chapel, she could see Mini talking urgently to Marcus, but they pulled apart as she approached, and she could see tears in Mini's eyes. Marcus turned and gave Ali a reassuring pat on the shoulder.

'Well done, Ali. You put on a great show there. It's been a long road for you both.' His voice cracked a little and Ali wondered what had just been said. 'I guess I won't see you for a while, but you know I'm always around if you need anything.'

The drive to the Fitzsimon Hotel was quiet. The 'family car', as the funeral directors called it, was a bit of an overstatement seeing as it was just Mini and Ali.

'So, did you just break up with your boyfriend at your husband's funeral?' Ali asked with a sardonic grin.

'Did you just announce that you're pregnant at your father's funeral?'

'You've got me there.' Ali sighed.

'Whose is it, Ali?' Mini peered at her, her tired face was deeply concerned.

'A guy I was seeing called Sam. He's actually really cool but I don't …' Ali paused to breathe. This was the most surreal day of her life. 'I don't think we're together anymore.'

'Ali, how did this happen?' Mini was shocked.

'Just the usual way.' Ali shrugged unhappily.

'Ali! For God's sake, how many times have we had the talk? Did you even think of the morning after pill? And what are you planning to do?' Mini shook her head, clearly trying to calm herself. 'Look, I'll help in any way I can – you know that, don't you? – whatever you decide. But for fuck's sake. Who is this boy? Is he even clean? What's his last name? Has he been tested?'

'Mu-um.' Ali squirmed, glancing towards the two undertakers in the front seats.

'Don't "Mu-um" me! You don't show up to your father's funeral with some stranger's baby in your belly, tell everyone mid-eulogy and then act like I'm the one being over the top when I have some questions.'

'All right, all right, I know. I *know*, Mum,' Ali pleaded as the car made its way through quiet Georgian squares, the mist still heavy outside. 'I didn't set out to do this but it's happening, and I feel like it's happening for a reason. This baby is my chance to make amends for how …' Ali grappled with her words '… for how I was with Dad. I'm going to take care of this baby. I'm going to be there for the baby the way I wasn't for him.'

Chapter 2

Shelly turned off the main light, stretched out in her large double bed and tried to luxuriate in having it all to herself. It was weeks since her husband, Dan, had moved out and the house still felt strange without him, not that he'd gone far – he was sleeping in the Seomra in the garden and apparently had no plans as yet to put any more distance between them. For this, Shelly was grateful. She couldn't shake the all-consuming dread that had seeped into her since the sunny morning the week before when Detective Bríd had rung to say that the person behind the sinister anonymous messages blackmailing her was not their suspect – a small-fry fashion blogger who went by @KellysKlobber – but was in fact something much more terrifying: a completely unknown entity.

As Ireland's premier Instagram influencer, with 260,000 followers, Shelly had had needy fans before but nothing like this. The anonymous account, whose username was just @_____, had thus far been flexing by sending candid and very personal pictures from the SHELLY annals. Pictures no one should have access to, pics showing Shelly had FaceFixed her own daughter, Georgie, in the past. And even more damning, snaps documenting an elaborate cover-up she and her social media analyst, Amy, had perpetrated a few months before back in February when they'd hired a Dan look-a-like to 'play' her husband at a PR event. Shelly squeezed her eyes tight and tried to ignore the memory of Dan ranting about this incident in their brief stint in couples counselling before the separation was finalised. The unpleasant memory was interrupted by another sound that had taken on unpleasant connotations of late: her Insta DM notification.

Shelly scooted up to sitting in her Insta-ready, high thread count bedsheets piled with satin and faux-fur throw pillows. Raking a manicured hand nervously through her shiny dark hair, she grabbed the phone from the marble and onyx side table. Aside from a single outfit of the day, she hadn't posted in days. She'd been feeling too exposed ever since her call with Bríd and she'd even started to wonder if she wanted to stay on Instagram. She wearily opened the message and felt a surge of sickly adrenaline on spotting the handle.

@_____: Nice #OOTD earlier but I hope you don't think I'm willing to let you off that easily. There are people on here who have supported you. We made you. You owe us consistency in your content. Remember … I have receipts.

Several blurred images appeared below and despite the dread swelling in her chest, Shelly clicked to bring them into focus. They were taken in the park. A series of about twelve shots that initially showed just Georgie and her nanny, Marni, playing on the swings. Then a couple showed Shelly arriving and taking over the playtime duties, pretending to push Georgie on the swing while Amy took shots – it had been for a #MummyAndMeMondays post, Shelly remembered.

The last pic showed Amy and Shelly returning to the car, leaving the little girl alone with her minder once more.

Shit, Shelly breathed. Who the hell could know the intricacies of her schedule to keep track of her like this? And who would bother sneaking around to capture this? It wasn't even a big deal – she was a working mum, she'd a minder, so what? Deeper down, Shelly felt a tug of unease. She always felt uncomfortable showing up and parenting for a photo op, then leaving again and whoever @_____ was had obviously sussed that.

Shelly suddenly felt acutely aware of how loud her breathing was. The room around her felt cavernous, the shadows beyond where the light from her bedside lamp fell looked deeper, threatening somehow. She slid out of bed and skirted the room, pushing aside the curtains and pulling the doors of her wardrobes open. She was alone.

'Relax, Shelly!' she muttered and drew her hand to her belly. Nearly seventeen weeks. Being pregnant and alone like this was making her feel vulnerable. There's no one here, she thought and tried to make herself believe it. She got back into bed and lay still for a few tense minutes, listening for any unusual noises. *I'll just check Georgie to put my mind at ease*, she thought before bolting upright again and charging out the door and down the stairs.

On the next floor down, she quietly peered into Georgie's room, where the small dark head of her nearly four-year-old was nestled on the pillows. All seemed well.

Shelly tucked the duvet back around the warm little body and tiptoed from the room. She wasn't done. She was too edgy. She made her way to the ground floor and peered around the door to the large open-plan kitchen-dining room. Empty.

She looked across to the sliding glass doors that led outside. With all the lights off, she could see clearly beyond them into the garden, which, just after midnight, was deep navy with swathes of dark green.

The windows of Dan's Seomra were blank and the surrounding shadows impenetrable. Behind that the furthest recesses of the garden disappeared into nothing. There was so much scope for someone to sit and watch and wait.

She checked the doors were locked and then quickly pulled herself away – all the glass was freaking her out. Back out in the hall, she started up the stairs but then stopped, her left hand hovering just above the banister. The alarm.

I put it on though, she thought, *didn't I?*

I did, I did, her mind insisted as she turned and started towards the little keypad on the wall by the front door. System disarmed. The words glowed, taunting her. Had she ever put it on? She always did. She'd never forget, especially not now with Dan gone and @_____ at her every hour of the day.

Her breathing was ragged.

No, I must've forgotten. I must have not turned it on at all.

She had to believe this. The alternative was too frightening. She hurriedly keyed in the commands to activate the alarm and dashed back up to her room. Settled once more in bed, she tried to slow her thrashing heart.

You're just freaking yourself out.

She picked up the phone for a nice calming scroll. It was still open to the DMs from @_____ and a new message had appeared while she was gone.

@_____ : *I really got to you there, didn't I?*

Shelly shoved the phone away and pulled the blankets up around her. It was a lucky guess, that was all. She killed the bedside light and stared into the darkness, watchful and frantic until at last sleep came at some point near dawn.

Chapter 3

The day after the funeral, Ali still couldn't shake a near constant free-floating anxiety that seemed to swell up and down every hour – a terrible tide of regret and foreboding.

She stood in the kitchen toiling over yet another greasy frying pan. The uncles didn't seem to know when to leave, which was beyond irritating. For days, she seemed to be caught in a never-ending cycle of making tea and cooking elaborate full Irish breakfasts – the North American lot needed to stockpile the Clonakilty black pudding in their systems before heading back Stateside, it seemed.

Thank God she was leaving today. Being back and trapped in her Harry Styles shrine in a room full of teenage promise was just compounding what a shambles her life was currently. The funeral had been a limbo period, Ali sensed – a temporary reprieve from having to face everything. She still hadn't gone through her inbox beyond a cursory glance, nor had she ventured onto Instagram since making her account private. It was a feeble attempt at damage control. She knew all the websites would be trawling for posts to include in their 'think pieces' so she'd locked them out.

I should just delete it, she'd thought at least ten times a day since her downfall.

Still, despite everything that had happened, the thought of deleting hundreds of thousands of followers was anathema to Ali. It went against her every impulse. She'd also noticed with bleak interest that notoriety didn't seem to hurt the numbers. In fact, quite the opposite – when she'd clicked in to set the account to private the day after the Glossie Influencer Awards, she thought there was a mistake at first because she'd gained about 8,000 new followers overnight.

Ali flipped the rashers lazily and slipped her phone from her pocket. She flicked over the screen to wake the phone and pulled up Instagram. She could see thousands of new follow requests – the number was growing daily. People couldn't resist a car crash.

Ali sighed, put the phone away and transferred the rashers to the oven, where various iterations of pork were warming on a tray. She checked the toast wasn't getting too crunchy in the lower oven, then walked to the head of the table and clapped her hands to shut the uncles up.

'I'm only making one type of egg this morning,' she announced. Immediately a chorus of 'POACHED! FRIED! CODDLED!' rang out and Ali raised her voice to be heard over the din. 'So, a show of hands for scrambled, please.' Three arms were held aloft. 'OK, three for scrambled, how many for scrambled?' Ali folded her arms and surveyed the toddler-like expressions of injustice spread over the uncles. 'Yeah, that's right. I'm not making four fucking egg varietals for you lads anymore. I'm pregnant and grieving so I'm making scrambled eggs and if any of ye want a *special* egg, you can get up there and make it yourself, OK?'

Ali cocked her head, making a stern face. The uncles were brats and needed a firm hand. She stormed back to the stove and began cracking eggs as passive-aggressively as she could muster. Whisking with one hand, she decided to chance a look at the email inbox. The level of bile and vitriol from strangers among the more measured disgust from people she'd been working with on Insta was just horrific. There were several subject lines referencing 'legal action' and 'payments made under false pretences' – Ali shuddered at the amount of money she was going to have to repay. She hadn't gone on a spending spree – she hadn't had the time, thank God, but the thought of having to hand over what she'd amassed over the last month was gutting. It would empty her account and then some.

Good thing you dicked in your job, you genius, she thought scathingly, flashing back on the blaze of temper that had precipitated her quitting her job mid-scene as production assistant on *Durty Aul' Town*, the soap that the influencer Shelly Divine was famous for.

She scanned the subject lines of her inbox and felt shaky.

You dumb stupid cunt

You deserve everything your getting right now

Notice of collaboration termination in light of recent events

Ali considered the time it took to type 'you dumb stupid cunt' and send it to a stranger on the internet. She poured the egg mixture into the biggest frying pan her mum had and stirred slowly, dragging her sleeve across her eyes to prevent the tears from dropping into the eggs. A swarm of emotions overwhelmed her: anger, rage, shame, guilt, pity for herself and pity for the baby inside her, who was surely going to be screwed up for life with her for a mother.

She also felt afraid – razor-sharp, relentless fear that seemed to knife her with each new vitriolic subject line.

You should die for what you've done

Ali shuddered.

X out of it. Delete the email account. You can't look at this. It will kill you.

She felt certain there was truth in this. She'd read stories about teenagers being cyberbullied who couldn't go on. Now she could see how attractive just giving in could be when you were already drowning in hate.

She put the phone down and pulled the eggs from the heat. They were a little overcooked but whatever. Ignoring the uncles, she set the pan on a mat in the middle of the kitchen table and brought over the meat and toast. *Let them serve themselves*, she thought impatiently, her focus still on the inbox.

She picked up the phone again. She knew she shouldn't look. She knew the hurt it would cause. Anxiety filled her body, squeezing her lungs and taking hold of her stomach. Still, she couldn't resist. It was like picking a scab or the feeling Ali sometimes got when standing too close to an edge. Peering over from a great height was terrifying but at the same time there was an irresistible pull, that strange urge to plunge forward anyway.

She brought up the inbox once more, swiped her thumb over the screen and watched the inbox scroll too fast to see the messages. She had around 800 unreads.

I'll read whichever one I land on, she vowed as she brought her thumb back down to arrest the messages speeding past.

Subject: Please read, Ali. I think I can help.

Ali grabbed the counter to steady herself as her brain caught up with the fact that among all the hate-filled, raging emails someone wanted to help her. She peered closer to read the sender: Amy@SocialSolutions.com.

'Alessandra? Are you OK?' Mini had suddenly appeared beside her and Ali stuffed the phone out of sight.

'Uh-huh.' Ali cleared her throat. One look at Mini's concerned face confirmed that she wasn't looking her best. She clawed at her hair self-consciously.

'Thanks for doing breakfast again, darling. They've really stayed far too long at this stage.' Mini raised her voice, throwing her words towards the table, but it didn't register with the rowdy brothers squabbling over the remaining rashers.

'I probably should be going home too. Time to get back to reality.' Ali couldn't quite meet her mother's gaze. They hadn't spoken about the baby since the day before. And Ali *still* hadn't told her anything about the Instagram scandal. In a very uncharacteristic move, Mini appeared to be respectfully waiting for Ali to open up.

She gently turned Ali around to face her.

'You're not looking after yourself,' was all she said. It was enough to crack Ali wide open and she drew her arms around her own body, stunned by the violence of her own sobs.

'I don't deserve to be looked after.' The words came up like vomit before she even had time to think about what she was saying.

'Alessandra, what do you mean?' Mini pulled her close and Ali stiffened, willing the hug to end. Mini would smell her hair, unwashed for how many days now? She'd know, somehow, all the bad she'd done. All the lies. Ali pulled back, certain Mini would sense the fear and guilt leaking out of her.

An awkward silence had descended on the whole kitchen – quite possibly the first in days, the uncles frozen at the sight of her tears. *Jesus, they must think I'm madder than ever. Little do they know*, Ali thought.

She turned to the table, hand on hip, ready to try to salvage the situation. 'So *that's* how to shut you guys up!' To her satisfaction, at least a couple of them looked contrite. Turning back to her mum, she dodged her probing stare and pulled her features into something she hoped resembled normal.

'I'm going to get my shit together – literally and metaphorically,' she announced and headed upstairs to pack.

'Ali?' Mini wasn't that easy to shake and she followed behind. 'What's the plan, Ali? What are you going to do about this baby? Liv said you'd left *Durty Aul' Town*? When? What on earth is going on?'

Ali hauled her suitcase out from under the bed and ignored the questions.

Fuck's sake, Liv. Ali made a mental note to give her a light bollocking the second she got home.

Mini watched her pack from the door, arms crossed. She looked faded by the recent events, drained of her usual vigour – her grey bob was sharp and neat as always, but without her slash of signature red lippie, her face seemed oddly expressionless.

'It's grand,' Ali said finally with a confidence that she did not in any way feel and lobbed a pair of Converse into the suitcase. 'What good's a dead dad card if you can't play it to claw back a job you stupidly jacked in while hepped up on pregnancy hormones?'

'I see. So that's what happened? Ali, we need to discuss this pregnancy.'

Ali could hear a bit of old authoritative Mini creeping back into the tone. 'Well,' Ali wavered. Her veneer of confidence and positivity couldn't withstand any kind of interrogation. Plus, any day now, Erasmus, Mini's nervy 20-something assistant, was going to have to inform his boss of the full extent of the mess Ali was in. Most social media shitstorms stayed contained to the platforms they originated on but cursory googles of her name had thrown up a terrifying search page. Every media outlet in the country had dredged up *someone* to have a hot take on the influencer who faked a pregnancy. The only reason Mini didn't already know was the funeral. Erasmus was probably at this very moment pacing Mini's gallery – she repped Ireland's biggest contemporary artists – crapping himself at the thought of broaching it with his newly widowed, always-volatile boss.

Deep breaths, Al, she tried to psych herself up.

'Well. There's a bit more to it than that.' She slumped down, allowing the clothes-swamp to engulf her. 'I fucked up.' She sighed. 'In fact, there isn't even a word strong enough to describe what I did.'

Mini stepped into the room, nudging clothes with her foot to make a path and closed the door behind her. She picked her way through the detritus and perched on the bed, her expression expectant.

Ali could barely meet her eyes. 'I'm sorry. I didn't want to dump this on you. Especially right now. That's kind of why I was getting out of here.'

'Alessandra.' Mini looked pained. 'I knew there was something eating at you. Beyond Miles and the week it's been, I mean. You look …' At this Mini seemed to struggle for words.

'Like shite?' Ali suggested. She'd barely looked in the mirror since getting ready for the funeral. She heaved herself up from the floor and walked to the dressing table. She started just a little at the sight of her own reflection. Ugh. Seven days of internet hounding had really taken its toll. Her eyes seemed to sag in their sockets; her skin was dull with vast continents of angry-looking dry skin crowding her chin and jaw. Her blonde hair was gathered in dirty, dark clumps and when she ran a hand through it, it held the new shape like a greasy hair-sculpture. She knew she hadn't been looking after herself. It was hard to bother when she felt so hopeless, but she knew she had to get it together for the baby's sake if not her own.

'So? What is going on? You're scaring me, Alessandra. Are you telling me whatever it is is *worse* than the pregnancy?'

Mini, at least, is getting back to her usual self, Ali thought ruefully.

'Yeah, Mini. It's worse. Can you believe it? There are things worse than your dumb bitch daughter getting preggers.'

'Oh God, I didn't mean that.' Mini looked stricken. 'Don't be coming after me now. I've just lost my husband.'

'Well, I've just lost my dad.' Ali crumpled. Christ, they were having some kind of grief-off. Thank God she was going home today.

Mini came and pulled Ali into a hug.

'Alessandra, please tell me. You know I love you. Whatever it is, we'll work it out.' Her voice was slightly muffled in their embrace, but the words were soothing. 'Also, you have to wash your hair, darling, it's vile.'

Yep, definitely getting back to her usual self. Ali smiled through her tears. She pulled away and wiped her face.

'OK, you better sit down,' she advised. Mini marched back to the bed and arranged herself with legs crossed and her listening face ready.

'When *did* you last wash your hair?'

'OK, are you going to be able to focus or do you need me to wash it before we start?' Just then a buzzing rang out from Mini's pocket.

'It's Erasmus. I'm sorry, I have to take this. He knows I'm still in mourning, so he wouldn't be calling if it wasn't urgent.'

Shite, Erasmus had to be calling about her. Before Ali could scream or lunge for the phone, Mini was holding it to her ear.

'Mm-hmmm, yes, I'm actually here with her now.' Mini's eyes flickered towards Ali and then she turned away slightly to continue the call. Ali resumed tossing things in her suitcase. Maybe it was easier for Erasmus to just fill her in. After all, she still hadn't come up with any 'good' way to say: 'I faked a pregnancy on Instagram and hundreds of thousands of people think I'm either an evil bitch or mentally disturbed.'

She'd cleared the floor and even made a start on the clothes-pile chair by the time Mini, who had barely spoken in her side of the conversation, finally got off the phone. She continued to sit in silence and Ali thought she was perhaps gripped by shock until she realised with a jolt of panic that she was reading something on her phone. *Oh God.* Ali cleared the chair and plonked herself down on it.

'Well?' She tentatively broke the silence.

'Well …' Mini looked at a complete loss, which was a brand-new look for her. 'Ehh—' She scrolled on her phone. 'I don't know what to say. This one is very creative.' She indicated an Instagram post where Ali'd put a speech bubble coming from her tummy with the words 'I. Want. A. Chicken. Fillet. Roll. NOW!' It was a screenshot embedded in a piece from Deborah Winters on Notions.ie.

Ali reached for the phone and scrolled through the piece. She tried to blur her eyes so none of the actual words could land, though the odd phrase like 'devious and conniving plot was not without its victims' still managed to penetrate. Lower down she saw mention of Sam, 'the twenty-nine-year-old has declined to comment but there was palpable pain in his solicitor's letter'. There was even a shot of this letter included below. Ali zoomed in on it. Deborah Winters was editorialising somewhat here – it was a very professional missive, devoid of emotion simply stating: 'My client will not be commenting on anything pertaining to Alessandra Jones.'

Well, thank God for that. Maybe it's a sign that he's going to warm up again. Not get back with her or anything but maybe answer her texts?

'So what exactly is this, Ali? Some kind of stunt? Are you pregnant right now?' Mini was clearly stumped. 'This woman is saying you were paid money to say you were pregnant? What's sponsored content?'

Ali tapped the chair leg nervously with her foot. Oh God, Mini was going to need an Insta primer just to get her head around BumpGate, as the incident was apparently being referred to in the media.

'So sponcon – sponsored content – is pictures and videos that influencers get paid to put on their feed—'

'And the feed is?'

'OK, one sec.' Ali dug out her phone, sat down beside Mini and embarked on a detailed rundown of the Insta world from #TBTs and #af. Mini was engrossed.

'My God, what's happened to this girl's other leg? Where is it?' Ali was showing Mini some of the other Influencer accounts to illustrate her little impromptu Insta 101.

'Oh, happens all the time,' Ali reassured her. 'She'd just gone bananas with the FaceFix and probably didn't notice the right leg had disappeared altogether.'

'And FaceFix is … ?'

A few minutes later, Mini was admiring a picture of herself that had just received the Insta treatment.

'Wow, it's like a dystopian nightmare but rendered in pastel shades.' Mini was fascinated scrolling through Ali's old feed. Ali resumed packing. She needed an activity, a crutch to help her through this awkward discussion.

'You know I'm really sorry, right?' Ali glanced at her mother. 'I never meant it to happen and then when it did, so many good things were coming my way. It wasn't the money. They're all acting like it was a money-grab.' She indicated the phone in Mini's hand. 'But it wasn't about that. Things were just so crap with Miles and this was something that took me away from all that. And then Sam showed up and I never expected in a million years that I'd fall for him. Or that he'd fall for me. At the time, it was just really convenient that he thought he was the dad. And then he was so sweet but fun too. Not like other guys.'

Ali glanced over at Mini, who had stopped on a video from a couple of months before. Ali leaned over her shoulder. Sam was flopped on her bed, lip synching 'Bigger' while poking Ali's tummy as she filmed.

'OK.' Mini sounded sceptical. 'So, you're telling me that you *didn't* think you'd fall for a gorgeous straight man who knows all the words to the Neil Patrick Harris opener from the 2013 Tonys?'

On the video, Sam was making up his own words to the song. *'Bigger. That's right it's bigger … Dunno how it's gonna get out of your vadge – be-cause it's bigger … every day it's bigger.'* He was grinning up at her as she swiped at him laughing. The video ended abruptly with her telling him to 'Shut the fuck up!'

'Well, if anything, I was falling for him in *spite* of the musical theatre tendencies …' Ali tried to downplay it and not let on to Mini how upsetting it was seeing how happy they'd been.

'Oh, don't be ridiculous. Nothing's sexier than that gay straight man thing. Miles had it in spades—'

'OK! No need for any more deets,' Ali cut across her in case Mini was about to land some horrific detail about her parents' sex life that she'd never be able to unhear. 'Anyway, yeah, Sam was a good guy. *Is* a good guy. And I knew it couldn't go on. I knew it had to end but I just wanted to win this stupid award. More and more people were following me. It was like this massive weight started to press down on me and I couldn't bear to lose face in front of so many people. Eighty thousand people were watching my stories every day.'

'But what did you *think* was going to happen?' Mini looked more baffled than angry. 'Did you … have a plan?'

'No.' Ali welled up again. She tried to focus on sorting the mess of make-up and jewellery strewn on top of the chest of drawers by the door. 'I just thought I'd sly off for a bit and that people would forget about it.'

'You thought a man who believed you were carrying his baby would forget about it? They're bad but they're not *that* bad. Well, not all of them.'

'I know. I know. I genuinely don't think I was right in the head.' Ali felt jangly and anxious right down to her fingertips. 'I basically have no answer,' she whispered and let the tears come.

'Ali.' Mini gathered her into a very comforting, unMini embrace. 'Maybe we can salvage this?' She pulled away and stood up. 'I think I can work with this.' She began to pace the room. 'We could draft a press release announcing you as a new and bold performance artist working in the medium of Instagram. You could be an exciting burgeoning talent, a kind of …' She pinched the air in front as she moved, searching for the words. 'I've got it: a *post-artist* working at the epicentre of this twenty-first-century collision of high art and the lowbrow concerns that devour our attention span. We could reframe the stunt as a kind of culture jamming that exposes the artifice of the social media world and unpicks our compulsion to package womanhood, and more specifically *motherhood*, as something contained and palatable. Your ... what did you call it? Bump journey?'

She is good, Ali allowed. *Could it really work?* she wondered.

Mini, meanwhile had immediately begun feverishly typing. 'Erasmus says there's a big art scene on Insta. Cindy Sherman is on there now.' Some more staccato tapping ensued, then she added, 'He's saying this could even have Biennale potential.'

Ali laughed weakly and resumed sorting the jewellery pile as she tried to get her thoughts straight. The art stunt angle was a thought. However, there would be a tsunami of follow-up questions, none of which Ali felt she'd be equipped to answer even if Mini and Erasmus were steering the ship. Plus, it didn't solve the Sam issue, it didn't solve the money issue and it sure as hell wouldn't solve the baby issue.

She interrupted Mini's machinations. 'I'm not totally sure that I should be lying my way out of this thing. Can you pause on the whole "Ali as the millennial Andy Warhol" plan for a minute? I know you're trying to help but layering lies on top of more lies feels a bit dodge. It's like trying to cover a wine stain by, I dunno, vomiting on it.'

Mini winced at the analogy but ploughed on with her indefatigable enthusiasm. 'But, Ali, it's inspired. This could be a great new direction for you. Erasmus and I would help you every step of the way.'

Maybe it's not my fault I wound up hoaxing everyone on Insta, Ali thought wryly. *The woman who raised me is seeing this as a career opportunity and thinks adding one hoax to another hoax is a totally reasonable solution.* She flashed on Sam at the funeral.

'Has it occurred to you that maybe you're unfit? That maybe I'd have a pretty good case to have sole custody of this child?'

His face had been thunderous and even though Ali'd been dismissive at the time, she couldn't help but worry that he might have a point. In which case, compounding her unhinged behaviour of recent weeks was definitely not a goer.

'I actually got an email earlier that might be worth reading before I make the leap into my new profession as full-time internet performance artist. At least, let me follow up on that first,' she implored Mini.

❖

Ali's inbox: 3654 unread

From: Amy@SocialSolutions.com
Subject: Please read, Ali. I think I can help.

Hi Ali,

Amy Donoghue here. I hope you don't mind me contacting you out of the blue like this, but I presume you are at least intelligent enough to know that I am your goddamn knight in shining armour right now.

While I'm certain I don't need to give you my full sales pitch about my services – this email is probably the first one you've received in a week that's NOT spewing trash your way – I'll give you the topline.

Social Solutions is a discreet side hustle of mine that I have been running successfully for years now in addition to my more prominent work as a social media analyst (most recently to Shelly Devine, as I'm sure you're aware).

With my insider knowledge of the Insta world, plus my experience and connections, I am perfectly positioned to clean up a mess of this kind. I have a track record for defusing situations of this sort.

Remember the blogger who faked her own engagement? No? Of course you don't. She hired me forty-eight hours before the story was due to break and I neutralised it. What about the politician who went on a tweet rampage after mixing meds and posted a series of racist slurs in the voice of his teddy bear?

I take it that's a no? And damn right it is, because I am good at my job.

I await your response,

Amy

Director, Social Solutions

Ali was rereading the email for the third time as Mini drove her home across the city.

They made their way by increments over the toll bridge. Even mid-morning traffic was a shitshow, though cutting through the city centre and crossing the river at any time of day was a bollox. She couldn't imagine leaving Liv, though, as they'd been living together for years now. And, anyway, she still didn't have a job. Liv would at least cut her some slack on rent until she got sorted. Ali sighed, leaning her head against the car window; the sun was persisting over the bay to the east of the city though the sky above looked heavy.

Opening the door of the tiny 1950s semi-d that used to belong to Liv's granny was overwhelmingly comforting. Liv rushed out of the kitchen and wrapped her arms around her.

'I'm so glad you're home. I've got a chicken in the oven.'

'So domesticated.' Ali was admiring as she drew back and wiped her eyes – she was like a ticking bomb right now, liable to weep all over anyone who showed her a hint of kindness. It must be a reaction to being universally hated by strangers on the internet, she'd decided.

'Mini, thanks for looking after this one.' Liv and Mini shared a look of amused exasperation, as if Ali were an unruly child. 'You haven't been feeding her, though?' Liv sounded jokey but Ali could hear concern fraying the edges of her words.

'Well, she's looking a bit thin but at least she didn't start social media world war three on my watch,' Mini retorted.

'Fair.' Liv nodded briskly. 'How are *you* holding up?' She moved to pat Mini awkwardly, which Mini neatly side-stepped as Ali grinned. You didn't pat Mini.

'I'm fine, Liv. In fact, I told your mum I'd meet her for a coffee this week. I've a lot on, though. I really need to get back to the gallery. Erasmus has been holding the fort, but really, he can't keep a handle on some of the artists. Edmund, particularly. Erasmus is frightened of him.'

'Will you not take a bit more of a breather?' Liv persisted. Having practically spent half her teens in the Joneses' house, Liv would always feel like family to Mini and, annoyingly for Ali, they got on. They were alike in their determined ambition and frequent despairing of Ali's ways. Also, Mini was worlds away from Liv's own flaky, hippy sex therapist mother, Meera, whom Liv had always felt was slightly disappointed in her strait-laced, academic youngest child.

'I'm going to head off.' Mini took them by the shoulders in turn and robotically pressed her cheek to theirs. Ali was unsettled by just how lost she looked. It was so unMini. At the door, she called back, 'Alessandra, let me know if you want me to come to the doctor's appointment with you tomorrow. I'm free any time.' And she was gone.

Chapter 4

Tuesday morning was a grey, quintessentially Irish day. Mist pressed against the windows and Shelly felt it matched her nihilistic mood. She checked her phone: 10 a.m. Amy would be arriving any minute, thank God. Shelly still felt nervy after @_____'s messages of the night before.

I really got to you there, didn't I?

It could've been a lucky guess. She tried to believe this.

Georgie was munching on toast and narrating her LOL dolls' every move on the table in front of her.

Shelly consulted the day's schedule – not too rammed, thankfully. With everything that had happened in the last few weeks, Shelly was embarking on a whole-life overhaul.

She was reducing Marni's hours so that she could spend more time with Georgie, the future of SHELLY was up in the air and she felt that maybe she needed this time to consider her options. Some brands had been cool towards her since footage of her truth-bombing a crowd of pregnant women at the Mothers of the Earth retreat had been leaked a few weeks ago. It was a ridiculous storm in a teacup that had been blown out of proportion. She'd merely been honest about how tough and lonely new motherhood could be sometimes, but whoever had edited the video had made her look like a ranting lunatic.

Shelly knew she needed to decide what she wanted to do: kill SHELLY, the Insta-maven, once and for all or try to salvage the brand and steer it in a new, hopefully better direction – one that wasn't quite such a drain on her and her family. Amy, of course, was full of vigour about a total rebrand, apparently unfazed by the fact that Shelly was wavering on the whole thing.

The sound of the front door slamming followed by the chink of metal – Amy Donoghue was singled-handedly keeping New Rocks boots in business – heralded her assistant's arrival. She stomped into the kitchen in a flurry of torn denim and neon fishnets.

'Morning!' She swung herself up onto one of the high stools at the kitchen peninsula. 'Thought I should tell you that I've been headhunted by @HolisticHazel to come onboard that crazy train.'

'Oh?' Shelly wasn't surprised. Hazel loved to pass snarky little comments on how Amy was the only reason SHELLY was such a success. At that very moment, a WhatsApp from @HolisticHazel dropped into the Insta-mums group.

Ladies, I think we need to get together this evening to discuss some developments of late. A lot of the brands I'm working with are getting shifty about future plans to collab. I've had words with Holly from GHM PR and she gave me a bit of the lowdown. I'm sharing the info because we need to stick together and show a united front. We can't let the behaviour of that

*desperate, delusional psychopath Ali Jones tarnish the work we
do. I'm proposing a #MamasNightOut to discuss and plan the
coming months – plus, good for optics to be seen out together.
Jenny has booked a table at The Landing so great for the
'gram. See you there and don't even bother crying 'childcare'
@Shelly, this is probably most vital for you.*

'So …' Shelly was careful to keep her tone light as she turned back to
Amy. 'Are you considering it?'

'Shelly, as if! Not a hope.' Amy laughed. 'I mean, she's got some
major stuff planned. She's launching a wellness summit called
W Y N D that's going to be held on an uninhabited island out west
called Inis Brí. She's talking about flying in mega names from the
international Insta scene. Dunno how she'll be delivering on her
promised "boutique luxe festival" vibes on what is essentially a remote
rock in the Atlantic. And while that might be an entertaining disaster
to watch – No. Thank. You.'

Shelly grinned. 'Maybe it'd be good for you, Amy. Realistically,
I don't know what's going to happen to SHELLY. How does an
aspirational lifestyle brand work with' – she dropped her voice to a
whisper – 'an estranged husband living in the back garden? And a
stalker raking up damning old pictures?'

'Any word from the guards since last week?'

'No, but I sent on another message from last night.' Shelly passed
her phone to Amy to catch her up on the latest.

'This is creepy.' Amy scanned the exchange. 'They're just trying
to rattle you, though, you know that. Let's get a meeting with Bríd
locked in anyway to be on the safe side.' She pulled out her iPad to
make a note of this. On Shelly's phone she scrolled back further to
look at the messages @_____ had sent over the weekend.

@_____: Me again! Where are you? You haven't been on much at all? What's my Insta feed without the Queen Bitch of Beige Shelly to brighten my day with your bullshit?

@_____: Bbz seriously I can't get through my day without an #OOTD update from the Queen of Bland. What EXACT combo of boots, skinny jeans and blazer are you 'rocking' today?

@_____: Shel, I am one of your most loyal Shell-Belles and I need you to dress up some bullshit sponcon collab as female empowerment so that I can feel good about myself when I'm shoving your Shellypons up my gee.

'They seem to both stan you and hate you! Can't believe they remember the Shellypons! Morto.' The Shellypons were an ill-judged collaboration with a tampon company from a few years before. 'The messages are so weird,' continued Amy. 'But not in the way you'd expect from a stalker. Like, can you even call it blackmail when the only demands being made are for you to keep your Insta-content consistent? And on this front, I'm afraid I have to agree with them. Shelly, we need you back posting ASAP. What is this faux soul-searching about quitting Insta? We will ride out the separation just like we have everything else.'

Shelly remained unconvinced. Money-wise she needed to keep her brand on track but everything with @_____ made her worry just what she was inviting with this level of exposure.

Amy headed off to the office while Shelly cleared up Georgie's breakfast. Dan texted:

Cool if I drop in for a quick Georgie kiss?

Shelly sent back a thumbs up.

They were slowly finding their way with co-parenting, but it was very early days. They had agreed that with Dan so close, it would be nice to not live completely separate lives.

He slipped in the sliding back door and Georgie sprang up.

'Dada! Muma's taking me to the park today.' She clapped her hands, her dark braids bouncing as she launched herself at Dan.

'Oh, that's gonna be cool! Aren't you the luckiest little puppy?'

Georgie did a few little yelps and gave his face a little lick.

'Hmmmmm, Puppy had porridge for breakfast.' Dan winked at Shelly as he discreetly wiped porridge from his cheek. Shelly grabbed a wet wipe and scrubbed the shoulder of his suit jacket, where more porridge was now smeared.

'Would you be around this evening to watch G if I head out with the girls?'

'Yeah, there's golf on so, cool, happy to chill in here and watch it.' Georgie was now scurrying around the floor between his feet.

'Have you much on today?' Dan gathered his bag and stood to leave.

'Just a couple of scenes this morning. I'm trying to cut back while I reassess things.'

Dan just nodded and pretended to pet Georgie, the puppy.

He's a good father, Shelly thought, tinged with regret. That was the thing you forgot when a relationship was in a nosedive for so long. In between all the cheap shots and resentments, you completely forgot who the person even was before you started hating each other. Dan was not a bad person. They had both changed. He didn't like the Insta-life and she didn't like the person she'd been pretending to be to keep him happy. They had both made mistakes, but if they could co-exist like this for the moment, Shelly was happy with that.

'You've got to mind yourself and this one.' He made to pat her slightly swollen stomach but thought better of it at the last minute and Shelly smiled awkwardly to hide the sadness rearing up inside.

This isn't how it was meant to be.

'Of course it isn't,' her therapist, Berna, had responded just the day before. 'You thought you'd be welcoming this second child as a couple. You need to feel sad about it. It is a sad thing. Feel that. Don't be afraid of feeling it.'

'So, who's going tonight?' Dan made his way to the door.

'The Insta-mums, Hazel and Polly.'

'Horseshit Hazel? Wasn't she tearing you down last week?' Dan grinned.

'What? Have you been reading Notions.ie?!' Shelly mugged.

'I may have been …' Dan looked sheepish. 'It's only 'cos I forgot to take the Google alert for your name off from when things were … a bit … heated there a few weeks ago. The sidebar on that Notions thing is addictive. It's worse than crack.'

Shelly laughed at the image of Dan stuck into the gossip on the Notions.ie sidebar of shame. 'Well, that was last week. This week, according to Hazel, we need each other. She says she's got some news and, well, I don't really know what's going to happen with SHELLY, but I probably need to hear what she has to say. Plus, that weird person is still in my DMs and I kind of actually wanna talk to Hazel and Polly about it. See if they've come across the account. Bríd, the guard, says lots of these trolls target loads of people at once. I might just be on her rotating roster of people who piss her off. The guards ruled out a suspect last week and seem to be having a lot of trouble attaching an IP address to the account.' Shelly shrugged unhappily. 'Meeting Hazel and Polly might be useful or at least comforting. Surely Hazel's been trolled online.'

'Yeah,' Dan agreed. 'You don't swan around the internet bad-mouthing epidurals and bottle-feeding without ruffling a few feathers.'

Chapter 5

After Mini left, Ali went into the living room and flopped onto the couch while Liv went to faff with the chicken for a bit. She flicked between Amy's email and the text she'd sent to Sam that was blue-ticked but remained unanswered:

My first appointment in the Rotunda is tomorrow at 10 a.m. You're welcome to come with me. Just let me know.

She'd deliberately left it till the last minute to give him the details. It was a bit of a defence mechanism – so that if he said no she could just blame it on not giving him proper notice.

'Chicken'll be another twenty,' Liv announced, joining Ali in the sitting room. 'So, how's it going?'

Ali burst out laughing and after a moment Liv joined in.

'Oh my gawd,' Ali gasped through her peals of laughter. 'How do I even *start* to answer that?'

'Well, you look shite,' Liv proffered cheerily.

'Yep, I do, thank you. Turns out public shaming is a real appetite killer.' Ali tugged her hoodie sleeves down over her hands.

'Is Mini still on the "pretend you were doing an art performance this whole time" train?' Ali had filled Liv in via text in the car on the way over.

'Well, I think she's coming around to the idea that it might be pouring petrol on an already raging dumpster fire. And I got an interesting email from Amy Donoghue, Shelly Devine's assistant.' She fired the phone displaying the message across to Liv and waited.

'Racist slurs in the voice of his teddy bear? Whoa, I think I know who that might be!' Liv peered once more at the phone. 'She sounds hilarious.'

'She's ... I dunno if "hilarious" is the word but she's certainly pretty intimidating. Think I should meet her?'

'Yes.' Liv was emphatic. 'Ali, you can't stall like this forever. Even if living out your days in internet exile was an option, the baby is going to happen whether you engage with life or not. You have got to clear the decks and make a fresh start. This looks like as good a step as any. Just see what she has to say. I'll come.'

'Yeah, I know. You're right.' Ali composed a short reply asking Amy to meet and hit Send. 'I dunno how I'm supposed to pay her, though.'

'What's the deal with the ill-gotten free swag? You've a fuck-ton of stuff down in your room – could you sell it?'

'I feel like that's probably not great, karma-wise.' Ali frowned. 'Ugh, my room. It's a frickin' hellhole in there. I can't face it.'

'Well ... I gave it a clean over the weekend and I cleared out the box room too ... for the baby.' Liv looked a bit awkward and turned back towards the kitchen. 'Chicken needs a poke, I'd say.'

Ali hopped up after her and watched her from the kitchen door fiddling with the oven glove. She seemed off and Ali slipped uneasily down the hall to her bedroom door – a quick glance told her why Liv was so uncomfortable. There were three black bin bags lined up on the right of the door. Ali had let things go pretty badly in there. She quaked at the thought of what Liv had found. She nudged the first bag, causing an unmistakable clink of bottles. She winced. When had she last done a bottle bank run? She shuddered to remember. The next bag was slightly smaller, but another nudge produced the same vaguely accusatory sound of glass on glass.

Ali felt sick at the idea of Liv finding all the bottles. She'd stashed them in the drawers, under her bed, even in the wardrobe. She'd never analysed her drinking and the hiding of her drinking. It had helped her to cope on the bad days and that was the most she'd been willing to explore. She didn't like to think about why she'd let it get so bad. Seeing the bags laid out like this was crushing the little line she'd been feeding herself – that it was all perfectly fine and nothing serious.

She eased herself down onto the edge of the bed opposite the incriminating bags. A pain low down in her abdomen had started up. The stretching pains. She bit her lip. Pregnant. It was so surreal. She'd figured out her dates and reckoned that the night she got pregnant for real was the night she had met Sam in Grogan's after he had called her panicking having seen her pregnancy announcement on her Instagram.

I wasn't drinking that *night*, she reasoned. But she knew she'd have been if she could have. Still, the unsheathed mickey was not a drunken slip but an act of pure stupidity on her part. But, argued Rational Brain, the whole reason you were there *was* a drunken slip.

You weren't stone cold sober when you announced at the Glossies launch party that you were preggers. *All right, all right.* Ali sighed. Rational Brain was such a fucking pedant.

Yes. I'd had a few drinks in the taxi on the way to the Glossies launch party. Everyone does that.

Even as she argued with herself right in front of the tangible evidence of her drinking, she could hear how illogical she sounded. Not everyone drinks by themselves in a taxi on the way to an event. Not everyone hides bottles and not everyone goes along with being pronounced pregnant by some random male Instahun while in the middle of a gin haze.

'They'd say, "Oh, weird, I'm actually NOT expecting lol!"' Ali muttered.

'What's that?' Liv appeared at the door.

'I'm just going over what I *should* have done at the Glossies launch night.' Ali budged over as Liv settled down beside her and put her arm around her shoulders.

'Never too late for self-reflection,' Liv said as they both stared straight ahead at the bin bags. 'It was like an episode of *Hoarders* in here.'

'Oh God.' Ali flopped backwards on the bed.

'I thought I was going to find a haunted tampon or at least some homegrown penicillin. There was a half-eaten spice bag from November, according to the receipt.'

Ali moaned. 'I don't know how I let it get so bad in here. I'm sorry.' She pulled a pillow – fresh sheets! – over her head.

'Mm-hmm. Well, let's just say nothing in here was sparking joy. Don't worry, I did get a precautionary tetanus shot afterwards just to be on the safe side.'

'So, I guess we need to go to the bottle bank?' Ali kept the pillow over her face. She couldn't look at Liv right now. Still, Liv picked up the corner of the pillow and peered down at her.

'Ali, we needed to go to the bottle bank, like, six months ago.'

Ali rolled over onto her stomach and then shot up.

'What? WHAT?' Liv yelped.

'Oh, I dunno. I suddenly thought maybe I shouldn't be lying on my tummy when I'm preggers.' Ali sat up and tucked her legs underneath her.

'We need a list of the shit you're not supposed to be doing. Like drinking, Ali, you shouldn't be drinking when you're pregnant.'

'I know.' Ali was quiet. 'Luckily, Sam was around so much the last few months I wasn't really having any. Hardly at all.'

Liv stared disbelieving at her. 'This looks like quite a fair bit.' She flicked her head at the bags.

'I was having a really hard time, Liv.' Ali's cheeks burned. 'I promise I wasn't drinking as much after I met Sam. Thank God.'

Liv pulled her in for a hug and kissed her cheeks. 'That's good. It'll be OK. My cousin, Rachel, found out she was preggers with her first after a hen do in Ibiza, sure.' She paused. 'You were drinking a lot, though. Before, I mean. I'm so sorry. I didn't realise.'

Ali rubbed her forearm self-consciously. 'I think I was trying to numb everything with Miles. I just didn't want to feel things.' She spoke carefully, aware of Liv's eyes on her. 'God, this is depressing,' she finished, trying to laugh.

'Yeah, it's bleak as fuck. Oh God, FUCK!' Liv jumped up. 'The chicken!' she roared and fled the room.

Chapter 6

'Mamas, how are you all on this beautiful April evening? I've just led the family in a cleansing meditation and now I'm off on a mamas' night out – hashtag balance! Orca is getting into the swing of shivasana now that I've realised he's more comfortable journeying within when strapped into his car seat …'

Shelly was catching up on Stories in the taxi into town. The eighteenth-month-old Orca was strapped, Hannibal Lector-style, into his car seat amid the flickering candles and sheepskin blankets where the rest of the brood obediently meditated for the 'gram. Orca, Hazel's youngest, hadn't played ball with the Holistic Hazel brand since the day he was born – a fact that Hazel valiantly coped with by killing the sound on most of the stories featuring him and occasionally sharing lengthy posts about overcoming the challenges of oppositional children through crystal work. Though it's hardly oppositional when a toddler doesn't want to down-dog all day. Shelly rolled her eyes.

'So I have to ask,' the taxi driver piped up from the front seat as they made their way to the city centre in fits and starts in trudging traffic. 'You're one of these influencers, right? So is yer one a mentaller or what? I heard she faked having a baby on Facebook.'

Shelly X'd out of the app and arranged her features into what she hoped was an impassive smile.

'Oh, I have no idea.' Experience had taught her that taxi drivers were *hounds* for gossip and there was no way she was giving him anything.

'My young one says she tricked a boy into thinking she was expecting and then started a Facebook page all about it – nasty little wagon.'

'Hmmmm.' Shelly remained staunchly non-committal. Better not to engage, even to correct him on his facts. Poor Ali Jones. It was an utterly bizarre and horrible thing to do but what little she knew of Ali, she felt there must be more to the story. She wasn't a 'mentaller', as this guy was so delicately putting it. She was young and she seemed so alone. Where was she right now? Shelly wondered, and how was she handling it all?

Shelly googled Ali Jones and pages and pages of headlines from the last week since Ali's downfall appeared:

Desperate Blogger Fakes Pregnancy

Conniving Instagrammer Goes to Ground after Pregnancy Revealed a Hoax

A New Low for Influencers as Instagrammer Ali Jones Outed as a Liar

Oh God. It was an online hounding made acceptable by sites like Notions.ie pretending to condemn Ali but actually *revelling* in the takedown. Shelly tried to imagine it was her at the centre of this venomous attention.

Shelly Devine's Marriage in Flames after Hiring an Actor to Play her Husband

Insta-maven Shelly Devine Used Photoshop on her Baby

Shelly Devine Fakes the Perfect Life for Money

She shuddered. It wasn't some remote possibility. She glanced down at the black screen of her phone. Mad to think this little device was a portal to so much. On the other side of the screen were all her adoring Shell-Belles and her success of the last few years. But there was also @_____ poised to take her down if she didn't comply with their strange demands. A heavy feeling lodged in her chest.

She pulled up Detective Bríd's email from earlier.

Hi All,

Shelly, since @_____ has escalated lately with images that appear to be taken in and around your home, not to mention images suggesting surveillance of your family, I have cc'd Detective Eamon Mitchell from the Garda National Cyber Crime Bureau to bring him up to speed on what's been going on. The GNCCB is the national unit for investigating these types of crimes and they have access to the most advanced facilities in the country. As I said last week, after our interview with Ms Kelly Byrne aka @KellysKlobber, the IP address linked to the @_____ Instagram account is not locatable. It appears the person(s) is using a VPN (virtual private network) to avoid detection.

Garda Mitchell is recommending we take your phone for examination, in case the person(s) has installed spyware without your knowledge.

Let me know a good time to arrange a meeting in the station. We imagine initial examination of the device shouldn't take longer than a day. In the meantime, keep up with the advised security measures.
Kind regards,
Detective Bríd Nolan

Shelly knew she should be relieved that the guards were taking this seriously but equally their official-sounding email was scary. VPNs and spyware made @_____ seem even more threatening. Had she really thought @_____ would just disappear back into the shadows? That a person with the drive to gather all these photos and lie in wait for so long would just give up so easily? Shelly picked at her nails, worrying a little bit of cuticle skin.

The taxi driver had started up about some other Insta girl but Shelly wasn't paying attention – a plan was coming into focus. She needed to appease @_____, keep them happy and do what they asked – at least until Bríd and this Mitchell guy came back with an update on the phone. She couldn't take a pile-on like the one Ali Jones was under. She also couldn't bear the thought of Georgie one day reading that her mother had FaceFixed her sweet little baby face. She couldn't risk it. She clicked into Insta and found the last few messages from @_____ demanding updates. An outfit of the day should do.

'We're going right down here, is it?' The taxi man glanced back at her.

'Yep, you can leave me anywhere here.' Shelly began gathering her bits. She was early but she could hang back a minute and get this post out. Luckily, the weather had cheered up. She handed over the fare, did a quick pic with the driver for his 'young one' and hopped out.

She uploaded an outfit of the day shot and hit Post, feeling a stab of trepidation. She'd been mostly hanging back from Insta since her video rant about how hard motherhood was. She'd been lucky that a few journalists had been quick with the hot takes lauding her 'bravery' in 'lifting the filter on the struggle of millennial motherhood', as Deborah Winters wrote on Notions.ie. Ironically, Hazel seemed to have suffered most for being less than supportive. It didn't go down well when she appeared on TV in the immediate aftermath apparently eager to chastise her fellow mumfluencer. Not very #WomenSupportingWomen of her.

Shelly watched the phone tensely, flicking down on the screen to refresh the post. Here they come. Likes and comments were cascading in and Shelly exhaled, relieved.

@RamonaT: Lookin stun, where's the blazer from?

@HeathersPix: Yay you're back, we missed you ❤️ ❤️ ❤️

@OrlaLuvs: So happy to have you back on. Screw those haterz, Shelly you were SET UP. We know it was a witch hunt.

Hmmm, it'd be better if they didn't keep bringing the video rant up but at least, so far so good, everyone was being supportive.

@MaireNicAnBhord: Yay looking GORGE, hope @HolisticHazel sees this and knows she won't be tearing you down ever again. The #Shell-Belles will see to that.

Uh oh, Christ. @MaireNicAnBhord was a bit intense.

Shelly fired off a rapid response:

@ShellyDevine: @MaireNicAnBhord you are so sweet to defend me but honestly me and @HolisticHazel are total #bffs, we're on a #MamasNightOut this very second. 💋 💋 💋 ❤️ ❤️ ❤️

Hopefully some storying with Hazel and Polly tonight would quell any rumours of trouble in the Insta-mum camp.

She checked her lipstick and headed into The Landing.

'Shelly!!!' Alan, the maître'd, was ecstatic. 'Good to see you out!'

Oh God, 'good to see you out' was basically Irish for 'good to see you out when you probably shouldn't be'.

'Yeah, I've been taking it easy with the little bump here.' She placed a perfectly manicured hand over her teeny belly, daring him to so much as *mention* the recent video scandal.

'Now that's a legit bump there, Shelly!' He winked. 'You're not another wan getting "pegnant" for the 'gram. Mad stuff altogether.' He led the way through the busy and highly decorated bar – The Landing was *the* spot for the Insta crowd, every inch of the place the perfect Insta backdrop. As they squeezed past tables of women dressed to the nines even on a Tuesday night, Alan kept up a stream of rambling hearsay he'd apparently gleaned about Ali Jones. 'I heard she was planning on getting out of it by faking a … well … you know.'

'Alan! No!' Shelly gasped. Poor Ali! God, the whole town was on this gossip train. 'I know Ali and she'd never have done that. Ever. I think she just let a little thing get way out of control.'

Even hearing herself saying that wasn't convincing to Shelly. How, she wondered, and not for the first time, *how* had Ali done this? She'd seemed normal enough any of the times they'd spent together on set. How do you 'accidentally' lead people to believe you're pregnant? And for nearly three months?

'Now, here are my favourite MILFs in the whole wide world,' announced Alan as they arrived at the large banquette where Hazel and Polly were both engrossed in their phones. Hazel was rocking her usual Gwyneth Paltrow homage, a well-judged tan, pale floaty slip dress, her blonde hair braided intricately around her head and studded with rose quartz. Polly, on the other hand, was draped in a uniform of various beiges with suede knee-high boots and a tan only a few shades lighter than her glossy brown hair.

'You're not ready for my mama jelly, Alan.' Hazel giggled, looking up coquettishly.

Yuck! Shelly grimaced, but Alan was happy to play along gamely. That was his job, after all.

'Oh, I don't know. If I wasn't betrothed to himself at home, I think I'd take a shot – a mama jello shot.'

Shelly slid in, giving Polly and Hazel pecks on the cheeks. As Alan headed back to his spot by the hallway, she wondered how he put up with all the schmoozing. He must go home to 'himself' just utterly fed up with it all.

'Right, group selfie,' Hazel announced, and Polly and Shelly obediently leaned in on either side of her. The miniature ring light mounted on the phone was blinding but when Hazel tagged her in the pic a few moments later, they looked amazing. All white teeth, glowing tans, tasteful extensions and delicate rose-gold jewellery.

'Don't forget the #MamasNightOut.' Hazel seemed even more het up than usual as she clapped her hands together to call the night to order. 'First things first: Shelly, well done on the first post in a week. I'm glad you're back. Maybe now you're active again the Shell-Belles will back the fuck off. My mentions are a goddamn mess. We need to pull back together. I don't want anymore "think pieces" from Deborah Winters on why Instagram is a microcosm of everything that's wrong with female friendships, thank you very much.'

Shelly and Polly exchanged a look, the tail end of which Hazel caught.

'You two can pretend that I'm the hysterical maniac all you want but this stuff matters. This is our livelihood. We have taken a serious hit with this Ali Jones crap. Holly from GHM agreed to meet with me and Jenny for a tête à tête and she was kind enough to appraise me of some of the sentiment floating around the agencies and marketing departments. The vibe is that some of the recent public debacles have seriously damaged the credibility of the influencer in the eyes of some of the more prestigious brands. Shelly, I know you're fannying about pretending that you "want out" or whatever, but you need to cop on, you can't quit in a blaze of viral rants and some wayward girl who, whether you like it or not, has some connection to you – you won't get acting gigs as a washed-up influencer.'

God, she's really off on one, Shelly thought darkly.

'I haven't even ordered a drink yet, Hazel. Can we take it down a notch?'

Hazel picked up her phone, still glaring at Shelly, held her thumb over the voicenote key and spoke into it:

'Alan, we need a non-alcoholic prosecco for Shelly.'

'Alan's a lovely guy,' Polly offered quietly, but Hazel ploughed on, barely listening to her.

'Gals, I'm afraid there's worse to come.' She paused as the waitress came to set Shelly's raspberry-topped faux-secco down. They all smiled tightly – you always had to be aware of being watched when you were high profile. Shelly murmured her thanks and the girl slipped away – probably to tell her co-workers just who was sitting in the back booth. 'Quick boomer for the 'gram,' Hazel hissed.

They picked up their glasses, Hazel held her phone high above to capture the best angle and Polly counted them in.

'Three, two, one …' They mimed a cheers and, a moment later, the boomerang appeared in their communal WhatsApp thread and Polly and Shelly set to work filtering it, customising with different GIFs and writing their captions.

'#chillaxing with my faves @HolisticHazel and @PollysFewBits #MamasNightOutOut #MamasOnTheLoose #partay #besties' typed Shelly and hit Share.

'OK, housekeeping done.' Hazel leaned closer in and lowered her voice. 'It's one of the old Jennys.' Hazel exclusively hired assistants called Jenny so the various brand managers and PRs wouldn't wise up to how many assistants she went through.

'She's gone rogue and is starting a podcast and I'm pretty sure it's a tell-all about the influencer scene.'

'What?' Polly's voice spiked with anxiety.

'Oh Christ.' Shelly sighed. It was one goddamn thing after another. Still, it was nice to hear that everything wasn't perfect in Hazel's positive-vibes-only camp.

'I'm totally safe, of course,' Hazel went on, as Polly's head snapped up in surprise. 'My non-disclosure agreements with staff are watertight – they have to be; she cannot speak about me or any of my dealings. But I'm afraid you guys are potentially vulnerable.' She sat back looking somewhat contrite but mostly relieved.

So typical of Hazel to cover her own ass, Shelly raged silently, *now we're the ones potentially going to suffer the fallout of her being a megalomaniacal nightmare who probably bullied this Jenny girl.*

'Well, thank God *you're* safe, Hazel. That's the bloody main thing,' she spat bitterly. 'I've enough going on without this.'

Hazel nodded. 'I can imagine,' she intoned calmly.

'How are you so sure this is what she's doing? The influencer thing, I mean.' Polly looked disturbed too, which seemed odd to Shelly. Polly, while a committed mumfluencer, was kind of small fry. What did she have to hide? She shared snippets of a very wholesome family life with her two boys and an ex-rugby-player husband, who occasionally did yoghurt ads and the like. She seemed to spend inordinate amounts of time crafting, if her Insta output was anything to go by, but she was so vanilla, so *nice*, Shelly couldn't imagine her embroiled in anything more nefarious than the usual heavy hand with the FaceFix and maybe a bit of mild trickery – the macaroni Hogwarts she did at Christmas *had* to have come from Etsy: it was way too perfect.

Hazel, too, looked surprised at Polly's concern but didn't have the tact to hide it. 'Really, Polly, I'm sure Jenny will be going after influencers with a bit more clout than you, hun, you're grand.'

A flicker of annoyance clouded Polly's otherwise polished features. It was probably the most Shelly had ever seen her react to one of Hazel's frequent put-downs. She shook it off immediately and arranged her mouth into a slightly pinched smile.

Shelly felt sorry for Polly, the tan-stained hands and laboured make-up – the contrast between her highlighter and darker shading gave her face a ghoulish, mask-like appearance – seemed to underscore just how much she wanted this Insta-life. And she wasn't a desperate nobody by any stretch. But she did have a considerably smaller following than Shelly and Hazel. At 80K, she got far less salubrious gigs – lots of supermarket swag, kids' stuff for Ben and Louis, her little boys, who were five and six, and she was brand ambassador for a detergent – it was hardly glam. Shelly knew she'd love a shot at more stylish brands – she was forever trying to push more of a fashion angle – but Shelly sensed the PRs didn't rate her.

'Shelly. Shelly!' Hazel barked impatiently and Shelly tuned back into what had rapidly become a crisis-management session.

'I was saying you need to think about potentially getting ahead of this thing. This Jenny could have been privy to some of your Insta doings, Shelly.'

'But, what do you know so far? Why are you so sure we've got anything to be concerned about? Did it end badly? Does she have something concrete on me and Polly?'

Hazel sighed testily as she flicked and tapped on the screen of her phone.

'Here—' She thrust it at Shelly.

Shelly peered at the phone open on a podcast in the iTunes app – the logo was like the painting nails emoji but reworked slightly. The red nails were cracked and an adjacent bottle of nail polish was tipped over, the words *Under the Influence* spilling out in red.

The blurb said it all:

Under the Influence *is an investigative podcast revealing the malignant lies we're sold on social media. Every week, join our host Jenny Delaney as she uncovers the sordid scams and bullshit pedalled by our so-called influencers; from white labelling to white lies and minor misdemeanours to mega misrepresentation. Former assistant to one of the most toxic and malignant influences in the Irish scene (who for legal reasons may not be named), Jenny has the tea and it's about to be SPILLED. Episode 1 coming soon …*

'She's been digging around, though I've no idea who the subject of her first episode is going to be.' Hazel was looking positively high on her supposed concern.

'What's this number? Sixty-eight thousand?' Shelly passed the phone on to Polly to give her a look.

'It's the number of subscribers, Shelly. This only went up this afternoon,' Hazel explained, her green eyes wide. 'She shared it on her social and it has spread like wildfire. She doesn't even have many followers, five or ten thousand tops, but I'd say it's all over the WhatsApp groups. People are gagging for these takedowns.'

Evidently. Shelly sighed and downed her drink glumly.

'Well, I may as well tell you guys since it'll probably be on *Under the Influence* next week, but Dan and I have separated.'

Hazel gasped, drawing looks from a nearby table of suits, while Polly looked up sharply but said nothing.

'Please calm down, Hazel. I'm OK. We're OK. It's been coming for a while and obviously we're still totally committed to co-parenting and being a family.'

Hazel's face remained aghast. 'But what are you going to do? No more @DivineMrDevine? The loss of earnings must be astronomical …' @DivineMrDevine, an account purporting to be Dan, had provided a lucrative arm of the SHELLY empire. Hazel was shaking her head in disbelief.

'Well, *I'm* fine, thanks for asking.' Shelly laughed.

'But how can you be? I mean, it's the whole identity of the SHELLY brand – this happy clappy families thing.' Hazel's expression was swinging wildly between horrified and slightly gleeful.

'It's not and I'll be fine.' Shelly was refusing to let Hazel see her rattled. She was already rethinking telling them about @_____. With *Under the Influence* on the horizon, she needed to keep a lid on anything potentially scandalicious.

'I know the brands still love you, Shelly,' said Hazel. 'But, gawd, the struggling single mother thing … it'll be a bit grim with Dan gone—'

'He's not gone, sure,' Polly interjected. 'He's in the Seomra in the garden. Leave her alone, Hazel!' Shelly was surprised to hear this from Polly. Not only Polly defending her, but Polly apparently being privy to their current living arrangements. However, before Shelly could ask her who had told her, Hazel was signalling for a waitress.

'Another round, good girl.' Hazel smiled tightly. 'Now, sorry to be blunt, Shelly, but I've a bit more business. This year the Holistic Hazel brand has been going from strength to strength, as I'm sure you'll have noticed. My meal-replacement Nourish Dust™ has been my biggest-selling product of the last five years, would you believe. But it's time to bring a more three-sixty approach to my devoted audience. As such, I am planning an event on a scale never before attempted by any Irish influencer.'

This was a dig at her, Shelly thought, as she recrossed her legs, trying to get comfortable. Hazel's pitches could be quite long.

'W Y N D summit,' Hazel continued, holding her bangle-adorned arms aloft to underscore the words that she uttered with reverence, 'will be a part of this new evolution of influence. A chance to connect more deeply and *authentically* with our followers. We've shown these women how to do an everyday no-make-up-make-up look. We've revealed the brow technicians who can change their lives. We've given them the interiors inspiration. We've shown them what fresh flowers, a well-judged tray arrangement and a column candle in a vase can do for a room. Now we need to bring them on the next phase of our journey. W Y N D summit will acquaint them with how we, Ireland's premier influencers, replenish our souls.'

'Riiight.' Shelly nodded along. 'And so, is it like a showcase? For the brand?'

'No.' Hazel's eyes flashed. 'It's the most unique lifestyle festival the world has ever seen.'

'OK.'

'Sounds amazing, Hazel,' Polly chimed in.

'I know.' Hazel nodded decisively. 'It'll be in an exquisite and unique location. I'll have all the top alternative practitioners. Huge influencers from around the world. Everyone who is anyone in the wellness sphere. And thousands of paying attendees. The luxury will be mega and the best part? All the attendees will be at the festival with the women they admire most in the world.'

'The Real Housewives?' Polly guessed.

'Us.' Hazel scowled at her. 'We will be the selling point.'

'Right.' Shelly was unsure. 'When are you thinking, Hazel? Small matter of a baby on the way.' She indicated the burgeoning bump.

'Launch will be in the summer, but the festival won't be till early September. Look, Shelly,' Hazel hurried on with the hard sell, 'you'll help front the launch. You can opt out of the actual festival. We'll work out payment plans for everyone proportionate to their input and personal *influence*.' Hazel, Shelly noticed, levelled a pointed look at Polly, lest she was getting any ideas above her station. Poor Polly. 'It'll be good money for your divorce, if nothing else,' Hazel finished bluntly.

'OK, relax, Hazel. We're separated. No one's talking about divorce.' Shelly was drained and eager to wind this up. 'I'll have Amy look at our schedule.'

Hazel gave a decisive little nod before accosting the waitress, who had returned with the drinks.

'Hey, will you be a darl and take a little candid shot for us?' She rummaged in her bag and pulled out a small box. 'It's just a quick bit of spon. You don't mind, do you, gals? It's a holistic haemorrhoid solution and the brief is "don't let haemorrhoids ruin a night out". So, everyone laughing and super carefree and casual,' Hazel instructed, playing around with poses herself, holding the box to the camera and fake laughing.

Once the sponcon was taken care of, the Insta-mums drifted their separate ways and Shelly, relieved they had wrapped up so early, got a taxi home. *Georgie might even still be awake for a cuddle*, she thought, as the car pulled up to their gates and the driver killed the engine. At that moment, she spotted the porch light go on, illuminating Dan and a young blonde woman standing in the doorway.

'Can you turn off the headlights, please.' She leaned forward to see what they were doing. A churn of revulsion as she realised he was holding her face and passionately kissing her. They pulled apart and he pointed down towards the side of the house where the path to the back garden was. The woman – though she couldn't be older than early twenties, Shelly realised – followed his direction and made her way around the side of their house. Dan appeared to scan the driveway without noticing the unlit taxi, then retreated back inside.

Shelly slumped against the back seat. 'Why are men so goddamn predictable?' she asked the taxi driver.

'Is he your fella, then?' the man responded grimly.

'Was. But we only decided to separate, like, a month ago.' Shelly shook her head. 'I'm expecting his second child.'

'Scumbag.'

'Thank you,' Shelly agreed. She paid up and let herself in the side gate.

Fuck him, fuck him, fuck him, she thought with every step towards the house. *Pretending to be so nice, all the while stashing some 20-year-old in the back garden.*

She felt sick. She paused at the front door, wondering what the hell she'd even say to him. She thought about the possibility of losing the house. And the divorce she'd dismissed an hour ago that they would now surely be getting, the inevitable custody agreements. The ammunition Dan had against her. He would probably throw her whole Insta-life in her face and @_____ would be all her fault.

Well, maybe this girl-woman was ammunition against him.

I should just sit on it, Shelly decided, *wait until I need something to throw in* his *face.*

She made her way inside and followed the sounds of tedious golf commentary to the living room. Dan had already jumped up from the sofa as she rounded the door.

'Hi.' She smiled tightly.

'Hey, hey.' He shoved a hand through his hair. 'You're home early.'

'Yeah, thank God, I'm wrecked.' She patted her bump. 'How was Georgie?'

Before he could answer, she heard Georgie bounding down the stairs.

'Ha!' Dan grinned. 'She was asleep, I swear.'

'Muma! Muma!' Georgie flung herself into Shelly's arms.

God, she was awake upstairs while you kissed that girl on the doorstep, she thought furiously, staring at Dan over Georgie's shoulder.

Dan started gathering up some official-looking pages from the coffee table.

'What's all that?' Shelly was sure she spotted her own name on the page closest.

'Um. Well, these are actually from the solicitor. It's a proposal about the s-e-p-a-r-a-t-i-o-n.' He finished the sentence spelling the word for Georgie's benefit.

Shelly felt a tug of alarm. 'Why do we need solicitors for the s-e-p-a-r-a-t-i-o-n?'

'Well, it's to iron out money and living arrangements in the meantime. So that the d-i-v-o-r-c-e, when we start the process, will be easier, and then there's this place.' He gestured around the room. 'We'll probably have to s-e-l-l. Unless one buys the other out.'

God, this was all moving so fast. This morning he was all 'dad of the year' and 'mind yourself' and now he was flinging this at her.

'Well, I'm not going to be able to buy you out, Dan,' she spat, thinking of the girl, sitting right at this moment in her fucking garden.

'Yeah,' Dan agreed quietly.

'So, what? You honestly expect me to move in this condition?'

'Move where?' Georgie had tuned into what her parents were saying. 'Are we leaving? I don't wanna go. I hate everywhere else.' Her anguished little voice was hitting a frantic pitch. 'This house has my dollies and the daddy house in the garden.'

'Shhh, it's OK, love,' Shelly rushed to reassure her. 'We're not going anywhere, OK? This is your house. It'll always be your house.' She cradled her daughter and glared at Dan. 'I think it's time for bed. We're a bit overtired, aren't we?' Shelly slipped into the soothing first person plural that oddly seemed to kick in for all parents when faced with a tantrum. 'Say "night" to Daddy and I'll tuck you in.'

'Nighty-night, Pup.' Dan kissed Georgie's head.

'You go on, sweetie. I'll meet you in the bathroom for teeth.' Shelly watched the little girl scampering off, then turned reluctantly back to Dan.

'I dunno why you would tell her something so definitive when you know it's not possible.' He shook his head.

'Well, I don't know why you would fling this at me at nine o'clock at night. Anyway, I'm not going to freak her out unnecessarily, Dan.'

'It's not unnecessary,' he argued. 'Look, I'm not going to be a dick about it, but the fact is you'd need at least a couple of hundred thousand to buy me out of this place, Shel. And that's probably me being too sound.'

'Oh yeah, you're "too sound", Dan.' Shelly made sarcastic little air quotes. 'There's been so much upheaval, we need things to be steady. Especially while Georgie is getting used to all this. What is the rush?' She crossed her arms and cocked an eyebrow.

'For one, it's a good time to sell. Two, I don't want to live in my own garden for ever. I want to be in your lives, but I need my own space. I've started looking at places.'

Shelly sighed and stormed into the kitchen where predictably Dan hadn't so much as washed a cup from dinner. She began clearing the table. It was so easy for men. He could just get some cool pad, probably in town, start going on Tinder, or whatever the equivalent is for snobby executives, scoring 20-somethings and she'd be stuck in some one-bed shithole in Ballyashtown commuting in to 5 a.m. calls on set and juggling his two kids.

'Good for you,' she eventually snapped. 'Do you wanna head on? I have to go and actually put Georgie to bed.'

'I can wash up,' Dan suggested, a peace offering but Shelly was over it.

'Nah. Don't bother. I'm sure you need to get back to your little …' Shelly wavered for a moment, sorely tempted to add 'Tinder bitch' or something equally damning, but now wasn't the time. '… your little bachelor pad.'

She whipped around and marched up to the hall without saying goodbye. Crossing the blush marble floor tiles, she flashed back on the day she'd picked them out. She'd been so proud of them. They had them shipped from Denmark.

She climbed up the stairs, her eye snagging on the series of family portraits that punctuated the ascent.

I should get rid of these and do one with me and my girls, she thought defiantly, patting the bump – she was certain it was another girl.

Even though, a few weeks before, she'd thought about downsizing, maybe renting for a while, she hadn't been in her right mind then. After the punishing week of exposure from the leaked viral footage, she'd daydreamed about slinking off to a simple life off the 'gram but that wasn't her either. At the end of the day, she was Shelly Devine. She couldn't live in some depressing hole – she'd made this house and she was not giving it up so Dan could buy a city centre fuck-flat without a fight.

She pulled out her phone and opened her thread with Amy to read Amy's last message.

> *You can't keep on like this, Shelly. One foot on the dock and one foot on the boat doesn't work for an influencer. If you're not committed, the followers will dump you. You need to decide if you're in or out once and for all.*

Curled up in bed and scrolling, Shelly came across Hazel's sponsored post from earlier. It was ridiculous. There they were, all shiny, bouncy hair and mouths gaping, supposedly laughing while the incongruous box of haemorrhoid cream sat front and centre.

> *#AboutLastNight ... Don't allow #MamasNightOut be ruined by discomfort. Pick up a tube of #SoulHole haemorrhoid cream by @HeavenlyHealth and get out there with your #besties – thanks for the lols @ShellyDevine and @PollysFewBits.*

Whatever anyone might think, Shelly mused, it was more or less an honest day's work and it was money she needed if she was going to make a home and a future without Dan Devine.

She dashed off a text to Amy.

> *I'm all in. No more pussyfooting around, I promise. We need to make some serious dosh before the new baby comes. Hazel's batshit Holistic hell-fest will be good bank. I'll explain all when I see you ...*

Chapter 7

Ali came in to breakfast the next morning giggling at a bit of sponcon from Hazel … #SoulHole. Ick. Hazel touting haemorrhoid cream was enough to put her off the breakfast she'd already been only half-sold on having.

Pregnancy genuinely feels like being hungover 24/7, she marvelled, stalking the fridge and cupboards for something that appealed. She'd noticed over the last week, she'd get a taste for something, salmon on a bagel or lasagne, and then as soon as she'd finally hunted it down and was about to tuck in, suddenly it became the most foul thing she could ever conceive of. So odd. *Coffee at least still tastes good*, she thought, as she got the pot together.

She felt so much better after last night, she realised. Telling Liv the truth about how far she'd sunk in the months before it all kicked off with the baby-faking was freeing. She felt that maybe Liv understood better how she'd gotten so deep into the Insta-sham. Loading the car with the bottles and purging her room had been cathartic and now, as she pottered about the sunny kitchen, a glowing atomic orange thanks to the lino covering the floor, walls and ceiling (Liv's granny's décor tastes were heavily 70s influenced), she finally felt a bit calmer and a bit more on top of things. Her first doctor's appointment was today, and she was getting together with Amy after to 'strategise', as her response had said.

It was so comforting to have another person in her corner. Even if it was someone she barely knew. Amy had wanted Ali's inbox password so that she could read all the hate mail and death threats. She said it was to 'collate data and get a read on public perceptions, in order to decide how best to proceed'. It sounded professional. Ali handed over the info without a second's pause. Public annihilation could do that to a person. What did it matter if anyone knew any more humiliating things about her? There was nothing left to hide.

She consulted her WhatsApp. Sam had finally responded to her message about the hospital appointment at 1 a.m. last night.

I will attend the appointment, but I will be keeping my dealings with you to an absolute minimum.

It didn't scream 'warmth' or 'reconciliation' but at least he'd be there, she figured.

Coffee made, she finally selected a packet of Skips from the press and settled herself to watch a bit of Insta. It was weird taking a break like this and then coming back to find everyone was still on there shiteing on about their 'secret projects' and their #goals diaries and fey veganism with a touch of leather when the #OOTD called for it. Why had she wanted this so much? She watched @PollysFewBits laying out a family breakfast for the beefy Mr Few Bits and the two little Few Bits, who seemed to communicate only through the medium of rage-screaming.

'Ah, Skips and coffee, the classic combo.' Liv rocked in wearing grey drainpipe jeans, boots and a flannel shirt.

'It's the breakfast of preggers champions.' Ali munched on, flicking past the rest of Polly's stories, amazed at how boring one woman could be. 'You look very good.' She took in Liv's ensemble, which was much sharper than her usual grungy vibe.

Liv waved her hand as if to say *this old thing* and poured a coffee. 'So where are we at on the hospital appointment? I can move college things around and come with you, no probs.'

'Well, Tinder Sam actually deigned to reply, just the fifteen hours after blue-ticking me.' She read the message to Liv.

'Keeping yer dealings minimum?!' Liv exhaled loudly. 'He's aware, right, that he left some of his DNA in you and that that DNA is now growing hands, feet and a head?'

'Yeah.' Ali furrowed her brow. 'Not really sure how he intends to pull it off. Maybe passing notes to the midwife? God knows. I'm just crossing everything that seeing the baby on the scan might get through to him somehow. He seems to be in denial.'

'Well, maybe people in glass houses Ali …'

'I know, I know. I don't have a leg to stand on. In a way, that's probably why there's no coming back from this whole disaster for me and Sam. He has the ultimate comeback for absolutely every potential row ever. If we managed to get over this, it'd never be his turn to make the tea or put the bins out *ever* because "Oh, remember that time you faked a baby?"'

'Yeah.' Liv shook her head sadly. 'There's nothing he couldn't get out of with that in the back pocket. Even if he banged someone. In your bed. On your *birthday*. I *still* think he'd have you on the fake foetus.'

'I know.' Ali was quiet as she rummaged in her backpack and threw in a just-in-case bag of Skips to bring with her. 'I can't stop thinking about how we'll have this baby and one day the baby's gonna grow up and be all "How did you and dada get together?"' She shuddered.

'It's going to be a race against time to get your version of events in first, ahead of Sam's,' Liv replied.

'Yup.' Ali shrugged bleakly. 'I suppose at least you'll be there. I can say "Ask Aunty Liv. She was there" and you'll back me up.'

'Yes, well, I won't lie to the child. Everyone needs to learn at as young an age as possible just how insane their parents are. But don't worry, I'll give context and explain that you were necking wine by the bin-liner load at the time.'

'So comforting to hear. Right, I'd better go. I'm meeting with Amy Donoghue here, by the way – she's coming at around 5 p.m. – she doesn't want to risk us being seen out together by any snap-happy Rants.ie users. She thinks it's bad for optics if I'm seen to be trying to *engineer* any kind of comeback or apology. She says it has to feel really *authentic*.'

'Jeez, my thesis is going to need a sequel.' Liv grinned. 'Insta's getting more batshit by the day.'

Chapter 8

'Oh my God, Shelly! You look amazing. I cannot believe we're bump twins! Let's do a bump shot!'

The woman in the hospital waiting room was verging on hysterical as she helped herself to Shelly's bump, pressing her own bump against Shelly's and snapping pics. Shelly tried hard to hide her irritation; she'd only just signed into the midwife clinic and hadn't even sat down yet. Still, she put on a bright smile – you had to be careful with the Shell-Belles. They were all love and light and would defend her to the end, but if they ever caught a whiff of ambivalence in the DMs or out and about, they'd be on Rants.ie saying Shelly was too fond of herself and above posing for pics. It was a very delicate balance and one that Amy had always been very handy for managing.

'Good luck with the next few months.'

Shelly gave her a hug. However, the woman's grip was vice-like and she hung on much longer than the traditional hug time.

'I have a YouTube channel. We could collab,' she whispered, urgently holding fast to Shelly's upper arms, their bumps pressed together. 'I'm documenting my bump journey. Your followers would love it. I'd love a shout-out.'

'OK.' Shelly tried to disengage and glanced around for help. The waiting room was mostly empty, the weekday morning clinic being the quiet slot. 'I'm happy to do that,' she panted slightly as she finally managed to extract herself from the YouTuber. 'What's your channel?'

'From Stressed to Blessed. I nearly had IVF so that's my hook.'

'What does "nearly had IVF" mean?' Shelly narrowed her eyes.

'Well, we were TTC for ages and I thought I'd have to get treatment but then, miracle of miracles, I got a BFP a few months ago, but I'm still kind of going with the IVF angle because not enough women are speaking out about these things.'

Shelly was about to say 'But you didn't have IVF?' but thought better of it. If this loon wanted to squeeze some content out of a difficult time that she'd *nearly* experienced, then so be it. Let them roast her in the comments.

'OK, good luck. I'll be sure to mention it, I promise.' Shelly moved off to find a seat and wait to be called.

The other two women sitting nearby were called into separate offices and thank God From Stressed to Blessed had been on her way out when she accosted Shelly to molest her bump. A young man sat looking nervous two seats over. Where was this guy's wife? Shelly wondered. Or his girlfriend? Or maybe it was a surrogate situation …? It was just the two of them sitting there now and he was looking everywhere but at her. He seemed oddly familiar.

'I'm not pregnant, in case you're wondering,' he blurted into the silent waiting room and something about the voice and the awkward grin made her realise where they'd met before.

'Sam? Ali's boyfr...' She trailed off awkwardly.

He visibly winced and Shelly wished she'd pretended to not know him.

'I'm not Ali's anything,' he muttered testily, then waved a hand apologetically. 'Sorry, I shouldn't be snapping at you. It's been a shitty week. You're one of the Insta-mums, right?'

'Shelly.' She leaned forward to shake his hand. 'I worked with Ali on *Durty Aul' Town*.' Sam nodded grimly and Shelly searched for something to say. 'Are you here with a friend?'

'Here? Oh right, a maternity hospital. No, I'm not here with a *friend*.' He was scathing. 'I'm here with a girl I met on Tinder, who turned out to be a complete psycho.' He delivered this in a monotone, but his clenched jaw betrayed his fury.

'Another one? Since Ali?' Shelly was lost. Didn't he meet Ali on Tinder? Though, in fairness, she wasn't sure how much of Ali's story about anything had been true.

'No, no, still the same psycho. Ali Foetus Faker Jones. Only now she's pregnant for real. Lucky me.'

'What? She ... she ...' Shelly was stunned.

'Well, she says she is anyway. Which obviously means fucking nothing.' He was venomous. 'I'm not believing a goddamn word until yer one in there' – he jerked his head towards the examining room – 'tells me so. I might even request a paternity test. It's a pity Jeremy Kyle's finished. We'd be the perfect guests and ITV could foot the bill.'

Oh my God, what was Ali playing at? Shelly's mind raced. *Could she actually be trying to continue with this lie? Surely no one was that mad?*

But no hospital would be taken in by a pregnancy faker, so it had to be true.

'So Ali's in with the midwife right now?' Shelly asked carefully.

Before Sam could answer, Ali walked out the door to the left of them and instantly froze on seeing Shelly. The midwife appeared behind her consulting her file and called, 'Eh, Mr Sam Healy? I'll see you now.'

Ali shuffled mutely to one side as Sam stood and marched past the midwife without a single word to her. Ali gazed at the floor and flinched as the door to the examination room banged shut beyond her. Shelly sat still, waiting to let Ali speak first.

Shelly had thought a lot about Ali in the last few days. At first, when the news broke, she'd been shocked and disgusted like everyone else. Then, with the messages from @_____ piling up in her DMs detailing her own Insta-shams, she'd begun to feel more than a little hypocritical for judging the girl so harshly. Seeing her now looking pale and impossibly young with no make-up or Insta trickery to hide her ashen face and bloodshot eyes, Shelly felt oddly protective of her. She realised she didn't know much about her. There'd been talk on the set coming from every direction. Some of the older cast members had said her dad had passed away but Shelly had assumed that was more lies. Now here she was in the midwife clinic.

'Ali?' Shelly spoke at last, as Ali seemed to be in some kind of trance.

'I can't believe *you're* here right now,' Ali whispered.

'Are you ... OK? Come sit down. You look pretty pale.' When the girl didn't budge, Shelly stood up and guided her gently to a seat. She still didn't speak.

'Are you expecting, Ali? Truly this time?' Shelly tried not to sound judgmental as she said this.

'I ... am.' Ali sounded as surprised by this as Shelly felt.

'Wow, that's a ... plot twist.'

Ali snorted. 'Yup,' she said flatly. She took a deep breath and finally looked at Shelly straight on. Shelly just about stopped herself from gasping. Ali looked tormented.

'I'm so sorry for lying to you. And everyone. It was not planned. I swear. It just kind of happened.'

Shelly couldn't really see how something like that 'just kind of happened', but she didn't feel that now was the time for an interrogation – the girl looked so fragile, plus it wasn't any of her business. Though, God, she did feel sorry for her right now. She'd read all the bile online that was directed at this girl, but she hadn't been prepared for the effects of it to be so obvious on her. It was writ large in her eyes and across her face and even her posture – she looked like a person who was being hunted.

'You don't have to believe me,' Ali continued. '*He* doesn't. I thought we'd come here today, and he'd see the little baby on the scan and come around a bit, but he wouldn't even go in with me, insisted on separate conversations with the midwife. It hardly matters, though, really. *Everything* is such a mess, that *this*' – she nodded at her tummy – 'is practically the least of it.' She laughed bitterly. 'Can you believe that? This isn't even the shittiest thing in my life right now!'

'What else is going on?' Shelly presumed she meant the online commenters. 'People can be so cruel online.'

'Ha! Oh God, *that's* not even it.' Ali took a long slow breath. 'My dad died just over a week ago.'

'Oh Ali!' Shelly didn't know what to say. She took Ali's hands – she wasn't much more than twenty-five, so young to lose a parent.

'It sounds so wrong,' Ali continued. 'You're the first person I've had to, ya know, *explain* it to. He was sick for a really long time. He didn't remember me, hadn't known who I was for a few years. Not since I was maybe twenty-two, twenty-three?'

Shelly put her arms around the girl, feeling Ali's tears seep through her cotton Breton top. 'I heard some talk on the set. But, to be honest, so many people were saying so many things, I just thought they'd gotten the wrong end of the stick somewhere.'

How, Shelly wondered, did the journalists writing damning stories about the influencer who faked a pregnancy not know this? Although, they probably didn't *want* to know; it would kill their precious story. They didn't want to humanise Ali; they just wanted to make her an object of hate. The fact that she was grieving would ruin their angle of 'malicious Instagrammer is a dangerous, desperate liar'.

Ali pulled back from the hug and wiped her face.

'Sorry. I am such a mess. Gawd, I don't even want to think about what's being said about me on set. I was sort of debating emailing them to see if I could have my job back but maybe it'd be a disaster. It's just that I'm going to need money for when the baby comes and anyone new will google my name and immediately be, like, "No, thanks". At least, Stephan and Terry know me. They'd have to consider me, right?'

Shelly was doubtful that the show would take Ali back but couldn't bear to bring further despair on her.

'I'm actually meeting with Amy, your social media analyst, later,' Ali confided quietly. 'She says she's going to help me get this whole fake pregnancy thing under control. I haven't told her about the real pregnancy yet. Or my dad.'

'Well, Amy is your woman.' Shelly tried to sound positive. 'I know about her little side hustle, though she's always been really discreet so don't worry, she never breathes a word of that stuff. Or anything. My husband and I are separating, and Amy's been a great support.'

'Oh no. I'm so sorry. That must be so hard.' Ali looked genuinely concerned.

'Well, it is what it is. In fact, you're one of the first people I've told it to.' Shelly shifted in her seat. Her name was probably about to be called any minute and she couldn't imagine leaving Ali looking so crumpled and despairing out here. 'Look, maybe I can help somehow, Ali? I can talk to Stephan and Terry for you, explain things a bit. I can be quite persuasive with Stephan. And between us, Ruairí's annoying the crap out of him. Since you left, he's been the only production assistant and he's a bit of a liability. He mixed up Stephan's meds on set last week. Apparently, he had sachets of Nourish Dust™ and sachets of laxative and, well, you can imagine.'

'Ick.' Ali shook her head to dispel the visual. 'Well, it'd be really good, yeah, if you could. I don't know what else to do really. I owe people money from the sponcon I was doing with, eh, Ali's Baba,' Ali said cautiously, checking to see that the door behind which Sam was presumably grilling the midwife was still closed.

'And are things with Sam—?'

Before Shelly could finish, the door whipped open and Sam marched out clutching a sheaf of photocopied pages. He didn't so much as glance their way. Ali shot up but he was already through reception and headed up the corridor. And after a moment, she sank back down, clearly deciding it wasn't worth pursuing him.

'Should you go after him?'

'I honestly don't think there's any point. He wouldn't speak to me before we were called and then when the midwife did call us, he stood up and announced to the room that I'd been gaslighting him during our relationship and he would be seeing her separately. There were at least ten people in here then. It was pretty intense.'

'Give me your number, Ali, and I'll see what I can do with *Durty Aul' Town*. Or if anything else comes up.'

Ali thanked her and got herself together while Shelly saved her details.

'So how far along are you anyway?' she asked as Ali pulled on her baby-pink faux-fur coat.

'I'm not even that far behind you.' Ali looked slightly bemused at this. 'I think I got pregnant, like, the night I told him I was, ya know, "pregnant".' She made awkward air quotes around the word. 'I'm nearly fifteen weeks. I'm due, like, about three weeks after you – second of October. The midwife says first pregnancies don't show until a bit later sometimes. Plus, I guess my appetite hasn't been its usual self with everything that's been going on. I'd been really tired for ages but, other than that, there weren't many signs. Maybe a little queasy, but I thought that was anxiety about lying to everyone. I had a lot on,' she finished, looking sheepish.

'Hmmm.' Shelly said non-commitally. 'You'd want to have a lot on to not notice you're pregnant while actually pretending to be pregnant.' Their eyes met and they both burst out laughing.

Through her peals of laughter, Ali gasped. 'I was googling pregnancy symptoms on the daily, like!'

Shelly doubled over at this. 'I'm sorry. It's too funny.'

'Oh God, I know. I'm a goddamn idiot.' Ali wiped her eyes. 'I kept thinking this monster period was about to start, never realising that all the cramping was this.' She waved her hands helplessly down at her stomach. 'It is *so* weird. It's like I keep forgetting and remembering. I thought seeing it on the scan would kind of ram it home for me but then it goes out of my head and all I can think about is "Oh, everyone hates me" or "Oh, my dad's dead" and then the pregnancy thing pops back in and I'm like "Wow, great. I'm gonna have a baby and everyone hates me and my dad is dead." It is non-stop craic in here right now.' She tapped her right temple.

Shelly was suddenly struck by how similar their situations were. She'd felt the exact same in the last few weeks as she and Dan became more distant, her pregnancy marched on and @_____ circled in the DMs.

'I know how it feels, Ali. All these things dragging out of you and you just wanna lie down and take a nap. I know you probably don't feel this right now. But with the whole Insta thing, you probably had a lucky escape. I know you were flying high on there, but it has a way of taking over your life and it's not always a good thing.' She paused, debating her next words. Maybe telling someone about @_____ would defuse some of their malignant power: keeping them a secret made it seem so much more frightening somehow.

'I've got this person messaging me non-stop and I don't know who they are, but they know everything about me. And a part of me is, like, that's what you signed up for. If you put everything out there, this is what happens, but this is different. It's really frightening. They have pictures of me and Georgie and Dan. Really private pictures, not things I've posted on Insta. Have you heard of anything like this?'

Ali shook her head and Shelly sighed, the disturbed expression on Ali's face not making her feel any better about @_____.

'Want to give me a look?' Ali suggested. 'Maybe I'll notice something? I've been bet into Insta for two years and I'm addicted to Bloggers Uncovered and Rants.ie.'

'Sure.' Shelly dug out her phone. She didn't even flinch spotting the new unread message from @_____. It was becoming such a grim routine at this point that she knew any time she didn't check for a few minutes, a new message would invariably be there taunting her.

Ali studied the phone. 'This username is creepy.'

'Yep,' Shelly replied. 'The account's private and there're no followers. They send me messages complaining if I don't post. Messages saying I'm the queen of bland if I do post. They seem to know everything about my every move.'

'Yeah.' Ali's brow was furrowed with concern. 'Have you said on your story that you're here right now?'

'No,' said Shelly cautiously. Ali handed the phone back and Shelly twisted it to read the latest message.

The maternity hospital solo is a depressing look on you, Shelly. Guess that's the end of the happy clappy Divine family. The Shell-Belles will be devo if you ever do come clean.

Shelly frowned. That phrase, 'happy clappy', was reminding her of something someone had said recently. She scrolled back up the messages from @_____ to see if they had said it before but there was no mention of it. *Think, Shelly.* Where had she heard it?

'So, how could they know you're here?' Ali was looking around the deserted waiting room nervously.

'God knows. How do they know anything they know? I can't figure it out. I've even gone to the police.'

'What have they said?'

'They ruled out someone whom I suspected. Which was awful. I'd been so certain it was her and then when it wasn't, it was like having the rug pulled out from under me. Other than checking her out, they're "looking into it". They have a task force for this stuff. God, it's so scary, though. I get really freaked out alone at night. A couple of nights ago, I was certain I'd put the alarm on but when I checked, it was off. Then they sent this creepy message saying how they'd really got to me. And I know it could've been a lucky guess. Just like this one could be a lucky guess. But still, it's just horrible.'

❖

After her appointment, which (thankfully) was routine, Shelly walked back to her car looking at the ultrasound pic. The baby currently looked like an amoeba with arms and legs but in the spirit of getting along she considered sending the pic on to Dan, then she flashed on the sexy *teenager* he'd stashed in the Seomra last night and him saying he was being 'too sound' about the house. *Fuck him!* A new voicenote from Amy provided a welcome distraction from her simmering rage.

Amy was talking 'separation reveal' and Shelly was oscillating wildly between being triumphant at the thought of how much that would piss Dan off and horror at the notion of such a thing.

'*Under the Influence* is growing by the DAY.' Amy was emphatic. 'This Jenny one is in everyone's inbox scouring for tea, and while there's lots of us with integrity who care about this industry, the audience for scandal is HUGE. I'm on my way up to do a consultation with Ali Jones and I've been analysing the data and the numbers don't lie. Her baby-faking has been a major boon for that account. Since being outed, she's been inundated with follows. The account is currently private but if I accepted all these friend requests, she'd overtake the SHELLY account instantly. That would put her at the top of the Irish Insta-scene. Now we know a hate-follow isn't exactly the ideal but hate-follow or not, it is still a follow.'

Shelly paused the message to get into the car parked at the back of the hospital. She'd been careful to park in an out-of-the-way spot – there was a Penneys one street over and there was always a high concentration of Shell-Belles within a two-mile radius of any Penneys. Once settled in the driver's seat, she resumed the voicenote.

'What I'm saying is Jenny What's-Her-Name is a major threat. I am positive that her first episode is about @VeganVanessa – apparently there's some video of her up to her tits in Korean barbecue. I'm certain Ali Jones won't escape the *Under the Influence* analysis and there's no way she's not going to start digging around for skeletons in the SHELLY closet. You're a big fish and it's clear with the recent video rant and your slapdash posting of late that things are afoot in camp SHELLY. So, I am strenuously advising that we get ahead on the separation front. I've been collating a lot of data re: the separation angle. We're still a bit of a provincial backwater here but, in the States and the UK, there's loads of influencers doing the struggling single mum thing. Now they'd be much more edgy than SHELLY tends to be, and UK audiences are considerably more open-minded. As we know a lot of the Shell-Belles are very "middle Ireland", but I think they'll come around. I'm going to pencil in some focus groups to float the concept of a single SHELLY and get a read on audience mood. It could potentially make you that bit more relatable. Plus, it may have the added bonus of taking the wind out of that At Underscore lunatic when they see that they can't blackmail you about Dan sleeping in the Seomra. Right. Off to deal with Ali Jones's little mess. Talk later. Over and out.'

Shelly started the car and carefully backed out of the spot. Where did Amy get her energy? She was a powerhouse. Even if a focus group to assess what follower response would be to the news of her separation did sound bonkers. What Shelly wouldn't give to be a fly on the wall later when Ali revealed her latest plot twist.

Chapter 9

'The important thing to remember is you're the one with the platform. You're the one with the voice. They can rant all they like in the comments and share their "receipts" on Rants.ie, but at the end of the day no one hears that noise. No one who matters, anyway.'

Amy was storming up and down the brown-carpeted living room in full flow.

'This new development is a stroke of genius,' she barked, furiously tapping and swiping on her iPad.

Ali nodded emphatically. Amy was calling the very real baby now at the centre of BumpGate 'this new development' and had been positively ecstatic when Ali nervously blurted out the news.

'In-fucking-genious,' she'd roared, looking Ali over with clear admiration. 'This'll make it even harder for them to tear you to shreds. They love a preggers bitch, though we're going to have to play this one very, very carefully. If you're caught so much as *smelling* a bit of pâté, they'll be down on you like a ton of bricks. We can't give them an INCH. You're going to have to be the most by-the-book pregnant woman to ever grace Insta.'

'Not a problem.' Ali tried to sound capable and collected. 'Sam's barely speaking to me but, since our hospital trip earlier, he's averaging about five links to pregnancy articles an hour in the WhatsApp. He has *got* to get off Facebook.'

Amy finally settled on a brown pouf across from Ali and put the iPad down to focus fully on her.

'Right. Obviously, this new development means my strategy needs rejigging but, to be honest, this couldn't be better news. We've got a full house of "don't come at me" cards.' Amy listed them on her fingers. 'Dead dad. Mental illness. Up the pole. Dumped. Unemployed. Ah-mazing.' Ali couldn't help but grin. Amy Donoghue was even more hardcore than Ali could have predicted. 'We're going to kill it, Ali. Now you currently look like complete shit, which is perfect. We need to record your statement while you still have this unfed *Girl, Interrupted* vibe going.'

Ali swallowed nervously. As much as she wanted Amy to sort out her life, the thought of going back onto Insta to talk to thousands of disgusted people did not appeal.

'Yes, that face is perfect for our purposes.' Amy held up her phone and Ali instinctively flinched away. 'Don't worry, it's not for posting, it's just research for my mood board.'

Ali nodded and steadied herself for the camera. A mood board for social media rehabilitation? Ali checked the time. Liv'd be home any minute and was going to lap up this shit. Amy was now absorbed in Ali's phone. She'd demanded the rest of her passwords the second the ink was dry on the confidentiality agreement they had both signed before Amy so much as said 'hello'.

'Right, I'm just setting up a shared Google calendar so that there are absolutely no goofs during the apology rollout.' She returned Ali's phone and Ali scanned the coming weeks.

'There're still sponcon slots in here?'

'Eh, yeah! How'd you think you're going to pay my fifteen per cent? Never mind pay for this baby and whatever rent you're forking out for this armpit of a house?'

'I guess … I just thought … Well, they've all fired me.'

'Yep. However, I've hand-selected a few to target for reconciling. I've emailed Holly at GHM to discuss how potentially good for optics it would be for GHM to show compassion and understanding to a collaborator who's suffered a mental breakdown. She was very interested. They've had some stick lately about paying lip service to the mental health issue without doing anything concrete to back it up. This could be their opportunity to look like, well, not a completely shallow PR operation. I think she's going to go for it and, when they do, the rest will follow.'

'Amy, that is really fucking clever.' Ali was awed.

'Now that I'm handling your dealings, it adds a layer of professionalism and trust. I've told them you are seeking treatment for your addiction issues and Holly reports that they're getting some final sign-off from higher-ups, but it looks good.'

Ali was stuck on the phrase 'addiction issues'. She quaked at the thought of people knowing about her secret drinking. She wasn't sure it had been a problem as such but more of a comfort blankey – a comfort blankey that was then replaced by followers and likes on Instagram – and Ali could honestly say she didn't miss drinking. She just missed having something to reach for and cling on to during the tough moments.

'I don't have addiction issues. And it wasn't a mental breakdown or whatever ...' She trailed off, sounding feeble and unconvincing even to herself, but to her surprise, Amy just shrugged.

'TBH, it doesn't even matter, Ali. We just need you to be seen to be seeking help. But it has to be credible. The programme of recovery I want you to enroll in is anonymous so it's not something we'll be discussing on your Insta in *explicit* terms. However, that doesn't mean that we can just pretend you are attending either. There can be no phoning it in or lying this time, Ali. It's too risky. Especially as one of Holistic Hazel's disgruntled ex-assistants has launched *Under the Influence* – a podcast exposing influencers' shenanigans. All eyes will be on you just dying to trip you up, so you will be going to Catfishers Anonymous meetings even though, technically speaking, no one could prove it one way or another.' Amy continued checking things off the list on her tablet as though she'd said nothing of note whatsoever.

'What's Catfishers Anonymous? Like Alcoholics Anonymous?' Ali yelped.

'Best place for her,' called Liv from the hall, having evidently entered the house stealthily to listen in.

Ali could hear Liv dumping her backpack on the hall table, disturbing the ceramic cat display in the process. She appeared at the door holding a tiny kitten, which was now without a tail.

'This is Liv. She's the one who's writing the thesis.' Ali gestured.

'Oh right, the famous thesis.' Amy jumped up to shake Liv's hand. 'It's a very interesting area you're working in. If I can ever be of any use at all for research purposes, let me know.'

'Oh thanks. That could be really brilliant actually.' Liv ran a hand over the shaved side of her head. The longer dark hair on the other side was arranged in an intricate plait. 'Anonymous, of course.' Liv gestured and the ceramic kitten flew from her hand and smashed against the wall.

Liv was nervous. Ali sat back to enjoy the awkwardness. *They're gonna bone.* She grinned to herself.

'Oops, sorry, sorry,' Liv muttered, bending to gather the pieces at the exact same moment Amy, too, stooped to help. They bumped heads and Amy's hair momentarily got caught on one of Liv's ear piercings. They stood close together apologising profusely and trying to extract Amy's hair.

'So, this is how Goths mate?' Ali chirped cheerily from the couch.

Liv, now freed from Amy's tangle of dyed red hair, straightened up, immediately regained her usual composure and shot Ali a warning look that seemed to say, *If you want any more roast chicken dinners from me, you'll shut it.*

'Ali,' she said sternly, 'maybe don't call the woman who's kindly taken on your shitshow of a cause a Goth.' Amy handed her a piece of the kitten and Liv flashed her a grin before turning and heading for the kitchen.

Amy returned to her seat on the pouf, a tentative smile playing on her lips.

'Right, so, where were we? Oh, CatAnon, yes. Catfishers Anonymous. So, it's an anonymous programme, very discreet. I just want you to attend meetings. Show face, etc. As I said, it's just to cover our backs should anyone probe any deeper into just what kind of treatment you're seeking.'

'Oh-kay.' Ali shrugged. 'But I guess, like, I'm not a catfisher.'

'Oh, no?' Amy raised an eyebrow behind her horn-rimmed glasses.

Shite. Ali sensed she'd just taken some kind of conversational bait.

'Well, the internet certainly seems to think you're a catfish, Ali. The definition on Urban Dictionary states: "A catfisher is an individual who uses the internet, and in particular, online dating websites, to lure people into a scam romance. The general goal of a catfisher is financial gain by developing an online relationship with another person and ultimately asking for money."'

'Urban dictionary has a definition for Bass Turd,' Ali replied flatly. 'It's hardly a trusted source. And I didn't set out to *lure* anybody and I didn't *ask* for money. Brands just started offering me money.' She leaned forward pleading her case.

'Well, Ali, if you want to go on a crusade, arguing your innocence based on semantics, that's your decision, but I'm advising you against it. There's no room for subtleties online. Everything is binary on the internet. Black or white. Guaranteed, those people won't even grasp the difference between "a premeditated scam" and, I dunno, what we'd call your stunt? A catfish crime of opportunity? All they hear at the end of the day is Girl Lied About Pregnancy. If we start overcomplicating the message and trying to say 'Girl Didn't Mean to Lie About Pregnancy, A Few People Picked It up Wrong and Girl Just Didn't Correct Them and Then It Snowballed', well, we've lost them. They're already mindlessly scrolling Insta. They've no attention span.'

Goddammit. Ali hated to admit it, but Amy definitely had a point. She knew herself from Rants.ie that people usually just heard a few key words from any bit of goss. It's how Shelly Devine's leaked video a few weeks ago before the Glossies had gone from *Woman Says Motherhood Is Hard* to *Woman Wanted to Harm Her Baby* in about two minutes flat.

'But the attention span thing worked for Shelly,' Ali argued. 'They forgot all about her in a matter of days.'

'Well, that's because elsewhere on the internet you were faking a pregnancy journey, Ali. To pull off the same deflection in this instance, we'd need Holistic Hazel herself to be caught at a BDSM party tit-feeding a guy on a dog leash who was not her husband.'

'OK, OK, I know. You're right,' Ali conceded unhappily.

'Right, next.' She consulted the tablet. 'Once you're rehabilitated, it's time to capitalise. You've now got one helluva compelling brand story and we wanna make the most of it. As soon as we reset your account to public, we're potentially looking at a captivated audience of two hundred and eighty thousand. There's no room for some half-baked fumbling rollout; everything needs to be choreographed to perfection. We need to get the apology done, then tease the new real baby reveal with a few #ExcitingNewsComing tidbits and then get some serious spon on the baby-reveal post. Leave that to me – this baby announcement post will get more eyes on it than Shelly's, Hazel's and Polly's announcements put together. It's unparalleled brand exposure and we're going to make sure they pay. I'll take care of that. There'll be a few brands that won't want to associate with us but don't worry, most of them don't have a shred of integrity. And when they see the figures on your stuff, they'll be all over it.'

'Won't people think it's kind of in poor taste?' Ali twisted her hands together nervously. It was way different planning sponcon with a real baby involved, she realised. *How do Polly, Hazel and Shelly do it?* she wondered. *How do they sleep at night and not worry about what they've signed their kids up to?*

'Well, yes.' Amy snapped with a grin. 'I certainly wouldn't be advising any ordinary client to do such a thing but, Ali, you're the baby-faker. *This* isn't in poor taste; *you're* in poor taste. They hate you anyway; you might as well get a little something out of it. This money'll give you a bit of stability after the baby's born. It's up to you how long you run with it. Beyond the rollout phase, this is hard to predict. In a couple of months, numbers might've have plummeted after their initial morbid fascination. You're *car-crash Insta* right now. They won't be able to look away. But depending on the public mood, they'll tire and drift off to some other bit of goss or, who knows, maybe they'll stick around? I watched you over the last couple of months and you've got something. It wasn't just the bogus baby journey and the Glossies WildCard nomination they were watching for. You're compelling on camera. You're a natural performer. Think about what you want out of this too, Ali.'

❧

In bed that night, Ali looked over her old video posts as she deleted them at Amy's instruction. She cringed at some but also found that others were actually pretty funny. She was definitely at her best when moaning about Sam or bitching about stuff – being herself basically. She combed the comments for clues as to why 68,000 people had watched this video of her talking about the etiquette of Netflix when you're coupled up.

@ElleG: Oh my gawd yassssss! You're so right Ali the absolute RAGE when he watches ahead in the series without me.

@YogaBae41: Ali on relationship ettiquette: 'You both need a personal Netflix show each and a shared show.' Best advice ever lol.

@SarahGreene: Pissed myself at your description of Sam finding out you'd already watched The Affair in secret!!!!! You guys are too cute.

Fuck's sake, they seemed to just like me. And I was too stupid to realise, she moaned internally. *And they liked me when I was just being me and not shiteing on about protein or matcha when I've never even touched the stuff.*

She flicked over to @HolisticHazel, who was in a bath with dried lavender and other blooms protecting her modesty and practising some #selfparenting, according to the text in the corner of the video. Apparently, #selfcare was over. 'For me, the self-care movement started with great ideals but it's since been co-opted by the media and has become a shallow term for little more than a scented candle and a bubble bath.'

She's not wrong, Ali thought. There was a time there when Ali was certain you could have posted a story of yourself shaving a cat, hashtagged it 'self-care' and everyone would have been totally fine with it.

'Self-parenting is simply a way for us to show compassion for ourselves and place our needs as mothers ahead of the demands of our families,' Hazel intoned calmly. 'So just for a few minutes a day, beautiful mamas, practise mindful self-parenting and allow yourself the luxury of being a child again with @lavenderlovlies, who do a fantastic range of bathing accessories from dried bath petals to natural sponges. Use the offer code "Holistic Hazel" for five per cent off your first purchase and don't forget to follow @lavenderlovlies. It means the world to me when you follow the accounts I shout out because that's more of what we need: women lifting up our fellow women. #WomenSupportingWomen #selfparenting #HazelsWisdom.'

#WomenSupportingWomen was being done to death. Ali rolled her eyes. *Let's be real here, Hazel, it's about you demonstrating your influence to brands.* She clicked the 'women supporting women' hashtag and found herself idly browsing the various posts earnestly extolling the power of supporting each other. The cynical voice in her head was bitching intensely, *No one's supporting me.* She thought of all the reams of hatred dropping into her inbox and DMs daily all coming from women. *It's such a goddamn sham. They only support you when you're perfect and you think like them and act like them. And don't fake pregnancies online... Okay, maybe they had a point.*

Chapter 10

'I wanna play Insta, Muma,' Georgie whined. Shelly leaned across her mother's kitchen table and unlocked the screen.

'She just likes the puppy and cat filters,' she explained to her mum.

'So how was the appointment?' Sandra's face was full of concern.

It had been a few days since her scan at the Rotunda and her encounter with Ali, but she was only just catching up with her mum now.

'Everything looks OK so far. They're happy with the size, she looked pretty chill in there. I was jealous! Imagine a cosy little nine-month nap.' Shelly sighed. 'I'm definitely feeling way better all round, thank God. Nausea is completely gone, and I feel like that soul-crushing tiredness is lifting.'

'You're doing great, pet. It's been a mad month but you're getting back on track. How's Dan?' Sandra put the kettle on and rooted out the biscuits.

'Well, he couldn't make it to the appointment. He's over in London for meetings this week.' Shelly dropped her voice, conscious of Georgie hearing them talk about their marriage. They weren't hiding things from her but, given that she was only just about to turn four, they figured they had a little more time before they would need to roll out a big explanation. 'I think he's started D-A-T-I-N-G. Already.'

'He didn't hang around.' Sandra looked appalled.

'I know! I keep thinking about how *I* was there walking on eggshells. Doing every little thing to anticipate his reaction to stuff. Hiding SHELLY work because I knew it'd cause a fight. That kind of thing. And then he's straight off with the first Tinder twat he catches.'

'Shelly!' Sandra admonished. 'I know you're angry but try to keep it pleasant. You have to. And how is the little madam?' Sandra cocked her head towards Georgie, who was pouting and preening into the phone screen. Shelly sighed as the little girl changed her poses and snapped a couple of pics from overhead. It was harmless play, though Dan would probably freak if he saw her at that. He'd blame Shelly for corrupting their daughter. *Everything is always the mother's fault*, she thought, feeling mutinous. Mothers can't win. If they're too focused on their kids, they've become mumsy and irrelevant, but if a dad is focused on his kids, he's a legend. Lauded for something as basic as supervising his own bloody child. Then if something goes wrong, all anyone wants to know is 'Where was the mother?' No one asks 'Where was the father?' because the bar for fathers is set so low that, short of just being absent entirely, they're winning at parenting.

'Berna says letting her just get used to the "new normal" is better than hitting her with a big talk that might scare her unduly,' she said softly, turning back to the debate at hand. 'She says we should just answer her questions honestly as they come up but not make a big deal out of things.'

'Yes.' Sandra poured the tea and nudged the milk towards Shelly. 'With a new bab on the way, she'll have plenty of upheaval without worrying about being a latchkey kid.'

'Why on earth would she be a latchkey kid, Mam? What even *is* a latchkey kid? It sounds like something you got from *EastEnders*.'

'Oh, I don't know what I'm saying.' Sandra waved her hands helplessly. 'A child from a broken home is all I mean.'

'That's WORSE,' Shelly erupted.

'What's worse, Muma?' Georgie had momentarily paused in her selfies and was looking up inquisitively.

'Nothing!' Shelly and Sandra both yelped in unison.

'What's worse?' she persisted. 'What is? What is?'

Shelly scrambled for something to appease her. Sometime in the last few months as four approached, Georgie had begun talking with the intensity and relentlessness of a cold caller trying to switch your internet provider. Shelly actually googled 'Four-year-old never …' and the search bar had automatically filled in 'stops talking'. It was cute but also could probably be used as torture against prisoners of war in combat situations.

'We were saying there's nothing worse than a melty Jaffa Cake,' said Sandra, coming to the rescue.

'Eww, yuck,' Georgie retorted, turning back to the phone and her own face peering back at her.

'Listen, Shelly. I'm sorry, pet. I'm saying the wrong things.' Sandra bit into a Jaffa Cake dolefully.

'I know, I know. It's OK,' Shelly reassured her and added milk to her cup. She watched the pale cloud bloom in the tea and tried not to get angry.

This was what it would be like for them now, she thought sadly. Dealing with people's everyday blunders; People feeling sorry for her. People assuming that her family wasn't perfect – that as a 'broken home', they were in some way in need of repair. She knew the last thing her mam wanted to do was make her feel bad but sometimes the intention didn't matter a damn, not *wanting* to hurt someone didn't make it any less painful when you did.

Thoughts of the mothers at the school gates next year and Georgie being the only kid in her class with separated parents converged on Shelly. She'd been going along trying her best not to think too far into the future.

'Georgie's doing great.' Her mother's voice brought her back to the present. 'She's a credit to you, pet. And you're doing great yourself in spite of everything you have on.' Sandra rubbed Shelly's arm and tilted her head sympathetically. 'Mairead said she's there any time you need help or to even just grab a break for a few minutes.'

God, this was torture. Was everyone just going to assume that she was some sad case now who was soldiering on? Saddled with her two kids instead of blessed with them? Her brother's wife, Mairead, was probably beside herself now that she and Dan were splitting up. Ever since they had become sisters-in-law, Shelly had detected a whiff of resentment from Mairead. She'd always suspected that Mairead and Johnny thought she and Dan were up themselves and she knew Mairead was always top of the watchers of Shelly's Insta-Stories, but she NEVER referred to SHELLY or any of her successes. They came to the launch of her coffee table book but didn't even ask her to sign a copy. Who did that?

Mairead did some blogging but Shelly wasn't sure if she was still at it. She'd been so busy with SHELLY – it was hard to keep track of everyone's lives. And here Mairead was now acting all concerned, offering help but most likely she just wanted a closer look at the slow demolition of Shelly and Dan's 'perfect life'.

❖

'Georgie! Dinner!' Back at home, Shelly fussed about with the gold cutlery and linen napkins. She'd set an extra place so it looked as if three people were having dinner. She chewed her bottom lip. It certainly wasn't the biggest lie she'd ever told on social media. She just wasn't ready to come clean yet about her new relationship status. She knew any announcement of the split would trigger an outpouring of pseudo-sympathy and an inevitable wave of headlines from online sites using her family's life for clicks.

She took a couple of flat-lay-style pics of the table. It looked gorgeous; along with their plates of quiche and salad, which Georgie would undoubtedly barely touch, she had a bowl of strawberries, a selection of crudités and breads, with wildflowers in a vase in the centre next to her marble tealight holder.

She called Georgie again. She was playing on the patio beyond the sliding kitchen doors. It was great to finally feel the days getting longer. It was nearly May, which always had such a hopeful vibe to it, though of course this year it would be hard. Shelly tried not to think about the anniversary coming up in a couple of weeks. She and Dan would have been seven years married this year. She snapped her mind shut to the thought and focused on editing the picture, bringing up the contrast and fiddling with the colour balance until the whole thing looked sharper and bathed in a rose-tinted haze. Georgie cantered in and clambered up to the table, stuffing a strawberry into her mouth.

'So pretty, Muma! Will I do "cheeeese"?' Georgie leaned her elbows on the table and perched her face on her small clenched fists, stretching her strawberry-stained lips into a perfect stage-child smile.

Shelly laughed at the pose and took a pic. 'Nailed it, sweetie!' Georgie happily tucked into the bread and ignored the crudités and quiche.

Shelly carried on editing the flat-lay and tried to enjoy the peace of the moment. She had found her guilt about her mothering had eased considerably since Georgie wasn't appearing so much on the SHELLY account anymore. This flat-lay was a sponsored post for the interiors brand that was supplying the tableware, not to mention Shelly's portion of the mortgage this month. Georgie wasn't needed for this kind of post and this was what Shelly was set on pursuing. It was tough, though. The Shell-Belles wanted the mum content and she'd dangled a bump journey in front of them only a few months ago and was now failing to deliver. The engagement on posts like this one was never as strong. The followers wanted the good stuff: the cute daughter and the perfect life, not sterile flat-lays. She added the requisite hashtags to the caption, tagged the relevant accounts, hit Post and slipped the phone into her pocket.

She took a reluctant bite of the quiche. Pregnancy seriously affected her appetite and, of course, @_____ hovering ominously at the edge of her mind wasn't helping. Any time she let more than a few hours lapse between posts, they were back in the DMs goading her and demanding she keep her 'Insta content more consistent'. It was a very particular kind of blackmail, as Detective Bríd had commented.

'It's difficult when their aim isn't clear like this. Usually we would expect them to have moved to demands for money or *something* by now.'

The fact that her stalker was confounding the police was not comforting. Shelly wished she could block the account but, as Amy had pointed out, they would be back within minutes with a new account.

'Trying to shake these trolls can be like whack-a-mole. You block one and they're immediately back with another account. And nothing pisses them off more than people trying to get rid of them,' she'd explained.

Amy was right, as @_____ could become very heated if Shelly didn't follow their low-grade demands to the letter. The first message she'd woken up to that morning was definitely verging on angry.

@_____: *Where was the bedtime skincare routine last night, Shelly? I TOLD you I wanted a 'get un-ready' with me on IGTV. Whatever happened to 'I'd be nothing without my Shell-Belles, without you guys I wouldn't have my amazing career and all these incredible opportunities'? You owe us, Shelly. You seem to be forgetting who holds all the power here. What would people say to this getting into the public domain????"*

Beneath the message was an old pic from the SHELLY account. They had put it up for breastfeeding awareness week. Shelly had swallowed uneasily.

How could @_____ know about this post? She remembered the day clearly. Hazel and Polly had been over at the time for an #InstaMamaMorning, Hazel banging on about how important it was to be seen to be empowering women on awareness weeks like this. She'd no Insta-worthy pics of nursing baby Georgie – taking nice pics had been the last thing on her mind as her experience of breastfeeding had been pretty rocky. She and Amy had been hard-pressed to find one where she wasn't looking despairing and ugly-crying, while Baby Georgie was wrinkled and red-faced screeching at her breast. Amy had dismissed them all for not being on-brand and then Hazel suggested they do a staged shot.

Shelly remembered burning with embarrassment. She couldn't be so bald as that. However, after Hazel and Polly had left, she'd given in and helped Amy concoct a tasteful portrait of Shelly breastfeeding a doll of Georgie's. It had been wrapped in a pink baby blanket.

@_____'s pic was from the same day, the same set-up but snapped from another angle. It showed Shelly smiling beatifically into the face of a small plastic doll, gently proffering a breast to it. Oh Jesus. This was bad, there was no way to couch it that didn't come off as pure batshit crazy. How did @_____ have all these photos? In darker moments lately she'd been suspicious of everyone. Amanda, her MUA? Marni? Even Amy herself – it had to be someone close, she decided. The level of access displayed in these pictures seemed to confirm this.

Shelly checked that Georgie was engrossed in the strawberry bowl and picked up the phone to look at the picture once more.

It was this same room, though before they had done the full light-filled-extension revamp. The sliding doors that now ran the full width of the kitchen-dining room had yet to be put in and instead that wall just had two large windows. This picture exposing the charade of the breastfeeding post had been taken from the window of the old back door.

Shelly twisted slightly to look at the spot where it had been. There were some floating shelves there now with tasteful Insta-essential accessories: a couple of ferns, a succulent, a glowing diffuser and a picture of resplendent pregnant Shelly. What a different story that pregnancy was compared with this one. She looked down.

At nineteen weeks, her bump was nearly as big now as it had ever gotten when she'd been expecting Georgie – she'd be massive by the end. Apparently, this happened on second pregnancies, the young midwife had sympathised before posing for a selfie for her own burgeoning account (@AWhiffOfMidwifery, 12,000 followers). 'It's 'cos the extension's already been built, know what I mean?'

Shelly grimaced just remembering her words. Ewww.

Of course, this latest incriminating photo knocked Marni firmly off the list of suspects. She hadn't joined them at that stage. And Shelly felt in her heart of hearts it couldn't be Amy. For starters, Amy was behind the camera when this picture had been taken. She'd have needed an accomplice. It was too ludicrous; Shelly shook the thought from her head. She'd seen Amy's reactions to some of these posts and, really, no one was that good an actor – Shelly should know, she'd studied with some seriously talented people at RADA. Of course, there was Hazel and Polly. There was always a little competition simmering between them. And they had been there earlier that day, but they had both left by the time this pic was taken. And if it was either of them it didn't make much sense. Wouldn't they be trying to get her off Insta? Not demanding she be more prolific in her posting?

Hazel was off on her own mad tangent of earth mama stuff and she surely had too much on her plate already for a committed campaign of blackmail, and Polly was just so nice and boring. Shelly felt bad thinking this, but it was true, she was so basic. There were always mortifying spelling mistakes in her captions. Shelly cringed. She genuinely appeared to not know the difference between 'you're' and 'your'. She just didn't seem to have the imagination for something like this.

Maybe it was a stranger? A Shell-Belle gone bad? She shivered at the idea of a stranger creeping around the property. She screengrabbed the latest shots and sent them to Detective Bríd. Hopefully they would get some time to discuss the case soon but Shelly knew from her email that Bríd was snowed under.

Chapter 11

Ali observed the crowd outside the Glasnevin community centre from the safety of her car at the far side of the car park. It was a fairly wide demographic, lots of old people, a few teenagers and every age in between. They mostly looked as if they had just come from work. She consulted the pin Amy had sent her the night before to double-check that she was indeed in the right place. They just didn't *look* like a bunch of crazy catfishers. The bulk of them looked like boring nine to fivers. The whole crew could have just as easily been a community choir or something. There was a little old man who looked about seventy. What was he doing on the internet full stop? Never mind catfishing people?

She checked the time on her phone. Twenty-five past. According to Amy's text, the meeting started at half and she could see people in the group stubbing out cigarettes and putting away their vapes as others began to file inside. It was now or never. Ali definitely didn't want to walk in after everyone. She'd always hated that feeling in school of everyone watching her while she tried to find a seat. Best to be among the crowd and remain anonymous. Though Ali was just about the least anonymous person in Dublin these days. Everywhere she went, she could see people doing double-takes, leaning in to whisper urgently to their friends or, worse, seizing their phones to snap a pic. Ugh. So many pics kept cropping up online of her looking shady ducking into the Spar near her and Liv's place. Notions.ie kept posting them alongside headlines like 'Not So Glam Now: Shamed Instagrammer Spotted Purchasing Findus Crispy Pancakes'.

Though Amy had promised her that anonymity wouldn't be a problem at CatAnon.

'It's in the title. Catfishers *Anonymous*. You don't even have to give your real name. I think lots of them go by initials or their old catfish handles – it's something to do with facing their actions or whatever. May the fourth be with you.'

Ali had grinned. Liv had said exactly the same to her first thing this morning. They were perfect for each other.

Shit. Ali could see the last of the CatAnons holding the door open for one another and she hopped out of the car and sprinted across. The tall, ginger guy heading inside just in front of her turned to greet her.

'Hi. I'm @SweetBabyAngel16.' He held out his hand to shake hers.

'Oh, yeah. Hi.' Ali tucked her hair nervously behind her ear. 'I'm, eh, @AlisBaba.' An unmistakable flicker of recognition crossed his face, but he simply smiled warmly and said, 'I think you've come to the right place, my friend.'

Ugh, God. Were the Catfishers going to be all peace and love and *healing*? Ali grimaced, making her way inside and slipping into a seat near the door at the back. @SweetBabyAngel16 had taken the one in front of her. She looked around the room. There were about sixteen people altogether. A few caught her eye and smiled, which she nervously dodged. Her tummy felt weird, but she couldn't tell if it was nerves or the first detectable little hum of life from the bab. She'd seen him on the scan. He looked like a kidney bean with wiggly little arms and legs and she'd felt certain he was a boy. She gave her non-existent bump a gentle pat and held her breath to feel the gentle pops within. It had to be the baby. She smiled to herself. There you are! The midwife at her last appointment reassured her she'd start showing soon. She was nineteen weeks after all. 'Everyone's body is different,' she'd said, patting Ali's arm.

Ali didn't like to dwell on the fact that while a large part of her was just excited to have a bump, a smaller part of her thought that once Sam saw her with a cute little pregnant belly, he'd finally soften towards her. Aaaand if she was being totally honest, another even smaller, darker part of her knew the bump'd better get on with popping soon, as Amy'd finalised an excellent sponsorship deal for Ali's return to Instagram. As the girl who'd previously cried 'baby', they needed there to be no niggling doubts in the followers' minds that this time it was #AlisNoBullshitBaba. That was literally the campaign's hashtag. They had partnered with Sweet Little Lies – Ireland's first and only private polygraph testing service – and Ali was constantly having to look at the final figure they'd agreed on to keep herself from backing out. After Amy's cut it was nearly a year's salary at *Durty Aul' Town*.

Amy was irritated by Ali's qualms. 'For God's sake, a few months ago you designed a pram for your fake baby, Ali. What's the problem? This campaign is about a *mea culpa*. It's about owning up to your bullshit. And coming clean. It's perfect.'

Ali gazed around the walls as more people came in and got settled. There were posters with slogans everywhere.

'Don't do the first post.'

'Keep it in the day.'

'Do no harm, tell no lies.'

'Put the phone down.'

A woman settled herself in one of the chairs at the desk at the top of the room, opened a large diary and began doing a headcount. Behind her hung two vast posters that looked like scrolls. One announced in large letters: 'The 12 Steps of Catfishers Anonymous' while the other proclaimed 'The 12 Beliefs of Catfishers Anonymous'. Ali started to read with interest when a last straggler bustled in and hurried to the empty chair at the desk.

Ali clamped her mouth shut in case she audibly gasped. She'd *not* been expecting to run into someone she knew at this little weirdo shindig but there, shrugging off her denim jacket and sitting primly facing the room, was none other than @PollysFewBits. What the actual fuck was she doing here? And not just here but, judging by her seat at the head of the room, here in some sort of position of seniority? Ali saw Polly see her and a look of mild panic swept across her usually serene features. Ali tried to smile in a reassuring fashion and Polly nodded brusquely, leaning to hear whatever the woman beside her was saying.

They confabbed for a second longer, then the woman beside Polly cleared her throat and began reading from a laminated sheet in front of her.

'Hello and welcome to this meeting of Catfishers Anonymous. My name is @BigDickY2K and I am a catfisher.'

The people around Ali drowned back: 'Hi @BigDickY2K.'

'This is a closed meeting of Catfishers Anonymous,' she continued. 'The only requirement for attendance is a desire to stop catfishing. Are there any newcomers here today who would like to introduce themselves?'

At least six people looked in Ali's direction. According to Amy, there was only one group like this in the whole of Dublin, so of course they were going to notice a newbie. Ali sighed and cleared her throat awkwardly.

'Hi, I'm … eh …'

@SweetBabyAngel16 turned back, coming to her rescue. 'You can say your name or use your old online handle,' he whispered. 'Then say you're a catfisher.' He finished with a wink.

'OK … I'm @AlisBaba and I'm a … catfisher.'

'Hi @AlisBaba,' chimed everyone, with lots of them giving her warm nods and encouraging smiles. The girl beside her, who looked about 30, shook her hand.

'We will begin today's meeting with @Always_Watching who has kindly agreed to share her story of recovery from catfishing addiction.'

'Thanks, M.' Polly smiled at the woman beside her and clasped her hands together on the table in front of her. 'I'm @Always_Watching and I'm a catfisher. So … where to start? I suppose the first time I ever made a fake profile was back in the MSN messenger days, which is a bit of a giveaway on my age!' A few appreciative chuckles rippled through the room. 'I'd go on there and pretend to be this really hot girl who was amazing at hockey and on the school team. It wasn't serious lies at first. I just wanted to feel like I could be someone different. I loved talking to the boys on there who were so gorgeous, and all seemed to be the most popular guys in their schools. Sure, who knows *who* they were. I was probably talking to some of you lot.' Polly grinned and the room erupted in guffaws. Ali spotted one of the older men getting a knowing nudge from the little old lady beside him.

'I suppose things got more serious when I got to college and there was more opportunity to be online. My parents had been pretty strict because it was all new back then. When I was a teenager, the family PC was the size of a small car and it was plonked in the living room, where the whole family hung out. But when I got to college, I could stay in the library all day. And, of course, that's when MySpace and Bebo became big and I had millions of profiles. I was lead singer in a band on one and I was really into dancing on another. I'd steal all the pictures from obscure blogs and tumblrs. It was a bit easier back then. You couldn't reverse search an image yet,' she added a little sadly, as though mourning a simpler time when catfishing was pure. Ali looked around the room at the sea of sympathetic faces. Some nodded at different things Polly said.

'I just loved my online life. I felt special online. People wanted to talk to me and be my friend. Whatever I wanted, I could make happen.'

Ali, to her surprise, found herself involuntarily nodding along. She got it. It was everything she'd been feeling these last few months.

'Then, of course,' Polly carried on, 'I met a boy online and he became my boyfriend. He was always trying to meet up. He lived down the country, so, at first, I could get by on excuses but eventually he decided to come up to Dublin and surprise me. He knew I lived on campus. I wasn't that good at catfishing back then. I used lots of the same details across my profiles. I didn't bother changing things like date of birth or location and I put up similar pics of my house and where I lived, that sort of thing. When I opened the door to him, I panicked and pretended to be Sylvie's roommate – that was the persona he'd been seeing online for nearly six months, "Sylvie". When he asked my name, I told him my real name, not realising he was already suspicious and had found my other profiles online. He said he'd come back later, and I remember just sitting on the floor panicking. I was too shocked to even make a plan. When he came back an hour later, I barely spoke. He had printouts of Sylvie's MySpace account and my own personal one – he'd gone to an internet café, remember those?' Polly smiled wanly. 'He called me a freak and a pathetic little bitch.'

The girl beside Ali murmured sympathetically. Ali noticed @SweetBabyAngel16 in front of her was wiping his eyes, his shoulders tensed. Ali thought of Sam holding Liv's thesis and spitting the same kind of furious words about her and she found she had to swallow hard to hold off the tears herself.

'That should have been my rock bottom.' Polly twisted her fingers nervously in front of her. 'I'm afraid I just got better at covering my tracks. Things got darker then and of course that's when @Always_Watching started, which was my last online identity before I found this wonderful programme. I've probably spoken for long enough but just to say CatAnon saved me and I have learned so much in these rooms. And for any newcomers' – Polly's eyes met Ali's and she looked deadly serious – 'anonymity is sacrosanct. It's so important for all our recoveries that we can trust each other.' She raised an eyebrow in Ali's direction, then smiled brightly, looking around to take in the whole room. 'I know it sounds mad to trust a roomful of catfishers, but there you have it. I'd trust you all with my passwords!' she finished with a little laugh.

Everyone applauded and @BigDickY2K made a couple of notes in her book and asked people not to talk for too long so that everyone had time to share. The sharing followed a circle around the room starting to Polly's left, meaning Ali would have to open her mouth pretty damn soon. *Shite.*

'Hi, I'm @User_4_h8,' said the little old lady, who had nudged the man beside her during Polly's speech. 'And I'm a catfisher.'

'Hi @User_4_h8,' the room answered.

'I got so much from your sharing, P. You always have such a great message. I have so much love for this programme too. You all know me. I didn't pick up a phone until well into my sixties. I barely knew there was an internet.' She laughed nervously, patting her white hair that was set into a neat little cap of waves. 'I first got started on TripAdvisor. It was an accident. My Jimmy had opened up a B&B in Kilkenny. Lovely place and then next thing they got a bad review on this yoke. I was beside myself. Jimmy was saying "Don't be worrying, Mam" but I couldn't sleep. I was sick on it. Then Jimmy's wife told me she reckoned it was a publican from town who'd put a bid on the property before they got it. Well, one night I'd had a sherry and was feeling braver than usual and I got the lad over the road to bring me his iPhone and he showed me how to set up an account and I was off. I gave that fecking publican a bollocking of the highest order. I said his pub was uglier than a bishop's bare arse!'

Ali was startled by the vitriol that was suddenly pouring out of this sweet little old lady.

'And bam! Just like that I was addicted to my catfishing. I got the lad from over the road to set me up on my own iPhone and then there was no stopping me. I went after everyone. The team manager at the GAA club who put Seamus Óg on the seconds. Biddy Meaney – meaney is RIGHT – down at bridge, who charged me for a class that I didn't turn up to because of her stupid fecking cancellation policy.'

Jaysus, she's on a roll, Ali thought. Maybe if she kept going Ali wouldn't have to speak at all.

'Anyway' – @User_4_h8 folded her hands primly in her lap – 'today I'm proud to say that I have deactivated every account and now I just use my phone to FaceTime the grandchildren, get the odd bit of shopping – oh, and I'm a divil for Candy Crush. I'll leave it at that.'

'Thanks, @User_4_h8,' chimed everyone.

The next man looked nervous. He was pulling at his shirt collar and the point where his thinning brown hair met his forehead was shiny with sweat.

'Hi everybody. I'm @OfficerMartin and I'm a catfisher.'

'Hi @OfficerMartin,' the room dutifully responded.

'Well, eh, gosh, thank you firstly for your incredibly honest share.' He nodded to Polly. 'I got a lot out of your story. It really brought me back to my rock bottom and reminded me how I never realised I was a catfisher. I just did these things and never saw that I was addicted to the power that my online persona gave me.' Around Ali, a few people nodded. 'For me, it started when I'd gone to the guards to give out about a neighbour who constantly parked his car up on the path, blocking the whole thing. Everyone had to step into the road to walk around it – it was so bloody inconsiderate. My wife would have the buggy for our youngest fella, and she'd be dragging that into bloody traffic, like!' He was getting heated and paused to breathe and calm himself.

'Sorry, it's just that kind of thing bothers me. Anyway, at the garda station they didn't give a crap. Told me I should just have a word with the neighbour. I was annoyed at being dismissed like that. The guard was on his computer on the other side of the glass at the reception and he was just so dismissive of me. That's when I spotted his name badge and got the idea.' @OfficerMartin swallowed and ran his fingers through his hair again. 'I went home and set up an email account in his name. It was just to give my neighbour a warning. I never thought I'd do anything else with it. Truly.' He licked his lips and then took a swig from his bottle of water.

God, he's so nervy, Ali thought, *where the hell is this going?*

'After "Officer Martin's" email, the guy stopped parking on the path, which was great and my wife was delighted, though I didn't tell her the ins and outs of it. And I should've just deleted the account …'

Fuck's sake, Ali wanted to shout, *this anecdote is giving us all blue-ball – spit it out – what did you* do*???*

'I started noticing that I could see the woman next door in her bedroom. We live in semi-ds, nineteen thirties – they're grand houses altogether. I'd know this woman to say hello to, very nice. She wears the yoga pants thingys.'

Oh, Ali perked up. *Officer Martin, are you a little perv?*

'I don't really know what possessed me but one day when I was in the older fella's bedroom – that's the room that looks onto their bedroom window – I got the idea to email her. I told her I was on an undercover covert op and that we were trying to snare a Peeping Tom in the neighbourhood.' He made another nervy raking of his hair and took a swig on the water bottle. 'I asked her to undress at the bedroom window so that we could flush out the Peeping Tom. I said it was her civic duty. She was concerned and I said it was for the safety of the whole road. So she did it. And I didn't expect to … ya know … eh, climax. But I did.' He was holding his face in his hands. 'I climaxed into the wee lad's Dublin jersey,' he finished in a whisper.

Jesus, that went real dark, real fast. Ali tugged her dress down in case @OfficerMartin was about to start 'climaxing' again. *God, just say 'jizzed in the jersey' or something.* She grimaced. *Why make it so much more gross with* climaxing*?*

The room roused itself from the shock of that graphic image and began muttering 'thanks' for his share.

'I also filmed it,' he blurted out and the chorus of 'thanks' trailed off awkwardly.

Now it was the turn of the girl to Ali's right. She straightened up and looked around nervously.

'Hiya, I'm @KellysKlobber and I'm a catfisher. I dunno how to follow *that*.' She laughed. 'That had everything! I didn't really think I had a problem at all. I had a fashion blog and used to do lots of fun ASOS and Penneys hauls on my Insta and that was all cool, used to get the odd free bits and bobs, but I didn't really have that many followers. Until my nanny got cancer and I don't know why but I decided it'd be better for my brand if I was the one who got cancer.'

'What???' *Oh shit*. Ali clamped a hand over her mouth to prevent anything else from escaping.

@KellysKlobber glanced her way momentarily and then carried on. 'I just thought #KellysKancer had a ring to it and I hadn't been feeling that well and a gal I knew had got loads of new followers when she was hospitalised with a UTI.' Kelly, obviously sensing judgement in the silence, was looking around the room with a beseeching expression. 'Look, I didn't wank at my neighbour! I just made a hashtag and did a cancer-reveal post.'

Oh my gawd! Wild! Ali was high at the revelation that at least two people here were definitely worse than her.

'No cross-sharing please,' @BigDickY2K piped up from the front. This, Ali realised, must be some rule to keep people from talking about what others had said.

'Sorry. Sorry. Anyway, the whole #KellysKancer thing didn't really get off the ground because my family staged an intervention and I ended up in treatment. Which is a good thing. Because I suppose after seeing what happened with' – she snuck a look at Ali – 'other people making things up on Insta, it's good that my family stopped me before anyone found out. In the hospital, I really started to understand that I didn't have cancer and just because I didn't have cancer didn't mean my Instagram couldn't be brave in other ways. So yeah, no more lying or catfishing. I even deleted all my burner accounts that I used to use to boost engagement! I'm in remission from my lying and from my fake cancer,' she concluded proudly.

'Thanks, @KellysKlobber,' the room somewhat grudgingly replied. The cancer thing had clearly not gone down well at all, Ali thought.

Shite. I'm up. Ali looked around at the expectant faces, many of whom were smiling and nodding encouragingly.

'Hi, so I'm Ali. I mean, @AlisBaba. And I'm a catfisher. I guess.'

'Welcome @AlisBaba.' The whole group seemed very interested once more. *I'm fresh meat*, Ali realised. *They're all probably listening to each other shite on about GAA jersey jizz endlessly. I'm new and exciting.*

'So, this is my first time here, obviously. Some of you might probably have heard about my little incident. I faked a pregnancy on Instagram and then everyone found out and now I'm a pariah. I'd just like to say, I didn't set out to make up a baby. Some people just assumed and then I didn't correct them.'

'Sounds like denial, Ali,' @KellysKlobber interrupted sagely.

'Excuse me, I'm just explaining the situation,' Ali snapped. 'And, anyway, is she not cross-talking or whatever?' she implored @BigDickY2K.

'Continue, Ali,' @BigDickY2K said in a placating voice.

'So *anyway*.' She glared at @KellysKlobber. 'Well, things got really out of hand when this guy I had sorta been seeing or, well, saw once and had sex with, showed up thinking the baby was his and I didn't quite correct him. So that was bad.' Ali sighed.

It was really horrible going back over it like this. She felt compelled to explain herself to these strangers. 'I just was going through a really tough time – my dad was really sick. He's dead now. He died the same night it all came out that I was lying.' Ali was now giving her hands twisting on her lap her full attention. She couldn't look around and risk seeing all the sympathetic head-tilts. Better wrap it up before she got upset. Pregnancy was like being possessed – one minute she was snapping like a premenstrual velociraptor and the next she was crying because one of the celebs on *Dancing with the Stars* had nailed the cha-cha. 'So, look, I'm here to get better and heal and all that shite. So, thanks.'

'Thanks, Ali.' The tone was considerably warm compared with Kelly's fake cancer. Ali shook her head. Even *she* could see that was low. Between Kelly's Kancer and Officer 'Spooge on my kid's stuff' Martin, BumpGate seemed positively *tame*. She flashed on Sam's stricken face when he found out she'd made up the pregnancy.

'I thought I was going to have a family, Ali.'

She swallowed dryly and dragged her attention back to the room.

'Hi, my name is @SweetBabyAngel16 and I am a catfisher.'

'Hi @SweetBabyAngel16 …'

❖

After the meeting everyone milled outside in the car park. The shares had been revelatory, mainly in the sense that there were people with much bigger problems than Ali. Kelly stood beside her sucking on a vaping device.

'So? What did you think?'

'I think @OfficerMartin is a criminal,' Ali returned casually.

'Shhhh, Ali! You can't refer to anything from inside unless the person who said it, like, specifically brings it up. Were you not listening at the end there?'

'Sorry, sorry! No, I was listening. Yep, first rule of Catfish Club, yadayadayada.'

Kelly chewed on the device.

'Can't believe you're Ali "Baby-Hoaxer" Jones!' Her look was halfway between disbelieving and admiring.

Ali shrugged at this dubious source of adulation. 'You're not supposed to talk to me about that unless I bring it up.'

'Well. That'd be true if you hadn't been the top story on every website for weeks there and trending on Twitter and all that.' She exhaled a plume of fragrant peppermint smoke.

'Fair.' Ali grinned. She was warming to Kelly. 'So, you're still on Instagram, then? Are we allowed to do that?' Ali dropped her voice and checked around. Polly was over by the entrance hugging @OfficerMartin. *Ick*. 'Like, Polly is still on Insta? She's on there loads, is that not against some rule?'

'Well, Polly's been in recovery a really long time, so I guess she has her shit together, ya know? She's my sponsor – she's been amazing. In treatment it was cold turkey, no devices or anything, but with CatAnon, nobody *makes* you do anything. You do the steps and learn how to manage your compulsion. Like, I think they're realistic. These days no one could NOT have a phone or be on social media!' Kelly straightened up, seeing Polly making her way over.

'Ali!' She leaned in to deliver a stiff hug. 'Kelly, you're showing her the ropes?'

'Yep.' Kelly beamed. 'Take my number, Ali, we can have coffee before the next meeting!'

'Cool.' Ali tapped in the digits and gave Kelly a missed call, so she'd have hers.

'I better go. My poor nanny's in the final stages and we said we'd rewatch all of *Daniel and Majella's B&B Road Trip* before she goes.' Kelly gave a jaunty little wave and bounded off to her car.

'She's sweet,' Polly murmured as they watched her go. Ali didn't know where to begin with this new Polly. She couldn't believe she was here. Of all the people, Polly had to be the most unlikely to harbour a deep, dark secret. She'd always faded into the background of Hazel and Shelly's infinitely more exciting worlds – just there to echo Hazel's views and admire Shelly's top – but now all that blankness seemed distinctly more sinister to Ali. Clearly, Polly wasn't boring; she was a cipher.

'It's so great you're seeking help, Ali.' Polly here was different to the Polly of the Insta-world. She seemed on edge without the Insta-mask to protect her. 'Now, I hope you've taken onboard the anonymity rule. It's essential for everyone to feel secure in the room.'

'I know. Kelly said it too. I promise I won't breathe a word. I just want to get better.'

'Good.' Polly gave a decisive little nod. 'Then you're in the right place. Here, take my number too in case you're ever tempted to go back to your old ways. This is my batphone, it's different to my other number.' She recited the digits, then looked Ali over, apparently considering a question before reneging at the last minute.

'What?' Ali sounded sharper than she'd meant to.

'Oh, I was just thinking you look different.' Polly tried a smile, but it looked stiff and forced.

She does not want me here, Ali realised. *Why?*

'Well, I'm preggers for real now, so that might be it.'

'What?' Polly was floored.

'Yep, it's a nightmare. I went method on the whole bullshit baby thing.' Ali grinned. 'Anyway, I should go. See you at the next meeting.'

Ali hurried back to her car, giving a couple of the others a wave as she passed. She lashed the car into gear and pulled out of the car park happy to be free of the weird, for the moment at least. She'd be back next week, of course. Amy was super adamant that if anyone ever went digging, it wouldn't just look like lip service or a publicity stunt.

Chapter 12

'This week's guest is just such an incredible gal – she is amazing. She is sharing her inspiring weight-loss journey with her fifteen thousand followers, who take comfort in her honesty and can also share their journey in the comments.'

'What is this bullshit?' Liv hissed. Ali had only just picked her up from the library and she was already in rant mode at the podcast playing through the car speakers.

'It's Crystal Doorley's new podcast, *Real Talk with Crystal.*' Ali kept her eyes on the road. They were expected in Liv's parents' house at six. 'Kate's the guest. That's who she's introducing there.'

'The Shredder?!'

'The very one. I'm listening 'cos I said we'd swing in to her later, maybe after family dinner? I'd feel bad if I hadn't caught up with it. It's been out for a week already. As it is, we haven't really spoken properly since the funeral.'

'Well, has she called you? Has she asked how you are? Or has she been too busy on her weight-loss journey?'

'Well, she is busy.'

'Pre-listening to her on a podcast is mad. It's like we all have to do homework before we see each other these days. Listen to each other's podcasts, watch each other's stories and then suffer through the same boring anecdote live when we see them.'

God, Liv's on a roll, Ali thought. She often got like this before Khan family get-togethers. It was the prospect of proximity to the extremely type A Nella, her older sister, not to mention her mother, Meera, who could rarely make it through a meal without referencing her 'immensely satisfying' sex life with Liv's dad, James, who was at least seventy.

'Without further ado,' Crystal Doorley piped up on the speakers, 'I am so thrilled to introduce my amazing guest, Kate from @ShreddingForTheWedding. Hi Kate!'

'Hi Crystal, thank you so much for having me. I am the biggest fan of *Real Talk with Crystal*. This is a dream for me,' Kate finished breathlessly.

'A dream!' Liv echoed scathingly.

'OK, what is with you?' Ali hit Pause on the podcast. 'Did something happen today?'

'No.' She rubbed the shaved side of her head, something she did when nervous. 'I just don't feel like seeing Meera and Nella tonight. They'll just be at me about if I am seeing anyone, "How's the thesis going?", that shite. I hate going there when I'm in flux like this. I prefer showing up with something to show for myself and then I hate myself for trying to impress them.'

Ali nodded sympathetically. The Khans were intense people. It was probably like having four Minis in your family, she figured.

James was a renowned professor of philosophy whereas Meera, a psychologist, seemed to have a host of additional qualifications as, among other things, a reiki practitioner and Pilates instructor – and she'd authored eleven bestselling books on sex, family and relationships. She'd mined her own life and the lives of her children extensively for her books, including an exposing and mortifying 'study' of the teenage Liv.

How to Talk to Your Sexually Naïve Teen about Love, Life and Mating Games came out when they had been in secondary school, which was pretty harsh timing. The Khans – James Devitt hadn't taken his wife's name but the family had always been known collectively by hers – had met in London in the mid-1970s and spent some years travelling (and expanding their minds, as they often liked to boast) before returning to Ireland and (to hear them tell it) starting something of a sexual revolution on the island in the early 1980s.

Liv was the afterthought baby. As Meera had written on page eighty-eight of *The Untold Orgasmic Joys of Middle Age*, 'the perimenopause ignited something of a sensual fervour in me'. Liv was nearly ten years younger than Nella, who was thirty-six.

As an only child, Ali struggled to understand why Liv felt inadequate around her siblings. They were high achieving, but so was she. Lex, the eldest at thirty-nine, spent much of his time working remotely from Bali on a tech start-up he'd founded. In West Clare, Nella enjoyed frequent donations from her parents to add new groundbreaking healing services for a tiny roster of loyal clients at the boutique retreat she ran with her 'husband'. (The legalities of their marriage were apparently shady, as Meera had performed the ceremony during a family ayahuasca trip that Liv did not take part in.)

They all acted as if Liv was the uptight one in the family, which baffled Ali.

'Sure, you're a bisexual!' Ali would often remark. 'You're as loose as they come!'

'That is a damaging stereotype,' Liv would sniff. 'But yeah, what the fuck, like!'

Ali drummed on the wheel and took the coast road south of the city.

'Why not tell them about Amy?' she asked coyly.

Liv's head shot up. 'Shut up. What do you mean?'

Ali snorted. 'Well, you like her. You're going to ask her out, right?'

Liv glared out the window, but then her expression softened. 'Would you mind?'

'No, of course not. I mean, I'm sorta surprised because she's deep into the Insta-sphere, which represents everything that you think is wrong with society, but I guess, maybe I get that too. It's like my Louis CK crush. You know it's wrong and that's half the reason.'

Liv grinned. 'I think it's a little different to that. Amy's working the system from within. She's smart. But anyway, I'm not going to announce we're dating to my parents when she has agreed to no such thing! Are you learning *nothing* at CatAnon?'

'I'm learning that people are way crazier than we even realise and that my little shitshow is practically small potatoes compared with what other people get up to.'

'Ohhh, juice?'

Ali caught herself just as she was about to squeal 'Try *man*-juice!!!'

'I can't say anything. The anonymity thing is super strict.' She flashed on Polly's stern, heavily made-up face. The make-up worked in a heavily filtered selfie but IRL made her look borderline demented.

Ali's phone buzzed and she handed it to Liv to check the message.

'It's Mini,' Liv reported. 'She says to pick her up on the way?'

'Whaaa?' Ali felt her shoulders rise up with tension reflexively. 'Goddammit. Why?'

'Meera must've invited her, she was muttering about "connecting" with Mini at Miles's funeral,' Liv explained. 'I'd assumed they'd keep us out of it, but I guess not. At least, now we're *both* dreading this,' she said brightly.

❖

Shortly after collecting Mini, they arrived at the '70s apartment block facing the sea at Sandycove, where Meera and James had relocated once their children had moved out of the family home in Bray. It was a generous two-bedroom apartment with wooden floors and French windows to a balcony looking onto the car park with a sliver of sea visible if you leaned forward and craned to your left.

'I just love my sea view,' Meera announced proudly while giving Mini the official tour. 'It's just the right amount of sea.' This was the party line and Meera stuck rigidly to it. While Ali was a frequent addition to the Khan family dinner table, Mini had never been invited before. In her red lipstick and various structural, black, asymmetrical garments, she looked completely at odds with Meera, who floated around in bare feet, her ankle bracelets tinkling and pendulous breasts swaying beneath a sheer maxi dress as she moved.

'We're so glad you could come,' James boomed, emerging from the kitchen laden down with platters of samosas and bhajis with minty yoghurt and pickled limes. He delivered the food to the large dining table and strode straight over to his wife. The Khans, Ali'd always thought, went way overboard with the PDAs. They were like a pair of randy cats, forever mewling and draped around each other. Maybe being a sex and relationships writer demanded these displays? From the look on Mini's face, she was evidently also not a fan of her proximity to Meera's grunts of pleasure as James kneaded her shoulders and managed to occasionally graze a bit of her very-nice-for-sixty-something-but-you-could-still-live-without-seeing-it side boob.

Thankfully, Nella's older son, Anish, ran in and shouted with alarm, 'What's Papa doing to Nanni?'

'Nothing, sweet.' Nella straggled in after him with the baby, Aziz, on her hip.

Meera tutted audibly and, rousing from the massage, fixed her grandson with a smile. 'It is foreplay, sweetie, the precursor to the physical act of love – a vital part of human connection.'

'Right, if foreplay time is over, can we eat? I'm starving,' Nella moaned, marching towards Ali and kissing her on the cheeks. 'Well, you've been busy since I saw you last!' She moved on without pause to Mini and pulled her into a one-armed hug with baby Aziz looking unimpressed at being shunted around. 'Mini,' Nella began, 'I'm so sorry for your loss. You must come down to Elysia for a break. When you're ready, of course.'

She plonked herself down at the table and started on a bhaji, as the others drifted over.

'We're actually waiting for one more,' Meera called just as the buzzer sounded. 'There he is now.' She pranced out to the hall and returned a moment later with a dazed-looking Sam.

'Gah.' Ali was mortified to realise that the weird little noise she heard had in fact escaped her own mouth. Her cheeks burned as Meera introduced Sam to Nella and James and lastly to Mini. 'Now, you two will have loads to talk about, I'm sure.' She winked and flitted away apparently unaware or unfazed by having just lobbed a grenade into the middle of the dinner party.

'Haha.' Mini laughed gamely. 'If this is a set-up for me, no offence, Sam, was it? But it's probably a bit soon, Meera.'

'Oh God.' Sam gulped audibly.

'No, no.' Meera clapped her hands, giggling and rushing over to Sam. Even in her state of shock, Ali couldn't help but grin. He looked shit scared at the approaching barely fettered breasts. 'Sam is the father of Ali's baby. I invited him because I think it is so crucial for a baby to feel a part of a family unit as early as possible and I know things have been tense between you and Ali but you need to get past this and put the hurt behind you.' She took Sam's and Ali's hands and Ali held her breath. He wasn't storming off, at least. *Please stay*, she willed.

'Thanks, Meera.' Sam shifted uncomfortably and Ali snuck a glance at his face. His cheeks were flushed and his hair tousled. Still so, so cute.

'Did he know I was going to be here?' Ali asked.

'I knew,' Sam whispered.

'How did she *find* you?' Ali looked disturbed at the long arm of Meera infiltrating this remote area of her life.

'LinkedIn,' he muttered back. 'Nowhere is safe.'

'Great,' Nella interjected. 'Can we eat now? I'm starving, this one's sucking the tit off me ten hours a day.' She indicated Aziz, who was holding said tit with both hands and guzzling like a tiny man downing a flagon of beer.

'They're having a moment, Nel, fuck's sake,' Liv hissed.

'We're not having a moment,' Sam blurted. 'I'm just holding your mum's hand! Out of politeness, like. I don't want to be.'

Ali burst out laughing. Hadn't seen him in weeks and two minutes back in his presence she could already feel how much she missed him.

Mini was looking at Sam with open curiosity.

'You're very tall. My husband was very tall, and I really wasn't able for his very long baby.'

Silence followed this strange pronouncement before James rescued everyone.

'Sam is tall. Long babies are tough. Let's eat!'

❖

Throughout the meal, Ali was bombarded by thoughts clamouring for her attention. On the one side, Sam was there. He came! He barely answered her text messages these days, but he came to this weird dinner party. He wasn't exactly looking at her with affection; he wasn't looking at her full stop. But still, he was suffering the slightly awkward boobfest at the dinner table. And she swore she saw his eyes widen when he spotted the tiny bump that was starting to pop under her Spice Girls tee shirt. Sam was an emoter and she was certain he wouldn't be able to maintain this cold front for much longer.

Across from Ali, meanwhile, Nella was in full flow about the daily torture of motherhood. Not exactly the most soothing thing to hear as the baby bounced in her belly. Nella was on full whinge-binge about how hard everything was with kids and it was starting to feel like exposure therapy to Ali – she'd seen a Netflix doc all about how they exposed people to their phobias to cure them, but more often than not it was even more traumatic. She could HARD relate.

'It's not the constant demands,' Nella went on, completely ignoring Anish looking glum at the far end of the table. 'It's just the whole talk, talk, talking. I swear Anish hasn't paused for a *breath* since he turned five. And I wouldn't mind if it wasn't such mindless stuff! And it's not like they're making memories. He won't remember if I'm hanging on his every word or not.'

Oh God, the poor kid. Ali cringed. *Someone shut her up*, she willed.

'I always remember my mum listening,' Sam said quietly. 'She'd stop whatever she was doing and sit down on the floor to be at my level and she always seemed so into whatever I was thinking about at the time. Space or dinosaurs or whatever.'

'Well, no offence, Sam, but they were different times. Your mum probably didn't have to work, and women had so much more support back then,' Nella snapped.

Ali could see Sam open his mouth then close it again, obviously debating whether to correct her. When he looked away and shrugged, Ali decided to do it for him.

'Actually, Sam's mum was a nurse and she didn't have Sam's dad around, Nella.'

'Oh, Sam, that's so hard,' Meera swooped. 'She must be so strong to have weathered all that. And in the nineties. Different times.'

Oh shite. Ali hadn't intended to throw Sam under the 'now you have to talk about your dead mother' bus. He glared at her and cocked an eyebrow, as if to say 'Happy now?' Damn. And right when she was sure they were making some kind of progress. She threw a helpless glance at Liv, who mobilised immediately.

'Isn't anyone going to ask me the Sad Single Person questions? Usually, I'd have got at least four "any romance lately?"s by now,' she heroically cut in, throwing herself to the 'interrogate the single person' wolves.

The whole table turned to Liv. Even the baby paused in his boob-chugging to look towards his aunt.

'Well?' James was eager. 'New development to report?'

Now put on the spot, Liv shifted uncomfortably. She clearly hadn't thought this far ahead.

'Em, I've been on a new app, SCISSR, which everyone is saying is way more queer-friendly. And, yeah, I might go on some dates soon. If I get matched.'

'Liv. That's hardly newsworthy.' Nella was scathing. 'You're such a third-born, anything to get attention. I was talking about my real problems and you somehow feel the need to cut across with your non-existent love life—' She was cut off by Aziz beginning to howl in her arms and Ali couldn't help but laugh. *Fair play, baby, you shut her up.* Nella picked up her boob and stuffed it unceremoniously back in the baby's mouth. He looked momentarily surprised and then resumed his rhythmic gulping.

'I can't even get my words out with these things suctioned onto me around the clock, Mummy,' she wailed to Meera.

'I know, sweetheart, it is so, so hard for you.' Meera was soothing, though to Ali, Nella sounded like a brat. She was thirty-six and telling on her own kids to her mum.

Christ, if Nella was finding it so hard, what was it going to be like for Ali?

'I found my babies awakened new depths in me spiritually,' Meera announced. 'But every woman's journey is different. Just as Ali's will be.' She smiled encouragingly at Ali and Ali sensed she was trying to communicate with her. The smile said 'Don't listen to my highly strung daughter. You'll be alright.' And Ali tried to believe it. She caught her mother's eyes flicking over to her. They had barely spoken about the baby, though Mini kept up a constant refrain of 'I'll support you in any way I can.'

In the early weeks, Ali knew what Mini meant by that was 'I'll support you when you get the abortion', but as the pregnancy continued, Ali got the sense that Mini's support did not.

Mini clearly hadn't anticipated 'her support' coming to mean 'I'll support you keeping this cursed child of a social media hoax.'

'And how does SCISSR work, Liv? D'ya remember you scissored once, Meer? At an orgy in '82.' James had a look of fond remembrance and both Liv and Nella winced.

'No scissor chat, please, Dad,' Liv implored. 'There's actually someone I like, not on the app. A real-life person, who I'm thinking of asking out.'

'That's fab, sweets,' Meera trilled. 'What's their name?'

'Amy. She's working with Ali on her Instagram things and she's really cool. I'm going to be interviewing her for a chapter of the thesis.'

Shite, Ali thought, spotting Sam's reaction to the mention of Insta and the dreaded thesis. They still had so much to talk about. Everything with the pregnancy announcement was set and she'd be making her return to the Insta-fray in a matter of days. She had to get him on his own.

After dinner and lengthy goodbyes, they all made their way out into the evening, which was balmy for May. She hung back, letting Liv and Mini go ahead to the car. Sam's hands were dug into his pockets, and even in the navy shadows of the car park, Ali could see him stealing glances at her bump. It had finally started to pop, and she'd had to leave the top of her leather skirt open just under the swell of her belly.

'You're getting a little roundier,' he said.

'Yeah,' Ali agreed quietly, careful not to push it. She felt that the moment was fragile. They hadn't spoken properly in over a month, just terse WhatsApp updates, but here finally was undeniable proof that they were bound together forever. 'I'm starting to feel it move a bit. It's amazing.'

'Wow, that must be freaky.' He looked around awkwardly, clearly unsure of where to go with this strange interlude.

'It is, seriously.' She relaxed a little. This was good. He was talking to her. Sort of.

'What did you mean when you said you were still doing Instagram stuff?'

Well, that lasted about two seconds. Ali sighed inwardly.

'I'm doing one last sponsored post. Amy Donoghue's helping me, like Liv said. Do you remember her? You probably met her at one of the Insta events a few months ago?'

'One last post? Like in a heist movie? One last job? Before you retire from your life of fakery and go straight for the rest of your days?' Sam looked sullen.

'Well, sorta yeah, but it's going to be an honest post. I just want to set the record straight. And Amy has found a really good sponsor, who is paying major money. Money that I'll need when the baby comes, Sam.'

He absorbed this without comment, just scuffing his trainers on the ground and avoiding her eye. *At least he's not railing at me*, she thought. She could see Liv and Mini waiting patiently, if presumably a little awkwardly, in the car and knew she needed to wrap this up.

'Why don't we meet and talk about it properly? Will you? Please, Sam, we have to find a way to at least still be friends.' She could see immediately this wasn't the way.

'Oh, as if it's me that's making all of this difficult! I'm the one refusing to play along, am I?'

'Sam—' Ali tried to protest but he was off. It was as if he had just suddenly detonated.

'I'm not punishing you, Ali, I'm fucking hurt. I'm completely fucking traumatised by all of this. *Prime Time* have actually approached me about giving an interview and I think I'm going to do it. They're offering private counselling if I go on. People need to know about this. It's fucked up and it could happen to someone else. I read about this girl who told her ex that they'd had a kid together and he spent years believing he had a son and paying maintenance and then it turned out she'd made the whole thing up.'

'OK, that's shitty, but I did not do that, Sam,' Ali pleaded.

'You as good as did that. You were on the way to doing that.'

Oh God, he was on a roll now. Ali felt panicky. She couldn't believe *Prime Time* were still sniffing around.

'Please just don't do *Prime Time*. If you do that, then this baby will always be able to see what happened and how she came about.'

'Fuck's sake, Ali! If this baby has a decent WiFi connection, she'll be able to see all that. You made sure of it with your #BullshitBabyJourney posts and the bloody hundreds of hot takes you've inspired.'

The sound of a car door slamming interrupted them both.

'Sam, you're angry but Ali is under a lot of pressure carrying this baby and you can't be attacking her forever.' Ali couldn't believe it – Mini coming to her defence. She continued towards them speaking firmly. 'She's made a horrendous mistake, but you don't know what she's been through losing her dad like that. Grief is different for everyone and we all cope with it in our own way.'

Sam's expression was still stormy, but he didn't argue. 'OK,' he muttered. 'I'll think about *Prime Time*. I haven't said yes yet.'

'Thank you,' Ali said softly.

They parted and Mini led her over to Liv's car.

'Thanks, Mini,' Ali whispered as they hopped in. She was quietly amazed her mum had come over and supported her like that.

'Well, you've a lot going on, pregnancy is no joke. You were like a parasite inside me, as I recall.'

Liv giggled and Ali couldn't help but grin too. 'It is like being possessed or something,' she piped up. 'One minute I'm crying over a really affecting home insurance ad and the next I want to murder everyone and eat two chicken fillet rolls back-to-back.'

'Oh pumpkin, don't be eating chicken fillet rolls.' Mini looked stricken at the thought.

Sam's headlights swung over them as he turned and sped through the gate of the car park.

'God, he's not thawing even one little bit.' Ali started the car, and tried to relax her shoulders. She was tense and exhausted from the angst of seeing him. They dropped Mini home and Ali resumed the Crystal Doorley podcast with the sound turned low.

'So many women have thanked me for being so brave and sharing my weight-loss journey, which makes it all worthwhile,' Kate was telling Crystal. 'With the bopo movement, many women are being shamed for wanting to be healthy and look good.'

'So true,' replied Crystal.

'You can't self-appoint as brave!' Liv shouted at the speakers. 'You have to wait until someone else calls you brave, Kate, and then modestly deny it!!! Considering she works in PR, she doesn't know shit about how to present herself. And, please, no one is being shamed for conforming to narrow beauty standards. Are you really going to call in to her or can we turn this crap off?'

'Yeah, it's late.' Ali sighed. 'I'll blame the foetus.' At the next traffic lights, she tapped out a message to Kate, blaming pregnancy tiredness. '*You were fab on Crystal's podcast. So brave. XXX*,' she concluded the message.

'*Fine*' was Kate's cold response, but Ali couldn't get caught up in her mood right now, not with the gnawing regret in her belly over her botched opportunity to get Sam back on side. Plus going to CatAnon meetings was really making her analyse her triggers around Instagram more. When they were better friends, she and Kate had communicated almost exclusively in bitchy screengrabs about other girls' Insta-posts. They didn't bring out the best in each other.

As they made their way toward the city, she mulled over the big picture. What were her options? If she did the Insta-post with the lie detector company, she'd be set for money for at least six months if she was smart about it. But judging by his reaction tonight, Sam would be a lost cause. She blinked to prevent the threatened tears from falling as the passing streetlights sped over the car. She realised a part of her had been certain that one way or another they would somehow work it out. That he would see her bump or see the baby hiccupping on the 22-week scan – only weeks away now – and finally put the hurt behind him. He said he was traumatised; the words landed like a blow to Ali. She'd done that. God, she had really fucked up.

'Hey, don't cry, Ali.' Liv reached over and rubbed her arm in a consoling gesture.

'Shit.' Ali wiped her cheeks. 'I didn't even notice I was.'

'Sam will come around, he will.' Liv sounded reassuringly confident, but Ali felt that hoping was dangerous at this point.

'Maybe I need to scrap the sponsored Insta apology post?' Ali was trying out the idea on herself as much as Liv.

As they turned towards the toll bridge, Ali glanced over at Liv, whose mouth was set in a firm line.

'Well, I'm always pro *not* putting stuff on Insta,' she said wryly.

'But how will you bone Amy if she's not around choreographing my image rehab?' Ali attempted to lighten the mood. 'It's you I've been doing all this for. The whole thing, fake preg and real preg, anything to get you back scissoring.'

'Oh gawd, shut up, no one *scissors*! I'm now officially unable to hear that word without thinking of my mother,' Liv groaned.

'My options are do the post and get a rake of cash and potentially not have to read about how pathetic and crazy I am on the internet for the rest of my life. Or stay quiet and go beg Stephan for my actual job back and just never look at the internet again.'

'If you stay quiet, maybe they will forget about you, Ali. It will blow over on its own eventually.'

'Yeah, but then every time anyone does anything crazy, I'll be this cultural touchstone for "bitches be crazy",' Ali argued. 'They'll mention me as the "disgraced blogger" and use whatever new scandal is going down to dredge up my humiliation. All those #BumpUpdates are out there forever.'

'What makes you think it'll be different if you speak up? It could just be giving them more ammo.'

'Well, at least I'll have had the chance to tell my side of the story. I'll get to own the narrative.' She was parroting Amy Donoghue nearly word for word as she handed over change for the toll bridge.

'Why don't you try *Durty Aul' Town* and that way you have options?' Liv suggested.

She had a point, Ali thought dolefully. Goddamn.

'I really don't want to have to see Stephan. I threw his Viagra at him in front of the whole set last time I was there. It was literally the day Sam nutted this baby into me so I can't even blame pregnancy hormones.'

Liv laughed grimly, then stopped abruptly.

'Stephan doesn't know that, though. You could blame the hormones with him?'

'I should probably downplay the pregnancy, though, if I really want that job back. I'm not sure if a pregnant production assistant is that attractive an option. Soon I'll be even less agile.'

'True,' Liv agreed. 'You look cute now but give it another few months and you'll be crowning in the middle of his set.'

'Thank you. I'll be attempting to keep that to myself.'

'Haha, not sure you'll have much of a choice. Remember, Nella delivered in the living room and, let me tell you, it was visceral.'

Chapter 13

'I'm back and hard at it on *Durty Aul' Town*, Shell-Belles! Here's my dressing room.' Shelly switched to the front camera to take in the rails of Imelda's clothes, her supply of sparkling water, the bouquet on her dressing table that was replenished every week and the bowl of fresh fruit on the coffee table.

'In today's scene,' she continued, switching the camera around so her face filled the phone screen once more, 'Imelda and her mam are having a row over the lingerie parties Imelda's been throwing because half the women in Maura's bridge club are scandalised and the other half are mad for it – another gritty storyline for me.' She winked and made a funny face, then added a filter and hit Share.

She flicked through her script, doing a last-minute run-through of her cues, then checked the time. Where was Amy? They were supposed to meet well ahead of her call time. She opened the dressing room door and started at the sight of Amy standing right there with Ali Jones.

'Ah, Shelly! Just on my way in to you.' Amy was blasé as per usual.

'You were not.' Shelly sulked, noting Ali squirm a little.

'Sorry, Shelly,' Ali piped up. 'It was me. We collided out here and she's just trying to talk me out of asking for my old job back.'

'Oh really?' Shelly softened immediately. She still felt protective towards Ali. She'd gone to Stephan on Ali's behalf after they had met in the hospital, but he had been characteristically dickish and she hadn't had the heart to mention it to Ali. Perhaps with Ali standing right in front of him, he would come around. 'How are you feeling?'

'Way better physically, thank god.'

The poor thing. Shelly gave her a hug, their bumps momentarily pressed together.

'Waah.' Ali laughed. 'That was intimate!'

'Great shot, gals. Insta loves some bump-on-bump action.' Amy turned her phone around to show Shelly and Ali the snap she'd just taken. *God, trust Amy.* Shelly grinned in spite of herself.

'You might share it after Ali makes her public statement, Shelly?'

'You're like an Insta-momager, Amy.' Ali giggled. 'Never not ON!'

'Get in here, Amy. Ali, come say hi before you go, yeah? Good luck with Stephan.' She blew her a kiss and Ali ambled on.

Amy shut the door behind her, holding up her phone where Shelly's stories were playing.

'Great stories this morning but watch your angles: ninety degrees is fine for some twenty-something in absolute mint condition but in your mid-thirties it's got to be a forty-five-degrees minimum. Now, I've been doing some major research and I think you're actually way ahead of the curve with this single-mum angle.'

Shelly didn't even bother correcting her on her cynical wording – single-mum angle! – as if she'd taken a wrecking ball to her life for something fresh for the 'gram.

'We're gonna play this smart. I think honesty is about to have a major comeback on Insta – I mean the right kind of honesty, obviously – and you and Ali Jones can ride this wave.' She spun her tablet around to show Shelly some infographics she'd put together.

'So, will you be continuing on with Ali?' Shelly couldn't help but feel a little territorial, especially now that keeping the house after divorcing Dan was riding on her Insta income.

'No, Ali's pretty sure this post I've negotiated for her comeback is a one-off. I'm not a good fit there anyway. If she does stick with the Insta thing, she's much more on the grittier side of things, which suits her. I think she's got real potential to be a great no-bullshit voice on the scene. She's good on camera.'

'Yeah, she was all right. From what I tuned into, she was funny about her and Sam. Plus, it'd be crazy to waste that following. What's she up to now?'

'Three hundred and twenty.'

'What!!! Three hundred and twenty thousand once she accepts all the follow requests?'

'Yep, notoriety sells. I keep telling her to capitalise, but she's all hung up on that Sam guy and I don't think she really knows what she wants out of any of this, except for Notions.ie to stop publishing their think-pieces. Beyond that I think she just wants to take care of the baby. Right, more importantly ... SHELLY. What is the plan?'

Shelly sat in front of the dressing table mirror and filled her in about the pressure to bring in some money.

'I'm ready to work. But with @_____ still lurking in my DMs, I just don't want to bring Georgie into too much Insta stuff. Plus, she's not a baby anymore and she's becoming more self-aware.'

'OK, brill. Well, I know you've been looking at the gender-reveal party offer with the booze company but I'm positive if you let me put it out to tender, I can come back with a more attractive package.'

'Yes. Fine.' Shelly checked the time. Ruairí would be along any minute to bring her to set. She started to gather her script and water bottle. 'But I think we should aim to do it quite close to the due date for maximum impact.'

'Yep, not a prob, boss. There's also the question of the birth.' Amy stood with one brow cocked.

'Is there?' Shelly narrowed her eyes.

'Well, it is a … unique marketing opportunity for the right brand,' Amy said plainly.

A tentative knock on the door interrupted them. 'Ms Devine?' called Ruairí nervously.

'Coming, one sec,' Shelly replied, then turned to Amy, dropping her voice. 'We'll have to see how desperate I get, I guess.'

'It's not desperate, it's savvy,' Amy argued quietly but insistently. 'I'll put together some profit projections and you can just think about it.'

❖

Ali still hadn't found Stephan when she saw Ruairi shepherding Shelly down to set and decided to follow. She hadn't wanted to plead her case on a set full of people, but when there was no sign of him in the production office or the canteen, she figured she'd just better get on with the humiliation.

As she neared Studio 4, she spotted Terry pop out of the writers' room just down the hall ahead of her and she had a mad urge to flee. It was one thing prostrating herself in front of Stephan after everything that had happened, but having to face someone she respected and admired was too much. She was just about to duck into one of the holding rooms they used for extras when Terry called out.

'Ali? Jesus, is that you?'

'Hi …' she said nervously, trying to pretend that she hadn't been about to dive into a random room to avoid him.

'Ali, it's so good to see you. I heard about your dad. I'm so sorry. I lost my aul' fella when I was forty-five and I found *that* hard. You're so young.' He made to give her a clumsy one-armed hug when the bump announced its presence by impeding the affectionate gesture.

'Woahhh.' He looked with alarm, as though her belly was re-enacting the scene from *Alien*.

'It's just a baby.' Ali laughed in spite of the awkwardness.

'Wow.' Terry rubbed his greying beard. 'You've had a lot on.'

'Yep.' Ali pressed her lips together and nodded. 'It's been pretty shite.' She surprised herself by being so honest. She'd always tried to put on a good front for Terry. She'd wanted to impress him since the day she joined *Durty Aul' Town*, sending him her spec scripts in the hopes of getting a shot in the writers' room.

'Look, I've an hour before my next meeting – want to grab a coffee?' Terry asked kindly.

Ali studied him carefully.

'I came to talk to Stephan, Terry. About getting my old job back.'

'Ali.' He sighed and started shaking his head. 'Do you actually want your old job back?'

The question stopped Ali in her tracks.

'Come and have a chat,' Terry persisted. 'You are better than being Stephan Delaney's on-set punching bag. Are you still writing?'

Ali paused, torn. He was right. If she went back to Stephan, nothing would change – she'd just be a slightly slower production assistant encumbered with a growing belly.

'I haven't really been writing,' she said, falling into step with Terry as he headed towards the coffee dock. 'Things have been way too hectic for that.'

'Obviously.' He grinned, gesturing at her bump.

'This isn't even the half of it.' She laughed grimly, tapping the bump. 'You don't want to know the shitshow my life has been – all my fault but, still, it's hitting Jerry Springer levels.'

'Ah well, I had heard a few mutterings around the production office.' Terry smiled kindly as they joined the end of the coffee dock queue. 'Instagram-something-something-something.' He waved his hand vaguely. 'Social media is like a foreign language. So, what happened?'

Once they had ordered and settled at a small table among the dusty fake plants and the other jaded-looking TV execs, Ali launched into the sorry saga. To her surprise, Terry was laughing with tears running down his cheeks by the end.

'I'm so sorry.' He was holding his head, his shoulders shaking with suppressed giggles. 'I know it's not funny, or it shouldn't be. It's fucking tragic, Ali. It's just the way you tell it.'

'Well, I'm glad my social media exile and Dad's death is bringing some joy to your day,' Ali deadpanned before cracking up herself. 'It is hilarious in a completely fucking bleak way, I guess.'

'Genuinely, Ali, I don't know if you're already thinking this or what, but you need to turn this into a one-woman show. It's perfect for the stage.'

'Oh God, WHAT?' Ali yelped.

'Seriously, what better way to turn all of this around? You could silence your detractors by taking back the narrative power, make the jokes before *they* get to make them.'

'I think they probably already have …'

'Whatever. Doesn't matter if they have, you're the star of this thing. You said, what, three hundred thousand people are on your Instagram thingy – *you* have the audience, *you* get to tell the story.'

Ali grinned slowly. He didn't quite have the lingo, but he knew what he was talking about. The show idea *was* kind of interesting. What did she have to lose?

'I'm not really a performer, though, is the only thing.' Ali rubbed absent-mindedly at her bump, where the foetus appeared to also be chiming in with a few little kicks of encouragement.

'Says who?' Terry stared at her. 'Even if your fake – what did you call it? – "bump journey" got people interested in you online, it was you they stuck around to watch. Yes?'

'I guess.' Ali felt an unfamiliar rush of excitement; she hadn't felt not-shite in so long, she was momentarily confused. *Oh yes, this is what feeling optimistic and hopeful is*, she thought wryly.

'I'll help you with it.' Terry was still in convincing mode. 'I'll happily read drafts. I have contacts in this town. I know I didn't develop your spec script from last year, but this seems like much more your thing. I haven't laughed that hard in ages – you're a real storyteller, Jones. This is a great opportunity.'

'OK, OK.' Ali was now blushing furiously. 'I swear I will ... try to put something down on paper.'

'Yes, thank God I intercepted you en route to grovel to Stephan.' Terry slapped the table, startling a group of downtrodden-looking extras at the next table. 'I saved you! Now, when is that baby due? You need to get this out there soon, by the looks of things? The bump really adds to the whole piece.'

'Yes, I suppose it does,' Ali agreed. 'I'm due in early October.'

'Ohhh, are you thinking what I'm thinking?' Terry had a definite glint in his eye.

'I seriously doubt it.'

'Three words, Ali: Dublin. Stage. Festival.' He underscored each word with a sweep of his right hand.

'But, like, it's in August. Wouldn't they have all the acts confirmed, plus don't I need a script to get a slot?'

'Yes, you do.' Terry leapt up, suddenly looking more like fifteen than fifty. 'You work on a script and leave the rest to me. Let me make a couple of calls. I'll be your agent, OK? You trust me?' He cocked his finger at her like a gun, closing one eye in a cheesy wink. 'This is my business, Ali, the business of show, and I will pull some strings, for I am the puppet master,' he finished triumphantly and a couple of the extras, clearly having recognised Terry as the head writer – and therefore someone to suck up to if they were ever to progress to the coveted role of 'featured extra' on *Durty Aul' Town* – clapped appreciatively.

Ali just laughed as he took several elaborate bows. She'd genuinely never seen him look this excited about anything. Years in TV could do that to a person. His newfound enthusiasm, however, was infectious and she found herself drifting back towards the exit, after agreeing to email him an outline, feeling positively high when she nearly collided with Shelly coming back from set looking harried. Amy was frantically tapping on her phone behind her.

'Hey, gals.' Ali tried to tamp down her good mood on seeing Shelly's anxious face. 'Tough scene?'

'No.' Shelly shook her head looking pained. 'Come into my dressing room. This probably affects you too, hun.'

Shite, what now? Ali glowered and obediently followed behind Shelly's immaculate dark waves and impossibly tiny skinny jeans. How was the woman even pregnant? Her arse was still miniscule. And, Ali wondered, what fresh hell had now come to wreck her buzz?

Amy shut the door behind them and bustled in.

'Ali, hi.' She was brusque even for her. 'Goddamn, I thought we'd have a bit more time.'

'What's going on?' Ali implored Shelly.

'The podcast that Jenny, Hazel's wayward assistant, was teasing has launched its first episode and apparently she's going straight for the jugular: Insta-mums. Amy saw it drop during that scene.' Shelly gulped and looked over to where Amy was, Ali now realised, half tethered to her phone with one headphone. 'She's been listening for half an hour at least,' Shelly whispered.

Ali didn't even bother getting her phone out. She didn't want to give it the click. Why help Jenny's audience figures if her whole mission was to take them down? She sat tensely beside Shelly waiting for Amy's verdict.

Finally, after another ten minutes, Amy pulled the earpiece out.

'Well, @MammasLittleMissus is fucked,' she announced starkly.

Ali drew a blank. She'd really only begun to pay attention to Mama Instagram after she had a fake bump to research. 'Who's that again?'

'She was very small fry, about twenty thousand followers until she gave birth "unexpectedly"' – Amy added air-quotes – 'in a Brown Thomas changing room.'

This did ring a bell all right. 'Oh ... yeah. Didn't she call the baby—'

'Brown-Motherfucking-Thomas, yes.' Amy looked in pain at the vulgarity.

'And she got a lifetime twenty-five per cent discount card,' Shelly threw in.

'And a shit-tonne of new followers,' Amy added.

'But Siobhan is lovely, though – that's her real name.' Shelly filled

Ali in. 'I can't imagine they dug up much on her. She's sweet. Always doing girly days out with the older one, the "little missus".'

Amy looked witheringly at Shelly.

'Please. You've been in this game long enough, Shelly. They went fucking deep on her. Jenny has a team of researchers. They had eyewitnesses talking about how she spent more time getting all the firemen's Insta-handles correct than looking at poor baby Brown Thomas after her "dramatic" birth.'

'But isn't that a bit flimsy?' Shelly wondered aloud. 'That's just people being mean and bitter, isn't it?'

'Yeah, but Jenny has *receipts*.' Amy scrolled and briefly tapped on her phone before turning it around to show the other two. 'CCTV footage.'

Shelly gasped. They both leaned in to see a heavily pregnant woman walk, apparently with some difficulty, into a changing room on the designer floor of BTs. The tape then sped forward, seemingly for a long time as countless people passed the camera and entered and exited other cubicles in the fitting room.

'Supposedly she was in there for close to two hours,' Amy explained. 'Then she alerts the shop to the fact that she's practically crowning on their cream carpet by – what else?! – posting to Instagram Stories. The fire brigade is called, and the rest is viral social media history.'

'Fucking hell.' Ali couldn't believe anyone would do something so outlandish for a few followers. 'Isn't that dangerous? What if something had gone wrong?'

Amy nodded grimly, now refreshing Twitter. Twitter always had a field day with the antics on Instagram.

'This takedown is going to be brutal.'

❖

By that evening, *Under the Influence* was at the top of the Irish podcast charts and Twitter was beside itself. GIFs of @MammasLittleMissus slipping into the Brown Thomas changing room were doing the rounds and the Twitteratti were in an all-out war for the best caption.

Ali scrolled.

TFW you birthing but you also need the bargs. #mammaslittlemishap

Can I get a size 6 in these and an epidural. #mammaslittlemishap

TL:DR For anyone not arsed, I'll sum it up: Instagram just being its usual batshit self

Another showed @MammasLittleMissus surreptitiously sneaking into the changing room and above it a somewhat baffling caption:

Everyone: Having a baby in a hospital is the safest practice.

@MammasLittleMissus, an intellectual:

'I don't think I get Twitter,' she remarked to Liv, who was lying silently under a facemask in front of the TV, watching *The Real Housewives of Atlanta*. 'You look like Leatherface by the way. Since when do you do face masks?'

'Since when do you do Twitter?'

'Touché. There's just been another major shitstorm on Insta and Twitter always offers a great bird's eye view of the action.'

'Gimme.' Liv held an arm straight up in the air.

'It's the *me, an intellectual* one I don't get.'

Liv peered up at the screen. 'Ah yeah, that started on Tumblr, I think. It's kind of evolved in meaning.' She scrolled on a bit, grinning. 'I love these days on Twitter.'

Ali grabbed the phone back. 'Says everyone who's never been the star of one,' she retorted, hopping back to the couch. 'God, though, people are such pricks. I don't mind the jokey people so much but it's the ones getting high off the outrage. Here's a complete bitch harping on about it. "it's the child I feel for, this woman shouldn't be allowed have kids". Fuck off, Sinead,' Ali roared at the phone. 'As if you'd be so concerned about this baby if it was beside you at brunch screaming its little face off! You'd want to drop kick it away from you if it was ruining your twenty-euro eggs benny.'

'You're in a rant hole tonight,' remarked Liv blandly and Ali stomped off to bed a few minutes later. Liv was right, so she figured it was best to just take herself away. Maybe it was the hormones, but this @MammasLittleMissus takedown was really getting to her. Who did all these people think they were judging this woman? She'd noticed her own glee in Shelly's dressing room earlier when Amy related the first juicy deets and then she'd felt disgusted for delighting in this woman's misfortune. It was obviously a really weird and stupid thing to do but the joy everyone was getting from dragging her down was making Ali sick to her stomach.

Meanwhile, Kate was pinging thoughts into their WhatsApp, the kind of sneering comments and screengrabs that had practically formed the backbone of their friendship for so long. *God, it is all so toxic*, thought Ali, scrolling away on the pillow beside her. A sudden thump in her side alerted her to the fact that the foetus was not appreciating her lying on her left and she shifted over and pulled the blanket away to get a look at her belly. Twenty-two weeks this week and nearly time for the big scan. The foetus moved again, and the taut skin of her bump rippled. She grinned. Weird. So, so weird. She gave it a poke and it poked back.

'Hello!'

A foot or an elbow or whatever it was emerged again, like a creature surfacing from the depths.

'Poke once for yes and twice for no,' she told it. 'Do you have a teeny tiny lil dick?'

She waited. And then came a firm thump right beside her belly button. She laughed.

'You better not be using it to poke me – that would be uncool in the extreme.'

Two thumps answered this statement.

'Do you want pancakes for breakfast?' A single thump.

'Good, Me too.' Ali grinned. She pulled up the camera app on her phone, aimed it at her belly and started to record.

'Is your dada ever going to forgive me, do you reckon?'

She held her breath the better to see the baby's movements. She gasped as a ripple spread from left to right across her belly followed by three fist-sized bumps. It felt so strange.

'Whoa! Three! What kind of answer is that!' Ali was indignant but the bump appeared to go silent again.

She watched the video. It didn't look quite as dramatic as she'd thought. Still, he couldn't ignore this, she reasoned. She killed the sound on it so Sam wouldn't hear her question and shared it on their WhatsApp thread.

The message blue-ticked right away and she could see he was typing.

Cool, when's the scan again? This one's the big one, yes?

Yep. It's the one where we can find out the flavour, 🍗 🥥 and they can tell us if things are looking ... OK. Health-wise, like. It's next Monday. 2 p.m. on the second floor.

Cool. See you then.

Sam?

The message blue-ticked but Sam seemed to be wavering on responding. Finally, he started typing again.

Yes.

I'm doing a post on my Instagram on the Friday before the scan.

It blue-ticked. He said nothing. Ali exhaled and ploughed on.

I'm apologising for my actions. I'll be explaining what happened, sort of. And ...

She hovered above the phone. His status read 'online'. He was waiting.

... I'll be telling them about this pregnancy.

She hit Send. He read it. Now she waited.

Fine, Ali. If that's what's important to you.

Oooof, that's not good. She cringed. She wanted to defend herself; she needed to apologise so she could get on with her life; still she felt there was little point in explaining. Anything she said, he would turn on her. He was a stubborn fuck. Well, she could be too.

What's important to me is having enough money when this baby arrives. I was offered a very lucrative one-off deal for this apology post and I'm taking it so that I can look after the baby when it comes. See you Monday.

Chapter 14

Ali paced the living room, checking out the front window every few minutes. Liv was edgy too, plumping and re-plumping the pillows on the couch.

'Where is she?' she demanded.

'Why are *you* so nervy?' Ali lashed back. 'I'm the one who's about to re-enter the Insta fray; you're just waiting for her to get here so you can hang around pretending to act nonchalant!'

'No, I'm not. Shut up!' Liv began pacing after Ali. 'I just want to say hello. It's polite to greet a guest in your home.'

'LOL. OK, whatever you say.' Ali grinned. 'But stop pacing after me. This room is too small and has too many clashing patterns for two people to pace in here at the same time.'

'Sorry, sorry.' Liv back off and checked her reflection in the mirror above the fireplace. 'It's just ... has she ever talked about me?'

'She said your thesis was "terrifyingly prescient".'

'Really?' Liv's eyes widened and a flush crept up her neck. 'She said that?'

Ali gave another glance out the window.

'Finally!'

Amy stomped up the driveway in a look that could only be described as 'off-duty' bondage – a neon-green fishnet bodysuit with various leather straps.

'She's definitely a change of pace from aging professor territory,' remarked Ali, referring to Liv's previous paramour, her college tutor, Emer Breen. 'Do you think she likes women? How do you tell? Is there some kind of divining rod?'

The doorbell rang.

'I feel like a divining rod would work better for the gay *boys*.' Liv winked. 'I'm gonna ask her out today.' She steeled herself.

Ali moved to the door and into the hall. 'You better. This is probably our last job together, so she won't be coming around again.'

Liv just nodded decisively.

'Hey.' Ali swung open the door to Amy's raised palm. She was glued to her phone and clearly in full rant mode to the person on the other end. Ali stood aside and ushered her in while Amy didn't even break flow.

'Well, I realise that, Hazel, but I'm not on your goddamn payroll and maybe you should've been vetting these Jennys more closely. I'm good at my job, hun, but I don't have the time to clean up every single mess. And I'm on a retainer with Shelly and Ali. Plus, my name ain't Jenny. I'll discuss the summit with my clients and then we'll get back to you.'

She ended the call and her focus snapped to Ali. 'Is this what you're wearing?'

Ali glanced down at her Courtney Love tee shirt and ripped jeans.

'What? I just put fresh tan on and everything.'

'I can see that.' Amy mimed being blinded. 'Wash it off ASAP. I've got a MUA coming to do your face. We need every detail of this *mea culpa* to be in keeping with the messaging. You can't go on there looking grand, Ali! You need to look stun, obvi, but in a kind of beaten by life, tragic way.'

Liv giggled from the living room door and Ali shot her a withering look, though Amy's whole demeanour changed at Liv's appearance.

'Liv! That last chapter you sent through is so spot on, gave me chills.'

'Not flutters?' Ali piped up mischievously.

'What?' Amy glanced over vaguely.

'Shut uu-up, A-li,' Liv was withering. 'Not everyone watches *Horn Island*!' She turned swiftly back to Amy. 'I'd actually love to sit down with you to really unpack some of the elements that are still a bit underdeveloped.'

'Sure, what about dinner?' Amy was already tapping on her calendar app. 'Tuesday?'

'Great.' Liv beamed. 'I'd love to try that new dim sum place on Camden.'

'Will I just go and rehab my own image so?' Ali interjected, pretending to be in a huff. 'I thought you said we're aiming to get it out before tonight at seven p.m. The Friday Insta rush?'

'Yep.' Amy smoothly switched back to her usual take-charge voice. 'Go take that Courtney Love top off. Could you have picked a more inappropriate one? We don't want to give them anything to bitch about in the comments, Ali, and Court, God love her, is just too divisive.'

'Right ...' Ali rolled her eyes, but Amy fixed her with a look.

'Ali, clothes are political. I want to see options in white, grey and dusty pink. Go.'

An hour later, the set up was nearly ready. Joanna, the MUA, had significantly toned down Ali's tan, and she looked wan and much closer to someone going through some personal issues, as Amy had demanded. She wore a simple white sweater and sat at the edge of her bed in front of an enormous ring light with Amy's phone mounted on a tripod before her. Amy was running through the stack of cue cards she'd made to keep Ali on track.

'How are you feeling?'

'Nervous.' *Really fucking nervous*, Ali added silently. This had the potential to go so horribly wrong. In preparation, she'd watched a load of apology videos on YouTube the night before and every one of them had been a train wreck. She'd struggled to find one decent example of a social media pariah pulling off a good apology video and it had given her The Fear.

Mostly people seemed to go in for crying but the all-important tears eluded them. The girls always looked perfect, completely hot, but you could tell they were suffering because their hair was in a messy topknot and there appeared to be an unofficial uniform of a grey hoodie. A lot of them seemed to hint at some undefined mental illness or 'exhaustion'. In a way, Ali had a bit more blame-material than that, but she couldn't bring herself to use Miles or his illness as an excuse. She pulled her sleeves down over her hands and waited for Amy to finish glaring at whatever she was typing on her tablet.

'She's unreal,' she muttered.

'Who? Shelly?'

'No.' Amy snorted. 'Shelly is my most obedient client ever, Ali! HellishHazel. She is fuh-reaking over the first episode of *Under the Influence*. She's calling me nonstop. Wants me to work my "Amy magic". I wouldn't touch that dumpster fire, though. God knows what else she's got to hide. She's talking about an Insta-mum Emergency Summit. She wants you there if this little statement goes OK. That's so her. She'll wait to see how this lands, then decide if you're a liability or potentially useful. OK, will we do a take?'

'Yep.' Ali shifted around and tried to get comfortable.

Amy tapped the phone to begin recording. 'When you're ready, Ali. Do you have the script?'

Ali glanced at the pages beside her.

I've learned a lot in these past few weeks. I've learned that I'm not perfect. In spite of my incredible success, I still need to do better. I'm sorry I disappointed you. I love my followers more than anything ...

Ali pushed them out of shot, took a deep breath and looked up into the camera.

'Hi guys, it feels like it's been a long time since I came on and obviously a lot has happened.' Ali tried a tentative grin at this. 'God, I don't even know where to begin. I am so, so sorry. I am so disgusted with myself. As you all know, I lied. I lied to you guys and I lied to my friends, everyone. I lied to Sam, who was my boyfriend, and I lied to the companies that worked with me on ads and collaborations.'

Amy was nodding encouragingly and holding up a cue card that said 'Sick Dad!!!!'

Ali rubbed her eyes and looked hopelessly into the camera.

'I feel like I could try and blame a whole bunch of things, but I'd just be making excuses. The fact is that life is hard for all of us sometimes and we don't all go around starting social media hoaxes and faking a pregnancy and hurting the people who believe in us. I was hurting and lonely and I felt like a failure but the real reason I did this was because I was jealous. It's pathetic but it's true. I was just jealous of everyone doing so well on Insta and I wanted to be the girl who had everything on Instagram.'

Amy was vigorously shaking a new cue card. 'DEAD dad!!!!'

'Since this has come out, I've lost a lot of people close to me and that's taught me how much I've hurt everyone with my lying. I'm so sorry. I really am. I have nothing to say to defend myself that wouldn't just be me trying to make excuses.'

Amy was rolling her eyes now and holding another cue card, each word writ large and underlined. 'Mention. The. Real. Fecking. Baby.'

'I'm sure lots of people will have lots of opinions about what I did and that's cool – you all have every right to think whatever you want about me. I can't take back what I've done. I wake up every morning and I feel sick with the regret and the shame but now I am going to get on with my life. I have to. I won't be talking about it again, especially 'cos I have some pretty big things coming up that I need to focus on.'

Ali ran her fingers through her hair. *Fuck it, Ali*, she thought. The bitches who wanna hate you will keep at it. There's nothing you can do.

'I'm kind of scared to spit this out TBH.' She laughed nervously. 'I'm literally girding my loins, like! Sooooo in the course of faking a pregnancy, I accidentally got pregnant for real.'

She leaned back to show her bump to the camera.

'It's real, before anyone starts up with conspiracy theories on Rants.ie!' She grinned, lifting her jumper and gazing down at the firm, round belly. 'It's so freaky too!' She rubbed the bump absent-mindedly, then straightened up, remembering the small matter of the apology video.

'I feel like posting this is probably inviting a lot more hate back in. I got a lot of messages after the Glossies and I deserved a lot of what was said. But just please know that I am seeking treatment to try and make sense of what I did and to …'

Amy's cue card said 'Grow as a person' but Ali didn't think she could come out with that without laughing.

'… try and change for the better. I need to work on myself, especially now that I'm going to be a mum! Looking after my baby is the most important thing for me now. I'll be doing this without a partner so I'm … ah fuck, gals, I am shit-scared. Like, WTF is HAPPENING???'

Amy held up her next cue card, which simply said 'You're so far off message, just plug the brand and wrap it up.'

'Anyway, if you have a liar like me in your life and you just want to get to the bottom of their bullshit, why not enlist the services of SweetLittleLies.ie – Ireland's first and only private lie detection agency. And before anyone in the comments says it – swipe for the video of me taking the test in case anyone thinks I'm spoofing this baby too! Byeeeeeeeeee!'

Amy stopped the recording. 'Well, that was a disaster.' She looked deeply irritated. 'Can we get touch-ups before the next take, Joanna?'

Joanna rushed forward with her palette and brush, but Ali waved her off.

'I'm not going again, Amy, there's no point. I'm never going to read off some script and at least this way it's real. I am sorry. I've apologised but if they want more out of me, they can all fuck off and calm down. It's not like they've any real beef with me. My fake baby has fuck all to do with them. They're just bored and if they want to judge me to feel better about themselves, there's nothing me saying "I've been suffering from exhaustion" or "I'm now on a journey toward healing" is going to do about that.'

Amy looked mutinous but said nothing.

'I thought it was good,' offered Joanna. 'It sounded like the old you and it was kinda funny too. Maybe it'll take the wind outta their sails?'

'Thanks, Joanna. Look, it is what it is. No matter what I say, people will be all over it. Let's just post this fucker.' Ali cocked an eyebrow at Amy, who shrugged in a slightly defeated fashion and solemnly tapped out a caption tagging SweetLittleLies.ie and rounding off with some relevant hashtags: #apologyvideo #socialmediaapology #Iamsorry #struggling.

'OK, you sure you're ready?' Amy stood with her finger poised over the phone screen.

'Oh my God, gimme.' Ali snatched the phone, made her account public again and hit Share. 'Now, let all the various judgements and hot takes roll in.'

Joanna started tidying her bits back into her mammoth wheelie make-up bag and Amy gave her details for invoicing. Liv poked her head around the door just as Joanna said goodbye and hurried on to her next job.

'All done? I'm ordering Thai. What do you want, Ali? Amy, are you gonna stay? We could all eat together.'

Liv looked blasé. It was probably taking everything she had to try to look so casual, Ali thought, grinning.

Amy seemed to consider the offer but then her tablet buzzed again and a strained look crept across her face.

'I'd really like to but Shelly's got a fashion event on tomorrow morning and I need to get ahead of the Insta admin on that.'

'How much does she make on one of those things?' Ali couldn't resist probing.

'Ali! You're one of us now. Instahuns don't spill the tea in front of Muggles.' She jerked her head at Liv. 'No offence. I mean, it's basically a compliment.'

Liv laughed and held her hands up. 'Hey, I'm an Insta Muggle and proud. So, I'll text you?'

'Yep, see you for dim sum.'

'And then some,' Ali threw in, then added a little drum effect. 'Ba-dum tsssshhhhh!'

'Uh-huh.' Amy looked scornful. She stepped past Liv, brushing her cheek with her lips. 'Can't wait,' she whispered. To Ali, she waved and said, 'I'm on the WhatsApp for the night if you need help fielding comments.'

And she was gone, leaving a dazed-looking Liv in her wake.

'Oh my God,' Ali squealed. 'You're so in there.'

Liv just nodded mutely, cradling her cheek where Amy had kissed her.

'This is so exciting.' Ali bounded over for a hug but was interrupted by the angry buzz of her phone which was lying on the bed. The Insta notification sound brought her right back.

'Oh, here we go.' She winced and hopped over to turn down the volume. Liv followed and peered over her shoulder at the notifications that were dropping in at a furious rate.

'When will we know how they're taking it? Massaman?' Liv asked, sitting down on the bed to order the food.

'Yes, Massaman please. In a way, there's no point in me even looking at these.' Ali waved the phone. 'I'm best just watching some soothing murder and eating my weight in prawn crackers. Then, in the morning, I'll get a pretty solid sense of the state of play from whatever Notions.ie puts up about the apology.'

'Ha, that's amazing.' Liv exhaled. 'You deffo think they'll cover it?'

'Oh yes, short of some other influencer getting up to some mad shit during the night, I'm guaranteed to be their bread and butter all weekend. The tabloid fodder should get a cut of the ad revenue. We're basically their raison d'être.'

'Well, you're not out of the woods yet, though, right? Careful, you're sounding way too cocky.'

Ali knew Liv was right but since her meeting with Terry, it was like emerging from a fog. She'd been so caught up for so long in this app, she'd practically forgotten about the whole other world that existed offline.

'I don't mean to be cocky. I'm just trying to care a bit less. I can't control what thousands of strangers think of me. Also, I kind of have an idea of what to do next.'

'Really?' Liv was still tapping the phone. 'I can't remember – do we get the sticky wings or the spicy ones?'

'Sticky.' Ali felt that it was still very soon to be talking about the show that might not happen, but since starting work on the outline the very same day as talking to Terry, she couldn't stop thinking about it. It had been so long since she'd written anything longer than an Insta caption, she'd completely forgotten how much she loved doing it.

'Well? You're smirking.' Liv cocked a brow in her direction.

'I'm working on a piece of writing, a script, like, for a one-woman show. All about the baby debacle. Terry from *Durty Aul' Town* is helping me.'

'Shut up! Are you serious?'

'Yeah, why?' Ali felt panicked at Liv's disbelief.

'That's fucking brilliant.' Liv leaped up and threw her arms around Ali. 'Ali! This is incredible. Yes. Finally! Jesus, I thought we'd lost you to Freakstagram forever. Tell me everything. This is what you're born to do, Ali. I hated that you lost confidence in yourself. Yes.' Liv was punching the air with glee. 'Good man Terry, he finally spotted your talent.'

'Well …' Ali was about to protest and get back to downplaying everything, but then she stopped herself. 'Yeah. He did a bit, I suppose.'

'Eeeek, what a day!' Liv was bounding around the place. 'I scored a date with Amy. You're writing again.'

'And I just earned practically a year's salary in under an hour. Who cares if they still hate me?' Ali danced around, rubbing her bump suggestively.

'Oh God.' Liv abruptly stopped dancing and shielded her eyes. 'Stop rubbing it. It's. Too. Much,' she shrieked.

'But me and the foetus have to express ourselves.' Ali started gyrating the bump at Liv, who fended her off, laughing.

'Right, what soothing murder will we have?'

'I'm in the mood for something horrif!' Ali said brightly.

'Jesus. All right. Fred and Rose West doc?'

'Eugh, no. I'm not that fucked up. Maybe Ed Gein?'

'Right.' Liv rolled her eyes, and then her gaze fell on Ali's phone on the bed, silent but blinking rhythmically with endless new comments. 'Are you leaving that here?'

Ali wavered for a moment. 'Yeah, fuck it. It'll just be a wreck-the-buzz. Let's have it just us tonight. And Ed. And his Lady Lamps.'

'I must admit, I am partial to his nipple belt.' Liv led the way towards the living room.

Chapter 15

'Shell-Belles, it is so exciting to be here in the Tullamore Swan Inn. I'm just with my glam squad getting prepped for my Shella-Bella Bumps Roadshow today! We'll be talking self-care for mamas-to-be, fashion tips for hiding your new unsightly lumps and styling that bump! Can't wait to see you all soon.'

Shelly put the phone down so Amanda could get back to the laborious task of getting her ready. In-persons were so stressful. The Shell-Belles could be hyper-critical, and she didn't want to end up on Rants.ie for looking sloppy. God knows they'd be up there bitching about the price of the ticket (€125 including faux-secco on arrival and a goodie bag). They moaned but they coughed up, as Amy always said. The whole tour had sold out in two hours. She was committed to traipsing around regional Swan Inns across the country every Saturday for the next six weeks. All in the name of unhitching from Dan and getting her life back, she reminded herself.

The door to the hotel room swung open and Amy ploughed in, head buried in her phone, headphones blotting out all but the, judging by the volume, highly stressful conversation she was engaged in.

'I realise that, but do you realise that your goofs are none of my responsibility? Now, I have two hundred bovine bitches coming in to be gussied up by Shelly in an hour and we have actual work to do.' She took a deep, steadying breath, evidently attempting to summon patience. 'We'll see you at the #MamasMorning tomorrow and, for God's sake, I presume you're giving your staff the day off.'

Amy hit End on the call and shook her head, looking profoundly irritated. Shelly was loath to say anything in front of Amanda, but equally was dying to know what Hazel was bitching about now.

'Mandy,' Amy snapped. 'Can you get the clothes rail? We need to run through the outfits.'

'No probs, hun. You're done for now, Shelly. I'll just top up the highlighter and do your lips once you're dressed.'

Amanda bustled out and Amy shoved the door closed behind her. Oh God, what was coming? Shelly tried to compose herself, pulling her silk robe tighter over her special SHELLY bump shapewear and recrossing her legs, careful not to disturb Amanda's leg contouring work.

'Right, Hazel is up to high doh because she's convinced one of her Jennys is a plant. Apparently, she was slow to sign the NDA and Hazel forgot to chase it until this podcast business started up. The Jenny in question's been AWOL since last Wednesday and when Hazel took out the NDA to double-check, she realised that instead of a signature, the Jenny had actually scribbled "Haha Fuck you".'

'Oh Jesus.' Shelly stifled a laugh. 'Sorry, it's not funny.'

'Oh, it is,' Amy said grimly. 'And so deserved. But she's been up my arse about everything for days. Paranoid that this is the perfect loophole for OG Jenny to finally reveal the truth about Hazel's one hundred per cent fake life for the 'gram on the podcast. I can't cope with her. She's so intense and she's also not getting that she's not my client, ergo she's not my problem. Appara she has some new guy leading her team but is still on to me endlessly.'

Amy shrugged and Shelly noticed her mini dress, which was red gingham and uncharacteristically demure.

'Love this,' she enthused.

'Oh. Thanks! Me too.' Amy did a little spin, revealing a plunging back held together with three leather belts and showing off a large tattoo of a tiger pouncing on a busty naked woman.

Shelly winced.

'Right, couple more things before Mandy comes back. We've the playdate tomorrow. Hazel is calling it the Insta-mums Emergency Summit. She's doing the big W Y N D hard sell, shooting some of the promotional materials and appara we'll be discussing how to counter all the negative press focus in the last few weeks.' Amy rolled her eyes.

'Ugh, I can't bear to read any of it.' Shelly sighed. She had enough depressing things crowding her mind without hearing the thoughts of Deborah Winters and the rabid commentators on Notions.ie saying that she and her ilk were a toxic influence and promoting an unrealistic lifestyle.

'Speaking of.' Amy was scrolling away on her phone. 'The jury is in on Ali's comeback post.'

'I saw the post. It was very …' Shelly searched for a diplomatic way to put it '… very her.'

'Oh, I know. She basically pissed on my script. But,' Amy continued grudgingly, 'I kind of do have to hand it to her. She went with her instinct and I think it's paid off.'

'Oh?' Shelly straightened up as Amanda returned with the rail of outfits. Six looks for a two-hour show was a lot but each retailer she wore paid a handsome fee and the shops were near guaranteed to sell out of any piece once Shelly wore it. Plus, if the Shell-Belles shopped via the swipe-up on Shelly's Insta, as they would be aggressively encouraged to do, she made a tidy percentage on the affiliate links. Every cog in the SHELLY machine was monetised and now, with the goal of buying Dan out of the house and ultimately divorcing him – seriously, if people knew the going rate for a divorce, they would skip the whole bloody wedding – she felt more invested in SHELLY than she had been in a long time. She'd even been letting Amy put together a sponsorship package for the birth of baby number two until the leaked footage of @MamasLittleMissus had scuppered them. The optics weren't great in the wake of that backlash, they had decided.

'Oooooh, are you talking about AlisBaba?' Amanda loved the goss.

'Yeah, what's your take?' Amy asked.

'I think she did a great job. No pretend crying, which you'd usually see. And no makey uppy excuses, just a straight up, sincere apology.'

'Hmmmm.' Amy was nodding and jotting a couple of notes into her phone. 'And what are your WhatsApp groups saying? General vibes?'

'Well, my school gals were all mad about her, so they just hope she keeps up the page now that she's put it behind her. The book club group think the apology was fair enough. She can't go around apologising for the rest of her life. And compared with that yoke @MammasLittleMissus and her antics, lying about a fake baby doesn't seem so bad, better than endangering a real one for a discount card and a bit of attention. And now Ali's really pregnant! You couldn't make it up!'

'You couldn't,' Amy agreed. 'And she definitely isn't. I've seen the bump with my own eyes.'

'What are they saying on Notions?' Shelly was pulling on the first look, a pair of white skinny maternity jeans with a flowing silk shirt and blazer in taupe.

'"Shamed Blogger Makes an Unexpectedly Heartfelt and REAL Social Media Mea Culpa",' read Amy. Amanda kneeled down to help Shelly step into the towering rose-gold strappy stilettos. 'Deborah Winters is commending her brave honesty,' Amy continued. 'Her.ie has "Did This Blogger Just Pull off the Most Perfect Social Media Apology of all Time?" The consensus seems to be yes,' Amy added, shaking her head incredulously. 'I knew it'd make waves but I did not think it'd go over this well. The lie detector lads are thrilled with the eyes on their website in the last twenty-four hours.'

'Good for her,' said Shelly, heaving the thick, stretchy waistband over her bump. 'I wonder if she'll keep going? Sam didn't seem too happy about any of it, and she could end up with a real struggle on her hands with him. Not sure #custodybattle would go down that well on the 'gram.'

'Oooh, I'd watch *that*,' Amanda piped up, giving Shelly's cheeks a final dust of highlighter. 'The things I end up watching on there. Sure, I was watching yer man, the influencer fella Blake Jordan, giving his cat a bath the other day.'

'My contract with her is up now so who knows.' Amy shrugged. 'It's deffo been a nice little boost to my holiday fund, so I know *she* won't be stuck for money for a while. Still, I feel like she's coming out of the whole Insta bubble a bit.'

'Lucky her.' Shelly sighed as Amy stepped forward to mic her up.

'Now, now,' she admonished. 'We want too-blessed-to-be-stressed Shelly, not some moany cow who is forgetting how good she has it. These Shell-Belles are your bread and butter and don't you forget it.'

✤

Coming off the stage after a gruelling three hours of Shell-Belles, Shelly was deflated. It was such tough work and, at twenty-six weeks pregnant, all the hopping in and out of outfits was like cardio. The SHELLY bump control pants made her feel like a zeppelin in a condom. And it wasn't just the constant changing that left her feeling so sapped. It was the relentless pep she needed to maintain all through the day.

She slumped in the hotel bedroom for a few minutes' peace while Amy wrapped up details with the hotel management downstairs. The Insta-mums WhatsApp group was hopping as Polly and Hazel shared links to the steady stream of articles about @MammasLittleMissus since her outing on *Under the Influence*.

Polly: Oh my God this has to be the worst one yet. www.notions.ie/ Disgraceful-act-by-MammasLittleMissus-proves-there-is-nothing-attention-obsessed-Insta-mums-won't-stoop-to.

Hazel: Oh God. She's been on looking for an invite to the playdate tomorrow. I blocked her. If either of you have any shots on your grid with her in them delete delete delete. She is TOXIC.

Shelly rolled her eyes. Really, people in glass houses should not be throwing stones. She flicked out of the WhatsApp and back to Insta. Her DMs were being hammered with mentions from all the Shell-Belles who had attended the Bella Bumps Roadshow. She flicked over to her notifications. There everyone was loving her outfit from this morning as per usual. *Amazing! Amazing! Amazing!* in the comments. *We need a new 'amazing'*, she thought ruefully, and she scrolled down, barely taking in the likers and commenters. She was trying to keep more of an eye on new followers. Amy had been closing in on a few of the bigger UK Insta-mums, dropping strategic likes and comments, and Shelly knew she needed to cultivate these kinds of connections. She went to London a handful of times a year to fashion events, but it was very hard to break the English market. Angela Scanlon had been very supportive, but she needed to break in on her own not just by riding the coat-tails of someone else. Sadly none of the new followers were anything to get excited about. Then a strange Insta handle caught her eye: @TheRealShellyDevine.

She snapped to attention, her weariness immediately drowned in an onslaught of unpleasant, anxious adrenaline. She tapped the account icon, which was, of course, her own smiling face.

'Oh God, oh God, oh God,' she gasped under her breath as the page loaded. *Don't be public, please don't be public.*

The account was private. She felt dizzy with relief, however short-lived it might be. She analysed what was visible. Two followers. Following one person. The bio read:

I think it's time to come clean. I can't go on like this.

She shuddered. It sounded dark. If anyone stumbled across this page, they'd be immediately stuck in. No one could resist that cryptic bio. Jesus. It was probably only a matter of time before word got out about this account. The anonymous ones grew so fast. Amy had told her they could go from zero to a hundred thousand followers in a matter of weeks. After all, they dealt in the drug of the masses: gossip. BloggersUncovered had gotten so big lately it was apparently close to imploding because whoever was behind it was mired in threats of legal action and couldn't keep up with the admin of the DMs.

Shelly snapped a screenshot and WhatsApped it to Amy. She tapped the two followers, but it was a futile effort. She knew that the followers wouldn't appear unless she requested to follow the account and was accepted. She needed to know what was on there, but she didn't know if requesting to follow would only make things worse. If the account got out and people noticed that she followed it, it would set off a tsunami of speculation and make it much harder for her to deny whatever it was they were saying about her on there.

Oh goddammit.

She checked on her WhatsApp. Amy hadn't seen the message yet. A new update in the Insta-mums group had come in.

Hazel: Shelly? You there? You're still on for tomorrow, I hope? We need you. We all need to stick together right now.

Shelly's earlier irritation had evaporated, and she felt comforted by this now in the light of the @TheRealShellyDevine account. Sure, Hazel was toxic but maybe they were all as toxic as each other. Shelly had as much to hide as any of them. She probably needed to get off her high horse and stop thinking she was any different.

'Yep I'm here,' she typed.

Hazel: Good good. I'm adding @AlisBaba to the group, gals. Welcome. Ali.

Ali: Hi Insta-mums! 👋 🤰 glad to be back in the fold 😁 looking forward to going on a playdate tomorrow and actually pregnant for real this time!

Polly: Hi Ali. Hi Shelly, well done today on the Shella-Bella Bumps Roadshow, looked fab. I shared it in my stories.

Hazel: Of course. The SHELLY Bump Shapewear looks magic. @Ali be sure to repost Shelly's event. We mamas SUPPORT each other. Speaking of, now that you are really pregnant, don't forget to download my app H-App-y Mama by Holistic Hazel. It's full of my favourite guided meditations, affirmations for expectant mamas and nutrition advice, etc. You'll put it on the 'gram this week.

Ali: Can't wait Hazel. ☺

Hazel: And don't forget, while tomorrow is emergency strategy, there'll also be lots of lovely piccies for the 'gram so dress code is Malibu Mamas with a tonal palette of blush and white. Ali, I know you're fond of your 'band tees' but these little get-togethers need to be cohesive, aesthetically speaking, for the 'gram. Also, there'll be a costume change for the W Y N D rollout. We'll have hair, make-up and wardrobe on hand. @Ali we'll fill you in tomorrow when you get here. ❤

Ali: Gotcha. 👍

Shelly X'd out of the group and checked in with Amy. *'Fuck. I'm on my way'* was all she'd written.

The door burst open and Amy staggered in panting.

'Ran here. Sorry. I was supervising security bodily removing the last of the Shell-Belles. Had to pay them off with some old SHELLY stock.' Amy flopped into the seat opposite Shelly. 'Car will be here in five. Now, you didn't request to follow, did you?'

Shelly shook her head violently. 'No! I'm not an idiot.'

'OK, OK, deep breaths, hun.' Amy was refreshing her phone furiously. 'I set up a quick burner and requested to follow to see if they'll bite. All we need is a quick look at what's on there and, if we can find out who these other two followers are. It'd be good to see @_____ there, as the best-case scenario for us is that this is them branching out.'

'Great.' Shelly couldn't believe this was what they were reduced to: hoping it was just one psycho being innovative in their approach, as opposed to many coming after her all at once.

'Boom.' Amy punched the air. 'We're in.' For a few minutes there was silence but for the clicks as Amy, hunched over her phone, snapped screenshot after screenshot of the account.

Shelly sat on her hands tensely. She was dying to rip off the maternity shapewear and get back into her joggers.

'Fuck, we're rumbled.' Amy sighed. 'That was quick. She blocked us. There's a DM, though. It says: "You think I don't know a burner when I see one? Hope you got a little taster of what's in store, Shelly. BYEEEEEE".'

'Shit. They think it was me.'

'Well, it is you technically. It doesn't matter anyhow, Shelly.' Amy pursed her lips and looked agitated. 'I got a good sense of it. It's gotta be @_____. It's loads of the pics they'd sent us. This is obviously them flexing, showing you exactly what they can do the second they feel like it.'

Shelly dug her fists into her eye sockets to try to relieve the headache gathering pace. *It's useless*, she thought, feeling tears seep between her fingers and gather in her palms. *This person just hates me so much. Why?*

'They could end me at any moment. They are messing with my livelihood. I could lose the house.' She sucked at the air but felt choked. 'They are messing with my family. What if I lose Georgie? Dan could use this as ammunition.'

'Shelly, it won't come to that. I promise.' Amy came over and wrapped her arms around her. 'The more moves they make, the more they risk making a mistake and when they do, we will be ready to catch them. I'll show these to Detective Bríd ahead of our meeting and she will see if there are any new clues, any personal information attached to the account. They will slip up. In the meantime, appease them in the DMs. If they reference our burner account, feign ignorance. Everything will be OK.' Amy was firm and Shelly tried to believe her but all the images @_____ had sent her in the past months played on a loop in her head – the breastfeeding ones most of all. She let go of trying to maintain any kind of composure and sobbed into her assistant's embrace.

Chapter 16

'Where are we even going?' Ali shifted around uncomfortably in the back seat of the cramped Honda Civic as Mini muttered urgent instructions to Erasmus, who was driving.

The sky was beginning to lighten at the horizon but the sea lapping in front of her parents' house was still dark. Mini settled back beside her and Erasmus pulled away from the curb and swung up the steep narrow street to the main road.

'I told you, we're doing the ashes. Your father has been languishing on top of the microwave in the kitchen for far too long. It's embarrassing. Everyone's been asking me where we put him and I can hardly say "he's resting peacefully near his favourite condiment".'

Ali grimaced. 'Sheeesh. He really did push the boundaries of Bovril's intended uses, didn't he?'

They both shuddered.

'The roast potatoes ...' Mini began but Ali halted her with a look.

'Please, no. I already feel like dogshit someone's set fire to without the image of Miles slathering Bovril on his spuds.'

'Is the nausea not gone yet?'

'Well, it has, but then you get me out of bed at stupid o'clock for an ashes-scattering and no one feels good at this time.'

'It's 4 a.m. Don't be so melodramatic. Anyway, we have to get there early. Before anyone arrives.'

'Where are we going?'

'Did I tell you I matched with someone on Tinder?'

Ali started at this conversational curveball. 'What?'

Her mother looked delighted at her surprise. 'Yes. He's twenty-four and his name is Solomon. He works in oils. We're meeting this week.'

'Oh gawd. Twenty-four? And he's a painter? Mini, he probably just wants you to represent him.'

Mini laughed. 'I don't *care*,' she said scathingly. 'I'm not going to date some old man, am I?'

'No? I guess not.' Ali tried to suppress the unpleasant image of Mini with a random old man and stifled another yawn. Yesterday had been tiring being back in the Insta-saddle. She'd forgotten all the admin of replying to comments and DMs but now that she had a real goal with the Dublin Stage Fest in a few months, it felt important to be responsive to the people who had come flocking back to her. The general sentiment was that, in comparison with all these ones and their insincere apologies online, Ali was a breath of fresh air. And they seemed to think she was gas – in Ireland people could be forgiven a lot so long as they were perceived to be gas.

The city streets were deserted and the streetlights were still lit, though the sky was beginning to streak with pink.

'Seriously, where are we going?' She studied her mother's profile.

She was acting crazier than usual. *Tinder? Ick.* She shifted and yanked on the thick waistband of the maternity jeans. Fucking hateful things. Why would you take an already uncomfortable, overheated, sweating, angry creature like a pregnant woman and then swathe her in a very thick, elastic waistband?

'It's so odd. I didn't show when I was expecting you until I was at least seven months pregnant. Are you sure it's not twins?'

Ali rolled her eyes so hard she actually felt a twinge in the right one. Could you pull a muscle from eye-rolling?

'Yep, I'm sure you were the dream preggers bitch, with zero stretch marks. Listen, Sam is very tall. It's probably just mega long. It's definitely only one foetus. I've seen it. I sent you the bloody pics, though, as I recall, you didn't even reply, even though it was a-fucking-dorable. It looks like a lava lamp, remember?' She pulled up WhatsApp to root out the pic she had sent to Mini. 'Behold the Tinder spawn.' She held the phone out to her mother.

'It's very nice.' She barely looked up from her swiping. 'Look, mine's good too, like a young Dustin Hoffman.' Mini proffered her own snap, a young guy in a flat cap and cheesecloth shirt with a monocle.

'What do you have, some kind of art school hipster setting on? He looks like he listens to the wireless and rides a penny-farthing to work in the charcoal chai coffee brewshop.'

'I just set my location to Dublin 8 permanently.' Mini shrugged. 'Erasmus's idea.'

'Excellent. Thanks, Erasmus. Can't wait for my chronically hipster step-dad.'

'Please, Ali, this is just sex, as you well know. Erasmus, go up Gardiner Street and then hang a left and left again. This one-way system is a pain.'

It was starting to dawn on Ali just where they might be heading.

'Mini ... ? We're not—' Her WhatsApp pinged in her hand, distracting her from what was a very unnerving realisation.

She X'd out of the pic of the foetus and spied a new message from Sam.

You're online. It's 4 a.m. What's wrong? Is everything all right? Is the Pea OK?

His nickname for the fake baby, the Sweet Pea, had been resurrected and seeing it here in the thread twanged on her heart unexpectedly. She was so consumed with trying to distract herself with her writing and re-engaging with Insta that she was able to avoid thinking about Sam for hours at a time. Then something like this was like catching her finger on a thorn. She didn't want to care, and she cursed the swoop of hope she felt at his apparent concern.

It's useless, he hates you, Ali. You fucked it all up. The rational voice in her head didn't want her to get her hopes up.

But he's checking on me, argued the part of her still nursing a persistent desire that they would somehow pull through this whole mess.

I'm OK, nothing's wrong no need to worry AT ALL. Mini just got me out ridiculously early. We're ...

She paused in typing her response. She didn't want it to look as if she was trawling for sympathy but maybe it would be good for him to be reminded that she'd lost her dad only a couple of months ago. Especially as they were having the big scan this week and her midwife had already warned that there was to be no more time-wasting with this going in separately business.

On Tuesday morning, they would be thrown together for at least a couple of hours in the hospital and Ali couldn't help it, she'd been buying and returning things to ASOS maternity for the last two weeks. It was hard trying to look appealing while also looking like that YouTube video of the snake eating the cow. She'd been experimenting with a Bardot neckline … Another WhatsApp dropped in from Sam. Shit, he was losing it.

Please, Ali, I can see you typing. Are you and the baby OK????

She hastily completed her message.

I'm OK. Nothing's wrong, no need to worry AT ALL. Mini just got me out ridiculously early. We're just going to scatter Miles's ashes. I'll talk to you later?

She waited but even though the message blue-ticked, he didn't write back. All the thrill she'd felt of him worrying about her ebbed away and she chucked the phone in her bag at her feet.

'OK, here we are.'

Ali squinted in the early morning gloom. They were on the corner of Abbey Street. Uh-oh.

It wasn't the most salubrious location in town, but Ali knew exactly what Mini was up to.

'There is no way this is legal, Mini.'

Mini was resolutely ignoring her daughter.

'Erasmus.' She leaned forward. 'Might be best to keep the engine running. Just in case.' She hopped out of the car and skipped down the street towards an inconspicuous maroon door.

Oh God, was this a grief-induced psychotic break? Should she be intervening? Though, at twenty-two weeks pregnant, short of lying on top of her mother she didn't think she could stop Mini.

'Mini, we can't. How do you think we're even going to get in?'

'One of the Tinder boys does usher Thursday to Saturday.' Mini produced a heavy set of keys with a flourish and jangled them in Ali's face. 'I can be very persuasive.'

'Oh my God.' Ali blanched. 'Please shut up, I can't cope with any more Tinder Mini visuals.'

Mini leaned back from the door and threw a quick glance up and down the deserted street, then hurriedly unlocked the door. She ducked inside. Ali threw a beseeching look back at Erasmus in the car, who simply shrugged helplessly. *Ugh, fuck it.* Ali dove into the narrow corridor behind Mini, who was grappling with the alarm code.

'This is bonkers,' hissed Ali.

Finally, the alarm was disabled and Mini hit the lights. The corridor was a deep red. Red walls, red threadbare carpet and even a peeling red ceiling overhead – it felt oppressive and ominous. The walls were lined with black and white pictures of actors playing in Behan, Beckett, Wilde and O'Casey. Ali knew somewhere among them was a young Miles playing Boy in Godot. She scanned the shots but Mini was already way ahead of her and Ali knew now wasn't the time to find the gawky teenage Miles acting opposite one of Irish theatre's greats, Séamus Mac Liammóir, in a now-famous production.

She jogged after Mini, who was crossing a small room cluttered with furniture and mouldy boxes of ancient programmes.

Weird how all theatres seem to have the same smell, Ali thought nostalgically. The smell wasn't exactly pleasant. It was a blend of cigarettes, burning dust and perfume and it always reminded her of Miles. She was certain she'd stood in this exact spot with him before. When she was little, he used to bring her around and annoy his actor friends during rehearsals. His restaurant was only a few minutes' walk away and every opening night the whole cast and crew would decamp there for the after party. Ali'd loved it, her parents' wild friends had the best fun and Miles and Mini were happiest directing the madness. She crossed the room after Mini. On the other side was the gap in the curtains that led to the stage. Some more lights came on as Mini fiddled with a bank of switches. It had to be close to 5 a.m. by now. The cleaning staff would surely be arriving soon. The Sunday matinee was usually at around 2 p.m. and by the looks of the set on stage, no one had cleaned after curtains the night before.

Ali wasn't even sure what was playing at the moment. She felt a gust of sadness sweep through her. When Miles was alive, this theatre was part of their family. They came here all the time – he knew the year's schedule. They would have celebrated opening night and he would have probably come again at least once during the run. How had she not been here in so long? She hadn't come once since he had gone to Ailesend, the nursing home he'd died in. She was suddenly gripped with guilt. She could have kept coming. That would have meant something to Miles.

'Ali? We can't dawdle.'

For once she was grateful for Mini's abrupt ways. She shrugged the guilt off. She could go down that hole. She'd been sucked down the guilt-spiral practically daily since the night he had died. Why did they call it grief? They should call it Guilt with a capital G.

She tentatively moved to the centre of the stage to join her mother.

'Well, this is batshit.' She sighed, resigned. 'Should we say something?'

Mini cleared her throat.

'Miles, I know you would have enjoyed knowing that the national theatre is your final resting place, not least for all the auditions you didn't get! Now you'll be on the Abbey stage for ever and there's nothing that fecker O'Shea can do about it.' She momentarily dropped the tone of gravitas to fill Ali in on O'Shea. 'Bitter little prig never gave

UNFILTERED

Miles a single bloody shot, not even in a minor role. Anyway,' she resumed her solemn speech, 'Miles. You always said you felt so lucky and I think you actually possessed the secret to being happy. You made the lives of everyone around you so full of fun and love and ...'

Ali pushed the tears from her cheeks as Mini's voice cracked on the empty stage. Ali stared at the seat Miles liked to reserve, B13, front and centre, and the sudden realisation that he would never sit there again, that he quite simply didn't exist anymore, hit her full force in the chest.

'I'm sorry,' Mini continued through her own tears. 'What I wanted to say, Miles, was that you were wrong. You weren't lucky; we were the lucky ones. We are the luckiest to have had you in our lives.' Mini twisted the lid of the plastic container the funeral home had given them. It was naff as hell, a plastic fake urn.

Ali stepped up and stood shoulder to shoulder with Mini. She closed her eyes and thought of Miles bashing out a song on the battered old piano backstage after a raucous closing show years ago. She could see him so clearly, tossing his blond hair back, his eyes half closed as he sang about the lucky old sun with nothing to do but roll around heaven all day ... She searched inside for a scrap of relief. The lucky old sun was Miles now, she told herself. He was free from the prison of his illness. She tried to believe this, to feel it.

'We love you, Miles darling,' Mini whispered. 'You're free.'

'Dada,' Ali murmured as the sobs rose through her chest. Then an odd whooshing sound and dust in her mouth. Her eyes snapped open to Mini's yelp of 'Oh feck!'

'Oh feck?' Ali leapt back from the dust cloud that was enveloping them and the rest of the stage. Mini had upended what looked like a bag of kitty litter right in the middle of stage left. 'What is this stuff?' Ali cried, spluttering.

'It's Miles.' Mini looked stricken. 'His ashes. I thought it'd be more like, well, ashes! This looks like fine-grade fecking gravel.'

'Jesus,' Ali whimpered, looking at the mound of Miles in front of them. 'There's so much of it! Did you not check it?'

Mini shook her head helplessly. 'I just assumed ... I've never scattered anyone before. I thought it'd be a very fine dust and it would kind of dissipate?'

'Well, we'd better put him back in.' Ali snorted, which in turn set off Mini. She covered her mouth but soon they were both bent over howling at the absurdity of the situation.

'Why did you upend the whole bloody thing?' Ali managed to gasp.

'I don't know. I misjudged,' Mini wailed. 'For God's sake, Miles, I'm blaming you!' she shot at the whitish-grey pile on the floor. 'Once I'd tipped it a tiny bit, he kind of threw his weight forward. He unbalanced it.' They both collapsed into giggles once more at this.

'Oh, I suppose ye think it's funny to give me even more work to do?'

A booming voice behind them abruptly silenced Ali and Mini. They wheeled around to find an intensely pissed-off-looking old woman standing with her hands on her hips.

Oh shit. What time was it? What was the cleaner doing here so early? Beside her, Mini, thanks to some kind of adrenaline-rush of instinct, shoved the plastic urn out of sight.

'Sorry.' Ali found her voice as the woman stormed over to the Miles mound and kicked at it with her foot. Ali winced as the ashes scattered.

'Absolutely outrageous. Grown adults effing around after hours with cat litter. Who are ye? Ye're not supposed to be in here before 9 a.m. This is my time.'

'We're terribly sorry—' Mini began, trying to appease her but she only raged on as she stormed back over to the side of the stage to retrieve …

'NO!' Ali shouted as the pissy woman shouldered a hoover and marched back towards them.

'What did you say, missy?'

'Don't hoover.' Ali scrambled to salvage the situation. 'We'll clean it up. We're really sorry. It was an accident.'

'I'll be cleaning my own theatre, thank you very much. Betty is the housekeeper here.' She thumped her chest. 'I've been tending to the Abbey since eighty-four, before you were born, I'd say, and this is my work. Some of us take pride in our work.'

She chucked the hoover down and stepped on the switch. It roared into life as Ali shot the panic-stricken Mini a pleading look.

'Stop, stop, you can't.' Mini threw herself in front of Miles. 'Betty, no! Please don't.'

Betty straightened up and, leaning on the hoover attachment, her eyes narrowed as she looked from Ali to Mini to the mound on the floor.

'Is this some kind of drugs thing?' She pulled out her phone. 'I'm calling the guards.'

'No!' Mini was vehement.

Betty looked suspicious.

'Well, if it's not crack marijuana, then why can't I hoover it up?' She cocked an eyebrow triumphantly.

'It's … it's …' Mini was clearly casting about for something convincing to say.

'It's not drugs,' Ali threw in feebly.

Betty pursed her lips and began to hoover the stage aggressively.

'Tell her,' Ali mouthed frantically at Mini.

'I … Betty! Please stop!' Mini roared over the hoover and tried to grab the cord.

Betty whipped around raging. 'Who are you anyway? Does Richard know you two are even here? You're not cast, are you? Are you? What's your name? I want to see ID.'

Mini froze. Ali flashed on the potential headlines that hovered like blades of a guillotine over this ridiculous moment.

'Failed Actor Dad of Shamed Influencer Wanted His Ashes Scattered on the Abbey Stage.'

Oh God, she gulped. She instinctively backed away. By the defeated look on Mini's face, she was clearly picturing a similar public humiliation.

'Sorry.' Mini held up her hands in acquiescence. 'You're right, Betty, we shouldn't be here.'

Betty smirked at them, delighted at having prevailed. 'Off you go, so. You've caused me enough grief, thank you very much.'

She turned and pushed the hoover straight through the pile of ashes with a kind of savage delight as Mini and Ali looked on in mute horror.

Finally, Ali shook herself. Goddammit, this megalomaniac cleaner was hoovering up her dad! She dove forward and grabbed what she could, a fistful of ashes, then turned and exited stage left. She tore across the storeroom, down the stage door corridor and back out into the pale morning light, where, mercifully, Erasmus still sat, engine running. She leapt into the back seat and hunkered down in case Betty was in hot pursuit.

'Where's Mini? What happened in there?' Erasmus looked terrified, which was, Ali reflected, pretty much his permanent natural state. Ali shoved the ashes she'd managed to grab into her coat pocket but, before she could answer, the stage door burst open again and

Mini tore out clinging to Betty's hoover. The door had barely banged shut behind her when Betty emerged, hair flying and shrieking, 'I knew it was drugs' at the top of her voice.

Mini managed to throw herself backwards into the passenger seat, screaming, 'Go, Go, GO!' while trying to fend off Betty with her foot. Erasmus burst into stress-tears and accidentally tried to start off in fifth gear.

'She's got the cord, Mini.' Ali rolled down her window and started grabbing at Betty.

'Get it together, Erasmus,' Mini shouted almost from his lap with the hoover hugged to her between her legs. A deranged and red-faced Betty was practically climbing into the car. Ali was struggling to fend her off while also protecting her bump. She leaned over the front seat and pushed Betty's head, managing to get her back out of the car. At that moment, Erasmus got into first and shot away from the curb.

'Jesus, she does not give up,' Mini exclaimed, realising Betty still had the cord, which was rapidly unspooling from inside the hoover.

'Shit, that's gonna take her hands off.' Ali craned backwards to see Betty, at least sixty years old, holding on to her hoover plug with the grim-faced determination of the Terminator. The car swung around the corner, looping the electrical cord around a lamppost and the hoover burst open. The bottom half fell out the passenger door leaving Mini with the top and Miles now billowing absolutely everywhere. Erasmus began coughing, the car swerved erratically and mounted the pavement before he braked hard.

'Fucking hell, leave the rest of the hoover, Mini!' Ali screamed. 'There's no point, she'll report us if we don't. There's probably CCTV cameras!'

Oh my God. Ali cringed. She had not anticipated the stress of this memorial. Or the fact that she should have come in some kind of disguise.

She hopped out of the car and hurried around to the front passenger side where a dazed-looking Mini was gazing at the spilled ashes. Ali grabbed the hoover and marched back to the corner, where Betty stood by the lower half.

'Here, we're really sorry. We've been going through a bit of a strange time. We should have just explained straight away – it was my dad's ashes. We … eh' – Ali was coming clean but she sensed she shouldn't come too clean – '… we spilled them by accident. Sorry, Betty.'

Ali turned and jogged back to the car before Betty could demand any further explanation.

'Drive!' Ali snapped the second her door was closed. 'I am sweating like a beast.' She shrugged off her coat and quickly clicked her seatbelt.

'Oh God, that was a disaster,' Mini groaned.

'I feel like I've been tarred and feathered back here,' Ali moaned. 'Only it's sweat and my dad's ashes. Let's never try having a heartfelt, sincere moment again. It's just not us.'

'Seriously, what happened? Are we in damage-control mode, Mini? Should I ring the office? Get them to start drafting a statement?' Erasmus was feverishly looking from the lights ahead to Mini to Ali and back to the road in front.

'No, no. It'll be fine,' Mini panted. 'Ali, you smoothed it over, didn't you?'

'Well, kind of … I wouldn't be counting on my garbled explanation to put Betty off complaining about us, though.'

'I'll text my little usher friend and, if all comes to all, I can call Richard Aster. He's the theatre director. It wouldn't be my preference to draw him into this, but I have his ear if need be.'

'Why didn't you just get his permission in the first place?' *Why do you have to be so unhinged?* Ali wanted to add.

'Oh, that would have killed the spirit of the thing. Miles would've loved all the sneaking in and the secrecy.' Mini smiled a little. 'He would've got a kick out of nearly making off with Betty's hoover.'

'Hmmm,' Ali said, unconvinced. 'And how would he have felt about the hoover being his eternal resting place?'

Mini ignored this and turned around to face her. 'You got some of him, didn't you?'

Ali was tempted to pretend she'd lost it in the kerfuffle and have her own private, non-slapstick moment with her dad, but she knew she couldn't do that to Mini. This freakish little outing had been oddly fun, good bonding for them she realised. Mini was loosening up and she was no longer wincing at the mere sight of the baby bump, which was definite progress.

'I have a little. It's here in my pocket but I'm only handing it over if you're willing to scatter it in the sea like normal people do.'

'I promise.' A satisfied Mini turned back to instruct Erasmus to take them home.

❧

After an infinitely more successful second go at the ashes-scattering in the sea in front of her parents' house, Ali retreated to her old bedroom to work on the show – working title: *My So-Called Best Life*.

She'd been struggling to decide whether it needed to be more like a piece of stand-up comedy or something closer to theatre. Currently the script was straight up storytelling but standing on the Abbey stage that morning had clarified things for her. Instagram was a virtual stage and the people who used it to tell a story about their lives were the actors and the directors. But it was more complex than that. It wasn't a one-way interaction. It was an exchange. The audience could influence the influencers.

She scribbled notes on the copybook she'd found among her old college notes.

In a way, Ali realised, *the audience influences the influencer way bloody more than anything. From the moment I started getting likes and followers, it started to direct my actions. I started tailoring my life to what I knew or guessed these people would want.*

She sat back. This was worth exploring.

What if the show was part stand up, part choose your own adventure? Only the audience gets to choose. Just like on Instagram.

She leaned forward and wrote 'interactive?' at the top of a fresh page. Below she added, 'Would people think I'm trying to blame my followers for the Insta-baby mess?'

She contemplated this.

Maybe I could have other characters who are also me who could show the internal struggle? Like Rational Ali and … she clicked her fingers searching for a good name …

Low Self-Esteem Ali? The Validation Whore?

She doubted Terry – or anyone else for that matter – would go for 'whore'.

Wait, wait … Thirsty *Ali.*

She grinned. *Perfect.*

She could pre-record the characters of Rational Ali and Thirsty Ali and play them as audio or even project them. And use them almost like a chorus. In the Greek tragedies, the chorus often provided commentary on the action. Plus, it would give a sense of populating the world of the play.

She checked the calendar on her phone and emailed Terry – subject line: 'So-Called Best Life epiphany!!!!' – to arrange their next meeting.

Chapter 17

When Hazel's charcoal-grey front door with gleaming rose-gold hardware swung open, Shelly was startled to come face to face with the woman herself. In all their years of faux-friendship, Hazel had never once answered her own door; one of the Jennys always did it so that Hazel could make a wafty entrance from some other part of the generous, light-filled, hemp-covered semi-d.

'Shelly! Quick, in. Now!' Hazel leaned out past her for a tense scan of the other houses in the cul de sac, then, satisfied no one was watching, pulled Shelly and Georgie inside.

'Hi, Hazel, I love your braid,' chirped Georgie.

Hazel aimed a chilly smile at the little girl and then steered her in the first door of the hall. 'All the kiddies are in here,' she said in a firm voice to communicate that this was not a suggestion but an order.

'Neil's mother is watching them,' she explained to Shelly, giving

Georgie a push into the room where *The Lion King* was blaring and shutting the door behind her. 'C'mon, everyone's in the back.'

'Everyone', Shelly realised, included quite a few new faces. Ali and Polly sat on huge beanbags in front of the glass doors that led to the vast deck and back garden. Nearby, standing at the kitchen peninsula in front of an open laptop, stood a young black guy in a bowler hat, a white tee-shirt and skinny suspenders holding up spray-on Levis. To his right, a vaguely familiar-looking girl with long brown hair hovered, pointing at different things on the screen. Amy sat on a stool on the other side of the peninsula and looked bored as Hazel beelined for her and immediately began delivering some impassioned hard sell about whatever they were emergency summiting about.

Shelly was surprised to see Siobhan from @MamasLittleMissus sitting apart from the others against the far wall along with Crystal Doorley. Hazel must've taken pity on her and invited her after all. Shelly took the stool beside Amy and Hazel moved to the centre of the room, clapping her hands together. Despite evidently being even more het up than usual, she still looked fab in a pale green kimono jacket over her simple white tee and jeans, layered with necklaces from her own range, Holistic Happiness by Hazel.

'OK, everyone.' She clicked her fingers unnecessarily; everyone was listening attentively for further instruction. 'Just for ease, Ezra has emailed an itinerary today so that we all know what we're doing and when, but first a few introductions. In light of recent security breaches, I've had to clean house at Holistic Hazel. No more Jennys. So, first I'd like to introduce the leader of the new administration, Ezra Ó Súilleabháin.' Ezra doffed his bowler hat and nodded solemnly to everyone.

'Ezra is returning from a stint in the UK, where he was working with a prominent influencer for the last three years. He is head of operations now and don't worry, girls, I have redrafted the NDAs so no more security breaches, I promise. Beside Ezra we have a promising up-and-coming young influencer, Kate from @ShreddingForTheWedding, who has been my right hand and such a great support during this trying era of mumfluencer-shaming.'

Shelly remembered her now. She was Ali's friend, the one with the #EngagementJourney.

'We also have Siobhan,' Hazel continued. Shelly smiled over sympathetically. 'A recent casualty of the appalling trend for mumfluencer takedowns and, of course, Crystal Doorley, who's no stranger to being cancelled. How many times is it now, Crystal?'

'Three, maybe four.' Crystal shrugged. 'The tan thing, the time I said I'd done the women's mini marathon and the whole hoopla about my "cruelty-free" eye palette being tested on honey badgers.'

'Ridiculous.' Hazel shook her head in sympathy. 'I mean, honey badgers are vicious. They would eat the face off your head, given half the chance!'

'Exactly what I said,' Crystal agreed.

'Ali Jones, meanwhile, has just this weekend delivered a masterclass in weathering a public shaming.' Hazel sounded openly bitter about this, but Ali just shrugged awkwardly and waved at the assembled crowd.

'Polly, on the other hand, is probably the most bland, uncontroversh person ever,' Hazel continued, characteristically unfazed at steamrolling anyone's feelings during the introductory speech. Shelly spotted Ali throw a strange look at Polly, who remained impassive while Hazel droned on. 'No skeletons in that closet, but she is in danger of being tarnished by association. And, finally, who else but Teflon Shelly herself. Nothing sticks to this woman,' Hazel announced through gritted teeth. 'A viral video rant, her marriage on the rocks and still she's top of the pile, thanks, I'm sure, in no small part to the brains of the SHELLY operation, Amy Donoghue, who is the child in the fetish wear there.' Amy took a sarcastic, little bow.

'Right, I'll be handing you over to Ezra now, who is going to outline my incredible vision.'

'Thank you, Hazel.' Ezra strode to the centre of the room, a slim remote in his hand. 'And thank you all for coming on this journey with us. I have been analysing shifts in public opinion towards Irish mumfluencers in the last six months and the results have been disappointing. Polls are suggesting that your once-loyal followers are becoming disenfranchised with the mumfluencer. Recent scandals have, of course, contributed. Deborah Winters has been spouting her hate speak and the general consensus seems to be that the mumfluencer is no longer empowering other women but instead fleecing them through affiliate links, flogging Ali Express products rebranded as bespoke luxury items and generally rinsing their own family's lives for sponcon. Now we are not by any means suggesting that you stop doing this. Absolutely not. We just want to demonstrate how women-centric you are and that yis're not all just money-grabbing melts.' Ali was the only one who laughed at this, but Ezra winked, unfazed, and stepped to the side, flicking the remote control at the projector.

A huge picture of Hazel appeared on the wall behind him. She sat naked, artfully draped in her children (also nude), all of them strewn with flowers on a cliff edge staring out at the ocean beyond. It was very Enya meets vintage Demi Moore. Panpipes played and the image was replaced by drone footage of miles of choppy sea, a tiny remote island emerging from the horizon. Hazel's voice rose over the music as the video cut from the air to a pristine, white, sandy beach.

'On the boundaries of the impossible, W Y N D is a festival and an experience.'

The camera picked up Hazel's footprints in the sand and then the woman herself striding majestically as the music soared in the background. The voiceover continued.

'Join Ireland's premier influencers for a weekend of empowerment, nourishing Michelin-star vegan feasts and self-discovery.'

On screen Hazel turned back to the camera and whispered, 'Learn to live how you've always dreamed. Workshops from the women you've always wanted to be on the things you thought you could never master …'

The scene cut to a barren limestone cliff, Hazel striding to the edge. Text appeared on the screen:

Luxury you could never conceive of, in a place wilder than your dreams. Finally, be your authentic self with the help of …

The text disappeared and onscreen Hazel appeared to dive from the cliffs, plunging into the pitch-black ocean miles below.

Pale pink words materialised dramatically:

W Y N D Summit

The screen went blank and the room erupted into reverential applause. Shelly clapped along but shrugged questioningly at Amy. Just what the hell were they clapping? What was that even an ad for?

Hazel got to her feet smiling and nodding at the effusive murmurs rippling around the room.

'Incredible, Hazel, truly.'

'You're a visionary.'

'Thank you, thank you. I know – it's amazing, right?' She grinned.

'So, as you can see, we're putting together an event so exclusive, so ambitious, nothing of its kind has ever been attempted before.'

'So, what is it? Some kind of culchie GOOP thing?' Ali asked. Shelly stifled a giggle. Ali, at least, could be counted on for a blunt take.

'No,' Hazel replied coolly. 'Some of us could do well to remember their place, Ali. Just because you've got a real baba en route now and you're the comeback queen shouldn't be any reason to forget your manners.'

A tense silence followed this reprimand until Ezra leaned forward and whispered in Hazel's ear. She gave an almost imperceptible nod and then cranked up a mechanical smile for Ali.

'How are you feeling by the way, lovelie?'

Ali blinked but played along.

'Ah good.' She rubbed her belly, smiling. 'We've got the big scan this week – I was actually a bit late getting the appointment – so fingers crossed Sam actually turns up.' She shrugged.

Shelly pressed her lips together. *The poor thing*, she thought. Ali looked tired too. Shelly was daunted enough getting ready to welcome this baby solo and at least *she* knew what was coming. Poor Ali was all alone and didn't have a clue. She resolved to invite her to the prenatal course she was attending. That would cheer her up, especially if Sam didn't rally soon.

Dan had at least attended their big scan a few weeks before, though things continued to be strained and they had ended up having a row afterwards about Georgie being filmed on her way into summer camp. The story was in exchange for a week at the camp, but Dan didn't want to hear it.

Speaking of quid pro quo, Shelly straightened up and tuned back into Hazel. Just what was their role to be in this W Y N D shindig?

'My vision is one of female empowerment.' Hazel was in full flow again. 'I summoned you here because you owe it to your followers – the women and gay men who made you into the Insta-success stories you all are – to lead the charge in this new era of Instagram. They look to us for influence, for guidance, for their self-esteem.'

'This sounds like a pyramid scheme,' Shelly caught Ali mutter to Polly, who only shook her head sternly in response, checking to ensure that Hazel hadn't heard.

'W Y N D will showcase the latest in restorative workshops, caffeine colonics, colostrum facials and laser gemstone therapy. It will be as beautiful and transformative as a destination wedding.'

'Riiiight, it sounds like the Hazel App in surround sound,' Amy piped up without taking her eyes off her tablet, on which her neon talons click-clacked incessantly. 'Where does my client come into this?' She sounded bored. Amy delighted in winding Hazel up.

'Well, Ms Donoghue, you may or may not have noticed that the Irish mumfluencers' reputations have seriously suffered in the last two months.' Virtually all the influencers shifted uneasily at this. 'W Y N D is an opportunity to give back, to prove that we're not all crazed liars out for a bit of sponcon at any cost.'

'OK, so it's a charity gig?' Amy set the tablet aside at last.

'Well, no, no, of course it won't be free, but the price point of the basic package will be accessible. And the luxury will be off the charts. Along with our own elite, I'm inviting some of the giants of the LA wellness influencer set. We'll be offering the followers access like they've never dreamed of to their fave online mavens. Twenty twenty is all about that authenticity buck and we are going to personify that. With this event, we can shove Deborah Effing Winters's hot takes about "toxic influence" and "negative beauty and lifestyle standards" up her own uncaffeinated hole.'

'So, are you paying my client for this unprecedented access, Hazel?' Shelly loved that she could count on Amy for keeping the bottom line in view at all times. This would be a decent boost before the bump popped in September.

'Appearance fees will be calculated according to your individual influence.' Hazel charged on with her notes. 'Now, selling this unique event will hinge on our collective magnetism. We want to have every one of our W Y N D ambassadors to appear in this promo, which is the second phase of today's itinerary.'

Both Polly and Ali were surprised by this news, with each of them protesting at the same time.

'I have a thing, Hazel,' said Polly urgently. 'I didn't realise we were doing the promo today.'

'I said we were doing promotional materials in the WhatsApp, Polly.' Hazel rounded on Polly and Ali viciously.

'I can't just hop off to Inis Whatever,' Ali yelped. 'We've got … I mean, I've to go to a meeting.'

'Don't worry, the island is far from habitable just yet,' Ezra reassured her as he distributed call sheets. 'The set up for filming today is all here on site.'

Shelly noted with relief that she was up first.

'We'll take you one by one through to hair and make-up and then to the green screen studio. The remaining women can enjoy a light lunch and we'll be through with everyone by 2, 3 p.m. tops. How does that sound?' He flashed a smooth, placating smile.

Shelly looked around to see how everyone else was taking this news.

Ali looked mutinous but was being soothed by Polly, which was definitely odd. Not only had she rarely seen them ever talk to one another, she could not imagine they would have much in common.

Ali was way too salty for Polly. Siobhan and Crystal, on the other hand, were looking delighted with themselves. They were essentially small fry, and this was probably the most salubrious Insta-event they had ever been involved with. Shelly pulled herself up to stretch the bump. As she neared the third trimester, a persistent pain in her ribs started up any time she sat for too long. This pregnancy was definitely proving to be more of a drain than her first. She doubted she'd even be able to attend W Y N D. It was very close to her due date.

She was just heading towards Ali and Polly when Ezra intercepted her.

'Shelly, pleasure to meet IRL. Your work has been a terrific source of inspo for me for years now. I just love what you've created with SHELLY. With the input of Amy, of course,' he added hastily as she appeared at his elbow, tablet raised for battle.

'Ezra, logistics at our end are tricky,' she announced, and Shelly relaxed, knowing the ever-on Amy was sorting things.

'Right, yes, I can see.' He gestured to the bump. 'You're about to go any day now by the looks of things.'

'No, Ezra, she's only twenty-seven weeks,' Amy shot back sternly. 'Now, W Y N D, as previously discussed, is too close to Shelly's due date. Shelly and Hazel did agree a certain amount of support in the lead up. I've mailed you the exact proposal along with our tiered rates for Shelly's appearances, stories and posts when she's on a bump journey.'

'Not a prob. I got them, Amy.' Ezra smiled. 'We've just this minute sent through the final and, might I say, very handsome offer and I think you'll be pleased.'

Shelly smiled blandly as Amy brought up her inbox. The financials could be awkward, but this would be a major dent in the money to buy Dan out of the house.

'OK, looks in order.' Amy snapped her tablet cover shut. 'Now, where's hair and make-up?'

Ezra beckoned Ali's friend Kate over, and she gushed as she kissed Shelly on the cheek.

'Oh my God, I just loved your IGTV on how you organise your clothes every week. I was like "Oh my God, ordering a rail immedj!"' Shelly smiled awkwardly as Kate absent-mindedly stroked the cashmere coatigan Shelly had unwrapped that very morning from BT's PR department.

'No touching,' barked Amy and Kate jumped.

'Sorry, of course, let's get you island-ready.' Kate smiled and hurried ahead, leading Shelly up Hazel's wide, sweeping staircase to the second-floor landing, where they were met by three different closed doors. Shelly marvelled at the plants and orchids tumbling from the tiny occasional tables that punctuated the hall. *How does she maintain this with five kids? Maybe the kids don't even come up here? Maybe they're bused off each evening to the real house that's full of handprints on the walls and the usual kid shite.* Shelly grinned at the thought. There was nothing she'd put past Hazel.

Kate led them through the middle door to a vast dressing room. The stylists and MUAs bustled about. The room was decorated to resemble a beachfront property in Bondi, bamboo panels lining the walls, the furniture mostly bleached-out wood. Shelly took a seat in an awkward hanging hammock chair beside a large cactus sitting in a woven basket.

Kate pulled up a wicker stool and leaned forward eagerly.

'I have followed you forever. I love you. So. Much.'

Her intense staring was a bit much and Shelly quickly swayed out of her reach as she noticed her start to stretch out for the coatigan again.

'Like, I love you,' Kate persisted.

'Thanks.' Shelly looked around desperately. Ever since @_____ had been hovering on the edges of her life, she'd found it more and more unnerving to come face to face with followers. *Follow me!* they had all said in the early days. Such a weird thing to ask for when you thought about it. *Watch me, follow me, like me!* Shelly made a mental note to follow up with Detective Bríd (their meeting kept being rescheduled) as she tried to fend off Kate.

Thankfully, before Kate could inch any closer, a perky stylist Shelly vaguely recognised from Hazel's events over the years skipped over, referring to the tablet she cradled in her left arm.

'Shelly! Great to see you blooming! I'm @FiFiStyles. Amy's just confirmed some particulars with Hazel and Ezra, so we've agreed a degree of bump for your shots. We have this sheer dress with a coral bikini for underneath. Our MUA, Jade, will be doing a little henna on the hands – can you believe it's having a comeback?! – along with a super-glowy, no-make-up make-up and, the pièce de résistance, Hazel's imported Caribbean sea water for the hair.' @FiFiStyles's eyes widened. 'Apparently, there's crushed pearls in it. We'll do the fitting when Jade' – who appeared on Shelly's other side at that exact moment – 'has done the face. My handle is spelled f-i-f-i-s-t-y-l-e-s BTW in case you wanted to tag me.'

'Uh-huh.' Shelly was feeling a bit cornered but tried to relax as Jade, who also oh-so helpfully spelled her Insta-handle for the all-important tagging, started removing the make-up she was already wearing.

Shelly closed her eyes but could sense Kate's burning presence pressing in on her.

'So, you're Ali's friend, Kate,' Shelly said brightly to attempt to defuse the fandom and just be normal.

'Well … kind of. I mean, if you can be friends with someone who has just completely lied to you. And then ignores you.'

'Well, she was going through a very rough time.' Shelly opened one eye to sneak a glance at Kate. She looked even more pissed off at hearing this.

'Ugh, that's what everyone's saying now. Poor Ali. And she's got more followers than ever, like. So typical.'

'Well, they're probably notoriety-follows, that's what Amy says.' Shelly didn't know why she felt she should soothe this girl. She definitely wouldn't be the kind of friend Ali would miss.

'Yeah.' Kate seemed to suddenly notice how she sounded and pulled herself together. 'Anyway, my own account is going amazing and Hazel has just been the most incredible mentor on this journey.'

'And what kind of journey are you on?' Shelly was half smiling as Jade dabbed concealer under her eyes, but Kate answered in all seriousness.

'Weight loss,' she said firmly. 'But it's weight loss with a wedding! See, I'm getting married in a few months so I'm actually working two angles: the bride journey and the weight-loss journey. It's been building steadily.'

Jade dusted highlighter on the tip of her nose. 'OK, you're done, Shelly! It was a pleasure to work with such a face. At least we know you're not all angles on the 'gram.' She winked. 'Sometimes I work with these girls who look like completely different people IRL – it's mad. Now you'll tag me in your snaps, right, hun? Right?'

'Sure, sure.' Shelly gathered herself and hopped off the stool. She accepted the sheer dress and bikini @FifiStyles was proffering and ducked behind a wooden screen to change. Then it was back out to Amy, who was waiting in the hall. 'All good?'

'"Good" is a strong word.' Shelly rolled her eyes. 'Let's get this over with.'

'This' turned out to be fifteen takes of Shelly, sitting on an enormous piece of driftwood in front of a green screen with a wind machine blowing, saying the same line – 'Beyond live, love, laugh is W Y N D' – over and over again.

'Great, Shelly, you are such a pro. Can we get just one more with a slightly breathier "W Y N D"?' Shelly wearily obliged. They didn't do this bloody many takes on *Durty Aul' Town*.

Ezra clapped his hands together.

'That's a wrap on scene fifty-four. Thank you, everyone. We'll take five. Kate, we'll get Ali and Polly down from hair and make-up, OK? They're leaving together at 2.45 so chop-chop, thanks.'

Where on earth would Polly and Ali be going together? Shelly couldn't quite get her head around this strange new alliance.

Chapter 18

Driving away from the W Y N D promo shoot, Ali felt like a fugitive fleeing from captivity.

'Christ, that was a bit of an ordeal,' she muttered to Polly, who was behind the wheel looking stony-faced. Ali had now attended five CatAnon meetings and she'd never once known Polly to be late. She was like the mayor of the thing.

'Well, there's almost always a few strings attached to invites from Hazel,' she responded primly.

It was so weird. Since starting CatAnon, Ali had gotten some fairly intense insights into Polly's pretty out there past as a catfisher, but she couldn't penetrate her studied front outside meetings. If anything, Polly was even more stiff and fake with her since they had this in common.

'I think I pulled something in that dancer pose she had us do,' Ali continued. 'I don't even do yoga *normally*, never mind when I have a whole other person stuffed inside me.'

'Well, she'll be happy to have got you. It's all coming up Ali this weekend, isn't it?'

Ali stole a look at Polly, but her face was inscrutable. She sounded pissed off.

'What? Are you mad?'

'Well,' said Polly, pursing her lips as if she had a bad taste in her mouth, 'I just think you'd better be careful. Of your recovery in CatAnon, I mean. All this praise and validation on Insta can be dangerous for us. You wouldn't want to get sucked back into old habits.'

Ali rubbed the spot on her side where she'd twanged herself while being an obedient little influencer. Polly had looked perfectly at home in front of the green screen, Ali thought, miffed. *Who's she to lecture me?* She was about to say as much, but she just had zero fight in her today. The pre-dawn ashes-scattering had left her feeling edgy and even though they'd managed to scatter at least some of the ashes in the sea, and she was jazzed about the breakthrough with *My So-Called Best Life*, she still had a niggling sense that she'd let Miles down yet again.

Why did it have to be so slapstick? He deserved better than that. She leaned against the car window and tried to focus on the passing housing estates to quiet the horrible little voice in her head. *He deserved better than you for a daughter*, it whispered. *Running around doing sponcon while he lay there alone and dying. You're a dumb, selfish bitch.*

She squeezed her eyes shut and tried to silence the hateful words. Not easy, she'd found. Especially not when they were your own.

The day had gone from slapstick to surreal with Holistic Hazel's stint as James Cameron. *Why do any of us bother actually doing anything for real anymore?* she mused. None of it needed to be real. Who needed a remote island when you had a sound stage built in the garden extension? Who needed to be beautiful for real when you could just stick a filter on your pix? Who needed to be smart or funny or any of those things when all that mattered was how it *looked?*

Her phone pinged with an email from Terry:

New direction is SPOT ON, Ali, I love it. Let's aim for a new draft in the next two weeks. I think ditch the interactive element – it's overly complicated and it doesn't need it. We can make the same point through Rational Ali and Thirsty Ali. With the proposed added production elements, we want to stay ahead of ourselves. Nothing kills a show like a rushed development schedule – and we didn't exactly have much time to begin with. Send over pages as and when you want feedback. Otherwise, I'll expect the reworked script before the 19th.

She thought back to the time she collabed with a buggy company to 'design' a new pram. It was the kind of thing she'd always thought she'd love to do when she watched other influencers bring out their tans and their accessory lines. However, in reality, it had been such a miserable experience, an utterly shallow process. She didn't 'design' anything; the designers just had her pick a colour and mocked up a new logo for the Insta post. This was infinitely more satisfying. She was writing something new and original, working on a real show with a real producer and a real director. She'd stick with Instagram for this alone. She needed to sell out four shows, after all. Plus, any money, even what Hazel's cult-like W Y N D summit brought in, would mean more stability for when the baby came. But between CatAnon and the posing and posturing of some of the more demented Instagrammers, she'd seen behind the Instagram curtain and she knew it would never again take hold of her the way it had before.

She spent the rest of the car journey making forced small talk with Polly and idly deleting pics and screengrabs to clear space on her phone when she found herself face to face with a photo of Sam from early March. From the date, she could see that they were only weeks from imploding. At the time she'd snapped the pic he had been cocking one eyebrow in a playfully mocking fashion, but now, in the wake of everything that had happened, she felt that he was gazing straight down the lens at her.

She was trying not to get her hopes up too much but a small (OK big) part of her was just the teeniest bit optimistic about their first face to face in weeks at tomorrow's scan. In the various daydreams she'd written in her head, the reunion was romcom-worthy. Sam would see the baby on the little TV yoke, see her blooming with his baby and, perhaps most importantly, see the mega preggo tit job she'd been enjoying since getting duffed up.

Of course, the daydream was constantly being interrupted by a far less enjoyable montage of Sam's face: when she'd found him holding Liv's thesis, in the graveyard at her dad's funeral and the last time she'd seen him, storming to his car after the dinner party at the Khans'.

She tried to shake the whirling thoughts from her head. *Focus, Ali.* Making the show work and getting her shit together for the baby had to be her first priorities.

Polly pulled into the community centre car park. Ali still hadn't really spoken at any of the meetings since the first one. She'd listened and, as the weeks had passed, she'd surprised herself by starting to feel that maybe she did belong there after all. At the beginning, she'd spent the hour listing the ways that she was so *not* like these people, insisting to herself that she wasn't a catfisher, just someone who'd stumbled into a lie and had failed to extract herself quickly enough. But slowly the denial had ebbed away. Especially as the words that were gradually becoming her Stage Fest show began to assemble into a cohesive narrative. Everyone in CatAnon had, at one stage, been on the run from reality and so had she.

Ali and Polly slipped into the meeting just as the secretary was introducing this morning's speaker. Ali eased herself into a chair beside Kelly, who immediately began affectionately mauling the bump. *People just cannot help themselves*, Ali noted with resigned exasperation.

The speaker cleared his throat awkwardly.

'Hi everyone. My name is @SecretRteProducer and I am a catfisher.'

'Hi @SecretRteProducer,' everyone chimed back at him.

Shit! Ali sat up a little straighter. *This should be interesting.* She wasn't that up on Twitter, but she vividly remembered the hoo-ha surrounding this account from a couple of years before. For a few weeks RTÉ had been more dynamic than she'd ever seen it, with people on an absolute mission to ferret out whoever was behind the tweets purporting to be coming from inside the national broadcaster.

It was the kind of thing that would have been considered small catfish fry in any other country, but given it was a national pastime of the Irish to bitch about the channel for having to pay the TV licence fee, an anonymous RTÉ truther was too delicious to resist and the public and the newspapers couldn't get enough of the tweets. She vividly remembered the one about how bad the RTÉ canteen food was and that the station's employees lived for Fridays, which were supposedly beans, bangers and chips day. The tweeter had also devoted many characters to complaining about the flabby layer of middle management stifling creativity in the company. She couldn't help but flash on Stephan, as she remembered that particular rant.

'So, firstly, I'd like to say thank you to @BigDickY2K for asking me along tonight to share my experience, strength and hope in recovering from my catfishing addiction with you all.' He nodded at the woman beside him. She smiled back graciously.

'I came to catfishing quite late, as you can all probably tell!' A few chuckles came from the older group members. 'I didn't really start using the social media things until a couple of years ago. Before that I was strictly a check the old email, read the *Guardian* kind of guy. Then a friend showed me Twitter and I started hanging around on there, "lurking", they call it. I've been working in TV for decades, but I've never been staff in RTÉ. I have my own production company. We do entertainment, bit of factual, the odd drama. I suppose the reason I liked Twitter so much at first was for the tweeting on a Saturday night. I could go on there and click the *Saturday Night In* show hashtag and see all these people bitching about how shite it was. It was immediately addictive. I'd notice myself reading back over it during the week while waiting for the next Saturday to roll around. Thirty years making telly – I've had some winners, but I've had some real losers too and you get resentments, you know. Few commissioning editors have really had it in for me over the years. I *know* entertainment. I put a pitch in to revamp the Saturday slot and was of course shot down. Then I'd see my segment trotted out the next month. Tubridy's *Tender Talent* was one of mine. Killer idea, he goes around the country looking for local talent but there's gotta be a sob story, see? Pathos. Great telly, and not tough on the budget.'

Ali snuck a look around. Jeez, he's really losing them. For someone who knew entertainment, he was having trouble keeping some of the assembled catfishers engaged.

@BigDickY2K's back story the week before had waaaay more juice. Ali had not seen the whole 'tweets were coming from inside the house' plot twist coming. It had been a bit unseemly for sure, very Oedipal, but damn, a good cautionary tale, which surely was the point of these soul-baring sessions.

Ali felt herself nodding off as @SecretRteProducer trotted out his litany of woes, the working title of which could have been 37 Times RTÉ Rejected My Proposal, The Wankers.

'By the time they didn't even invite me for a face to face for the doc I proposed about why so many of our older celebrities are dying these days, I'd just fucking had it with the mediocrity and lack of vision. I got pissed one night and took a taxi out there to Montrose. I walked straight up to RTÉ and I punched it. Just fucking punched the fuck out of the building. Wrecked my hand that night but I knew just what I had to do. I set up the account while waiting in A&E down in Vincent's and by the next day I had a million followers.'

Did you? Ali crossed her arms sceptically. This guy was pissing her off. He seemed thrilled with himself. They were here to get better, not revel in all the bullshit schemes they had perpetrated.

She did wish she could tell Sam about the fistfight with the RTÉ reception building – that was hilarious. She sighed. It would be breaking anonymity. Maybe she could tell him about the W Y N D craziness. That shit was ridiculous. Hazel had sent them all a tile to post on Insta at an agreed time to herald the launch; it was cryptic, showing only rose-gold glitter strewn across limestone rock. It was hard to gauge, though. It could just piss Sam off further. Anything could. Her continued existence was probably pissing him off at this point. Maybe she could make him a present, something to remind him of all the fun they had before she'd turned out to be a total psychopath.

She was tempted to pull out her phone and research *Law & Order: SVU* merchandise but phones were heavily frowned upon for obvious reasons. She zoned back into the room to see if @SecretRTEProducer was wrapping up any time soon.

'Thank you so much for that exhaustive history, @SecretRte Producer.' @BigDickY2K was looking slightly dazed by the tirade they had all just endured, but she gave him an encouraging little wink. 'We'll open the meeting for general sharing now, please, though I would love to encourage any of our newer members to speak up if you feel ready.'

Shite, she is so talking about me … Since the first meeting when she'd spoken briefly, Ali hadn't said a word. She knew she'd been avoiding this quite crucial element of the meeting for too long for it to have gone unnoticed.

She cleared her throat and awkwardly introduced herself.

'My name is @AlisBaba and I am a catfisher.'

'Hello @AlisBaba', 'Welcome @Alisbaba', 'Hi @AlisBaba' came the various replies around the room.

'So, I'm pretty new to this, as you can probably tell. I haven't shared since my first meeting. Lots of you might remember I had an Instagram account – well, I still have it – and I sort of accidentally told my followers that I was pregnant. This is real by the way. It's not a pillow up the old jumper trick. Anyway, the whole thing got completely out of control. I've just been so messed up. My dad died the day everything came out and everyone on the internet totally hated me but it's the thought of Sam hating me – he's the baby daddy – I really can't cope with that. I just wish there was some way to make him see me the way he used to see me. He loved me and I was too stupid and too obsessed with getting big on Insta to realise that. I let my Insta-obsession overshadow everything. I destroyed Sam and I wasn't there for my dad.'

Ali's voice broke as the last words tumbled out and Kelly gave her a reassuring pat, which only served to undo her completely.

'I'm sorry, oh Jesus, I'm fully crying now.' She tried to laugh. 'It's somehow even harder to cope with people being nice to me. I don't deserve it. Anyway, coming here is helping me so much. I know I can't take back what I've done but I have this baby to think about now and I'm going to be better for little Miles or little Millie – whoever is floating around in there.'

The catfishers thanked her for her share and Ali sat back feeling lighter. A few seats over, Polly cleared her throat.

'My name's @Always_Watching and I'm a catfisher.'

'Hi @Always_Watching.'

'@AlisBaba's share just really brought so much up for me there. I've been having a really tough time lately and … well, I feel like some old habits might be slipping back in … My husband has been spending a lot of time abroad for work. And when he is home, he's so into his VR gaming. He's great with the boys, don't get me wrong. Very present and he loves them to bits. But every night once they're gone to bed and it's just us, he puts the helmet on and it's like I may as well not even exist.'

This bleak set-up flashed in Ali's mind. Polly arranging a flat-lay of nibbles, wine and a scented candle captioned:

#datenight on the couch with this one #mylove #marriage #soulmates

while some burly husband-type sat in a VR helmet beside her. That was possibly one of the most depressing things she'd ever heard.

Unbidden, a memory of Sam jumping up and perfectly lip synching the opening monologue of *SVU* one night when they were curled up on the couch popped into her head. She'd accidentally inhaled a Banshee Bone from laughing so hard, which had naturally led to a heated debate regarding the potential for death-by-crisp. It was the kind of shite-talk that couldn't be explained to anyone really. She pictured someone asking, 'Oh, what do you miss most about Sam?' And her responding: 'His appetite for pointless analysis of crisp varieties?'

But maybe that was kind of what love was, finding that person who knew you so well that they knew you would be more embarrassed dying choking on a Dorito than a Banshee Bone. There's no shame in being felled by a crisp Titan, she remembered telling him, to which he solemnly agreed. You couldn't even get Banshee Bones anymore. RIP Banshee Bones and RIP her and Sam.

Polly was still outlining the grim details of her marriage to the wannabe third member of Daft Punk when Ali picked up the thread of her share.

'… I was getting so down about it all and I was feeling lonely. I didn't think at first that what I was doing was a problem. I set up a new Insta account just to follow Bloggers Uncovered. I couldn't be seen to be following as my real self – that would be a huge problem for me.' She was staring down at her lap, clearly too ashamed to make eye contact with any of the catfishers. She'd tucked her hands under her legs and looked like a guilty little girl caught being bold.

'It was just such a slippery slope. I was only using the account to make sure nothing was being said about me on these vicious pages and then the next thing I knew, I was checking every hour and starting to comment on things.' She shrugged, looking bereft. 'It just got such a hold of me again. I want to get back to where I was a few months ago. That's why I'm sharing this now. I need to be honest and accountable. Thank you all for listening.'

'Thank you, @Always_Watching.'

The meeting concluded and the catfishers filed out looking much more solemn than usual. It had been a heavy one. Ali looked for Polly outside, but she'd scarpered, probably to avoid any well-meaning tête-à-têtes from the veterans about relapsing.

Ali started towards home. It was a good twenty-minute walk, but she needed time to clear her head. She hadn't woken up that morning thinking 'I must cry in front of a roomful of strangers today' but, damn, she actually felt strangely lighter. Admitting how hard the last months and even years had been seemed to have gone some way towards her forgiving herself. She hadn't realised just how guilty she'd been feeling about Miles and Sam until she'd said the words aloud in there. Everything in the last while had been about keeping her head down and trying to weather everything, trying to hide her pain and trying to perch just out of reach of the crushing words and comments about her online.

You deserve it, she'd cruelly told herself every day when the fresh onslaught came and she swallowed the rising guilt and hurt.

Punishing herself seemed like the right thing to do, but at the end of the day it couldn't go on for ever. She turned left and continued towards the gates to the Botanical Gardens.

Maybe I did something bad, but I'm not a goddamn monster, she mused. *I can't feel shitty about this every day for the rest of my life. Sam thinks I was pretending to be someone I wasn't but it's not true. I was completely myself with him, maybe more than I've ever been with anyone else, even Liv.*

She saw a chalkboard proclaiming 'Carvery All Day' outside O'Hara's pub and veered through the doors practically on autopilot.

This was how pregnancy cravings worked, it seemed. The pregnant appetite was powerfully suggestible. In this moment everything else in the entire world seemed disgusting. Right now, all she wanted was some cooked-to-fuck meat, powdered gravy and a bowl of potatoes.

Once the meal arrived, she took a grinning selfie. She looked cute, the carvery looked almost aggressively unattractive – *it's not the most photogenic genre of food*, she observed. She sent it to her thread with Sam and followed up with a message:

TFW the foetus who is possessing your uterus won't stand for anything but a completely disgusting but oddly iconic meal #carveryvirgin

It was time to stop apologising and instead try to remind him of who she was and why they had worked so well together in the first place.

Chapter 19

'Can I ask again, what is the fucking point of this?' Liv was grappling with the stencil Ali had carefully made the night before after getting back from solo carvery.

'I want to him to remember why he ever liked me in the first place.' Ali shifted around on the living room carpet so that Liv could get better purchase on the bump.

'This seems like a weird way to do that?' Liv observed, pressing the card to lie flat on the belly and trying to position the black marker to draw on Ali's taut skin.

'It's a gesture, Liv.' Ali didn't need any unsolicited editorial feedback from Liv at this late stage. She'd been awake most of the night trying to come up with *something* and this flimsy scheme was what she'd arrived at at 3 a.m. after watching countless YouTube roundups of favourite romcom moments of all time and best romantic gestures ever.

'Well, I suppose it's less creepy than some of the shite men are going on with in movies.' Liv shook her head ruefully.

'Yeah, what is with that?' Ali giggled. 'I mean, the cue cards in *Love Actually*? Though Sam would probably love something like that. He has a misguided *grá* for that film.' She was feeling flickers of optimisim since he had sent her a *Parks and Recreation* GIF in reply to her message about the carvery. Sure, it wasn't words exactly but a GIF was promising.

'Can you just lie still,' Liv muttered. 'What if the midwife sees this and is familiar with the *Law & Order* canon? She might think you two are totally fucked up and pre-emptively confiscate this foetus.'

'Look, you're nearly finished the first line. We're going with it,' Ali barked. 'I have zero other ideas so this'll have to do.'

Once Liv had finished, Ali went to survey her lettering work in the mirror. She'd done a very good job – it was perfect. She pulled her dress back down, snapped a quick #OOTD and grabbed her bag. She was getting the bus so she could catch up on emails. Now that she was back in the Insta fold, there was a pile of messages from various PRs, who were apparently interested in having her tout their products again. She was polite in her responses. She'd be using her Insta very selectively from now on. She wanted to be herself. No more 'aligning with brands' and other wankery. She'd chat to her followers – she needed to keep up a level of interest in her ahead of *My So-Called Best Life* – and she'd do the well-paid prestige stuff like W Y N D to add to the baby fund, but beyond that 'no, thanks'.

Once she was settled on the upper deck, she uploaded her outfit pic to Stories. She'd gone with a stretchy navy polka-dot dress that looked cute and retro, plus it showed off 'the milkers', as Liv had taken to calling her new pregnancy mega boobs, with some neon trainers and a denim jacket. She'd taken care with her make-up, but it was a fair bit more toned down, her love affair with contouring having waned slightly. She'd barely bothered with her tan in the last few months, but now that she was doing a bit more on the 'gram it actually gave her a bit of impetus to make an effort with her appearance again. She considered the caption for the outfit of the day.

TFW your outfit needs to say 'Yes, I was a lying psycho but also I love the hell out of you – please forgive me?'

She nervously swiped to try a couple of filters before settling on the unedited image. She considered the consequences of sharing it. Would Sam see? Would he be mad? Madder than he already was?

She stared out the window at town rushing by and tried to imagine his reaction, then she caught herself.

No, Ali! You can't be changing the way you act to appease him. She thought back to Mini walking in on her and Liv watching *Grease* when they were thirteen.

'Turn that shite off.' She'd been withering and Ali was mortified.

'My mum is such a snob,' she'd told Liv by way of explanation at the time and later she'd whinged at Mini over dinner.

'Why'd you always go out of your way to embarrass me? It was just a stupid film. Everyone in school loves it.'

'It is a stupid film,' Mini agreed. 'Watch it if you want but the message is bullshit. Remember Sandy wearing different clothes and changing herself to be with Danny, Alessandra. It's never a good idea. Always remember that. Oh, and leather is very unforgiving.'

Ali leaned her head against the window, smiling at the memory. Miles had chimed in at that point.

'Remember, I had leather pants in eighty-three? One of the most uncomfortable years of my life. Ever heard of trench foot? The soldiers in World War I got it from never, ever having dry feet. Well, those leather pants gave me trench crotch. It was a moist hell of my own making.' He had sighed, shaking his head regretfully before they all shouted him down.

Trench crotch! She shuddered at the memory and then smiled weakly to herself. So unfair that Miles and his idiosyncratic wit was no more. He would never gross her out or make her laugh again. Sure, he hadn't really said much in his last years but, as time crawled by in this new world that didn't contain her sweet, funny dad, she'd found that she remembered more and more of the real Miles.

Even after he had become vague and vacant from the illness, she'd occasionally get glimpses of the real Miles. She remembered a late autumn afternoon in Ailesend when the nurse had presented him with his various pills and he had looked up with a flash of the trademark glint in his eye and said, 'Yum! The red ones are my favourite!'

Ali turned back to the phone and hit Share on her pic. She was sorry. But she wouldn't be spending the rest of her life apologising and pretending to be something she wasn't. Life, after all, was finite and if Sam wasn't going to come around, then so be it.

She strolled from the bus stop on O'Connell Street to the Rotunda and practised her opening gambit.

'Hey, you might remember me from such public debacles as the doomed family dinner with the Khans or the great foetus fakery of 2019?'

Hmmm, maybe too glib, even for me. She sighed as the sliding doors into reception eased open for her. She hurried to the lift and made her way to the second-floor neonatal assessment unit. Seeing the sign directing her to the small waiting room set off a whoosh of anxiety. With all her Sam angst, she'd virtually forgotten that this was the 'big scan'. Lil Pea felt chipper enough in there, bopping around when she lay down at night, but a sudden hollow feeling in her stomach reminded her how much was unknown in this baby-making business.

She took her seat among a selection of similarly nervy-looking pregnant women and tried not to think about what the sonographer might see on the screen. The minutes ticked by and she tried to calm the mounting anxiety. She typed a message to Liv.

I should've forced you to come with. He's late. Maybe he's gonna jilt me at the baby scan. ☹

Liv's reply dropped in in a matter of seconds.

Don't catastrophise, remember the gif. A gif is very positive. Playful, even. I would never give gif if I wasn't feeling fairly warm towards the person.

Liv followed this with a reassuring Maya Rudolph blowing kisses gif.

'*Yes, you're right, it'll be fine, it will all work out,*' Ali typed, adding a gif of people dressed as poodles doing an '80s-style workout.

She flicked over to Insta to check in on her #OOTD post. There were loads of comments. More than 30 already. *Oh God.* She hit the icon with trepidation. She couldn't face a barrage of negativity right now. She looked at the phone side on as the messages loaded, as though not looking directly at it could shield her from the hate. '*Yay go, Ali! We're rooting for ya*', the first one cheered. The next were equally encouraging.

Lying psycho!!!! 😁 *Never change Ali!*

He'll come around bbz, we'll start an Uplift.ie petition to get yis back together if he's holding out on you #TakeHerBackSam 💪

'Ali Jones?' a young man called from the door to the waiting room.

'Yep, that's me.' Ali rose reluctantly and moved towards the door. She couldn't believe Sam hadn't turned up. She checked the clock. It was five past two. What if she went in and then he arrived? He wouldn't know where to go.

'Ms Jones?' The sonographer was waiting expectantly down the hall.

'Yeah, em. I'm coming, it's just my ... eh ... the—'

'We've a lot of appointments to get through, Ms Jones,' he cut her off abruptly.

'Ali?' Ali whipped around to see which of the pregnant women still waiting behind her had just said her name.

'Hey!' A girl to her right waved shyly. 'I follow you on Insta.' She grinned. 'We can tell Sam you've gone in.' She lowered her voice delicately to add, 'If he comes.'

'Yeah, he's a dick if he doesn't show,' chimed another woman across from the first. 'We'll show him where you are. Good luck!'

'Everything's crossed for ya, Ali,' called another woman sitting at the very back. 'Well, my legs are crossed 'cos I'm on my third and the old pelvic floor isn't up to much anymore. One sneeze and the floodgates are open. But we're all behind ya.'

Ali smiled gratefully at her unlikely allies.

'Room four, Ms Jones,' the sonographer called impatiently, and Ali jogged after him slightly dazed from the sudden outpouring of support.

'Right, sorry for rushing you along there but we're under immense pressure in here each day. I'm sure you can understand. I'll assess now and if there's anything we need to discuss further we will of course wait until you have your partner or family or whoever present for a bit of hand-holding, K? Hop up there now and pull that dress up, thanks,' he finished in a bored voice.

Ali obeyed in slightly stunned silence. *Thanks for the fucking shred of consideration*, she huffed inwardly. *What a prick*. She lay back on the bed and hiked her dress up over her bump, drawing the cardboardy hospital blanket over her knickers. Dumb pink knickers she'd worn in the hope that Sam would see them, although romancing the father of your child during a foetal assessment is probably considered somewhat problematic anyway. She glared at the ceiling waiting for the Prickologist to get on with his job.

'Jesus Christ! Is that a tattoo?' he yelped, momentarily distracting her from her grump. *Oh God, the stencil*. She'd completely forgotten it said …

Executive Producer
Dick Wolf

… in giant letters across her bump.

In romcom-worthy timing the door to the examination room burst open at that exact moment and a sweating, discombobulated Sam practically fell in.

'Jesus Christ! Is that a tattoo?' he unwittingly echoed the sonographer.

'Yep, it was a hormonal decision but one I'm happy with,' Ali deadpanned. 'I just want lil Pea to understand his heritage.'

Sam's face hung in a stunned expression for a nano-second before he looked at the horrified look on the sonographer's face and burst out laughing.

'She's messing,' Sam reassured him.

The guy was looking more bewildered, not less, at this information.

'Why is that funny?'

Sam fully doubled up at this.

'It isn't really.' He laughed. 'But your face is now making it seem hilarious.'

'Right,' the sonographer said coldly. 'We'll get on with the exam now.'

Ali grinned from the bed, delighted with the sudden turn things had taken, as Sam wiped his eyes and took his place on a little stool beside her.

'Don't worry, he was being kind of a dick before you even got here,' Ali explained matter-of-factly, as the sonographer paused in squeezing cold jelly on her belly to glare at her. She beamed back at him and Sam snorted again.

Ali didn't want to hope but somehow this really was feeling like old times. She caught Sam's eye and grinned. He looked back at her, but she couldn't quite decide just what he might be thinking. His smile seemed suddenly dimmed, tinged with regret.

The sound of their baby's heartbeat drew her focus instinctively towards the screen, where the grainy, grey image showed a very baby-like creature with a strong, rhythmic flicker of life blinking at the centre. The moment was more momentous than Ali had anticipated. She suddenly wondered had Miles and Mini looked at her on the screen like this twenty-six years ago. They would've been young, like her and Sam, though presumably less dumb and more united, more prepared for this unknown about to take over their lives.

She didn't notice that tears were streaming from her eyes into the hair at her temples until Sam brushed them away gently. He laid his hand against her cheek, and more of her tears spilled into the creases of his palm.

'Right.' The sonographer was either oblivious to or bored by new parents emoting in front of him. 'All looks good here. I'll just take some measurements, and I can get you some piccies for the grandparents.'

'Huh.' Sam stayed staring at the screen. 'We're a bit short on those. How's Mini with babies?' He cocked a playful eyebrow at Ali.

Ali grimaced to try to cover how bereft she suddenly felt about the fact that Miles would never know her baby, nor would Sam's mum. And Sam's dad barely knew about Sam. It was all so unfair. Why did the good parents die?

'Hah. I can't quite picture her grandmothering, but I'm sure she'll schedule Erasmus in for any of her obligatory granny duties!'

'Poor Erasmus.' Sam grinned. 'How is he?'

'Tormented. He's still getting over driving our getaway car a couple of days ago. Let's just say Mini's idea of a moving, low-key ashes-scattering diverges quite significantly from what any normal person would come up with.'

'Oh ho, you can't give me that clickbaity headline and leave me hanging ...' The sonographer moved to the printer to retrieve the pictures of the baby. 'Will I buy you a carvery after?' Sam suggested.

'Wow, overcooked meat! I thought you'd never ask.' Ali made a stab at trying to sound flirty. Though, with a giant veiny belly covered in scan jizz, it was a pretty futile attempt. Sam pulled his hand back and rubbed it awkwardly. It must be wet from her tears, she realised. He pulled himself upright and seemed to shake off something of the sentimental glow that had settled around them just seconds before.

'Well, yeah, of course, I mean, you're providing a meat cave rent-free to my kid so, I guess, I owe you.'

'Yeah, cool,' Ali agreed and tried not to sound as disappointed as she felt. She was certain they'd been having a moment there. She accepted the roll of paper held out to her by the sonographer and began scraping the jelly from her bump. She pulled her dress back down and slid off the bed. 'Thanks for the lil show and tell there. I'll be leaving a full review on Yelp but some top-line feedback? It wouldn't kill you to be just a shade nicer to these preggo bitches, especially the ones that come in alone.' She flounced out of the room, leaving Sam to just grin awkwardly at the guy.

Walking back past the waiting room, Ali found several of her cheerleaders from earlier still parked, waiting to heave their bellies down the hall to be jellied up.

'He's not the worst,' called one, smiling. 'He came, that must mean something, Ali.' She offered a big thumbs up.

Ali grinned and mouthed 'thank you' just as Sam caught up to her.

'Aw, yous two are so good together, would ya not forgive her, Sam?' one of the others piped up as she snapped a quick pic of Sam's startled face. Ali seized his hand and half dragged him down the hall to the exit.

Once out on the street, she tried to brush it off as nothing, but she could tell Sam was preoccupied.

'So, how's everything been going?' Ali needed to distract him. 'How're the lads?'

She'd never grasped the individual identities of Sam's friend gang. In her mind they were an amorphous mass of pasty, freckly Irishman all called some variation of Sean or Schmiddy or Murph, working in the kind of places where they had nap pods, free lunches and a statement wall with artful graffiti on it. She realised now that she'd always resisted his attempts to include her on nights out with 'the lads' because the less face-to-face contact she had with people in Sam's life, the easier it had been to lie to him day in, day out.

'Yeah, they're grand.' Sam was carefully maintaining a distance of about two feet from her at all times. *He's really making sure he's not sending the wrong signal*, Ali thought ruefully. 'Schmiddy and

Sinead are actually getting married in a couple of weeks. The first to succumb.'

'Wow, that's so proper,' Ali marvelled.

'Ha, well, so's this thing.' Sam tapped her bump and then snatched his hand back as though it had burned.

'You can touch it.' Ali took his hand and pressed it to her belly. She watched his face, searching for anything of the old way he used to look at her, but he was studiously avoiding her eyes. Instead, he gazed at the firm little bump. It seemed so insistent, always right there between them, binding them in spite of everything.

'Can you feel it yet? Move, I mean.'

His eyes flickered to hers and the desolate look there felt like a punch to Ali.

'Yep, starting to. It's lovely. You'll be able to feel it soon too if … if you're around, like …' she trailed off awkwardly, letting his hand drop and resumed walking. 'Anyway. So dying to murder this carvery! Not something I think I've ever said before.'

'Yeah.' Sam seemed thoughtful and neither of them spoke until they came to the Merry Cobbler, which seemed to be emanating a powerful gravy fug.

'You sure this is what you want to eat?' He looked sceptical but Ali was already feeling the crazed hunger setting in.

'Tinder, we are not above a carvery. Now, in!' Ali was adamant that she was going to make the most of this non-date. 'It's demented how hungry you get when you're preggers – you can go from zero to this crazed cannibalistic hunger in minutes,' she explained as they found seats. 'And it's always this, like, really specific thing. The other night I could not rest until Liv went down to the shops for mushrooms for me. She fried them and I ate them straight out of the pan. It was weird. Then other things you normally like are suddenly completely foul. I read that some women eat things that are not even food!'

'Like carvery?' Sam grinned.

'You're such a snob.' She mugged. 'Though Miles would be turning in his grave if he knew I was about to pound back some leathery meat drenched in demi-glaze and served with scoops of smash. If he had a grave, obvi. What can ashes do?' she mused. 'Rustle in their jar?'

Sam laughed awkwardly. 'So, what did happen with that? And why was Erasmus there? Where did you scatter Miles?'

'Oh. You do not want to know.' Ali grimaced. 'It was so bad. It might even be slightly illegal. I'm not sure.' A server appeared with plates and instructions on the carvery, which was laid out under glowing heat lamps in the centre of the dark pub.

'You can help yourselves to our buffet-style carvery. Feel free to go up as many times as you like. There's also a cold buffet with starters like prawn cocktails and crab salad,' he advised.

'Brill, thank you.' Ali smiled and, tucking the plate under her arm, moved toward the trays of meat and veg.

'Hang on, wait up.' Sam hurried after her.

'I'm sorry, Sam. I'm only the host body.' She shrugged as she slapped a slab of meat-like something on her plate. 'The lil parasite is in charge. I'm just doing its bidding, ya know? I think I'm going to need a separate potato plate,' she muttered thoughtfully, scanning for the server.

Once they were settled back at the table, Sam began to fill her in on Schmiddy and Sinead's wedding.

'It's huge. They're having about 300 in Strokestown House. I'm a groomsman and I'll be doing a short speech after the best man.'

'Oooh, pressure. I wish I could be of some help, but we all know what happened the last time I was hauled up in front of a crowd.' It was a gamble, she knew, to refer to the fateful night that Blake Jordan had announced she was pregnant at the Glossies WildCard launch. Luckily, Sam managed a laugh.

'Yeah, maybe I could say I was pregnant and just kind of stun them into not even noticing how shit my speech is.' He winked.

'Just, please, whatever you do, don't spend the whole speech going on about what a gas lad Schmiddy is and then be all "fair play to Sinead for taking him on, she's a lovely girl". I hate that. It always makes women out to be so boring. Just these totally bland, anodyne girls who will be "taking on" the burden of some "mad gas man". Women are way fucking better than that. Dig up a bit of dirt on her too!'

'Yeah, Sinead's very cool,' he agreed. 'It'll be weird to see her in a wedding dress,' he added thoughtfully. 'I've seen her arse so many times. She's a real flasher when she's drunk.'

'Ha, brilliant. I love an arse flash.' Ali nodded, scooping up her mash and gravy. 'It's such a whimsical brand of grossness. It's sort of adorable, isn't it?'

Sam laughed in agreement. 'Though I saw my uncle do it once and it wasn't great. Weird, almost stubbly arse.'

'Shheeeesh, I suppose it is always the wrong person getting it out. So, do you have a plus one?'

'Eh, yeah, I do 'cos of being in the bridal party.' Sam was suddenly focused on his Yorkshire pudding.

'Relax. It's grand with me, of course. Who is she?' Ali plastered a smile on her face, ready to play the cool girl if it killed her.

'Oh no. I haven't invited anyone yet. I just have the option.'

Ali messed with the last of the mash on her carb plate and debated throwing caution to the wind. She flashed on her new resolve to stop grovelling and just be herself. It was a gamble but fuck it. The man's child was in her. She'd nothing to lose.

'You should bring me!' she announced brightly. 'It'd be great fun. A nice chance for lil parasite here to get to know the sound of your voice ahead of him busting out all over you on a wave of gore. We could just go as friends, separate rooms and everything.'

Sam looked deeply uncertain and Ali figured it was best not to let him answer right away.

'Sure, have a think,' she quickly continued. 'And if you want some company, I'd love to come. It'd be good to meet your friends and show them that I'm not a complete lunatic.'

'Yeah ...' Sam was looking a little blindsided by her enthusiasm and undeniably dubious.

'Look, no presh,' Ali rushed on to change the subject, so that before he could reject it outright the idea could settle inside him and maybe he would start to think that he had come up with it in the first place.

'Right.' Ali mopped up the last of her gravy with a chunk of Yorkshire pudding. 'Dessert? I feel like a doughnut might be in order.' The buzz of her phone interrupted with a calendar notification.

W Y N D Summit announcement countdown post.

Ugh. Ali checked the time: 4 p.m. All the influencers were supposed to be posting the W Y N D tile at exactly 4.45 p.m. and adding a countdown function, which would expire at midnight when W Y N D would be unveiled on Holistic Hazel's feed.

'You're still yoked to the phone, I see.' Sam sat back and Ali sensed a chill permeate what had up until then been quite a good almost-date.

Ali ignored her immediate urge, which was deny, deny, deny.

'Yep, kind of.' She held his gaze. 'I need money for carveries! And the small matter of your bastard child. But it is completely different now. No gaslighting. No pathological lying. And I'm not trying to make a career of it or anything. After the internet found out I was lying about the pregnancy it was totally shit, but there is something freeing about losing everything.' She took a breath to steady herself. She didn't want to get upset and make it seem like a manipulative sympathy-grab. 'I'd lost my job, my dad and you. And I know it was my fault,' she added quickly, 'but, well, anyway I just thought "Fuck it". I wanna make something positive out of all this mess. For me and for the baby. And whether it's because I'm a crazy lying bitch who they hate or whatever, all these people follow me so I'm going to use it. But for something real, something important. I've been writing again and Terry from *Durty Aul' Town* is helping me. I'm hoping to perform it in the Dublin Stage Fest.'

'Oh.' Sam looked uncertain. 'Congratulations, I suppose?'

'And I'm in this group therapy programme that's really helping me to kind of get to the bottom of my problem with Instagram. So anyway, yeah, I'm not on there talking shit every day and I'm not pretending to design a range of prams or bollixing on about random supplements for an #ad but I'm still dabbling a bit. Just in a less obsessive, destructive way.'

'Cool, cool.' Sam was scanning the room to signal for the bill and Ali tried not to feel too defeated. She couldn't have expected him to want to jump straight back on board her crazy train but this did seem like such a dud note to end on.

'Sam? I'm not sure if you've thought about the birth at all. Liv has said that if I need her, she'll be my partner, but I just wanted you to know that I would love you to be there. But it's totally up to you. There's a class I'm going to in a few weeks, so you don't need to decide now. Just let me know,' she finished quietly.

They parted ways with a clumsy hug outside the Merry Cobbler and Ali had to concentrate hard on not getting upset. His Sam smell and lovely Sam arms were still her kryptonite.

He seemed to hear her thoughts.

'That Ali smell.' He allowed his fingers to linger in her hair and she could feel the crackle of that impossible to explain, impossible to ignore chemical compatibility that she'd never had with anyone else.

For a wild moment she considered just blurting out 'Wanna bone?' but before she could ruin a perfectly lovely moment with her trademark subtlety, Sam stepped towards her and practically mashed his face into hers.

She just about had time to think: *My God, we're kissing* when it was over in a muddle of lips and tongues, her hands on his rough jaw and his on her neck. He looked dazed, even more shocked than *she* felt despite him being the instigator.

He took a few steps back and then gave her a slightly baffling thumbs up, his cheeks burning adorably.

Ali, not knowing what else to do, gave him an enthusiastic thumbs up too.

'Well, see you in the WhatsApp, I guess.' Sam spun around and immediately lurched away. Even his back looked mortified.

Ali positively floated to the bus, posting the W Y N D Insta to her Story and feed, unable to believe the turn the day had taken. All afternoon at her desk she tried to write and eventually settled into scrolling through pics of her and Sam on her phone while listening to the soundtrack from *The OC* for good measure. She kept checking WhatsApp to see if he had sent anything but there were only tumbleweeds. Eventually, when she heard Liv's key in the door, she abandoned all attempts at pretending to work and drifted down to the kitchen, where Liv appeared to be in similar buzzed form. She'd cranked The Distillers and was bopping around cheerily doing the dishes Ali had ignored earlier. Ali sidled up and grabbed the tea towel to dry and Liv caught a peek at her face.

'Uh oh, what's got you so happy? Have you hit the half a mil on Instagram?'

Ali shook her head, unable to stop smiling. 'I could ask the same of you?' she deflected.

'Ah well, tonight's the dinner with Amy.' Liv ducked her head, also apparently unable to stop smiling.

'Of course!' Ali shouted. 'Finally! Boom!' She whipped Liv playfully with the tea towel and then started a little victory twerk.

'Gahhh, please.' Liv pretended to shield her eyes in horror. 'No preg twerking, it's so jarring,' she pleaded.

'Fine.' Ali modified the dance into some lascivious gyrating.

'That is worse,' Liv wailed.

'What? It's medicinal, I've got to do my pelvic thrusts.'

Liv laughed. 'Seriously, what is up? This is the most jazzed I've seen you since that parasite moved in. I take it the scan went well?'

'Yep.' Ali continued thrusting and smiling, 'But that's not all … Sam kissed me and now I have hurty smiley face.' She flung her arms around Liv's waist and spooned her at the sink.

'Wow, that's … unexpected.' Liv stopped washing the dishes and turned to face Ali.

'I know.' Ali spun over to the biscuit cupboard and grabbed the Jaffa Cakes. 'I'm trying not to overthink it. I don't really think he meant to and then suddenly it was happening. He cut it off kind of abruptly but I'm not dwelling on that.' She crammed two biscuits in her mouth triumphantly and handed one to Liv.

'Quite the plot twist.' Liv munched absent-mindedly on the Jaffa Cake. 'But seems positive?'

'Deffo.' Ali's reply was muffled by sponge and orange jelly and she swallowed thickly before continuing. 'I think the best plan now is to totally ignore him and just try not to spook him. We don't want him suddenly coming to his senses.'

'No.' Liv smiled.

'Still, though, etiquette-wise, he's on thin ice. It's not a good idea to get your estranged girlfriend all riled up right in the middle of the second trimester. I have a raging pregnant horn and now I have to go action that myself. Like, not only is this kind of thing way better as a team sport but also logistically it's very tricky right now. My reach just isn't what it was even a few weeks ago.' She regarded the obstructive bump sadly.

'Oh, I'm sure you'll manage, nature finds a way.' Liv grinned. 'Right, I'll leave you … eh … all' – she awkwardly indicated the bump – 'to it. I'm gonna head. Need to meet Amy at seven.'

'Have fun!' Ali called. 'Text me how it's going. I'm living vicariously through you.'

Chapter 20

Shelly walked through the quiet house rubbing her back. At thirty-three weeks pregnant, she was aching everywhere now. She was doing her final check for the evening. She hated that she'd become so antsy in her own home. At least it was still bright out. In late July the garden just beyond the vast kitchen windows was still visible in many shades of violet and deep purple.

She dreaded next winter, when the night would press in on her and all she'd see from inside was her own tense face reflected. She cursed her determination to have as much glass as possible in the kitchen extension. Of course, she'd never pictured a future where she'd be alone here night after night, held hostage by some unknown threat. How had it been nearly six months of @_____? Of constantly looking over her shoulder for who or what, she didn't even know?

Movement in the garden startled her but it was just Dan. Instinctively she retreated from the doors in the hope that he hadn't seen her. Ever since the night she'd spotted him kissing that girl a few months before, she'd been waiting to see if he would bring any more women back to her house. *The absolute neck of him.* She still got furious when she thought about him admonishing her for taking photos of Georgie when he was bringing strange women around while he 'babysat' his own daughter. Now she could see Dan was heading straight for her back doors and she slipped over to unlock them.

'Hey.' He nodded, clutching a large brown envelope as he stepped over the threshold.

'Hi?' Shelly made no effort to hide her irritation. 'Did you say you were coming by? I'm just going to bed. I'm exhausted and I have an early appointment.'

'Sorry, I didn't.' Dan moved past her, and Shelly bridled at the entitled way he settled on the couch and crossed his legs without even being invited in. 'I'll be quick. I just wanted you to take a look at the new separation agreement my solicitor drew up – he's amended it to include a suggested custody arrangement. He says it'll make the divorce easier in due course. In your own time, anyway.' He tossed the envelope down beside him. 'Also, I need to take some pics of the kitchen extension to send on to the valuer.'

Shelly crossed her arms. 'Why are you sending pics to a valuer?'

'C'mon, Shelly, you know why.' Dan actually had the nerve to look exasperated. 'Neither of us will be able to buy the other out, so the sooner we get this place valued the better we can decide what comes next.'

Shelly snatched up the envelope. 'Take whatever pictures you want. Do it quickly, please. I'm tired. I'm about a million years pregnant and I need to go to bed. I'll send this to my solicitor.'

Just as soon as I get one, she added silently, seething.

As soon as Dan had left, Shelly pulled out her phone to resume her checks. *Fucking fucker, as if I need this house stress on top of everything else*, she fumed as she deleted the previous night's videos then hit Record as she tested the sliding glass doors. Locked. Of course they were, Dan had only left minutes before. However, the security in the house had become an all-consuming paranoia. Hence the video. She'd started to record the nightly check so that in an hour or so up in bed when she became convinced she'd heard some unfamiliar creak downstairs she could check the video and be reassured she'd left no door or window unchecked.

She moved into the flat-lay studio to pull on each of the windows in turn, her phone capturing each tug. She returned to the kitchen, scanning the table as she passed.

Amy had set it immaculately for the Morning Routine LIVE they had scheduled for first thing tomorrow. It was sponsored by Kanavan Oats and Shelly was apprehensive. Amy priced the LIVEs very high on their services because they were tricky. You had to nail everything in one perfect take, which left little room for any Insta trickery. However, Kanavan's had coughed up for an hour of Instagram LIVE and that was a serious spend for any client. So, in the morning Amanda was coming at the crack of dawn to do her make-up before Amy would arrive and kick off the LIVE. Shelly would rise refreshed and apparently perfectly made up from sleep to take the viewers through her morning routine.

The Shell-Belles were setting their alarms if the comments under her post announcing the collab were anything to go by and they had been promised a Q&A session at the end of the show. Exhausting. Shelly sighed as she knocked out the lights in the kitchen, repeated the filming process with the windows in the reception rooms, checked the front door and turned on the alarm.

On the second floor, she slipped into Georgie's room to kiss her on the temples. Mama perk, she smiled to herself and then double-checked the child's outfit was in order, grey and pink skirt and top to complement the grey maternity jeans and pink cashmere sweater she'd hung up for herself in the dressing room upstairs.

In her bedroom, she spritzed her pillow with something claiming to be calming lavender oil. She massaged her bump with some body butter Hazel assured her was the best stretch-mark-preventing unguent on the market and tried to do some of her breathing techniques.

She hadn't been going to her therapist, Berna, quite as much in the last few weeks. Things were just so hectic with the weekly trips to various hotels pedalling her perfect life and her perfect wardrobe tips. Plus being at Hazel's beck and call with the W Y N D summit barely six weeks away had been … taxing. Still, if she made the money to buy out the house meant it would be all worth it. She'd worked so hard for it. She could do it, couldn't she?

In the dim light of her side lamp, she took some steadying breaths to stave off the thoughts that crowded in unbidden at night …

Could she realistically sort the house? She could. She would. Whatever it took. The anxious monologue changed tack. How would she manage a nearly four-year-old and a newborn?

'Oh my God!' she blurted out loud, shooting up from the sea of throw pillows.

How, how, HOW could I have forgotten this?

She raced from the room and back downstairs as fast as she could without waking Georgie. In the kitchen she scoured drawers for candles or balloons, anything birthday-ish. Nothing.

She looked at the wall calendar in the kitchen. Wednesday, 25 July: Georgie's birthday. For God's sake. The coming Saturday was highlighted and circled many times over because that was the day of her party but the anniversary of her bloody birth was tomorrow. Poor Georgie probably didn't even know that tomorrow was the actual day but still Shelly couldn't believe it had gone so far out of her head. Plus, many of the Shell-Belles were invested enough to remember specific dates. Last year it was only thanks to a few Shell-Belles messaging to say happy anniversary that she remembered it was her and Dan's sixth wedding anniversary. *Morto.* Shelly pulled out a few more drawers but couldn't find so much as a streamer to put on the breakfast table for the morning. Not wanting to give Dan the satisfaction of her having forgotten something so key, she dug out her phone to send Amy a voicenote.

'I've messed up. Is there any way you can pick up some balloons and candles on your way over in the morning? It's Georgie's goddamn birthday and I am officially the worst mother in the world.'

She trudged back up the stairs feeling slightly better. Amy would pick up that message in the morning and Georgie would never know Shelly'd forgotten. She hopped back into bed and pulled the sheets over her. It'd all be fine in the morning was her final thought as she drifted away on a tide of sleep.

'Shelly? Shell hun?'

Shelly opened her eyes to Amanda's whispers tugging her from a chaotic dream where she'd left the baby and Georgie in the back of a taxi and was racing around the city trying to find them. They were the kind of dreams that had plagued her during her pregnancy with Georgie. Anxiety was a bitch.

'I'm awake, Mandy. Thanks.' Shelly sat up and Amanda gave her a little wave and ducked back out to set up in the dressing room. It was 6 a.m. They had an hour tops before Amy would arrive and she'd go LIVE for the Shell-Belles. Luckily, Mandy worked quickly, and

Shelly was back in bed and ready to fake wake up when Amy strode up the stairs an hour later.

'Hey bbz.' Amy kept her voice low so as not to disturb Georgie and came around to the side of the bed to put an alarm clock on the bedside table. 'Right, let's get going. We'll aim to do the Q&A while you're cooking the porridge. So just rock through the morning meditation, journalling and intention-setting, get yourself dressed, wake Georgie et cetera and we'll be down in the kitchen by half. This is set for twenty seconds, right?'

Shelly nodded and settled herself under the sheet to pretend to wake up as Amy began to roll the Insta LIVE recording. Just as the alarm began to sound, she realised she forgot to check if Amy had brought the party stuff. *Oh feck.* It was impossible to interrupt the LIVE now. The Shell-Belles missed nothing, and no doubt would be swarming all over Rants.ie with *theories* if anything were amiss in the LIVE.

Shelly rolled over and hit the alarm.

'Good morning, Shell-Belles! I am so excited to be bringing you through my morning routine LIVE today with special thanks to our sponsor Kanavan Oats, the oattiest oats you'll find on the market and the only oats milled right here in Leinster using power from the River Bán. They are the only brand of oats I use.' She tried not to cringe visibly at the marketing spiel. Clients never got that less was more with these things.

'So, join me now as I prepare myself mentally for my day as a busy mama-of-one and soon to be two! I like to start with some meditation and journaling in my SHELLY journals. Click the link in my bio to order your own if you want to get into intention-setting like me.'

Pretending to meditate, cross legged on the floor for ten minutes while Amy filmed was in fact a pretty stressful start to the day. She kept fretting that she'd get gas or fall over, but somehow she kept it together through all the fake mindfulness and led Amy and the by now thousands of viewers into her dressing room.

'I always choose my clothes the night before.' She smiled at the camera. 'It means I'm not worrying about what to wear in the morning. If any of you have picked up my coffee table book, you'll know all about my brilliant system from the No Stress to Dress section.' Amy panned to an artfully arranged tray boasting a scented candle and a couple of framed pics of Shelly and Georgie along with none other than the aforementioned SHELLY book to allow some modesty for Shelly to pull on her jeans, fur-lined loafers and cashmere top. She gave Amy the nod and the camera swung back to her as she fastened her delicate rose-gold bracelets.

'When I'm doing my regular "working mama" day, I always rock my Glam Mama range in collaboration with Newbridge silverware. They're just so easy to wear and add that bit of sparkle to even a plain old Wednesday. Hit that link in my bio if you wanna treat yourself, Mama!'

Shelly proceeded down the stairs and called out to rouse the miraculously still-sleeping Georgie.

'Hey, baby girl! Time to get up.'

She threw a playful wink back at the camera and could see Amy visibly cringe. Whatever, Shelly thought, bustling into the little girl's room. That's just the Shelly character. Give the Shell-Belles what they want.

'Mam! Mam!' Georgie leapt into her arms while Shelly tried to gently but quickly correct her. 'It's Mama, pumpkin. Not Mam.'

She rolled her eyes at the camera as if to say, 'Kids!', then she noticed the outfit she'd put out last night was gone and in its place was a manky old Elsa costume that they'd practically had to surgically remove Georgie from when it got too small.

'What did you do with the clothes I put out for you, sweetie?' Shelly began pulling out drawers, searching.

'I wanna wear Elsa, Mama!'

Shelly spun around and marched to the white wardrobe in the far alcove. *I did put it out. I did. Didn't I?* She flung open the doors but no sign in there either.

What the f—? She noticed Amy motioning at her to wrap it up and move on. With the LIVE rolling, Shelly couldn't explain why the missing skirt and top seemed so sinister.

'Right, yes, sweetie, of course you can wear Elsa.' She knelt down to help her daughter into it. 'And you didn't move other clothes that were right there?' she reiterated but Georgie just shook her head.

'No, Mama.'

'Right, OK. Well, down we go anyway for our delicious and nutritious Kanavan oats. Packed with that all-important slow-release energy to fuel mums and kids all day.' She concluded the sales speak with a slightly maniacal smile to camera and jogged downstairs after Georgie, whom she could hear squealing with delight.

She rounded the corner into the kitchen and immediately let out a relieved exhale. Amy had done an amazing job. Thank God. Helium balloons in gold and silver covered the ceiling, and a tiara, a wand and even a wrapped gift decorated Georgie's place at the table.

'So, we have a very special day in the Devine house, don't we, pumpkin? How old are you today?'

'Four.' Georgie grinned into the camera, holding up her fingers. Under her other arm was a wrapped gift. 'Can I open it, Mama?'

'Of course, you can, sweetie.' Shelly stood back to give Amy a better angle on the child and mouthed a grateful 'thank you' in her direction.

Amy's brow furrowed but she kept the camera steady on Georgie.

'Ahhhh, yaya the Share Bear.' Georgie was jumping up and down, hugging the white furry teddy, and then she flung herself into Shelly's arms. 'Thank you, Mama.'

'Oh, happy birthday, my best pumpkin, now sit up and I'll make you your favourite: Kanavan oats with banana and melty chocolate chips.'

Amy kept the camera on her as she went over to the kitchen to get the porridge on.

'So, Shell-Belles, I've got a couple of minutes for questions while I stir the porridge. You can speed up the cooking process by pre-soaking overnight and for more top tips on top toppings, go to www. Kanavans.ie.'

Amy read the first question from behind the camera.

'@MummyLovesABargain asks: How do you make it all look so easy, Shelly?'

Oh, this stuff made Shelly's skin crawl. She could hear herself giving these saccharine beige answers and always pictured the people who hate-followed her laughing their asses off.

'Well, I think the biggest thing that I use to keep calm and focused and not let myself get overwhelmed is gratitude. If I'm ever feeling the pressure from my hectic, always-on for my job, always-on for my baby girl lifestyle, I just take a minute to breathe and count three things I'm grateful for.'

'@LizzieGG says: Your skin's amazing, what's your biggest skincare tip?'

'Well, eating right, so starting my day with a big bowl of Kanavan's porridge! Then lots of water and smoothies – oats are a great addition to any smoothie, plus I often make an old-fashioned face mask by mixing soaked oats with honey and an egg white. So, oats, oats and more oats! OK, last question because my lil monkey is getting hungry!'

'@ShinyHappySinead asks: Do you ever get tired of being so fake all the time?'

Shelly's stomach dropped and she gripped the counter to steady herself for a moment.

'Wha … What?'

Amy looked irritated and repeated in a bored voice, '@ShinyHappySinead wants to know if you ever get tired of being so fab all the time?'

'Oh, ha. Right.' Shelly scrambled after her thoughts and tried to calm her jangling nerves. 'Fab. Well, no, I mean, not no. I mean, I don't really think of myself as fab. At all. But thank you for saying that, eh, ShinyHappySinead. On that lovely note, I'm going to give my birthday girl her brekkie, so thanks for joining me for my Morning Routine and thank you so much, Kanavan Oats, for supporting hard-working mamas. Happy Wednesday, everyone!'

Shelly waved and concentrated on tipping the porridge out into bowls and then, as soon as the camera was off, into the bin. Georgie wouldn't touch the stuff. She quickly got the cereal out from the cupboard and turned the coffee machine on.

Amy plonked herself on a stool on the other side of the island. 'Well, that is one thing off this never-ending list. How are you?'

'I'm fine now. Obviously, I was freaking last night! God, what am I like to forget?!' Shelly dropped the Coco Pops to Georgie along with her iPad to keep her entertained.

'Oh yeah,' Amy murmured, head in phone. 'So, you got sorted anyway. Sorry I didn't grab anything. I was up against it timewise.'

'What? You mean you didn't do this?' Shelly swayed as if the floor were tipping and grabbed the empty chair beside Georgie to regain her balance but accidentally tipped it over in her unsteadiness.

'Jesus.' Amy sprang up. 'What's the matter?' She righted the chair and steered Shelly to a stool at the peninsula away from Georgie.

'You ...' Shelly was struggling, groping in darkness to make sense of what this meant. 'You didn't do this?' She waved a hand to take in the room full of balloons and birthday paraphernalia.

'No.' Amy looked questioning.

Shelly dashed to the sliding doors. They were locked. She began to run from window to window. All locked. Just as they had been the night before. She flew out to the hallway calling for Amanda, who appeared at the top of the stairs, evidently startled by the note of panic in Shelly's voice. Shelly tried to calm herself.

'Amanda, did you put out balloons and stuff for Georgie's birthday?'

Why are you bothering? You know the answer, she thought grimly.

'No, luv, sure I was in the door and straight up to you. I didn't even go into the kitchen.'

By this point Amy had joined her in the hall.

'What is going on?'

Shelly ignored her.

'Was the alarm on when you came in, Mandy?'

'Yes, hun.' Amanda came down and stood by Amy. Shelly could feel their concerned looks as she hurtled into the living room and continued her frantic check of all the entry points. The windows in there were all secured. She rushed back to Amy and Amanda in the hall and tried to compose herself.

'I think we need to call the guards. Someone came in here last night. There's no doubt. They disabled the alarms and they set up the party stuff.'

'Shelly, calm down.' Amy was using her 'take charge' voice, which usually comforted Shelly, but Shelly could see her assistant glancing around the hall nervously. *Even she's freaked out.*

'What about Dan? Could he have come in?' Amanda suggested.

Shelly pulled out her phone. Dan was the last person in the world who would think of laying out a birthday surprise but still Shelly dashed off a quick WhatsApp.

Did you come back to the house last night? And leave out birthday bits for Georgie? Balloons and stuff?

She knew it wasn't him. Men didn't think like that. In the four years since Georgie's birth, Dan had never once so much as cut his daughter's nails, for God's sake. *What does he think? That the child has some magical self-trimming nails?* No, it wasn't Dan. She just knew it.

She saw him typing and a message appeared seconds later.

Nope. Tell Georgie I'm bringing her prezzie on Saturday, K?

The Direct Message icon flickered as always over the Insta app. Shelly tapped it. The latest message was from @_____. *Surprise, sur-fucking-prise.*

'What is it, Shell? Is it Dan?' Amy's tense voice sounded far away, as if she were in the next room and not right beside Shelly. Anxiety was strange like that. It could turn down the volume of any room and dial up the roaring terror inside in seconds.

'It's a message from @_____,' she heard herself say.

Good thing I'm Always Watching and listening, right? I have your back, hun. ♀ ♀ ♀

Amy peered at the message over Shelly's shoulder. 'Fuck,' she breathed. 'Right, I'm calling the guards. And your mum. You can't stay here until the locks are changed and the alarm is reset.'

Amy immediately launched into action, hustling Amanda upstairs and embarking on a series of frenetic calls to get the house secured. Shelly drifted back into the mercifully quiet living room and sank onto the sofa.

She felt raw and exposed. While she'd known that @_____ had been around the house, peering in windows and capturing private moments, the thought that they had walked right in last night while she and her daughter were asleep upstairs made her feel sick to her stomach. How had she not sensed the intruder? Had @_____ padded gently up the stairs to watch them sleep? Then Shelly remembered the clothes in Georgie's room and helpless tears pushed through her feeble attempt at remaining calm. This person had stood within feet, maybe inches, of her sleeping child. And it was all Shelly's fault. All because she'd wanted the likes and the attention. The free stuff. To be admired and envied.

Her stomach roiled with fear and disgust at herself and what she'd brought on them. This psychopath had trained her gaze on Shelly's life and Shelly had practically ushered them in. And now they weren't safe in their own home because Shelly hadn't taken it seriously enough. She'd only been thinking about her reputation and the embarrassment of people seeing her dumb photos. She'd never considered that she'd been offering her daughter up on a platter.

A heavy weight settled over her, a weight that went far beyond the gargantuan bump that felt as if it literally couldn't get any bigger. It was exhaustion and fear, but she knew she needed to get back in control of the situation. Shelly shivered despite the mid-morning sun streaming through the taupe velvet curtains. Her mind was reeling. @_____ could be anyone and it was looking more and more likely that they were a complete stranger. And a dangerous one at that. A dreadful thought veered into her head:

I could meet them at an event, in the street, anywhere and have no idea, Shelly thought bleakly.

❖

Shelly passed the day in a haze. She couldn't focus on any of the upcoming events Amy was pressing her for answers on. By 7 p.m., the locksmith had redone every ground floor door and the alarm company had reprogrammed the codes. Her mum and dad were installed in the spare room and Shelly was counting the minutes until she could just hit the pillow and put this horrible day behind her. She'd been unable to get a hold of Detective Bríd. Contact had been patchy since their last communication just over two months before. Some backlog in the department had pushed Shelly's complaint way down the list and they still hadn't examined her phone. Shelly felt stupid for not having followed it up. The truth was she'd had a lot on between the W Y N D rollout, *Durty Aul' Town* and researching her rights regarding the house. It was weird what you could get used to over time. She hadn't taken @_____ seriously enough and now they'd been inside her daughter's bedroom.

The young guards who'd come to take her statement had looked positively bored at her anguished retelling of the morning's events.

'So, someone set up a birthday party? And you're … upset?' said the dark-haired one with the patchy, ginger beard.

Amy had nearly gone for him and Shelly'd lost a nail trying to hold her back. It definitely felt as if they were all barely keeping it together.

Shelly'd even had a complete meltdown during Georgie's bedtime. Georgie was kicking off about what pyjamas she wanted to wear and at that point Shelly's sanity was holding on by a thread.

Shelly'd actually given the little girl the finger when she'd turned around and flounced over to her frilly princess bed. It was unbelievably childish, Shelly knew, but also unbelievably satisfying in that maddening and frustrating moment.

She walked through the house performing her nightly check for the camera on her phone. It was a shitty end to a shitty day, but she was relieved Sandra and Jim were up in the spare room watching *Bake Off*. As well as the doors and windows, she carefully checked the utility room and the cupboard in the hall under the stairs.

This is what it's come to, she thought bitterly. *I'm frightened in my own home.* @_____ was getting exactly what they wanted. Shelly climbed to the third floor and tried to immerse herself in her evening routine. She massaged her bump and then her face and even took a few drops of the CBD oil her mother had brought over. She got into bed and tried to relax but the weight had settled once more on her chest and she found she was having trouble getting a full breath. The panic was circling, and she knew if she allowed her mind to wander back once more to thoughts of a stranger prowling through her house, it would easily grip her.

'Calm, calm, calm,' she whispered just as Berna had advised. 'I'm calm, I'm safe.'

They can't get you now, Shelly thought while trying not to think too hard about how close they'd come. All this time, she'd felt she was overreacting or imagining things, but the balloons were real. As was the message: *I'm Always Watching and listening.* @_____ had heard her leave the voicenote for Amy. She was sure of it. How else could they know?

Shelly's phone vibrated beside her and she grabbed it before she thought to question whether it was a good idea to check the notification.

A message from @_____.

Don't read it, Shelly, some sensible part of her warned but her fingers moved as though of their own accord. @_____ had sent a story from another account. Shelly tapped it and came face to face with herself. It was footage from just hours before of her shouting and then giving Georgie the finger. How did they have this? It was posted to the @TheRealShellyDevine account. There were still no followers on the account but now the threat of exposure hung like an axe above Shelly's head.

Chapter 21

'OK, can I get a bit of hush?' Terry shot a look at Liv and Amy, who were front row centre, heads together, whispering and quietly laughing.

They'd arrived just minutes before to catch the last run-through of the day and Terry was desperately trying to keep focus among the crew. With *My So-Called Best Life* now a multimedia piece of theatre, the pressure to nail cues and monitor the pace of Ali's delivery was considerably more intense. With two characters being pre-recorded projections, Ali couldn't so much as draw an unrehearsed breath in her own delivery or it could throw the timings for the rest of the play.

'Scene one, cue Ali, cue Thirsty Ali.' Johnny, one of the techs, pushed the life-sized smartphone onto which the pre-recorded character of Thirsty Ali was projected for all her dialogue to centre stage. Ali stepped up to her mark, a tiny 'x' at stage left, as Terry continued directing. 'Cue Rational Ali and lights.' An actor called

Martina 'played' Rational Ali. She stepped up to stage right in her all-white bodysuit and white balaclava. Ali's performance of all Rational Ali's dialogue was projected onto Martina and she moved perfectly in sync with Ali's original movements.

Ali stood in the lights, holding a plastic tub in the shape of an urn, regarding a mound of cat litter scattered on the stage beside her. In more than five weeks of development and rehearsals, the show had certainly become a lot more ambitious, but Terry was ecstatic with their progress.

'Shoot for the moon,' he'd said grinning when she'd brought him the concept for projecting additional 'Ali' characters. In just a few weeks there'd be a lot more people than Liv and Amy sitting out there and Ali's nerves were mounting.

'OK, from the top,' Terry called.

Ali counted the beats in her head, then looked up into the audience, mercifully impossible to see with the lights on her.

'Have you ever tried to scatter someone's ashes before? If you have, you'll probably know they're not very ashes-like.' She glared at the tub. 'They should put a warning on this thing, something like "FYI your loved one now resembles cat litter".'

Ali sighed.

'This is my dad.' She indicated the mound by her feet. 'Dad, this is everyone.' She swept her hand towards the audience. 'They're here to find out how I went from being an average nobody to faking a pregnancy online – not this one, obvi, this one is legit – to being the most hated woman on the internet and all in just three months. I'm nothing if not efficient with my downfalls. And *now* they're probably wondering a) what you have to do with it and b) what you're doing down there.' She looked back up at the audience. 'And by "there" I mean the stage of the National Theatre. Yep, Dad, somehow, I found time in my busy, being-shamed-on-social-media schedule to tip you out onto the stage of the Abbey. But I can explain. Before all this, I was just your average thirsty Instahun with a mild addiction to lying my balls off for the 'gram …'

Ali's spot went down and the phone at the front of the stage emitted a notification buzz. Thirsty Ali appeared on screen, perfectly filtered and made up in bed purporting to be just awake.

'Good morning and *namaste*, bitches! I'm just about to do my morning routine. I love to kick off my day by setting some positive intentions in my journal, then I'll drink my green juice and kick this lil butt into gear. I have a full day of exciting meetings scheduled, so many amazing projects are in the pipeline, I can't wait to tell you all.'

Rational Ali, now illuminated on the other side of the stage, took over.

'Yeah, Thirsty, you've soooo much in the pipeline. Keep breadcrumbing those fictional exciting projects, hun.'

'Well, to be fair,' Real Ali interjected, 'she doesn't have a whole lot else to be peddling on there. Shit jobs and sick dads aren't exactly the stuff of aspirational Insta-content.'

Forty-five minutes later the run-through wrapped up and Liv and Amy were applauding from their seats.

'OK, everyone, good job today.' Terry emerged from the wings. 'We'll reset for the morning and I'll see everyone back here at 10 a.m. Ali, good job. I've marked a couple of passages that need to be tightened up but, overall, it's really getting there. Any more thoughts on the ending, though? We *have* to get that locked in. With the technical elements being so demanding, there's no time for a rush job.'

'I know, I know …' Ali sighed. 'It's so hard 'cos, well, it's still unfolding.'

Terry smiled. 'Keep thinking. It'll come into focus. These things always do.'

✤

'Ali, it is brilliant.' Liv and Ali had relocated to the café across from the theatre for a debrief. Amy was pacing out front on the phone to Shelly, trying to calm her down by the looks of things.

'You're not just saying that? Promise, like? 'Cos I'm relying on you to save me from any more public humiliation.'

'Ali,' Amy had just caught the end of Ali's plea as she slipped into the seat opposite beside Liv. 'Saving you from public humiliation would be a full-time job! This one doesn't have the *time*.'

'Yeah, yeah, hilarious.' Ali rolled her eyes. 'Look, easy with the "this one" stuff. You've both been tolerable these last couple of months. Just promise me you two won't turn into the couple who only want to go out when the other one's away or busy. Single people know what's up, you know.' Ali narrowed her eyes.

'We would never,' Liv was indignant.

'So, Ali, that was excellent.' Amy pulled out her phone, back to her comfort mode: business. 'We need to market the shit out of this show. We need to make sure people know that the appeal is broader than just Insta-users. The themes you touch on, the darkness at its core. No offence, but I just was not expecting it to be that good.'

'Really?' Ali grinned. She'd been sick at the thought of performing the show for them. After working so intensely on it for months, she felt that she'd no idea what it was like anymore.

'I loved the three Alis,' Liv added. 'It could've been convoluted but you completely pulled it off. And I even sort of forgot that it was you playing all three by the end, I was so invested in all the Alis! I can't wait to see what you do for the ending.'

'Ugh, me either.' Ali shrugged. 'The ending is turning into my personal Everest. Plus, I need to run everything else by Mini first.

'So, when's opening night again?' Amy was making notes.

'Three and a half weeks.' Ali clutched her face in mock horror that didn't even feel like a joke.

'OK ...' Amy scrolled through her calendar. 'It's tight, but I can make you a little promo campaign for the 'gram if you like. Pro bono. Consider it my baby gift.'

'Ah, thank you so much. That would be amazing.' Ali beamed.

Amy hopped back up abruptly. Another call. Once she was pacing outside once more, Ali leaned over to Liv. 'What is going on with that? Trouble in Camp SHELLY?'

'Isn't there always?' Liv grimaced.

Chapter 22

'So, Shell-Belles, thanks so much for tuning into my What I Put in My Hospital Bag video brought to you by the lovely gals at MamaAndMe.ie. I can't believe in another couple of months, I'll be meeting this one and my perfect little family will be complete. Feeling so hashtag blessed, as they say! Love and light, especially to all my fellow expecting mamas.' Shelly blew a kiss and ended the video.

Amy took the phone and began adding the campaign hashtags, along with the required 'ad' and 'spon' hashtags, as Shelly got ready to leave.

'When will you be back?' Amy looked up anxiously. 'We have several events this evening. We really need you back out there, Shelly. It's been noted by several of the PRs that your profile is slipping. Plus, we need you out in some of the outfits the Princess Closet sent over. The feed is all #MamaUniform, and there's only so much "simple marl tees, jeans and boots" I can tolerate. It's too one-note.'

'Right.' Shelly was not in the mood for a lecture. 'I'll be back when I'm done but you realise meeting the Gardaí is something of a priority?'

'Of course, of course.' Amy waved her off. 'Just be back for 5 p.m. Mandy is booked for make-up. Good luck with the guards.'

✣

At the police station Sandra and Shelly were led by a young guard into a small windowless room at the back of a busy open-plan office. A desk and a few plastic chairs stood in the centre and the walls were covered in posters from ancient police initiatives. Slogans like 'Drugs take lives' and 'You wouldn't steal a car: video piracy is a crime!' were splashed around them. Shelly slipped into the seat beside her mum. Crime had moved on since they'd taped up these warnings. Video piracy seemed antiquated compared with the thefts of funds and identities possible online now and, as much as drugs were still a problem, Shelly supposed there was a new, more socially acceptable addiction epidemic in the form of phones.

Detective Bríd joined them and Shelly stood to greet her.

'I am sorry it's been so long since we caught up properly about everything that's been going on. Donal?' Bríd beckoned the young guard forward. 'Will you bring Ms Devine's phone up to Mitchell on the third floor for examination and can you organise some tea and bickies on your way back? I wouldn't punish you with what passes for coffee round here,' she confided as Donal took Shelly's phone and left, pulling the door shut behind him.

'Now, firstly,' Bríd continued, 'I am so, so sorry about the attitude you encountered when you spoke to law enforcement after the incident of the' – she consulted her notes – 'the twenty-fifth of the seventh in your home. At the time the call came in, I was in an interrogation – as you know we had a major case that took up a lot of resources – and when I saw the dispatch notes later I was so upset that two unbriefed beat cops were sent. I'm so sorry that they didn't bring appropriate professionalism to their dealings with you all. It must have been incredibly upsetting.'

'Thank you, Bríd. Look, it's OK. I knew these guys just didn't understand what they were looking at. I'm just really keen to get more of a sense that we are closer to finding out who @_____ is.'

'Absolutely.' The detective pushed her short blonde hair back behind her ears and pulled out a blank page. 'Can you quickly give me a rundown of security measures you put in place since the twenty-fifth?'

'Changed the locks on all ground-floor doors and windows. Changed alarm codes. My mum and dad are staying with me. I've alerted my husband – he lives in the garden currently – he says he'll try not to be away as much until we get sorted. I've also got that new doorbell app, the one with the camera. Not that @_____ has ever just rocked up and rung the doorbell.'

'That we know of,' Bríd muttered darkly as she continued to note down Shelly's information.

Shelly glanced at her mother, who, if possible, looked even more terrified than Shelly felt. Maybe it had been a mistake to ask her to come. Though Jim, her dad, would have been even worse – he was prone to histrionics, hence tasking him with bringing Georgie to the cinema while they were at the station.

'So, does that mean you think Shelly definitely knows @_____ in real life?'

'Shelly, did you bring the lists I asked you to make?' Bríd skilfully skirted Sandra's question.

Shelly unfolded and smoothed out two sheets of A4 paper: on one, everyone she could think of who'd ever been given the alarm code, and on the other, the people who could've got a hold of and made copies of keys to the house.

'The keys to the house one is, in our opinion, the more crucial,' Bríd explained. 'Mitchell strongly suspects that info about your whereabouts, alarm codes, your conversations with the likes of Amy and your husband could be gleaned through spyware installed on your phone, if we find any. However, the fact that @_____ gained entry and locked the door after themselves on the night of the seventeenth suggests someone trusted, potentially someone close to you, Shelly.'

'I see.' Shelly clasped and re-clasped her hands on the table in front of her until Sandra gently placed her hand on top to calm Shelly's agitated movements.

Bríd took the lists and slid them into a brown file to her left. 'I'll be working on ruling out the people on these lists. And there is still a possibility it's not someone you know.'

Shelly was rueful. This was not the comfort Bríd intended it as.

A knock at the door startled everyone.

'Come in,' called Bríd. 'Ah, Detective Mitchell. Great. Please meet Shelly Devine and her mother, Sandra.'

Mitchell came over and shook hands before joining them at the table beside Bríd. Donal, who had slipped in behind Mitchell, placed a fully loaded tea tray down on the table and scuttled back out the door.

'So, I have good news and bad news.' Mitchell slid the phone back across the table to Shelly. 'We have detected and removed a malicious spyware app called YourEveryMove. That's the good news.'

'Really?' Shelly had to laugh. This constituted good news now?

'The bad news is that it's actually a very sophisticated piece of spyware,' Mitchell continued in his oddly robotic manner. 'Most of the spyware we'd see being used among civilians is crude and usually easily attributed to the person who installed it. YourEveryMove has layers of encryption, however. We do know that it would be impossible to install remotely and that it was installed sometime between January and March of this year. We may be able to narrow that installation window as we examine our findings in more detail, but we need you to create an exhaustive list of people who may have had access to this device. Bear in mind, they could have reconfigured your device's settings and installed YourEveryMove in mere minutes. So, try to remember every instance that your phone was out of your sight for even five minutes. Hell, a slick operator could have done the installation while pretending to take a photo of you with the phone.'

Mitchell went on to explain some of the grubby ins and outs of spyware before filling his suit pockets with most of the biscuits from the plate on the table and ducking back out of the interview room.

'He's an odd one,' Sandra remarked as the door clicked shut.

'He's odd but very thorough.' Bríd was quick to come to Mitchell's defence. 'Everyone on the tech unit says he's their best guy. Look, I know none of it feels that positive but in a way it is. The spyware is providing @_____ with so much of the access and information they've been taunting you with. The time they knew you were in the hospital, the old photographs, even the voicenote you sent to Amy about the birthday. Yes, they gained entry to the house and planted the decorations and the nanny cam concealed in the teddy bear that captured you getting, eh, frustrated with your daughter but at least now we know it was likely an isolated incident.'

❖

Shelly was exhausted from the meeting with the guards but knew skipping any more press events could jeopardise her standing with the various PRs and brand managers who were an essential part of the ecosystem of her precarious career. She walked the red carpet leading into The Landing for the beauty launch she'd promised Amy she wouldn't bail on. She posed for the social pics, swishing the long Rixo dress on loan from the Princess Closet and placing her hand on her bump lest anyone confuse it for – horror of horrors – weight gain. She'd swung home for make-up and wardrobe and to get Georgie bathed and dressed for bed. Then she headed out, leaving her parents messing with the TV settings. It was amazing to have them there, built-in babysitters for Georgie and nice company in the evenings, but still, she resented how @_____ had made her afraid in her own home. The guards, Bríd assured her, were devoting all their resources to identifying who installed the spyware, though she'd looked a little daunted when Shelly handed her the tally of every person who'd had access to her phone during a two-month period. There were close to thirty names. Still, at least the phone was clean now. And Mitchell's team had installed an anti-spyware app.

Shelly stepped off the red carpet and into the party, waving to several key influencers already inside.

'Shelly!!!' Alan, the maître d', hustled over, elbowing small fry bloggers out of his way. 'Shelly!' He pulled her in for an air-kiss. 'I did not know you were coming tonight. You look stun, hun. STUN!'

'Thanks, Alan. Any sign of Hazel or Polly yet?' She flashed guiltily on their names at the top of the list she'd made for Bríd.

'No, hun, not yet.' He took her elbow and began to steer her towards a secluded table that said 'Reserved' off to the left of the main entrance, away from the bar area. *Why is he being so pushy?*

Shelly wondered as she scanned the ornate bar-cum-restaurant. Then she spotted Hazel and Polly at the far end of the central bar area.

'Alan, they're right over there.' She pointed.

'Ah … oh … yeah.' Alan was being very shifty, and Shelly got a pang of fear. What was wrong? Had @_____ released something incriminating? Did Alan know something? She spotted that Hazel and Polly were both staring in complete silence at something in the restaurant area.

Shelly shook off Alan's hand and rushed forward to get a look at whatever they were so engrossed in.

'Shelly, I'm sorry.' She was just about aware of Alan's pleading voice behind her but one look at the source of Hazel and Polly's fascination – a couple at the booth by the window – had the effect of turning everything down but the pounding of her own heart.

Dan and a young brunette were chatting over what looked to be dessert and a bottle of champagne. A date. In the middle of one of the most Insta venues in the city. For fuck sake. With a great effort, Shelly stretched a bland smile across her face and tried to look unruffled. Giving a cheery little wave to Polly and Hazel, she beelined for Dan's table.

'Hi!' she announced brightly, sliding into their booth beside the girl and giving her a huge hug.

'Shelly, what the—' Dan was clearly shook at her sudden appearance.

'Everyone play the fuck along,' Shelly muttered sweetly through clenched teeth. She turned to the brunette. 'I'm saying it's nice to fucking see you and you're gonna say it's nice to see me and ask me how I'm getting on.'

'Dan?' The girl looked like a startled deer. 'Who is she?'

Dan wearily poured another drink. 'Do it, Lydia. I'll explain after, I promise,' he said quietly, making no eye contact.

'Wow ... it's so nice to see you. How are you?' Lydia gave a faltering delivery, but it'd do.

Shelly smiled icily. 'I'm great,' she returned peppily, then reached across the table to lay a manicured hand on Dan's cheek. 'And how are you, Dan?'

He stiffened but didn't shake her off. 'Shelly—'

'Listen,' Shelly cut him off. 'I don't give a fuck what you're doing with Lil Lydia here, but I do give a fuck *where* you're doing it. Do you realise that The Landing is *the* venue for Insta-events? At this very moment, a ton of PRs, journos, photographers and other influencers are about twenty feet away wondering why my husband is here on a date. That's why it's "so funny",' she put on a faux cheery voice, ' and "such a coincidence" that you're here with' – she glanced at Lydia, assessing her age – 'your niece to chat about her career plans.'

'Shelly, I am not lying about my life. That's really more your buzz.' His lip curled, betraying a level of disdain she'd become all too familiar with. God, was it just impossible to get through a separation without too much animosity?

'Well, Dan, if you don't want me to bring up how you brought young women into our home when you were supposed to be looking after your child during custody negotiations, I'd suggest you play along.'

Dan was clearly raging but didn't argue further. Shelly pretended to chat nicely for a couple more minutes, then slid back out of the booth. She leaned down and kissed Dan passionately. It was so bizarre to be kissing him after having not touched him in months and she was relieved that there was no sense of nostalgia or longing, just a desire to get this shitty moment and this shitty day over with. She straightened up briskly and walked back to the side of the room reserved for the beauty launch. Hazel and Polly looked utterly flabbergasted. Shelly only smiled and waved. Some lesser influencers were hovering beside them so Shelly was quick to get in her explanation before the other two could say anything.

'So funny! I knew Dan was out having dinner with his niece but no idea he'd booked in here!'

Hazel nodded her approval at the cover up and they all turned to the podium where the CEO of the beauty brand was preparing to say a few words.

Chapter 23

'Week thirty-one must be the charm. My tits look amazing!' Ali grinned, stuffing them into a denim shirt as she came into the early morning kitchen. 'I suppose they're gonna deflate the second the parasite has had a go of them.'

'Yeah, they're great all right, so veiny, though.' Liv was groggy despite the nearly empty pot of coffee in front of her. Juggling college work and her new loved-up status with Amy had taken its toll, Ali observed. Though, my God, a loved-up Liv was a very cheery Liv. 'So, you honestly think you're going to seduce him at the antenatal course, then?' Liv sat back looking beyond amused.

'Stop mocking. It's not your classic foreplay but I'm an innovator. And at the antenatal class, like, they'll be talking all about our baby and that's a big trigger for him. He can get very feelingsy, just like he did back at the scan. He's been giving me a very wide berth ever since The Kiss – I think he's all "don't get sucked back in", but he won't be able to hold out for ever. I mean, who could resist these?' Ali gave her boobs a poke. She and Sam had been texting on and off since the kiss and Ali had been careful to let him go at his own pace, but she'd been planning this day down to her lace knickers for the last two weeks. They were going to talk about adorable lil parasite at the class and then she'd suggest a bit of *Law & Order: SVU* for old time's sake and one thing would lead to another.

Liv continued to look dubious.

'How many weeks did you say you were? Does it not say in the books that you should throw in the towel on sex once it becomes, ya know, a bit bestial?'

'Fuck you!' Ali laughed. 'I say if you can't fancy me at my most bovine, you don't deserve me at my … least bovine.'

'A well-known maxim,' Liv deadpanned. 'Well, just don't smother him.'

Ali rolled her eyes. 'I'm just so excited to see him. I really hope he is too.'

'What time is kick-off on this foetus-fest?'

'Shit, it's 10 a.m, but all the way over in Harold's Cross.' Ali grabbed her jacket. 'Right, have a lovely Saturday. I will hopefully not see you later.' She winked and ducked out the door.

Even though she splurged on a taxi, she was still fifteen minutes late rushing into the health and education building, where the one-day intensive course was being held. Sam sat buried in his phone on a small folding chair just inside the large revolving doors.

'I am so sorry.' Ali heaved herself and the belly into his eyeline. 'Liv was having a crisis and I was trying to extract myself. How come you're not in there?'

'Well, the midwife man-shamed me out!' Sam's neck and ears were flushed, which definitely confirmed he'd had some kind of public altercation. The man could not maintain his chill – it was very cute.

'What do you mean she "man-shamed" you?' Ali hissed, looking over at the door behind which presumably the cosy little chat about parenthood was well underway by now.

'She didn't believe me when I said you were late. She said I was clearly some creepy pregnancy enthusiast here for, and I quote, "your sick kicks".'

'Oh no, sorry.' Ali stifled a giggle with her hand.

'Laugh away,' Sam said dryly. 'But it's not a good look for a man to be flying solo in antenatal class.' He paused and glanced down at the immense bump between them. 'This thing is really something now, isn't it?'

'Yeah, I guess it's been like two months since you've seen me.' Ali smiled shyly.

'Well, I'm watching you on the 'gram a bit.' He shifted awkwardly, kicked one scuffed trainer against the other. 'You're good on there,' he allowed. 'Much more like, well, you.'

'Yeah,' Ali replied. 'Being myself is way easier.' She laughed a little and ducked her head. 'It's good I still have some followers on there. Ticket sales for the show are going really well. Just over a week to go! And then that might lead to who knows what?' She shrugged. '*Fleabag* started as a one-woman show at the Edinburgh Festival. Maybe I could wind up getting back on *Durty Aul' Town* in the writers' room this time? Dream big, Ali!' She grinned ruefully. 'I don't mind either way. I've loved writing it. It's really helped with everything that's happened …' She trailed off awkwardly.

'It'll be really good, Ali.' Sam sounded so certain. Ali wished she could siphon off a bit of his confidence. 'I'll be there,' he added softly.

The words took immediate effect, giving her a whoosh of excitement in her tummy.

'I'm really glad to hear that,' she said solemnly.

'OK.' Sam clapped his hands and started towards the lecture hall. 'Time to show this bitch I've got me a legit pregnant woman and am not some creep who gets boners from hearing about episiotomies.'

'Wait, about what?' Ali stopped just short of the door.

'Episiotomies, Ali. You know, snip-snip?' He made a scissors motion with his hand.

'Snip what exactly?'

'Your lady area.' Sam looked highly amused at being the one to explain episiotomies to her. 'If the baby's trying to get out but your vadge is … ya know … then the doctor just …' He made to do the cutting action again and Ali instinctively blocked her ears and clamped her legs shut.

'Shhhhh, stop,' she squealed.

'What's the matter? What did you think this class was for? It's all about how to get that thing out of you.'

'I thought it'd be nice little chats about how to be a parent,' Ali wailed. 'I thought we'd talk about how to give it a bath and what to do if it cries.'

'Haha, God no.' Sam laughed. 'This is the whole blood and guts shitshow. As far as I know, they don't tell you how to raise the thing until … never, like. Or you might get a lecture after you've already cocked it all up completely. They'll probably be dying to tell us then. Nah, nah, my sister gave me the rundown on this class.'

'And? What did she say?'

'Well, she told me to bring a sick bag.' Sam pulled a small neatly folded paper sack from his pocket.

'Fucking great. Well, lead the way, Episiotomy Enthusiast.' Ali gestured at the door huffily.

So much for reminding him of how much he liked her vagina at this thing. This was like bringing someone to an abattoir before treating them to a lovely steak dinner.

Sam pushed open the door and the room inside abruptly fell silent. A woman at the head of the class looked up from the squat she was assuming.

'I told you, a lone man in the room is not appropriate—' She paused, peering past him to Ali.

'Look, I found a woman,' Sam announced triumphantly. 'I even impregnated her thirty-one weeks ago. Handy.' He cocked a snarky eyebrow at the squatting woman.

'All right, all right.' Ali shoved him forward. 'I'm supposed to be the hormonal one. Sorry for being late.' She waved awkwardly at the room and mouthed 'hello' at Shelly, who was sitting front and centre beside Dan Devine.

Shelly had recommended the course to Ali. She'd barely seen Shelly since shooting the W Y N D promo and she didn't look her usual radiant self. She was wan and it looked as if she hadn't slept in weeks. Still, she mustered up a warm smile for Ali as she and Sam found seats at the back.

'As I was saying before I was interrupted' – the midwife glared up at them before resuming her squat – 'in an ideal world this is how the baby would come out. Gravity is on your side. Mum is bearing down while Dad is supporting her in any way he can. Remember, the baby's head is about the circumference of a large coconut and the cervix can only dilate to ten centimetres, which is – and I'm not supposed to tell you this – well, it's not big enough, ladies.' She pulled a face that seemed to say 'Glad it's you, not me' and Ali instinctively crossed her legs.

'I'm supposed to pump you all full of the party line, which is all "Oh, your bodies are built for this" and "It'll be fiiiiiiiiine". Well, let me tell you, I have seen women ripped in half by these things.' She indicated the pile of dolls sitting off to one side. 'It's barbaric that in this, the year of our Lord two thousand and nineteen, we're still insisting on growing human young inside – INSIDE – women. People don't fit in people. That's just basic maths.'

'Is it?' Ali whispered to Sam.

'We're in the right room but I feel like we've stumbled on some very specific Reddit obstetric conspiracy thread,' he muttered back.

'We have put a man on the moon and invented actual flying machines, but still women have to give birth. I wouldn't mind but if it were men, sorting out this whole birth issue would've been straight at the top of the technological advancement to-do list.' She paused in front of a man in the front row. 'Well? Am I right?'

'Ehhhh …' The man shifted uncomfortably.

'Have you apologised yet to this woman for what you are putting her through? For what you are about to do to her?'

'I … em … I love my wife,' he blurted in a panicked voice.

'Indeed,' the midwife sneered at him and resumed her rant. 'Anyway, they've done nothing about this dire state of affairs so here we are, ladies. So, you all chose to come to my class, which means you're not interested in the systemic rose-tinting of childbirth that has taken place in the medical establishment over the last century.'

'Oh Jesus.' Ali leaned into Sam. 'I think I kinda *do* want the rose-tinting. Is this going to give me nightmares?'

'I think I can hear your vadge screaming from here.'

Ali snorted and most unfortunately drew the attention and ire of the midwife.

'Do you think there's something funny about the infantilisation and disempowerment of women in the obstetric services?'

'No, absolutely not,' Ali firmly replied, keeping her face as bland and impassive as possible.

'Good. Laugh now while you can. You won't be laughing when you're able to wear your vagina as a sarong after that ten-pound baby has ripped its way out of your body.'

'Jesus Christ,' Sam muttered, threatening to set her off again.

'If you want some rosy spiel about how birth is one of life's miracles, you're in the wrong place. I'm here to give you the facts. We're talking about an event where the best possible outcome is one where everyone involved LIVES. So, buckle up, burn your birth plan and enjoy your pelvic floor while you've still got one.'

Ali spotted a woman two rows in front who appeared to be sobbing quietly, her partner gingerly patting her back in a gesture of comfort.

'We'll take a short break so that some of you can compose yourselves.' The tyrannical midwife glared at the crying woman disdainfully.

Ali glanced at Sam, who looked as queasy as she felt.

'Fuck this. This is terrifying. Will we just go home and YouTube it?' Ali whispered urgently as they watched the weeping woman ushered outside by her partner.

Shelly, Ali spotted, was making her way over to them, followed closely by a weary-looking Dan Devine.

'Hi.' Ali waved brightly. 'So, what the fuck is this? Why would you suggest this … this … hazing?'

'I'm sorry. The website listed this wonderful woman whom Hazel swears by but, when we got here, the management announced that she'd been called to deliver a baby and they'd had to find a last-minute replacement. Don't let her put you off, though. Birth is fine. She's just trying to give everyone …'

'Nightmares?' Sam suggested.

'… realistic expectations,' Shelly finished firmly.

'I don't want realistic *now*! It's too late for realistic. I want someone to lie to me and say it'll all be fine,' Ali wailed. 'This is horrific. I don't need this info now when there's no way out. I needed this mad bitch ten years ago in school. Or thirty-one weeks ago in Tinder Sam's grotty bedsit.'

'It's a very coveted garden-level apartment,' Sam interjected, outraged. 'In this rental climate, a lot of people would kill for a basement flat with rear access and a colony of silverfish.'

'It's much too late for talk of rear access now, Sam,' Ali deadpanned and they both cracked up. Shelly shook her head, wincing while Dan looked utterly horrified, which only made Ali laugh harder.

'Sorry, sorry.' She wiped her eyes. 'How's it going anyway? Not long now for you, huh?'

Shelly folded her arms over the huge bump that she'd swathed in a dusty-rose cashmere cardigan over pale grey skinny jeans.

'Yeah.' She was looking tensely around the room, where other couples were grouped chatting in low voices. Her features were sharpened by anxiety and Ali felt a pang of pity. Amy had been hanging out at their place more and more and, though she wouldn't get into specifics, she'd mentioned things were not easy for Shelly at the moment.

'You OK, Shelly? I'm Sam. We met at the hospital a few months back.' Shelly seemed startled by Sam's concern and Ali couldn't help but feel proud of him. He was a sweet person, when he wasn't treating her to his patented, epic cold shoulder.

'Yeah, I'm fine. I just, sometimes I feel a bit exposed in these kinds of situations.' Absently she pulled the cardigan even tighter around her. Ali spotted a flicker of a sneer cross Dan's face and felt even more protective of Shelly.

'Oh, I know what you mean,' Ali agreed. 'Like, whose Story will you end up on later? It's a real thing,' she shot at Dan and Sam, probably sounding a bit more defensive than she intended.

'Uh-huh.' Dan was clearly bored and not in any way bothered to hide it. *What a prick.* 'Look.' He shrugged. 'If you insist on putting yourself out there, you have to take the good with the bad.'

'What is that supposed to mean?' Shelly whipped around with a force that surprised Ali. Sam shifted awkwardly beside her.

'You know what it means, Shelly. You brought this on yourself and now you're acting like a victim in this whole thing. Typical. You're so self-obsessed. Never a thought for who you are really putting at risk. Our daughter.'

Jesus. Ali glanced furtively around. There were several interested couples now openly watching the exchange.

'Hey man, maybe you should keep it down a bit?' Sam spoke quietly but firmly and Dan looked furious, as if he might storm off at any minute. Ali admired Sam for speaking up for Shelly but maybe this wasn't something to get involved in. Dan was clearly talking about more than a few posts on Instagram.

'I'll keep it down.' Dan held up his hands in mock-surrender. 'I'm fucking out of here anyway. Coming today was a mistake. I'm not ready to play nice, Shelly, not with all this shit going down.'

Shelly was staring at the ground and barely reacted to Dan turning on heel and marching from the room in a wake of open-mouthed stares from the rest of the class.

God, they're all so obvious, Ali thought. Everyone was lapping up the dramz. Why is the sight of other husbands and wives fighting like crack to couples?

'Shelly?' Ali tugged on Shelly's sleeve gently. 'Want to come get some carvery with us? You'd be amazed at the medicinal properties of a meat buffet.'

'You don't think we should stay?' Sam asked. Around them pregnant women were lumbering back to their seats with dazed and, in many cases, queasy-looking men drifting after them.

'No way.' Ali was scrambling to pick up her bag before the malevolent midwife returned and tried to detain them. 'Listen, we all got out of our mum's vadge one way or another. I don't need this one psyching me out. Shelly can give us the lowdown on the way to the carvery, sure.'

Sam grinned. 'Liv told me not to give you any carvery, that you'd had enough carvery this week.'

'If I have to manslaughter you for a bowl of mash and gravy, I fucking will, Sam. Don't push me.' Ali grabbed Shelly's hand and pulled her out of the auditorium. Sam hurried after them, casting an anxious eye around to make sure the midwife wasn't about to appear and stop them.

'Sam, tell me you drove,' Ali pleaded once they were safely free of the place.

'Yep.' He dangled his keys. 'I'll nip around for the car and pick you both up.'

He jogged off and Shelly watched him go, looking wistful.

'Things seem to be going well between you two,' she said quietly.

'Well, it's very hit and miss. I get the impression that every time he catches himself warming to me again, he sort of shakes himself to pull out of it. I'm really working on it, though. I miss him. Plus, every episode of *Teen Mum* I watch, I'm like "shit, I do not wanna be dealing with a baby on my own".' Ali finished the sentence before realising what she'd said. 'Gah, oh shite. I'm sorry, Shelly. I'm a knob.'

'Oh, don't worry about it. You're right. A newborn solo is probably most people's idea of hell but I won't be on my own. My parents are being really supportive and I have Amy and Marni my nanny will do more hours. I'll be throwing money at this issue – it's the only way to stay sane, believe me,' she finished with an oddly hollow laugh.

'Are you OK? I mean apart from …' Ali cast a hand around awkwardly, searching for a good way to put Shelly's troubles.

'Apart from what? Everything?' Shelly suggested wryly.

'Well, yeah.'

Shelly gazed across the car park. Despite the belly, she looked tiny, Ali thought, and vulnerable.

'Have you lost weight, Shelly?'

'It's just stress.' Shelly sighed. 'Everything has been so full on.'

She met Ali's eyes and the look of bald fear startled Ali.

'What's going on? Are you OK?'

'I'm not,' Shelly replied plainly. 'I have this person who is wrecking my life, and no one is taking it seriously. The guards can't seem to find any answers. They don't seem to understand half of what we do on Instagram. My parents are freaking, which is not comforting. And as you probably gathered, Dan is blaming me completely for the whole thing.'

'Shit. Is this still the person in the DMs? The one getting ratty every time you forget to do an outfit post?'

'Yes, I think so. Only it's really escalated.' She looked uncertain about whatever she was about to say next but appeared to steel herself. 'They came into my home, Ali.'

'What? So, you've seen them—'

'No,' Shelly interrupted sharply. 'Not exactly. I dunno if you remember, it was Georgie's birthday about a month ago and I actually forgot to set up the balloons the night before. I sent Amy a voicenote asking her to pick up stuff. Anyway, when I came down in the morning, it was all laid out perfectly. Except Amy hadn't done it.'

Ali shivered despite the warm late August day.

'What. The. Fuck. That's so creepy. What was set up? Balloons and shit?'

'Yeah, they sent a message being all "I've always got your back. Lucky, I'm always watching and listening".'

'God.' Ali was reeling. 'It's just so, so freaky. How did they get in?'

Shelly just shrugged helplessly. Something niggled at Ali about the message Shelly had just related but she couldn't put her finger on it.

'No idea. Still. Obviously, I've put in way more security measures since. I've got a camera on the front door that links to my phone. All the alarm codes and locks are changed but they're relentless.' Ali folded Shelly into an awkward hug. She looked so worn out and desperate.

'Here's Sam. C'mon let's get you fed. You look tiny, like someone's FaceFixed you into oblivion.'

Shelly mustered a thin, bloodless smile.

Sam pulled up beside them and Ali ushered Shelly into the passenger seat. 'Mega preggos get shotgun,' she chirped, trying to sound cheery.

'Sorry that took so long.' Sam slipped into gear and headed back down the avenue to the exit. 'Your one actually clocked me making my "getaway" and gave me the bollocking of my life. She said I deserved to be sterilised if I couldn't sit through one antenatal class. It was a bit much,' he trailed off, spotting Shelly's upset.

'Crap, are you OK? What'd I miss? Is it your husband? He seemed … eh … nice?' Sam finished clumsily.

Shelly, to Ali's relief, managed a laugh at this.

'Dan is the least of my problems. I was just telling Ali about this complete psycho who is wrecking my life currently.'

As Ali directed them to the nearest carvery – she was keeping an active list on her phone, colour-coded according to which establishments were 'weekend-only' carveries versus which provided leather-meat all week – Shelly brought Sam up to speed on @_____.

'It's so twisted. They basically want you to keep performing for them.' Sam shook his head.

Shelly nodded emphatically. 'I didn't understand it at first but that totally is what it seems to be about. Berna, my therapist, says the stalker has a form of addiction. They seem to hate me but need me in equal measure. The thing is they've amassed so much on me.'

'Like what?' Ali had spent the journey leaning forward with her elbows propped on the front seats lest she miss a single detail.

Shelly shifted uneasily. 'Stupid stuff like posed photographs.'

'But everyone does that. It's Instagram! Anyone who thinks they're not watching a complete sham probably has some undiagnosed brain injury,' Ali pointed out.

'Some of these things are … pretty dishonest. It'd be embarrassing if they came out.'

'Liiike … ?' Sam prompted as he pulled into the pub Ali had indicated and she was amused at how invested he was. She'd forgotten about his love of tea-spilling.

'Well, I lied a bit about breastfeeding. So, there might be misleading pictures on my grid … that were staged. With a doll instead of a baby.'

Ali and Sam snorted in unison.

'Oh my God! You just snorted,' Sam roared.

'So did you! Shut up! OK, so you boobed a doll but that's not exactly the craziest thing anyone's lied about on Insta.' Ali tried to sound soothing.

'Yeah, Ali knows!' Sam chimed in as he swung into a parking space.

'Well, yeah, none of the pictures are as bad as …' Shelly hesitated then seemed to make up her mind. 'Well, see for yourselves,' she said, pulling out her phone and tapping and swiping until she found what she was looking for. She passed it to Ali and Sam. Ali was dying to see what could've spooked Shelly so badly, but she was also very, very aware of how close Sam was at that moment. His body just seemed to emanate some undefined aura that called to her, a magnetic pull she found irresistible. Goddamn, it was potent stuff. His shocked exclamation broke the spell.

'Oh shit! Did you just give your kid—'

'The finger? Yeah.' Shelly rolled her eyes. 'Sometimes they are really asking for it. Give it three years and you two will understand. Ugh, if this got out, it'd be a disaster,' she said as Sam replayed the clip and Ali shifted her focus, with some difficulty, back to the video and away from the curls of dark hair on his neck.

'Well, the kid has her back to you,' Ali noted. 'She can't see it. Seems grand to me. Sure, you don't have to have kids to know that they can be complete pricks. Just go to the supermarket and follow the sound of screaming and you'll find some bastard kid breaking their mother's gentle spirit in the cereal aisle.'

'Yeah!' Sam chimed in. 'I was deffo a little shit to my mum. I barely remember her, but I remember her telling me to "go the fuck to sleep" one night! Must've worn her way down that day.'

'C'mon to the meat.' Ali was antsy. 'I can focus better when the carvery is locked in.'

Inside the dimly lit pub a Saturday match blared, and the punters gave them barely a glance as they loaded up plates and settled in a pleather banquette in the corner.

Shelly had skipped the carvery in favour of the salad bar, which Ali was sure she'd never seen anyone go for. *God, she seems so repressed,* Ali thought as she watched Shelly take genteel bites of what had to be the most disgusting mélange of vegetables masquerading as a salad ever to grace a plate.

'Look, I have a theory.' All that *SVU* seemed to have paid off. Sam was seriously all over the stalker situation. '@_____ is obsessed with you, right? You're her – look I think we can assume it's a "her" – you're her oxygen. She threatens you when you aren't supplying her with what she craves. YOU. You said any time you're slow to post to Insta, she's in the DMs. She might hate you, but she also needs you. She's addicted to you, see?'

'Yes. I *see*, Sam, but that doesn't exactly help when she's coming into my house to hang up decorations and watch me sleep.'

'But wait, he's onto something.' Ali picked up the thread. 'You think she's got stuff on you, that she holds all the power. But in reality you have way, way more power. If she loses you, she's got nothing.'

'Yeah, but how does she lose me? She has me on the hook with all these pictures and videos.'

'But power is relative,' Ali argued, swallowing a forkful of mash doused in gravy. 'Can we just take a minute for this gravy, lads ... fuckin' gorge.' She sighed contentedly before continuing. 'This video to me is nothing. You should post it. You're not being a bitch to your kid, you're not hurting her, she doesn't even know you're flipping her off. You post this and write a caption about how some psycho troll is trying to mum-shame you and BAM, everyone will be on your side.

The tide is turning on all this call-out culture. Mark my words, you'll win this. You'll be brave for "being real",' Ali concluded.

'Instagram.' Sam shook his head ruefully. 'You get praise on there for just not being completely full of shit.'

Shelly pushed her depressing wilted iceberg lettuce around her plate, evidently considering Ali's words.

'Ali deffo has a point, though,' Sam continued. 'You need to get ahead of this. That's what we'd be advising in work.'

'What do you do, Sam?' Shelly asked. Ali straightened up. This was her chance to finally nail this info down. Back when they were together, Ali had zoned out a few too many times on the early dates, planning Insta captions for her feed, and had never gotten to the bottom of Sam's job beyond that he went to an office. It had then gone on too long and it seemed too late to ask.

'Well, I'm in communications ostensibly, in a big software company, but with the way things are these days, we spend a lot of our time managing micro shitstorms on Twitter. It's sensitive stuff. I can't really talk in depth about it because it'd defeat the purpose of my job – put it this way, if you've heard about it, it means I didn't do my job right.' He gave a little exasperated wink.

Aha, Ali thought, *finally, I can confidently tell people what my boyfriend's job is. Kind of.*

He's not your boyfriend, luv, the bitchy inner monologue was quick to point out. *Was he ever?*

All right, all right. Ali was refusing to end this day on a downer. *My sort-of near-boyfriend – we were definitely relationship-adjacent at some point and he'll be my baby's dad for ever so piss off.*

'He's so right.' Ali turned to Shelly. 'Post it and you are basically castrating this horrible person. It's the perfect solution.'

Shelly looked as if she was coming around to the idea and for the rest of their lunch they composed the caption. Sam, Ali couldn't help but notice, was particularly good at the Insta-spin. He dictated a pitch-perfect caption:

'It is not OK to terrorise another person. Instagram is a wonderful, positive space and I am so, so grateful for the career and connections I have forged here. This person has hidden behind their anonymity while threatening to expose intimate moments from my life. I am not perfect but every day I am trying my best. I am showing up and trying to be a good mum and role model for my little girl. I don't always succeed one hundred per cent, but I try, just like all us mums are constantly trying. The holder of this anonymous account illegally gained entry to my home, set up a camera and captured footage of me at the end of my mum-tether, then threatened to expose me. But I say NO MORE. No one has the right to publish the private moments of others ...'

Sam briefly trailed off, switching back to his normal voice.

'You want to subtly hint that you're throwing yourself under a bus for the good of others ...' He pondered for a minute while Shelly waited, finger poised to tap.

'OK, I've got it.

'No one has the right to publish the private moments of others and if I am criticised for my actions with my daughter, which came at the end of a long day and which I am not proud of, well, then so be it. I am taking this stand because I don't want others to be shamed or harassed or bullied in the manner in which I have for the past six months.'

'Mention your pregnancy,' Ali cut in. 'You're at a particularly vulnerable time in your life or whatever.'

'Good idea.' Shelly amended the caption.

'Now, we need a hashtag that can get everyone talking,' Ali said.

'What about #CallOutCallingOut?' Sam suggested.

'That's good.' Shelly typed feverishly.

'Is #TakeBackPowerFromTrolls too long?' Ali wondered.

'Tighten it up.' Sam drummed his fingers on the table. '#TakeTrollPrisoners works.'

They read the caption through a couple more times before pronouncing it perfect.

'You're good at this, Sam,' Shelly said admiringly.

'Yeah, you could've helped with my Insta comeback.' Ali grinned, risking a reference to the dreaded baby lie.

'Nah, yours was good.' His face was infuriatingly hard to read. 'It needed that rawness. Anything too polished and people would've hated it.'

He suddenly looked solemn and Ali sensed it was probably still too soon to be making cracks about her Insta downfall. But it would always be too soon unless they just talked about it. To get past it, they had to get it out there. It was just like what they'd been saying to Shelly, hiding from something only feeds its power.

Shelly, clearly sensing the change in mood, signalled a lounge boy to bring the bill.

'I'd better be getting home. My mum's got Georgie but I don't want to miss bath and bedtime. I'm getting this.' She handed her card to the waiter. 'You guys really cheered me up and, seriously, I'm starting to feel so much better about this. I'm going to give it to Amy for a final edit but then, screw it, you're absolutely right. Taking back the power is the only way.'

They piled into the car and, as Sam headed towards the health centre, Ali mulled over how to swing it so that she and Sam were alone together. He hadn't mentioned giving her a lift home and it made no sense for him to cross the entire city and then go back to his place in Rathmines. But maybe he—

'I can drop you to the bus, Ali?' His abrupt stop by the side of the road shut down any hopeful thoughts in her head. 'It goes from here back into town, yeah?'

'Yeah, cool, here's perfect. Thanks.' Ali said her goodbyes and heaved herself out of the car, wishing she wasn't leaving Sam with the lasting visual of her looking distinctly ungraceful and struggling to get out.

She thanked them and waved as they drove out of sight.

It seemed like he couldn't wait to get rid of her, she thought sadly as she ambled to the bench at the bus stop and stood practically pelvis to eye level with a guy on his phone until he got the message and grudgingly gave up his seat for her.

She WhatsApped Liv.

It seemed to be going great. We went for lunch with Shelly, but then he dumped me out at the bus stop and is now driving her back to her car.

Also, we ducked out of the class early because it was like a hellish combination of Social and Personal Education class in fourth year and the final scenes from Event Horizon. I need cheering up ASAP and to find out how to birth a baby.

She added a GIF of Sam Neill losing it in that last scene of the movie and began rooting for her Leap card.

Liv's response a few minutes later was comforting.

I got you covered …

It was accompanied by a picture of the coffee table in the living room where Liv had arranged a load of snacks and some latex gloves with *One Born Every Minute* loading on the TV in the background.

Thank you. I don't want to know why you just HAPPENED to have latex gloves to hand like that ;) See you soon. xx

❖

Shelly felt bad that Sam was bringing her back to her car. Maybe if she hadn't been there, Sam and Ali would've spent the evening together. It was such a shame those two had gotten off on the wrong foot – though that was, Shelly knew, definitely putting it mildly.

Still, the connection they had was just so obvious. Even in the early days, she and Dan had never had that.

'So' – she turned to Sam – 'you didn't want to invite Ali back to the very coveted garden-level apartment, then?' She was pretty sure it was OK to ask, given how much he had learned about *her* life in the preceding two hours.

Sam shrugged, keeping his eyes on the road, the turn for the health centre coming up. 'I don't want to be sending mixed signals.'

'What constitutes mixed signals when you clearly still have feelings for her and she's having your child?'

'It's more complicated than that,' he returned tersely.

He didn't deny he had feelings for her. Shelly made a mental note to WhatsApp Ali as much as soon as she got to her car. She sensed Ali needed cheering up on this matter.

'How many serious relationships have you had, Sam?'

He looked unhappy with this line of questioning.

'None really, unless you count Ali and I don't really count it.' He sighed. 'Not with how it ended,' he added quietly.

'Can I be your annoying big sister for a minute?'

He shrugged again and indicated left for the health centre. Shelly opted to take his silence as a grudging agreement.

'You don't get what you have with Ali with a lot of people.' She held up a hand as he began to argue. 'Wait, let me finish. Just park her dumb lie for a minute. You two get each other. You have fun together. You fit. I've never had that with anyone, you know. Not even Dan. Never with Dan. From day one, I tried to fit him and then it didn't work and look at us now. That's why I can't bear to watch you talk yourself out of being with Ali. You'll probably go on and meet someone and she'll be nice, but she'll never be Ali. She'll never be that person who makes you laugh and smells just right, feels right, *is* right. I truly wish I'd had that, and if I found it, I wouldn't be tossing it out over one thing that, yes, was brutal and so wrong but my God, Sam, her dad was dying – she was not in her right mind.'

'I know that.' He pulled into the car park. 'Where are you parked?'

'Up there on the right,' she directed him. 'I'm not trying to annoy you. I just like you two. Plus, I guess I know what's coming down the line. Newborns are a miracle and all but they're also like someone just chucked a sweet-smelling bomb into the middle of your life. She's going to need someone to mind her.'

'I'll be involved. I was there today, wasn't I?'

'Yeah, but it's more than doing half the nappies and rocking the baby.' Shelly flashed back on her own lonely, dark days as a new mother. Among her memories of Georgie wailing and her crying helplessly along with her, there was never any sign of Dan. And, worse, Shelly distinctly remembered forcing a brave mask over her shattered face whenever he was around. She couldn't have him see how much she was struggling.

At the time, she'd felt that her struggling – she'd only recently been able to admit with Berna's help that it was in fact postnatal depression – would've been an inconvenience for Dan, which was probably unfair. She'd never even given him a chance to help her, but she'd never felt able to let him in. That's why they didn't fit.

'Sam, she's going to need someone who loves her and minds her as much as loving and minding the baby.'

He seemed to soften at these words. He pulled up beside her car and turned the engine off.

'I do love her.' He looked so desolate, Shelly had to fight the urge to hug him. 'I want to move on and not feel bad about any of these things anymore. I started seeing a therapist to try and get all my thoughts in order.'

'That's great, Sam.'

'The therapist thinks Ali is a narcissist and that I should cut ties.'

'Oh.' Shelly floundered at this damning assessment. 'Well, therapists aren't always right. My therapist is amazing. She's helped me so much, but I wouldn't take her word on everything.'

'Everyone's in therapy except Ali, the one person who definitely needs it.' Sam grinned.

'In fairness to her, she joined a group therapy thing months ago.' Shelly was careful with her words, not knowing how much Sam knew or didn't know about CatAnon.

'Yeah, I know.' He sighed. 'She's been making an effort. And I know she's completely cut the crap on Insta. Except for this W Y N D thing – what's that all about? "Excavate your soul and prepare to soar with Holistic Hazel"?' He mimed wanking and Shelly had to laugh.

'God, I know. I'm so glad I won't have to attend. It's too close to the birth of this one.' She patted her belly. 'Still, it's money in the bank for Ali. Good with a baby on the way.'

'So, Ali's going to the festival? Is that safe with a baby on the way?'

'Oh God, yeah. It's not like Electric Picnic. This is a luxury wellness summit thing, according to all the press releases. She'll be completely fine. It'll be the same as staying in a hotel. Probably better. So, are you going to give her another chance?'

'I do have a wedding coming up. I've got a plus one. I would really like my friends to get to know her outside of all that craziness.'

'That's perfect, Sam. Definitely ask her. She will be so, so happy. I just know it.'

'Yeah,' Sam replied thoughtfully. 'I really do want to just get over this.'

'You guys will. You're so good together.' Shelly leaned over and gave him a little side hug. 'Thanks for today. You made me feel so much more normal about everything. In fact, I'm not going to hold off any longer. I'm posting the video. I'm a grown woman and I don't need Amy's signoff for every little thing.' She got out her phone and found the video still captioned and saved in her drafts. 'After everything @_____'s done to me in the last months, all the misery and worry, now I get to wreck her day for a change.'

She hit Post and grinned triumphantly at Sam.

Chapter 24

The CatAnon crew were especially chatty before the Monday evening meeting. Kelly came in and beelined for Ali the second she spotted her.

'OMG! Did you see Shelly Devine's post???'

Ali glanced around and lowered her voice. 'Yeah, actually I was hanging out with her on Saturday. We went to the same antenatal course. It sounds like she's had a terrible time.' She was careful not to let slip that she knew any more than anyone else about the stalker saga.

'It really makes you think, though, doesn't it? I mean about how there's a person on the other side of the account. Even if it's little miss perfect Shelly Devine.'

'Yeah.' Ali kept her tone vague. She really didn't want to inadvertently say anything to Kelly that might add fuel to the SHELLY fire. The post itself had gone down well, with tonnes of people condemning the stalkers and catfishers of the world, though a smattering of commenters did question whether influencers like Shelly weren't asking for it by flaunting their best lives online and rubbing other people's faces in their success. And a couple of the middle-aged male radio broadcasters had tried to rouse a debate about whether giving your child the finger behind their back was unacceptable, but they were rapidly shouted down by virtually every woman in the country.

As one Radio 1 listener, Mairead Ní Mhuracú, put it on the phone-in show:

'Get back to me when you've spent your days at home raising your own kids, ya smug shite.'

Shelly was relieved at the overwhelming outpouring of support but, she told Ali on Sunday evening via WhatsApp, she was no closer to figuring out who @_____ was. As yet, there had been no response from the account. The silence struck Ali as even more ominous.

The whole thing had made her rethink some of her own actions on the 'gram. She'd shared a snap of Liv at the front door a few weeks ago and a follower had DM'd to say she passed their house on her way to work every day. It was a harmless bit of chat but, with hundreds of thousands of followers, Ali was more and more aware of the odds that at least someone in the bunch was a bit of a psycho. How did she not think of it sooner, sitting in CatAnon every week, *FFS*?

'Right, we'll get started, shall we?' called the man sitting at the desk at the head of the room, whom Ali knew only as @sluttycheerleader69. He was cute and before her belly had really kicked in, she'd spotted him looking at her with interest, an interest that unexpectedly only seemed to intensify the more pregnant she got.

@sluttycheerleader69 was rattling through the preamble now and

Ali's mind drifted back to Sam unceremoniously dumping her out of his car at the bus stop on Saturday evening. *We're like a car stalling,* she thought bleakly. Shelly had insisted Sam was coming round – they'd apparently had a heart to heart after Ali got out at the bus stop on Saturday – but still it was two steps forward one step back. One week he was chatting in the WhatsApp and slagging her about her questionable taste in baby names and the next he was running a mile again the second he seemed to notice that they're getting on.

I should just go on a date, move on. Maybe that'd make him realise that I'm not gonna be hanging around for ever for him to bestow some fucking magical, hard-won forgiveness on me.

She rubbed her belly and looked up to find @sluttycheerleader69 eyeing her up exactly like someone appraising livestock.

Shit no. Her mind went hard into reverse. *Anyone willing to date me at thirty-two weeks gone has way more issues than even* I'm *up for dealing with.* The door of the meeting banged open, startling @sluttycheerleader69 and the people nearby. @PollysFewBits hurled herself into the nearest available chair, not even apologising for her lateness or the commotion. Kelly shot Ali a meaningful, wide-eyed look and mouthed 'WTF?'

Ali tried not to stare at Polly, but she couldn't help noticing her dishevelled appearance. Polly, who was always so immaculate, was barely even fully dressed. She wore a ragged coffee-coloured cardigan over grotty sweats and a battered pair of UGG boots that looked closer to roadkill than actual footwear. Her usually bronzed-to-oblivion face was pale and bore remnants of what looked like last night's make-up. To Ali's shock and then pity, Polly started to cry, loud gasping sobs that sounded so desperate Ali immediately made to stand up and go over. She went to put her arms around Polly, but Polly reared back and shoved Ali away.

'Oh, fuck off,' she spat.

@sluttycheerleader69 stood abruptly and hurried through the chairs to Ali's aid. 'Are you OK?'

'Yeah.' Ali inched backwards. She couldn't believe Polly had lashed out at her. What was going on?

'What is going on?' @sluttycheerleader69 was stern. 'You cannot touch another member, @AlwaysWatching. Do I need to ask you to leave?'

Polly was shaking her head but still looking furious.

'She touched me first. I was only—' Polly was arguing but Ali barely heard the rest. Always Watching. @sluttycheerleader69 had called Polly by her original catfish name because he probably had only ever heard her go by that handle.

Always Watching. The phrase tugged at Ali. She'd heard it recently. There was something familiar and horribly sinister in the words. Why were they bothering her?

@sluttycheerleader69 was now talking calmly and quietly to Polly. 'As you seem to be intent on disrupting the whole meeting, would you like to share first? We're here for you,' he added in a gentler tone.

'I'm sorry, OK?' Polly seemed to be trying to wrest back some control over her emotions. 'I can't just sit here and pretend anymore. I've had a slip.'

A gasp rippled through the room. Ali was a bit lost until Kelly leaned closer to whisper, 'It means she's been catfishing again.'

Ali nodded, her mind racing. Always Watching. The message @_____ had sent to Shelly said something like 'lucky, I'm always watching'. Ali stared at Polly, but she couldn't find any sense in the idea that Polly was stalking Shelly. Why would she stalk a woman she was already sort of friends with? Well, Ali corrected herself, as friends as any 'friends for the 'gram' really were.

Polly took a deep breath.

'I set up an Instagram account when my boys were small. I thought I had put my issues so far behind me that a little bit of social media would be fine. And it was fine. At first. Instagram meant so much to me when the boys were tiny babies. I was so lonely. I loved being a mum, but we were living in an estate in the middle of nowhere. My husband was gone all day. Here was a way to make friends. To feel connected even when I was home all day with a small baby. I knew that it could be risky, given my history. But at the time, Instagram was a much more basic thing. Just people posting their crappy holiday snaps and things. Not like now.' She raised her hands to her face, overcome. 'Now I see, now I … know.' She was struggling to get the words out and Ali felt a pang of pity. 'It was like bringing an alcoholic to a brewery,' she continued. 'Instagram is a bloody catfishing *machine*. No one is their real selves on there. No one.'

Ali and Kelly each shifted uncomfortably. Ali could feel the eyes of the other catfishers drifting over to them. Most of the others were older. They catfished on gmail or Twitter or Facebook. Ali had always sensed a bit of judgement from them over the fact that she and Polly still had Instagram accounts – which Polly now sadly was proving right.

'I became addicted to the thing. Every time I put up a picture and got likes and comments, it just felt so good. I started to think I really was somebody because 20,000 people I knew nothing about followed me on this app. I knew I was drifting away from the CA programme but the more followers I got, the more I felt like I couldn't give it up. I became obsessed with my numbers. I knew I was losing control when I began pretending to be someone else on the 'gram. It wasn't exactly like my @AlwaysWatching days. Back then, all my aliases were like elaborate fictions I made up.

'This time I just began to make subtle tweaks to who I was. I was me. Kind of. But better. I was obsessed with one woman and at some point, I started modelling myself on her. She got a peninsula in her kitchen, so I got a peninsula put in. She had dark hair, so I went dark. She did her bedroom in beige with textures of gold and chocolate; I did mine in beige with textures of gold and chocolate. I even had my second child because I wanted to have a girl just like Shelly did.' Polly shook her head sadly. 'Such a stupid, stupid obsession. But you don't understand … it took hold of me.' She looked around the room, something pleading in her expression. Kind faces looked back. Many people were nodding, herself included, Ali realised. Polly was describing exactly what her own descent into Insta-insanity had been like.

Illogical yet irresistible. Why did she want strangers to like her or think well of her or envy her? It was a ludicrous pursuit but impossible to stop once you were sucked in.

Thanks in no small part to these meetings, since returning to Instagram, Ali had largely shed the obsession. After losing Miles and screwing things up with Sam, the hearts and comments of strangers just didn't buoy her the way they had before. She wasn't even sure how many people followed her anymore. She didn't quite want to chuck it all in – she still needed to sell tickets to her show! – but now her Instagram was a means to an end instead of the entire point of her life. It was a crucial difference.

Polly was still clearly in the grip of her addiction. She'd been talking now for longer than was usually permitted at the meeting, but everyone could sense there was more to say.

'I became so addicted to this woman and to comparing my life to hers. I set up Google Alerts for her name. I started an account that only followed her so that I never had to wade through any other users to find her latest updates. I guess this was the beginning of the end of my catfishing sobriety. I didn't put my name on the account. I had a new handle and before long I was using it to control this woman. And hurt her. I wanted to hurt her. She'd begun to post less online and I became furious. She was taking away the thing I needed most in the world. Herself. It just escalated and escalated but I didn't realise how much I was enjoying tormenting her until she suddenly put a stop to it. She outed me to her followers. Or not me exactly but what I was doing. She's ruined everything. Now, she's taken away the one thing that was giving my life meaning. She has everything. Everything goes right for her. She gives her child the finger on video and everyone still fucking loves her. She doesn't even know what she has.' Polly was working herself up into another fury now. 'She has the perfect house and her perfect little girl. You can do so much shit on Insta with a little girl. I can't bring my fucking son on a #MamaAndMe pamper day, can I? Can I?'

This was met with stunned silence. No one was nodding sympathetically anymore, and Polly looked furious.

'Oh, fuck this place. You're all talk but the second anyone has a real problem, no one really wants to help.'

Polly stood up with such force that her folding chair collapsed backwards. She grabbed her bag and made for the door but at the last minute whipped back around to point in Ali's direction.

'I better not hear a fucking whisper of this out there, Ali. Anonymity is the foundation of all our beliefs.'

Ali rose. She had to say *something*, as apparently no one else was going to. 'You should delete the app, Polly. You need to put this all behind you. It's not too late to make a fresh start. Just delete the app and leave Shelly alone. I won't breathe a word, I promise. I swear on this baby's life, I won't betray your confidence, but you have to stop. Do you understand?'

For a moment longer, the sneer remained on Polly's wild features but then she crumpled, folding in on herself, starting to cry once more.

Ali moved towards her and pulled her into a hug, patting Polly's matted hair and trying to soothe her ragged sobs.

Ali felt torn about promising not to tell Shelly but she couldn't betray the group and break the anonymity rule. Polly and the CatAnon group had helped her so much these last months. Plus, Polly coming clean had to mean something; it had to mean that she truly did want to end this madness.

As they embraced, the other catfishers seemed to finally find their voices again and several clapped and muttered encouraging words.

'Well done for facing your behaviour.' @sluttycheerleader69 tentatively patted Polly's shoulder before resting a hand on Ali's lower back.

He leaned in to whisper, 'Nice work, Ali.'

❖

Later, as they cruised around the IKEA car park looking for a spot, Ali idly related @sluttycheerleader69's interest to Liv, though she was careful not to name him or reveal any identifying details.

'Ugh. He's a confirmed bump-banger, so.' Liv rolled her eyes, pulling into a family space near the entrance.

Ali briefly considered the contortions that would be necessary for them to even do it, then shrugged off the idea swiftly. Ick.

'Do you think we can park here?' she asked as they got out.

Liv shrugged. 'We've got a baby in tow. We're a family. Of sorts!'

Ali nodded. It was very reassuring that Liv was getting on board. 'So happy you're willing to sacrifice your youth with me and raise this baby together.'

'Well, somewhat.' Liv grabbed a trolley and they joined the stream of other young couples heading for the entrance. Virtually every woman in the vicinity had a burgeoning bump – obviously the IKEA trip was mandatory for soon-to-be parents. 'Let's say you can absolutely count on me if absolutely all else fails. Maybe give yer man – the bump-banger – a try first!' Liv mugged.

'Ew, no. Don't encourage me, the problem is I'm super … randy.'

'Randy? Ewww,' Liv moaned as they took the packed lift up to the showroom.

'I know,' Ali wailed as she stood wedged between the other shoppers. 'I mean, I wish I could call it something else but "randy" is the only word for it. I'm in heat or something. Are you having this at all?' Ali turned to a wary-looking pregnant woman beside them. 'I thought it would have gone away by now but it's only intensifying,' Ali continued, ignoring the horrified looks of the others in the lift. 'Genuinely the only thing stopping me from giving him a go is the thoughts of him then wank-banking it for life, ya know? It feels unfair to the baby somehow.'

'It must be some biological quirk to keep pregnant women faithful to their baby-daddies,' Liv offered as the doors to the lift slid open and several people burst out ahead of them.

'Which is why I've set my sights on seducing Sam. At the wedding! It's Friday week. He finally caved and invited me as his plus one.' Ali grinned. 'I am going to seduce the shite out of him.'

'Well, you've never looked more alluring.' Liv brought up the list for the baby's room on her phone.

'Thank you. I happen to agree.'

The IKEA trip was eye-opening for Ali. 'I'd no idea babies needed so much bullshit,' she remarked as they finished loading up the car.

'Yeah,' Liv agreed, swinging into the driver's seat. 'Imagine how much crap it'd be if Nella wasn't donating some of *her* old stuff.'

Ali hopped in beside her, pulling out her phone to check the time.

'Right, I've gotta get home and finalise everything before rehearsals tomorrow. I cannot believe this is really going to happen!'

'I know,' Liv agreed, steering them out of the car park. 'I'll be honest, when you first told me, I would have bet my life on you never getting a word of it down on paper.'

'Thank you!' Ali would have been pissed off if she wasn't also completely stunned that she'd done it. 'I'm really hoping this leads to more things. I know it's stupid to put too much on one four-night show, but I just feel this real pressure to make my mark before the kid comes and my life is over and I turn into a one-woman buffet for this grabby baby.'

'I get that,' Liv replied. 'I'm like that about the thesis, well, apart from the life-ending bit. My life will be continuing apace.' She winked. 'Though Amy and I have been talking about trying to get away for a bit after the deadline.'

'What?' Ali tried to keep the terror out of her voice, but Liv's hasty backtracking suggested she hadn't been that successful.

'Just for a couple of months, maybe. I've been doing this thesis for a year and a half. I just need a breather. And Amy thinks the Insta-game is this close to imploding, so she wants to plan her career pivot.'

Liv's deadline was just months after the baby was due. Ali knew it was selfish to expect Liv to co-parent her Tinder Baby, but whenever she'd thought ahead to those newborn days, it was a montage of her and Liv doing the baby thing. Always. She wouldn't allow herself to imagine Sam in that picture out of self-preservation. Suddenly it seemed more crucial than ever to get Sam back.

Unless she wanted to move in with Mini. But, oh God, no way. Frankly, it would probably lead to a murder-suicide situation. Safer for everyone concerned for Mini and Ali to only see each other for finite periods in neutral locations. Speaking of, she'd completely forgotten her mother was coming to the rehearsal tomorrow. They had agreed she could vet any of the lines she didn't like. It had seemed like the sane thing to do when she announced the planned show to Mini but now, with the prospect looming, she was nervous.

My So-Called Best Life had become something much more personal as the weeks and months of development had passed. What she'd thought originally was a funny, quippy show about how crazy Instagram was had ultimately become a hopefully funny, quippy show about how crazy *she* was. And Instagram. But mainly her. She'd also written far more about Miles and Mini than she'd planned, and she knew Mini could very well object. It was definitely going to be tricky. Terry had agreed to come along as moral support and perhaps to help if Mini needed convincing.

'Ali?' Liv's alarm cut through Ali's churning thoughts. 'Please don't look so worried. It's not even definite yet.'

'Oh God. No. Sorry, it's not you and Amy going off. That sounds really good.' Ali pulled a smile together as best she could. 'Sorry, I was just thinking about Mini. I'm showing her the show during rehearsal tomorrow.'

'Ahh. OK. Shit.'

Ali laughed. 'Yep, that sums it up, just about, I'd say.'

'Maybe she'll like it?' Liv sounded doubtful.

❖

'I hate it.'

The production tech was trying very hard to look as if he wasn't listening in to Mini's assessment of *My So-Called Best Life* as he fussed with leads in the corner of the stage.

Mini was front row centre with Erasmus, as always, by her side, on his phone.

Ali stood onstage feeling winded from the gut-punch of Mini's words and exhausted from her second full run-through of the day. She was fully off-book now, which was amazing, but the look on Mini's face was draining the life out of her. *Fuck. She hates it. Great. Whatever she wants changed will need to be rewritten and re-learned and, if it's dialogue from either Rational Ali or Thirsty Ali, re-shot. Great, great, great.*

'So just to clarify' – Terry was stepping out from his seat behind the curtain – 'you hate … all of it?'

'All of it?' Mini repeated vaguely, momentarily distracted by Erasmus showing her something on his phone. She muttered instructions to him and then returned to the matter at hand. 'Where were we? Ah yes, the ending. Look, I hate the ending. It's too flaccid. You need more of an emotional climax there. In my opinion,' she added as a diplomatic afterthought.

'OK, so you just hate the ending.' Ali rolled her eyes. 'You know, when you're giving feedback, just a blanket "I hate it" is kind of misleading.'

'Hmmmmm?' Mini was back leaning into Erasmus's phone. 'No! Tell him that, Turner or no Turner, there's no way he's withdrawing any more blood this week. Good God.'

Erasmus nodded and resumed tapping.

'Edmund.' Mini sighed exasperated. 'Ali, it's excellent, pumpkin. Well done. I love the bit about Miles and the dumb-waiter at the restaurant. I'd forgotten that story. I think you need to sort the ending, though. Ali and Sam need to get together at the end.'

'But it's not fiction, Mini. I can't just pretend we do when we haven't.'

'Why can't you? He's not coming to the show, is he?'

'Well, I don't know. I hope so. I don't know for definite. But, no! That is too demented. Stop it with your lunatic suggestions.'

'All right,' Mini replied mildly. 'Just a thought. Maybe a song at the end or something. That always gets people going, emotions-wise.'

Ali had to laugh. Mini talked about emotions as if they were a completely distant, oddly quaint concept.

'Maybe a song is a thought, Ali,' Terry interjected. 'Like, conclude with an announcement, like a title card in a film, sort of wrapping up the narrative and then play them out with a song.'

'I like it.' Ali grinned. 'It's very Miles, actually. Something like "At the time of going into production, Ali and Sam are still only tentatively communicating through flirty GIFs".' Ali scoffed slightly. 'Then I could do 'Que Sera Sera' on the ukulele. There won't be a dry eye in the house.'

Chapter 25

'When Schmiddy told me he'd asked Sinead to marry him, I assumed he'd got her pregnant and I was like "Careful now, man, get proper confirmation of that, there's a lot of 'pregnant for the 'gram-itis' going around".' The groomsman, Paddy, roared laughing at his own opener while, beside her, Ali felt Sam tense.

'You see our mate, Sam, who'll be up next to tell you all about the J1 in San Diego, was caught out like this and since then it's been kind of a cautionary tale.' Paddy grinned at Sam mischievously. 'And tonight, he's actually brought the cautionary *Whale* here with him.' He accompanied this with an exaggerated wink, clearly thrilled at his own wit. 'Welcome, Sam's not-so-little-bit-on-the-side, Ali! Now you have checked that bump's not a pillow, right, Sam?'

Oh Jesus. Ali made sure to keep smiling awkwardly, hyper-aware that now most of the room was craning to get a look at her.

At this point, Schmiddy grabbed the mic and in a moment of

extremely honourable self-sacrifice barked, 'It's me you're supposed to be slagging, you eejit.'

'Hahaha, yeah, sorry, mate, couldn't resist. Back to the man of the hour: Schmiddy-boy.' Paddy recovered the mic and ploughed on with the kind of terminally unfunny slaggology all best-man speeches seemed to be made of.

Sam remained stony-faced beside her and Ali wanted to maim this Paddy fucker. They had been getting on quite nicely up until this point. The drive from Dublin to Strokestown House, where the festivities were on, was nice. She'd regaled him with tales of the show preparations and generally tried to sound as normal as possible. She couldn't help but feel like she was trying to re-audition for a gig she'd already once had: Sam's girlfriend.

Now this idiot – she tuned back in momentarily to catch him saying 'when the under-nineteens would go on tour, what happened on tour stayed on tour, if you know what I mean? Except for Schmiddy Óg. He brought the herpes back from Carrick-On-Shannon as a souvenir, heh heh heh' – was reminding Sam publicly of the humiliation she'd inflicted on him.

'Is Paddy a bit of an arsehole?' She leaned into Sam.

'Yep,' he said through tight lips.

'Right, we'll leave it there, Paddy.' Schmiddy's father, whom all the lads revered and feared and inexplicably called Macky, snatched the microphone back from the still-guffawing Paddy. 'Glad *you* were entertained by that drivel, yeh gobsheen. Right, good man, Sam, your turn.' Macky passed the mic across the top table and Sam stood to address the room.

'Cheers, Macky. So, as Paddy already mentioned, I'm Sam. I've been friends with Schmiddy and Sinead for years and when they told me they were getting married, I assumed it was 'cos of the rental crisis. That's an upside no one's really acknowledging – crippling rates are actually bringing people together and reviving the lost art of getting married young. Now, I love you both equally but sorry, Sinead, Schmiddy has the edge. You see, back on our J1 in San Diego, Schmiddy was the mammy of the house and once a man brings you a full Irish in bed after a night on the sesh, well, you know yourself, he'll have your heart for ever. Anyway, I don't know shit about true love, but I know that you two are the best team, the best allies I've ever known. And as much as Sinead doesn't deserve Schmiddy, Schmiddy doesn't deserve Sinead either. They're two of my favourite people in the world. When Schmiddy had Delhi belly when they were travelling, Sinead was amazing. She didn't have anything to do with him, of course. She has way too much self-respect for that, I'm happy to report. But she took pictures of him at his lowest moments and shared them in the group chat, which was one of the greatest acts of giving I have ever witnessed. Like I said, I don't know dick about marriage but if on your wedding day you're beside your favourite person in the world, then you've got a pretty good chance and after that it's just about compromising all the time, fighting over dumb stuff, taking the bins out, making the tea, taking pictures when Schmiddy's in bits for the group chat and never, ever forgetting that you're each other's favourite person. To Schmiddy and Sinead.'

Ali tried to keep her head down. It was very exposing here at the top table and she hadn't expected to be quite so moved by Sam's speech.

Don't cry Ali, she warned silently, *they already think of you as unhinged. Do not make this wedding all about you and your botched relationship.*

'To Schmiddy and Sinead,' the room shouted gaily, clinking glasses.

'And to you for a really fucking nice speech,' Ali whispered to Sam. He smiled back tightly. She sensed the very nice and conventional wedding was throwing their own dysfunctional situation into unpleasantly sharp relief for him. 'I always wanted a real family,' he had told her the day he realised she'd lied to him for months about a fictitious baby. Weddings were shit for people with fractured families, Ali mused. She herself had sat through the father-of-the-bride speech practically holding her breath the entire time, afraid that any exhale would draw out an unstoppable and wildly inappropriate gush of grief.

Ali didn't think she'd particularly like a big wedding with top tables and party favours and father-of-the-bride speeches but, still, now she'd never get the chance to sit through a corny speech, rolling her eyes at the cringey dad-jokes. If she and Sam got married, their top table would be fairly cobbled together, she sighed. Poor Sam had no one but his sisters – his dad had never been on the scene. She, at least, had Mini. She wasn't the most maternal, but Ali knew for a fact that Mini would provide her with an alibi should that ever be necessary and, really, if that wasn't suffocating maternal love, then what was? Sam lost that demented devotion when he was just a little boy, Ali reflected. He was up now having the arm yanked off him by Macky and a stream of other burly, red-faced men all moulded in the likeness of Schmiddy.

'Good man, Sam. Good man.'

The speeches had, mercifully, concluded and Sam had been the only person to talk about Sinead beyond how beautiful she looked. *God, weddings are the pits.* People were beginning to mingle now, and Ali started to carefully drift away from the top table. It had been very, very odd sitting there among complete strangers, who only knew that she was a dangerous, pathological liar. Ali wished she could knock back about nine proseccos and skip straight to tomorrow's hangover.

'Ali! We did not think you would come!'

Ali spun round to find the WAGs of Sam's BoysLyfe WhatsApp group descending in a blur of taffeta, tulle and spidery eyelash extensions.

'Hi, yeah, well, I heard there would be cake.' She smiled.

'Oh my God, you are huge.' Orlaith's eyes widened and she leaned back as if she couldn't quite fully take in Ali's vastness. 'Huge.'

'Yeah.' Ali was feeling dangerously kamikaze after Paddy's little speech. 'That's what happens when there's a real one in there.' She shrugged.

This had the desired effect of stopping them in their tracks.

'Ha ha, yeah,' said Ellen, the one with the misfortune to be hitched to Paddy. She looked uncomfortable at Ali's abrupt pronouncement and Ali softened slightly. *This is stupid*, she realised. *You need to get these women onside if you are ever going to get Sam back. Women are the brains of every operation, Ali, even Sam's WhatsApp group.* If she could charm the WAGs, the boyfriends would fall into line.

She smiled at each of them. 'Sorry, I just figured I'd say it before anyone else did.' She squirmed a little, letting them see her unease. 'I know what you all must think of me. God, you should hear what I think of myself these days. It's a dark place in here sometimes.' She tapped her head. 'I know it must sound weird, but I'm really glad that all the shit hit the fan in a way. I hate that I hurt Sam so much but I was out of control, sick in the head, like, and I needed reality to smack me in the face for me to realise how bad I'd been for so long. Obsessing over Instagram, watching my numbers like a crazed bitch.'

Ali could see that something in their expressions was shifting.

'I even set up fake accounts to like and comment on my own posts,' Ali continued. 'So pathetic, but I was completely addicted.' Ellen, Ali noticed, was beginning to nod slightly.

'Yeah,' she breathed. 'It can be really easy to just be sucked in. In my line of work in the wellness sphere, it can be so toxic. I'm a life coach,' she filled Ali in. 'I'm there supposed to be counselling young women on how to resist comparison syndrome and then I'll be on the couch at night fuming over all the life coaches I know getting massive followings online.' She shook her head sadly.

'But, Ali, you are still on Insta, right?' This slightly barbed question came from Rhona, the longest-running and, therefore, chief WAG. She'd gone to school with Sam and the lads before getting together with Ed in college. 'You can't be that cured.' She folded her arms and narrowed her eyes.

'I'm working on it.' Ali tried to keep her tone light.

'I heard you were "working on" a one-woman show about humiliating Sam.' Rhona clearly wasn't interested in any bridge-building.

Jeez, chill your tits, Rhona, Ali thought, while outwardly she was just about clinging to a shard of a smile in the face of this oh-so-polite interrogation.

'The show is mainly about what a complete dick I've been,' she replied flatly. 'Anyway, I think I'm going to go soon. It was so nice to be here, but I don't want to make it awkward. Plus, I'm so freakin' tired from being pregnant.' She shrugged and smiled wearily. The WAGs now looked quite divided: Ellen and Orlaith were nodding sympathetically while Rhona was clearly still sceptical. 'Hopefully I'll see you guys at the show. I'm giving Sam a whole bunch of tickets.' Ali turned and plunged back into the swarm of wedding guests still milling around the top table. She grabbed her coat from her chair and her clutch bag from the table. She scanned for Sam but couldn't see him in the scrum around the bar or in the mosh pit on the dancefloor where, in the grand tradition of Irish weddings, everyone was jumping around to Riverdance while a lone uncle was slumped on a chair, apparently sleeping, in the middle of the chaos.

Ali loved a bit of wedding shenanigans but with a ten-pound lump sporadically kicking her in the vadge from the inside, she knew there was no point hanging around, plus Sam had remained oddly stiff and formal with her. Thank God the wedding was not too far a drive from Dublin. She'd catch up with the latest episode of *Under the Influence* on the way home and go to bed with a bag of M&Ms and a bit of Benson and Stabler – the lead detectives in the Special Victims Unit. *I really need a new show*, Ali mused as she ducked through the crowd into the jacks for a safety pee – pregnancy seemed to be an endless exercise in bladder management. The urge could hit her with barely a moment's notice, and all she needed was a rogue sneeze while trying to hold a pee in and game over, knickers full of wee.

She settled on the jacks and was watching some Stories with the sound down when she heard voices outside by the sinks.

'Did you see Sam's face when Paddy started up?'

'Oh God, poor guy. But even more juice, did you see Rhona when he walked in with your one, Ali? I bet Rhoners thought she'd nab Sam no probs after BumpGate.'

Ali X'd out of Insta to focus better on what was being said just outside her stall.

'What about Ed?'

'Ah, they've been going through the motions since he went off to do the master's. I bet she just wants to make sure Sam's up for it before dropping him. Ed's a dope anyway. She shouldn't have stayed with her third-year boyf. That's the lesson here. Hot in third year is a totally different story to hot in his twenties. She basically picked a hot child in school and now, well, let's just say Sam's had the better glow up.'

'Ick, yeah. D'you remember we all fancied Ed when he was, like, twelve? We were such pervs.' The girl laughed.

'Do you think Sam will get back with Ali?'

'Yeah, Schmiddy told me that he said he wants to but he's nervous about what everyone will say. Plus, he doesn't want to do anything that might upset Ali 'cos of her being so far along. I think he's pretty confused.'

'Yeah,' the other replied thoughtfully before suddenly shouting. 'Oh my fucking gee, they're playing "Lady in Red"!!!'

There was a clatter of heels and handbags and then Ali was alone once more. She fixed her dress and slipped out just after them. She texted as she headed for the main door of the old house.

LIV! Gleaned some great intel in the pisser. I love #OverheardAtWeddings ;) Turns out Shelly was right. These girls were saying Sam still likes me. Also, one of the WAGs fancies him which makes total sense 'cos she was super harsh to me after dinner. These schoolfriend groups are always so incestuous. Makes me thank fuck we were no-friend losers in secondary school. Gonna quit while I'm ahead. Coming home now for SVU and munch.

Ali pushed through the heavy front door and down the steps to the gravel driveway leading to the car park, composing another message.

Hey Sam, I couldn't find you to say goodbye. Think it's best I go after Paddy's speech and some of the girls weren't that happy I was there. I just didn't want to make things awkward or tricky for you. I loved being there with you tonight. I miss us.

She read it back carefully. She needed to get the tone just right.

No, wait, I fucking don't, she thought. *No games, Ali*, and she hit Send decisively.

A phone notification coming from the shadows in front of the house jolted her and she whipped around.

'Sam?' she called. 'Please say that's you and not some serial killer or handsy-uncle type.'

'It's me.' Sam smiled as he stepped into the pool of light streaming from the hall door. He was flicking his thumb over his phone. 'So. You're leaving?'

'Well, I thought maybe I should.' Ali shifted on the spot, hardly daring to meet his eye. She was suddenly hyper-aware of how alone they were. They hadn't really been alone together since that clumsy kiss after the ultrasound scan. He was, she realised, still coming towards her.

'I miss us too.' He came to a stop right in front of her.

'Really?' The word caught in Ali's throat. She didn't want to show just how overwhelmed she felt at hearing him say it, so she kept her gaze focused on the tiny space that remained between them, a space her bump nearly filled.

Sam ran his hand lightly over her hair and trailed his fingers down the back of her neck as he gently tilted her face towards him. He dropped his head to the sensitive place where her neck curved into her shoulder and breathed in deeply, hungrily almost. The heat of him and the tickle of his breath was tormenting her. She could feel herself revving up and she pressed herself against him as best she could, given certain obstacles. She willed him to touch her, kiss her. Anything.

'Fuck,' he breathed in her ear. Then he covered her mouth with his and pushed his tongue in and she moaned a little.

'Shhh,' he muttered but barely pulled out of the kiss.

They continued kissing and Sam's hands were tantalisingly close to her breasts. She loved the things he did to her tits. Goddammit, they had to go somewhere.

'Sam,' she whispered. 'We're kind of visible.'

'Mhhmmmm.' He barely stopped kissing her but began to push her back towards where he had stood watching her leaving just moments before. Now in the shadows, his hands roamed everywhere. He thrust his knee between her thighs to part them and then his hand was in her knickers.

'I'm gonna come really fast, Sam.'

Suddenly she felt Sam freeze. She opened her eyes. His horrified face was just inches from hers.

'What's wrong?' She looked around to see if someone had caught them, but the front of the house was still deserted.

'Your ...' A pained expression clouded his features. 'Your boob is, like, hissing at me or something.' He pulled his hand away to inspect it, leaving her boob loose where he had scooped it out of her dress. 'It's moist,' he yelped. Abruptly he pulled his other hand out of her knickers to cradle the wet hand looking freaked. 'You're leaking.'

Ali laughed. 'Fuck off! That's not even possible.' She investigated the boob, which did feel not exactly wet but certainly sticky. Then she gave it a squeeze and nearly died of shock to see a vaguely milk-like substance come out of her tit. 'Holy fuck!'

'See!' Sam sounded as gleeful as he was horrified. 'I told you.'

'Well, maybe you shouldn't have been milking me,' Ali retorted, grinning. 'C'mon, it's OK, just do what you were doing but don't touch the boobs.'

'I dunno.' Sam looked dubious. 'That's going to be quite hard to come back from. Maybe it's the baby's way of cock-blocking me. It seems like a hostile warning.'

'Oh, for God's sake. It's fine. The baby was loving it!'

'Ali! Too far.'

'OK, sorry. Look, the tits were just overexcited. C'mon, let's just go to my car and nail this thing.' She winked in what she hoped was at least in some way inviting and watched an agonising war wage across Sam's face. He was clearly struggling with the pregnant fuck as a concept but also the tension between them was unbearable.

She took his hand and pulled him to the car park. Fortunately, the other guests were probably still balls-deep in 'Rock the Boat' and the place was empty.

When they got to the little battered Punto, the reality of boning in the car hit Ali. *Shite.* She could literally barely get into this thing in her current state, never mind perform sexual gymnastics in there. Afraid of spooking Sam further, she said nothing and crawled into the back seat, where they resumed kissing and began to grapple like a pair of frustrated eels.

She couldn't lie on her stomach, which was one of their faves. He couldn't get on top. She tried to climb into his lap and actually managed to get a nice bit of gyrating going when Sam's muffled, plaintive voice could be heard from somewhere beyond the crest of the bump. 'Ali! Ali! I can't ... breathe. The bump is ... like ... attacking me.'

'Oh shite, sorry.' Ali dismounted as quickly as the belly would allow. Eventually, with all the logistics required to land a 747, they managed to get a position that seemed to work, kind of a sideways doggie style with elements of spooning.

'It's in.' Sam was jubilant, before asking approximately 400 more times if she was sure this was OK for the baby.

'Jesus, shut up about the baby. It's barely sentient – it's just sloshing around in there. Please just go a bit faster and a bit harder.' Between the milky tits and him gingerly rutting away back there, it was doing nothing to make Ali feel less bovine.

Finally, they seemed to settle in themselves. And the awkwardness and livestock vibes drifted away.

'Fuck, I've missed you,' Sam moaned into the back of her neck as he reached around to stroke her. She gasped into her hair strewn over the car seat as she tried not to make too much noise as she came. A few seconds later, Sam shuddered against her and practically roared 'Fuuuuuck' into her back.

'Jesus, Sam!' Ali laughed. She'd completely forgotten how loud and unhinged he sounded during sex. 'Keep it together!'

'Sorry, sorry, but fuuuuuck.' He squeezed her gently. 'That was good.'

Typically, at that exact moment the baby kicked the place where his hand was resting on the bump.

'Whaaa.' He sprang back. 'That had to be retaliation.'

Ali grinned and sat up, her dress was half off and she pulled and twisted to try to rearrange it while Sam did up his pants. Eventually they both looked dishevelled but reasonably respectable. They sat in silence, staring straight ahead, flushed and slightly panting.

'So …' Ali eventually broke the silence.

'Soooooo …' Sam nodded. 'Do you think we should, like, start going out again?'

Ali gazed down at their knees nearly touching. He sounded nervous. His hand lay on the seat between them and he kept tapping his fingertips against the pad of his thumb. The frenzied tension had passed and now she felt a powerful wave of fondness for him wash over her.

'I think,' she began, then they both jumped as Ali's phone buzzed loudly on the floor where it had landed in the comotion.

'Shite, it's Liv. I told her I was leaving ages ago. Hang on.' Ali hit the green button. 'Hi, hi, hi, sorry. I'm not dead. I'm still here at the wedding.'

'Delighted to hear you're alive.' Liv laughed. 'Why are you still there?'

'I'm ... eh ... I got held up with Sam. He's here beside me,' she added in case Liv came out with anything controversial that Sam would hear.

'Oh, OK, that's good?' Liv wondered mildly.

'Yep, it was good. I mean, it's good.'

'Oh, fuck off, Ali. Is he, like, *inside* you right now? What have I told you about that?'

'Shhhhh.' Ali could feel giggles welling up inside. 'He's not, we're done.'

'Oh God, well, just go easy, Ali. You're just about to crap a baby out with all the head-fuckery that entails. Maybe now's not the time to jump back into a relationship that didn't end so well the last time. That's not the movie you're in right now. You're not in a romcom, ya know? You're not Zooey Fucking Deschanel, you're in some sci-fi horror shit right now. You're Ripley with a goddamn alien about to plough out of your vadge any minute.'

'OK, thanks. Love you too, byeeeee.' Ali ended the call before Liv could get on any more of a roll. Still, Liv's warning crept across the pit of her stomach, dampening the simmering excitement that had been bubbling just moments before. What if this wasn't a good idea at all? She'd been so focused on getting Sam back that she hadn't stopped to think about what it would mean if it didn't work. What would it mean for the baby? Right now, she and Sam were able to be in the same room and be friendly but what if they got together only to become one of those couples who imploded and hated each other's guts until the end of time? Suddenly she felt utterly drained. Maybe it was hormones but suddenly the thrill of the evening had leaked away and was replaced by a dreadful angst. She felt scared for the baby. For the future. All that uncertainty.

'Ali?' Sam was leaning over to catch her eye and Ali frantically scrolled through possible scenarios and outcomes in her head. 'Hey?' He waved a hand in front of her face with a playful grin, then he cupped her cheek and whispered, 'I love you, Ali.'

I love you too, she thought but couldn't say.

If she said it back, she was staking everything on this one person. On them loving each other for ever. And it wasn't just about her anymore. She had to think of the baby as well. It was all too much.

'I think I need to go home, Sam. I feel a bit overwhelmed.' She tried to clear the lump from her throat and smile gently at him. 'Maybe we should …' She ducked her head, embarrassed. 'Maybe we should go on a date?' She felt uneasy. Was she just buying time? But no, if they took it slow, she could control her feelings and maybe that would keep her and the baby safe from any uncertainty.

'A date?' Sam sat back abruptly. 'Are you fucking kidding me?'

'No.' Ali was defensive. 'I'm just …'

'Just what?' Sam's eyes were steely. It was like the day he'd read the thesis all over again. 'Just a fucking game-player? Fuck you, Ali. You're conning me again.'

'Sam!'

He started pulling his trainers back on. *Only Sam would wear battered Reeboks to a wedding*, Ali thought. *It's why I like him*. He shoved his way out of the car.

'Sam, please!' she tried again.

He turned back to her. 'What?'

'I'm just ...' Ali hesitated. She let the silence drag for a beat too long and Sam slammed the door shut.

'I'm just scared,' Ali said, but it was too late.

She sat and cried in the empty car for a long time before she eventually managed to pull herself into the front seat to start the engine. She had no more tears, her throat was raw and a strange numbness had invaded her. She drove home carefully and burrowed into her bed without going in to Liv, as she usually would've done. Under the blanket in the darkness she cradled the bump.

'I'm sorry. I think I've fucked it up with him. Again,' she whispered.

A foot or an arm poked her either in agreement or exasperation, she couldn't quite tell. Probably both.

Chapter 26

A week later, Ali paced her tiny dressing room as the sound of the audience taking their seats beyond the door rose from a low hum to a wall of noise. The opening night of *My So-Called Best Life* had finally arrived, and it was already being heralded as the commercial hit of the festival. Ticket sales had been unbelievable, and they had even added matinees to the run when the original four shows had sold out.

Every time Ali felt the churning terror start up at the thought of performing for a real live audience, she looked at the total sales on the website. Selling out a 500-seat theatre for eight shows was a tidy sum, even minus the overheads. She and the baby would be making out with a rake of cash. Plus, Terry had even said he wanted to donate his cut to the Baby Jones fund. Ali couldn't believe how kind everyone had been: the whole of Dublin Insta was coming, and the Twitterati had rallied, presumably ironically but still, sales were sales, and even the theatre luvvies had been wildly supportive, probably because of Miles.

Now, all I have to do is live up to all the bloody hype. Ali glared at her reflection in the mirror over her dressing table. The table was crowded with flowers and cards from Liv, Amy, Mini and even Shelly. She checked her WhatsApp thread to see if Sam had responded to her last message. She'd put a ticket on the door for him. The message was blue-ticked but no sign of a GIF or answer.

Given how silent he had been since their botched car sex at the wedding, it seemed highly unlikely that Sam would come.

When she'd related the incident to Liv and Amy later, they had all agreed she did not play it well and that Sam's reaction was understandable. It would have been a cancelling offence if a guy banged his pregnant ex in the back of his car, then, instead of getting back together, suggested they go on a date.

'Everyone would be, like, what a toxic asshole! Put him in the bin,' Amy had mused.

A knock on the door was Ali's signal for ten minutes to curtain. She scrolled Insta to distract herself.

'We're at the opening night of @AliJones new one-woman show and cannot WAIT to see what she's come up with,' @CrystalDoorley was gushing on Stories, seated in the auditorium just down the hall.

Oh God, the pressure! Ali sat at her dressing table to run through her little pre-show ritual, which she'd established before the first full dress rehearsal and was now too superstitious to abandon. She tapped the table three times, the mirror twice and knocked once on her chest, muttering 'Miles, Miles, Miles' as she went.

She stepped into the corridor where Emma, the assistant stage manager, was ready to bring her to the stage.

'Deep breaths, Ali.' She smiled, adjusting her earpiece. 'Full house out there. Even B13.'

'Sam? Really?' Ali couldn't decide if this made her more nervous or less.

'Yep, he's there. We're all rooting for you, pal.' Emma squeezed her hand and gave her the plastic urn for the first scene.

❖

Ali could feel the audience relaxing into the swing of things after Blake Jordan's erroneous pregnancy announcement, which played out onstage with Real Ali seamlessly slipping into the role of Blake and delighting the man himself, who was sitting near the front, while Rational Ali begged Thirsty Ali to be reasonable. There were audible gasps and laughs at Thirsty Ali's kamikaze decision to play along and pretend to be pregnant. Ali was so thoroughly rehearsed she found she could both stay in the moment onstage and simultaneously freak about Sam sitting in the second row. As yet, he hadn't registered a single visible reaction to the play and she was tense as her reenactment of their meeting, when she told him she was pregnant, approached. It wasn't written to be slapstick. If it was deprecating towards anyone it was her, but you couldn't always predict audience reaction.

Luckily, the spectacle of Ali lying to Sam in Grogan's while Rational Ali begged her to see sense played out to horrified silence in the theatre.

Thank God, Ali thought as the lights shifted for the next scene. She couldn't have coped with them thinking it was funny while Sam sat right there.

The following scenes of Ali's misadventures in Instaland were lighter and the crowd was laughing in all the right places. But as the play drew closer to the climax in Miles's hospital room, the tone palpably shifted, and many people were wiping their eyes by the time Real Ali stood in a lone spotlight cradling her ukulele in the wake of her father's death.

'So that's the true story.' Ali sighed. 'I'm a villain. I'm a liar. I'm thirsty. I'm selfish. I'm flawed. I'm rational – sometimes. I knew what I was doing. I knew the potential for hurting a good person, but I did it anyway. And my punishment? I'm bigger than ever on the 'gram!'

The audience laughed and she waved her hand as if to bat away the guffaws.

'Jokes, jokes.' She grinned. 'My punishment is that I lost two people I loved, and I have to live every day with the knowledge that I didn't treat them right.

'I know the #bestlife thing is an Insta-sham, but for a while there I had a good life. I had my dad and Sam said I was his favourite person. And what I've learned is I can have a good life again, maybe not the one I thought I wanted, but this lil baba, this cursed child of a social media hoax, will definitely have a good life. That's my job now. And who knows, maybe Sam'll see me crowning and see me in a whole new light.

'Or maybe not! Endings are hard, especially in real life ... I wanted to do some grand gesture like in the movies. A declaration of love? A proposal? At one point, I legit thought "What would Tom Hanks do?"'

Ali wavered over the final lines. It was hard to do it with Sam right there. What if he felt compelled to answer and said 'no'? There was no room for stalling. The title card would be projected on the phone shortly.

'Sam, will you ...' Ali sank to her knees as the audience seemed to hold their breath.

'Will you forgive me?'

After a beat, the spot went black and text appeared on the screen of the phone accompanied by the sound of texting.

At the time of going into production, Ali and Sam are in communication regarding their expected child ... but nothing else.

The words faded and were replaced by:

In loving memory of Miles Jones.

Ali's spotlight came up again and she began to strum 'Que Sera Sera' on the ukulele. When the audience twigged the song, they stood as one and swayed and clapped along. Ali couldn't believe it. *They're really with me*, she marvelled. *If Miles could see this ...*

At the chorus, the whole place sang '*what will be, will be*' with her and Ali smiled through tears.

But when the house lights came up, seat B13 was empty.

Chapter 27

Shelly's dad, under Amy's directions, was heaving an enormous papier mâché baby into the house when Shelly came down the stairs on the morning of the gender-reveal party shoot. She hadn't intended to do the baby reveal quite so close to her due date – she had just weeks to go – but everything with the guards and @_____ had really thrown the schedule.

'This thing is terrifying,' Jim panted. 'What have ye got planned for it?'

He lugged it into the front reception room with Shelly close behind him craning to get a better look.

The baby's head was about the size of her inflatable pregnancy ball but lumpy and misshapen with livid red cheeks and eerie black eyes. A smattering of what looked to be real hair covered the crown of the head while the body was comically tiny by comparison and was dressed in a real baby's romper suit.

'The eyes follow you,' Jim leaned in to whisper.

'It is horrific.' Shelly shook her head. How would they ever make this look not completely frightening never mind actually good?

'I know what you're thinking.' Amy appeared at the door laden with balloons, decorations and a pink and blue baseball bat. 'Believe me, this piñata was the best of a bad lot among the gender-reveal options. They had another hideous creation – a papier mâché giant pregnant woman for the dad-to-be to jump out of dressed as a baby. They even had these poor live animals on offer to chew through things with pink or blue slime inside. Crazy shit.' Amy shook her head.

'But, like, we're supposed to beat this fake baby with a bat?' Shelly was dubious. It felt like a viral disaster waiting to happen.

'Hmmm, yeah or rip it apart with your bare hands, I guess?' Amy was distracted. 'Jim, the flower arch guys are at the gate. Will you show them to the nursery, please? Maybe we could let Georgie do it – it'd be like a funny sibling gag.'

'Yeah, that'd definitely be better,' Shelly agreed. 'So, what time are guests arriving? Who's even coming? I'm sorry, I've been so checked out of the planning of this. Pregnancy has really overtaken me. I don't know how I'd be coping if @_____ was still lurking around. I am so glad that's not hanging over me anymore. I can't believe how she completely stopped all communication after that one post pushing back. It's been such a relief.'

'It's amazing,' Amy agreed. 'Now, I need you up and in full make-up and wardrobe. The cast'll be here any minute.'

'"The cast"?'

'The cast, Shelly. When you greenlight a sponcon proposal two days before your due date, I have to get creative. I couldn't guarantee numbers for real guests at such short notice.'

'It's not two days, Amy. I've two *weeks* to go … but okay, point taken. Are Ali, Polly and Hazel coming? Who are the cast?'

'I used the rent-a-crowd from the *Room to Improve* parties. They're seasoned. Polly and Hazel are a yes. Unfortunately, Ali's not – Liv arranged her baby shower for this afternoon, not realising. I'll probably head over there after this to help her out.'

'Of course, right. I'll get dressed.' Shelly made her way through the hall, dodging delivery guys left and right, and headed up to her dressing room.

❖

'Bash! Bash! Bash!' the Room-to-Improvers chanted, clearly well into the gender-reveal piñata. They were raucous as Georgie whacked the baby with the bat.

'Kill it with fire,' screamed one particularly zealous crowd member.

Shelly winced. Amy, who was moving through the crowd filming, swung close. 'Don't worry, we'll mute the sound in post. It'll all be fixed in post.'

Shelly grinned. Just then the giant baby swung back on one of Georgie's swings and knocked her to the floor. Shelly rushed to help Georgie up.

'Yes! Revenge of the baby,' the zealous Room-to-Improver roared. 'This is way better than one of Dermo Bannon's tight-arse shindigs.'

Together Shelly and Georgie took a final swing and an explosion of blue confetti filled the room.

'Yessss, a BOY!' Jim raised his prosecco and pulled the Room-to-Improver into a warm embrace.

Through the cheers and the commotion, Shelly was the only witness to Dan's entrance. He took in the scene, clearly fuming, turned and immediately stormed back out.

Ugh, dammit. She'd better go soothe whatever toys-out-of-pram tantrum he was about to have. She mouthed 'Be right back' to Amy, who was taking snaps of Georgie kicking up the confetti.

Shelly marched out the front door and took the path down the side of the house to Dan's place. He was at the door fumbling with the lock.

'Hey.' Shelly kept her tone light.

'Hey, yourself.' He didn't turn around.

'Why are you mad? You knew we were having a boy. I told you weeks ago when you asked me.'

'Why am I mad?' He sighed and turned to face her. He leaned against the front door. 'You're taking the piss. You're there still peddling our kids for the 'gram and, Shelly' – he sighed – 'I'm gonna have to take legal action because I don't want them to grow up and fucking hate us.'

'Will you please calm down. This is a little light sponcon, involving a child who isn't even born yet.'

'Listen to yourself, Shelly. Look, I'm going now. I need to grab some files. My flight's in two hours. Shelly, I mean it about the kids. I'm their parent too and you're abusing their privacy. People know Georgie's face. When I am out in public with her, I see people *recognising* her.'

Shelly hated when he brought up the ethics of using the kids for her work. Mainly because she didn't entirely disagree with him. But what option did she have?

'Well, if you weren't pushing the house sale, I wouldn't be under so much pressure to sell sponcon.' She knew she sounded defensive.

'What pressure, Shelly? I haven't been at you about it at all. And I should be. I'm the one living in a shed for months.'

'You don't have to be "at me". Bringing random women back

is pressure enough to get you out of here. And humiliating me around town with these women when I haven't even announced our separation yet.'

Things were getting heated and Shelly just wasn't feeling up to it. Their every interaction had become so fraught.

'Listen,' she continued, trying to calm down – she was feeling achy and drained from the conversation – 'I'm prepared to make an offer for your share of the house. A lump sum – I think I can get €100K together to start with – and then monthly instalments of €3,000 until the next lump sum. My parents are going to rent their place out and we'll pay off your share of the house as quickly as we can. This is a solid plan, Dan. We can't go on like this, angry and hostile. You're right, you need to move on and so do I. And this way, Georgie and this lil guy will have their grandparents around all the time. I'll sign the agreement regarding the kids, I promise. I just don't want to lose our home.'

Dan seemed to consider this offer. Finally, he relented, and his expression softened. 'Put something down on paper with your solicitor and we'll get it ironed out. I'm going to rent anyway before I commit to another mortgage. If I can even get one, I'm nearly forty! The bank'll probably say I'm a dud investment. You'd agree no doubt.'

'You were never a dud investment. Look at Georgie and whoever this guy's going to be, he'll be magic.' Shelly sighed sadly. 'Go get your flight, I need to go lie down for ever. I'm wrecked.'

✤

The gender-reveal party had more or less wrapped when Shelly came back inside. She did a few promo videos about the full range of products available from ArtOfTheReveal.ie and then, once Sandra had agreed to watch Georgie, she slipped upstairs and gratefully burrowed beneath her crisp sheets. *I've got to nap while I can*. She rubbed her belly, which was taut and crampy, probably from tiredness. *At least Dan's being receptive about the house*, she thought as she drifted off to sleep.

Shelly was dreaming. She was in labour and the Room-to-Improve guy was cheering her on. The scene changed and Shelly rushed from room to room searching for her phone. *The baby's coming and I need to capture it for the 'gram.* Just then she spied a figure holding her phone. Their face was obscured by a giant ring light. 'Don't worry, I'm always watching,' they said and snapped a photo. Shelly howled in pain and seemed to feel the click of the picture being taken way down in her pelvis.

'Shelly? Shelly?' Shelly's eyes popped open. Sandra was shaking her. 'You were moaning in your sleep. Are you OK?

It took a few moments for Shelly to register that the pain from the dream was still roiling low down in her abdomen. Also, the bed was drenched.

Groggily she clenched her fists and curled into a ball until the contraction passed.

'Mam, my waters have gone.'

Chapter 28

'Good morning, Insta-bitches.' Ali rubbed sleep from her eyes blearily as she posted stories from her bed. 'In an unprecedented move, Liv is throwing me a baby shower today. Now, Liv usually hates ... pretty much everything, but I think she feels sorry for me since I have been continually fucking up my life for the last nine months so I cannot wait to see what she's come up with. Expect intensely cynical vibes in place of the usually cutesy stuff.'

Ali checked the video and dragged a couple of different filters across the screen to try to smooth her skin and brighten up the slightly dank-looking sheets of the bed. The filters made her look less blotchy for sure but equally, Ali thought, *why bother?*

Of course I'm blotchy. I'm clearly just awake with no make-up on and Sudocrem on my spots. I've just finished a run of my hit one-woman show. I'm a gazillion years pregnant. Why wouldn't I be blotchy? Why am I adding to this bullshit idea of perfection? Why do I want some other girl to watch this and feel shit because she doesn't look like my filtered face first thing in the morning? Ali added a baby shower sticker to the video and posted it unfiltered.

Shit, it's not first thing in the morning, though, she suddenly realised. It was nearly noon and people would be arriving in less than an hour to toast the baby and aggressively fondle the bump.

Ali searched for something stretchy and not too depressing to wear for the party. She pulled on a jersey leopard print skirt, her Docs and an *Alien* tee shirt. Smoothing it down, the sight of Xenomorph jolted her briefly back to the Punto and Liv's comment about Ali's life being a sci-fi horror movie as opposed to a romcom. It had been three weeks since the wedding and Sam had reverted to perfunctory responses in the WhatsApp, clearly still stinging from Ali's suggestion that they date. He had shown up at *My So-Called Best Life* but his ducking out right before the end did not seem promising.

If her life was a romcom, this would be the final frustrating 'will they, won't they?' before the big grand-gesture finale. Going by Sam's one-word messages, however, he was definitely not planning on showing up to serenade her with a boombox or channelling any other iconic romcom moments.

She snapped her outfit in the mirror a couple of times and then uploaded the best shot to Insta before heading down the hall to the kitchen. A few months ago, the #OOTD would've been a laborious exercise in editing and adjusting in FaceFix lest anyone actually saw that she was a real person with cellulite. Now she couldn't summon the will to care. It was incredibly liberating. She flicked through the morning's Stories, stopping to allow @PollysFewBits to play through. Ali'd felt deeply conflicted about not telling Shelly the truth about Polly, but she'd given her word. Instead, she'd just tried to be as reassuring as possible in their now frequent WhatsApps.

And Polly did seem to have totally backed off from Shelly's DMs and Insta in general. Ali'd felt reassured that she had been taking a break but here, she could see, were a couple of new Stories. Each was white type on a black background. The kind of cryptic epitaphs designed to pique a follower's interest in whatever undisclosed beef was going on behind the scenes. Ali didn't like the tone.

Let people underestimate you, that way they'll never know for sure what you are capable of.

Followed by:

Go ahead, underestimate me. You won't be the first. You won't be the last. But you will be wrong.

'Good morning!' Liv was cutting up an array of tiny sandwiches as Ali walked in.

'Hey.' Ali dropped the phone on the table and swooped on a teeny cucumber sandwich. 'These are adorable, yum.'

'You may eat one of each thing and no more,' said Liv primly, knowing Ali's propensity for devouring miniature savouries. 'The guests will be coming soon.'

'Can't wait.' Ali waddle-ambled to the kettle and began making coffee. 'Where's lover-girl?'

'She's working till later but will be here for the movie, hopefully.'

'Excellent. Who else did you invite?'

'I invited Mini, a couple of the school gang said they'd come, plus Emma and the production lads from the *My So-Called Best Life* crew. It'll be intimate but fun. Also, Nella insisted on coming so, whatever you do, do not get into a conversational hostage situation with her. She's dying to truth-bomb you about childbirth.'

❧

After a few rousing games of Pin the Episiotomy on the Vagina and a piñata that sprayed black confetti everywhere – Liv insisted that there was too much emphasis on the *Gender* Reveals and that we needed more *Sociopath* Reveals – everyone filled their plates at the crisp buffet and settled in to watch *We Need to Talk About Kevin* or, as Mini pronounced it, 'the most accurate portrayal of the anxiety and anguish of late capitalist motherhood ever committed to celluloid'.

Ali couldn't help but notice that Erasmus was in attendance as Mini's plus one and was waiting for the right moment to corner him and pummel him for answers. Her phone buzzed. It was Liv texting from across the room.

Are they dating?

'*I am actually scared to contemplate it,*' Ali wrote back.

A commotion in the hall interrupted the exchange and Ali hopped up to find Amy grappling with the Sociopath Reveal Piñata, having just let herself in.

'Hey, happy baby shower! What is all the black confetti?' Amy was kicking her way through it.

'Don't ask! My baby is apparently going to be a psychopath with persistent antisocial behaviour. You got here in time. Liv thought you mightn't make the movie.'

'Yeah, you won't believe it! Shelly is in labour right now!'

'No way.' Ali whistled. 'That's early, right?'

'Just a couple of weeks but of course Dan has just boarded a plane and no one can reach him.' Amy rolled her eyes. 'Her mum and dad have gone in with her. TG, I was terrified she was going to hit me up for the hand-holding shit. I've a very weak stomach – it'd be way too much.'

'So, where's Georgie?'

'Polly offered to watch her. I've just left them playing "salon". Poor Polly. She's starved for a girl baby … What?' Amy spied Ali's horror at this. 'What's wrong?'

'Polly's got Georgie?' Ali whimpered.

'Yeah … ?'

'She can't …' Ali scrambled for something to say that wouldn't dob Polly in entirely '… She can't be alone with her. We have to go over and help her.'

'Do we? She's grand, Ali. She has two kids herself. She knows what's up.'

Ali whipped around and kicked the piñata detritus out of her way to grab her jacket.

'Get Liv. I'll start the car.' She hurried out the door, leaving Amy no more time to question her.

❖

Approaching the Devine compound, Ali had a sick feeling in her stomach. Since her outburst, Polly hadn't been seen at a single CatAnon meeting, nor at any of the Insta-mum outings. Ali just needed to get inside the house and see that everything was OK.

'I still don't understand this complete overreaction,' Amy insisted from the back seat.

'Is it pregnancy anxiety, Ali?' Liv implored.

'Yeah, maybe it is. Humour me. I just want to make sure they're all right.' Ali didn't want to betray Polly, not until she knew there was definitely something up anyway.

They approached the large gates and Amy keyed in the code. Ali swung into the drive and parked the car haphazardly. They hurried to the door, with Amy looking around puzzled. 'I think her car's gone,' she said as she let them into the house.

Inside, all seemed quiet. Too quiet.

'Polly? Georgie?' Ali walked through to the kitchen extension. Georgie's toys were scattered across the table but nothing seemed off. There was, thank God, no sign of a struggle.

'Ali?' Amy called from upstairs. 'Ali? Come up. This is a bit weird.'

Up two flights of stairs, Ali arrived panting at a room full to bursting with clothes and cosmetics and a professional studio lighting rig. She recognised it as the SHELLY dressing room/office. Apart from some clothes scattered on the floor, nothing looked out of place.

Liv was marvelling, stunned at the sheer volume of brand-new products on the various shelves. 'She only has one face, like. There aren't enough hours in a lifetime to put all this crap on.'

'Ha,' Amy barked. 'This is only the stuff in circulation. There's more in storage and the guest room's full to the brim with swag. But listen, this seems really off.' She toed the clothes on the floor with her boot. 'I am positive this is what Polly was wearing when she arrived earlier and I know for a fact this was Georgie's #OOTD – it was a bit of sponcon.' Amy held out her phone with the @GeorgieDevine feed displayed. There was Georgie mugging in head-to-toe floral.

Can't wait to meet my new baby brother today! I'll be wearing my fave new #OOTD. I love the new florals campaign by @KidsByKatlyn, they're the perfect clothes to go see my mamma in the hospital later. #ad #spon #kidswear #coolgirls

'So, Polly changed them both into new outfits?' Liv was absent-mindedly running a jade roller over her face. 'Weird.'

'We have to find them.' Ali tore back downstairs to the second floor on the off chance they were, in fact, doing something perfectly innocent in one of the other rooms she hadn't checked.

I should've told Shelly, her thoughts raced as she ducked into each room off the landing. *Fuck anonymity. What if Georgie's in danger?*

'Ali, please calm down.' Liv jogged down behind her. 'You're about to pop, don't stress yourself into labour prematurely.'

'Yeah.' Amy joined them on the landing. 'I mean, the outfit change seems weird but you never know, Georgie could've insisted. She's like that. So demanding.' Amy turned to Liv and added, 'She's a complete melt, to be honest. We're never having kids.'

'You don't understand. I know stuff about Polly,' Ali said quietly.

At this Amy snapped her attention back to Ali.

'What stuff?'

'She is @_____.'

Amy's eyes widened.

'What does that mean? At underscore underscore underscore?!' Liv was confused.

'It means Polly's been stalking and harassing Shelly for months,' Ali explained. 'I only found out a few weeks ago, Amy, I swear. And I would've told you and Shelly, but it was at CatAnon and I felt like I couldn't say. It's against the rules.'

'Oh Jaysus-fuck,' Amy moaned. Ali had never seen her anything other than completely unruffled – this reaction was making Ali feel even worse. '@_____ is a fucking nutjob, Ali. If it *is* Polly, it means that she has broken into the house at night to mess with Shelly. God knows what she is capable of.'

'I know, why do you think I dragged us all over here? I should've told Shelly. I just felt torn.'

'OK, both of you chill your tits.' Liv tried to soothe them. 'We will sort this. Like, no offence to you two and your industry, but she's an Instagram stalker. I'm sure Georgie's not in danger. Polly or Underscore-whatever is probably just off somewhere tryna get some content for the 'gram or something.'

Ali glared at Liv.

'Right,' Amy snapped. 'I'll call our Garda contact and get a plan together. Ali, obviously I don't need to say this but nothing on the 'gram about what you're doing. I know Shelly's dilating right now but if she gets the epidural she'll probably be right back on the phone. We can't have her see a whiff of this.'

'Of course, I wouldn't be 'gramming how I let an insane stalker steal my friend's child.' Ali was outraged.

'Well.' Amy shrugged. 'It'd deffo get a lot of eyes on it is all I'm saying.'

Amy returned to the office to make her calls and Ali and Liv headed downstairs.

'Do you think she means it about no kids?' Liv looked concerned.

'Let's just find this real kid before we start concerning ourselves with your hypothetical ones, please.' Ali flung herself unhappily on one of the many mink-grey couches down in the kitchen. This was all her fault. She pulled out her phone and automatically opened Insta – it was like a nervous tic.

'*Under the Influence* with Jenny is doing an Insta LIVE,' she reported.

'I understand the words but have no idea what that sentence means.' Liv plonked down beside her to look at the phone.

It was Jenny in the passenger seat of a car that seemed to be travelling at speed down the M50.

'We are sharing updates as and when we're getting them but it seems that police are in pursuit of a high profile Instagrammer who was initially detained in the car park of Bellissimo's Beauty Salon in Malahide when she was spotted trying to load an unwilling child into the boot of her car. She managed to evade capture and flee with the child. Police have caught up with her and are imploring her to surrender to authorities.'

'Shit, I'll get Amy.' Liv hopped up and pounded up the stairs.

Ali could see the comments streaming in at the bottom of the screen.

@PoppyLovesTheGoss: My cousin works in Bellissimo's and she's confirmed it's @PollysFewBits. Appara she was in there with Georgie Devine trying to get the Mama-Daughter Special when the little girl freaked saying she wasn't her mother and that she'd stolen her.

@ModernMaven: No fucking way. Madness. She's always seemed disappointed that she only had boys. No spa days with the wee fellas. Poor kids to be dragged into this.

@Jenzer2000: Is Georgie still in the boot of the car?

@PoppyLovesTheGoss: @Jenzer2000 no, don't think so. Under the Influence got closer a while back and it looked like Georgie was in the car seat behind Polly. Front-facing though, I can't believe these parents with their front-facing car seats. ☹

@ModernMaven: Omg gal, just went over to @PollysFewBits and she is fucking on there shiteing on about how she's taken her little princess off for a #PamperDay. The child looks terrified. This is Polly's nervy b happening in realtime.

Ali switched hurriedly to Polly's Insta as Amy and Liv rushed back in.

'The guards are already all over it, TG,' Amy panted. 'They've got some negotiator en route to try to talk her down.'

'She's bloody 'gramming everything,' Ali whimpered. 'What is happening?'

She held the phone out so Liv and Amy could sit and watch.

The @PollysFewBits LIVE was rolling. It showed Polly driving and smiling maniacally while, beyond her left shoulder, Georgie was trying to bravely answer Polly's inane questions through the silent tears streaming down her cheeks. From the angle, Polly had the phone in a holder on the dash, but it was clear that she was driving erratically.

'Aren't we having the best mama-daughter bonding day? We're even TWINNING!!!!! Do you love spending time with Mama, sweetie pumpkin pie?'

'Ye … yes, Polly,' Georgie gasped.

Polly whipped around to the back seat. 'What did you just call me???'

'I … mean … Mama. I love spending time with you, Mama.' Georgie's tiny voice was cracking with fear.

'Oh my God. I can't watch this.' Liv looked stricken. 'We need to turn this off. It's exploitative. She's clearly having an episode. Fuck, they have to get that child out of the car. What are all these fuckers saying?' Liv indicated the bottom of the screen, where more comments were flying.

@PennysFromHeaven: This is the best thing to happen to Sunday in the history of for ever. 🫳 🗑️

@HelenMellon: Oh my God she is unhinged. Can't. Look. Away. 😬

Meanwhile, Polly had fixed her mask of manic cheeriness back over the momentary annoyance.

'Sweetie, oh my goodness,' she squealed in a syrupy voice. 'There's over three hundred thousand people watching our #MamaDaughterPamperDay! Bet those cunts at Bellissimo's wish they hadn't made such a fuss now?'

'Yes, Mama,' Georgie whispered.

On Amy's phone, from the *Under the Influence* LIVE they could see the car swerving dangerously.

'This is car crash stuff about to become a real goddamn car crash.' Liv buried her face in her hands.

'I have to do something.' Ali stood and began to pace.

'I'm not sure there's anything you can do,' Amy said sadly. 'The guards are on their way. They have to handle this. I'm gonna call Shelly's parents to update them. They have to keep this from her.' Amy slipped out of the kitchen.

The schoolgirls WhatsApp group was hopping with the breaking scandal. Ali couldn't bear to look at any of the messages. She knew they'd all be gleeful or sanctimonious. Everyone on social media talked about the importance of 'mental health' but no one wanted to know about 'mental illness', which was exactly what they were all making a spectacle of with their views and shares and comments.

She X'd out of the Insta app and called Polly's number. Presumably a million people were trying to call her at this moment, but Ali knew this was not her main phone. How many people had the number to what she'd called her 'batphone'? Ali had to try something. She dialled the number Polly had given her at the first CatAnon.

Incredibly the phone didn't ring for long.

'Ali!!!!!' Polly's voice was shrill and overly jolly. 'If it isn't the little influencer who could.'

'Polly!' *Shite.* Ali had not anticipated her answering and had given no thought whatsoever to what to say should she actually pick up. 'Polly, it's so great to hear from you ...' Ali flailed for something to say. 'Are you going to CatAnon later?'

'I dunno. I'm pretty tied up today, Ali. I'm doing an Insta LIVE right now.'

'Oh, are you?'

'Yep, three hundred thousand people and counting are watching,' Polly said with relish. 'That's the appeal of Mama-Daughter content on Insta. Do you think all these people would be watching me bring the lads to Gaelic? No way, José. Not glam or cutesy enough. But if you can breed a fucking little mini-me to twin with, everyone eats that shit up. You better hope that bump you've got is a little girl – a little boy would kill your brand,' she spat with venom.

Liv, who was following Polly's side of the conversation on Insta, looked utterly baffled.

'So, Polly, could you do me a favour? Will you pull over? It's just ... I have something to tell you. And I'm really nervous telling you this big, exciting news while you're driving.'

'What are you on about?' Liv hissed.

'I dunno,' Ali said, covering the phone. 'Everyone is mad for a bit of "exciting news" on the 'gram. I'm breadcrumbing her.'

'Exciting news?' Polly sounded suddenly engaged. 'Exciting news relating to me?'

'Yep, it's really big, Polly. I was just talking to an agency that represents influencers and they said something I think you're going to want to be sitting down to hear.'

'Oh my gawd!!!!! Do they want to rep me? None of the fucking agents have ever come neeeeear me,' Polly squealed.

'I can't say until you pull over, Polly, seriously. It's too big. I can't risk you crashing with the excitement.'

'It's mother-fucking-working!' Liv was shout-whispering and holding out the phone to show Polly indicating, carefully pulling over to the hard shoulder and popping her hazards on.

'OK, Ali. I'm stopped. Spit it out!!!! I can't take the suspense.'

Ali paused, watching as three Garda cars pulled up behind Polly with several guards in high vis jackets spilling out and carefully approaching her.

'Madam?' Ali could hear the one closest on her end of the call. 'Madam, kindly hand me the phone and step out of the vehicle.'

'Officer, I'm on a very important call,' Ali heard Polly say as Georgie started screaming in the back seat.

'She's not my muma. She stole me.'

The line went dead and Ali heaved a grateful sigh of relief as Liv hugged her.

'You genius! I'll let Amy know.'

Ali sank back onto the sofa and texted Polly.

I'm sorry for tricking you, there's no exciting news, Polly. Hope you get the help you need.

Chapter 29

Shelly lay on the bed in her private room, dark only for the bedside lamp and the room diffuser she'd brought from home. She gazed in elated disbelief at the new baby wriggling beside her. She was alone with him for the first time since his birth four hours earlier. Sandra had slipped out for another frantic whispered phone call. She'd been antsy and distracted all afternoon. Presumably Dan was in constant communication – it had not been a part of the plan for her to give birth while he was at the conference in London. She knew he was probably in Heathrow right at this very moment trying to hijack a plane to get back.

Though, honestly, it was, Shelly realised, something of a relief that he wasn't there. She couldn't imagine doing the whole wild, frightening, beautiful mess of birth with him. Not anymore. They were more like strangers now and frankly she couldn't bear the thought of being so vulnerable in front of him.

She ran her fingertip softly around the baby's face.

'Hello you!' she murmured, her lips pressed to his temple. *Oh my God, that smell. If you could bottle it …*

The birth itself had been much better than she'd expected. Sandra, despite her intermittent phone calls to Dan, had been a very comforting and soothing presence. It made Shelly feel impossibly young to have her mother there with her, encouraging her to breathe and cheering her on during the pushing.

'What will we call you, my sweet baby?'

He didn't so much as sigh in response. Four hours old and he barely seemed to realise that he had indeed been born. Since his initial upset at being wrenched from her, he had been sleeping. For the first time since groggily waking from her nap to the pains of birth, Shelly groped for her phone in the bag beside the bed. She was still moving gingerly, though no episiotomy this time, thank God.

She snapped a picture of the baby and herself looking wrung out but delighted. There were hundreds of notifications on her Insta, but she couldn't face taking so much as a glance and bursting her new-baby bubble. She shared the pic with Amy along with a dozen heart emojis.

Sandra slipped in the door quietly. 'Ah, I was hoping you'd be getting some sleep. Wait.' Sandra's eyes widened. 'Have you been on the phone?' She rushed forward and snatched the device from Shelly's hand.

'Jesus! What's wrong? I was just taking a picture.'

Her mother scrutinised her, looking worried and sceptical.

'What did you see?'

'Nothing.' Shelly felt a spike of fear puncture the momentary oasis of calm she'd been revelling in just moments before. 'What is it? What's happened?'

'Nothing's happened. I just want you to be in this moment with your baby and not online.' Sandra was brusque.

'Mam! That's horrible. Of course I wouldn't be on the internet at a time like this.' Shelly could feel her mood flipping abruptly. Hormones. 'Why are you being like this?'

'I'm not being like anything. I just want you to get a proper rest, that's all.'

She's being weird. Shelly felt a stab of anxiety. What is she so tense about? Luckily, the midwives came around shortly after to kick out visitors. Shelly needed a break from Sandra's strange edginess.

Sandra was clearly reluctant to leave. 'Don't stay up now, Shelly.' She turned to the midwife. 'Make sure she rests. No internet – she needs to relax.'

'No probs, Mammy, I'll be keeping an eye on her,' the midwife promised, smiling.

'I'm grand, Mam! Nighty-night. I'll see you tomorrow. You need to get some rest too.' Shelly blew her a kiss.

As soon as she was certain Sandra must have left the building, Shelly scrambled for the phone. Her mam was acting way too crazy for there *not* to be something brewing online that she was worrying about her seeing, but what now?

She flicked through her phone rapidly searching for any whiff of scandal. It took about two seconds to find the cause of Sandra's unease.

'Influencer Goes Postal on M50 with Kidnapped Child'.

A wave of nausea crashed over her. A smiling picture of Polly with her children's faces blurred out was the lead image under the headline.

Scrolling quickly through the article, Shelly felt as though every scrap of oxygen had been sucked from the tiny room. Every paragraph revealed a new level of anguish. Georgie being stuffed into the back of Polly's car? A high-speed chase on the M50? An Insta LIVE of the whole bloody thing?

Shelly struggled to breath. *Oh my God. All day I've been here in this baby bubble while Georgie must have been terrified.* She started crying hysterically and fumbled to dial her mother.

When Sandra answered, Shelly could barely get a full sentence together and Sandra didn't need her to.

'I'm coming back, darling. I'll be right there. Stay calm. Georgie is fine. Everything is fine.'

Shelly could only muster a strangled sob in reply. Incredibly the baby slept on while Shelly wept and tortured herself with clips of Polly's deranged spree on her phone.

The one relief was that in the media reports Georgie's identity was being protected but it was clear that everyone on the internet knew exactly who had allowed her child to be kidnapped.

Sandra slipped back in the door, clearly fending off the ire of a midwife intent on enforcing the ward's visiting hours.

'My daughter is very distressed.' She shoved the door closed decisively behind her before rushing to put her arms around Shelly. 'Oh pet, please don't cry. Everything is fine now. Georgie is fine now. We just didn't want to upset you in the middle of the birth. Georgie is with your dad, Dan will be landing shortly and I'm going home to them. Everyone is safe.'

'Mam.' Shelly held her mother's gaze. 'I have to go with you. I have to hold her. She must've been so frightened.'

Shelly began to ease herself off the bed. Sandra looked uncertain but surely her mam knew there would be no arguing with her on this.

An hour later and after jumping through several logistical hoops to sign Baby Devine out of the hospital early, Shelly and her mum were sitting tensely in a taxi back to the house.

It was nearly 11 p.m. and the streets were deserted. Shelly had given the baby a feed before they left the hospital, but it seemed as if he had still not woken up to life quite yet. He had gone straight back to sleep once they'd bundled him up in the car seat.

As they came through the door into the warm house, Jim dashed out to the hall and crushed Shelly in a hug.

'My darling girl! I heard you were wonderful.'

Over his shoulder, Shelly could see Amy, Ali and Ali's roommate Liv hovering awkwardly. She didn't even bother asking what they were doing there.

'Where's Georgie?'

'I just this second carried her up to bed. Wired.' Jim grinned. 'You'd swear being almost kidnapped was the best day of her life.'

'Dad, Jesus.' Shelly could feel tears overcoming her again as she gingerly hurried up the stairs – she was tender from the birth. She tried to calm her breathing outside Georgie's room, then she tiptoed in and carefully crouched by her sleeping daughter, burying her face in her warm, familiar smell. The relief of holding her after reading the accounts of her hideous ordeal. Shelly stayed like that for a while until she realised her own tears were making a damp patch on the little girl's pillow.

Chapter 30

The fallout from Polly's M50 meltdown was more far reaching than any Insta-scandal ever before. The media was addicted to the bizarre story and all week the internet had been awash with updates and hot takes that Ali felt certain would surely herald an implosion of the Irish Insta-sphere, yet @HolisticHazel was intent on going ahead with W Y N D festival.

'I don't think you should go, Ali. It's too close to your due date. Where is it on anyway?' Liv had asked that morning as Ali packed a final few bits and downed some coffee in the kitchen.

'It's on some uninhabited island off the west coast.' Ali had sighed. 'Look, I know it's close, but I feel totally fine. Vadge-mageddon is four weeks away and this thing is showing no sign of budging plus the appearance fee is whopper. Anyway, we need this, it's the last time I'll be making any bank for potentially months and we still haven't bought the bloody travel-system yoke.'

'Oh yeah.' Liv scrambled for her phone. 'I've added some new ones to the spreadsheet for you to look at.'

'It's so bizarre that you've become the gear nerd for this baby.' Ali grinned.

'Well, someone had to.' Liv sniffed.

'Well, I'm bringing in the money and cooking the bloody thing. Now I will be gone for less than forty-eight hours, you don't have to worry. The influencers don't have to stay for the whole thing, we just show up to add a bit of prestige, Hazel says.'

'I'm worried about the world when a bunch of women talking to themselves in their phones constitutes prestige.' Liv slumped bleakly at the kitchen table. She pulled up the W Y N D hashtag.

@HolisticHazel had posted a video of herself perched, hair streaming behind her, on the prow of a boat speeding towards an outcrop of rocks at dawn. Beyond, on a sliver of white, sandy beach, dancers twirled fire poi and drums were beating.

Liv scrolled on. Selfie after selfie of festival attendees, young women in mirrored sunnies, tie-dyed bikinis and Docs making the peace sign in Athlone services. #FestivalBound #WYND #BestFest #Chillax #BestLife.

More pics showed fire pits surrounded by cabanas and hammocks, with pristine white villas grouped along dramatic cliff paths.

'This is unreal,' Liv breathed.

'Yeah, they've done so much since the launch meeting. In only two, three months, like? Unbelievable.'

'What was here? Before, I mean? How did Hazel get the permits and the planning? There's a vintage carousel on the beach. Incredible! You sure, Hazel isn't spoofing and these aren't Coachella shots?'

Ali peered at Liv's phone. 'Well, the tagline is "Beyond the bounds of the impossible lies ... W Y N D"!' Ali grinned. 'Sure, I'd say they've been generously touched up. I mean, it looks practically tropical. But even if it pisses rain, it's gonna be class. You don't know how badly I want to lie down and be pampered. I am so over being pregnant. I just wish you were coming.'

'Well, it's not often Amy gets unexpected time off, so with Shelly on early mat leave we figured, ya know, make hay and all that. We're only going to Kildare. Besides, once the baby comes, we won't be going anywhere for ages.' Liv looked apologetic.

'Don't worry, I fully get it. She's your laaa-day.' Ali segued into a rendition of the Styx song. 'I get it. It's like *your* babymoon. Soak it up. In another few weeks, it's gonna be baby ka-boom.'

❖

'So has she been arrested or what?'

'I dunno, it's not like she got very far with the kid—'

'Yeah, but just because you're crap at kidnapping doesn't mean you should get let off.'

'Still, it'd be obvious to any judge or jury that she wasn't in her right mind. That Insta LIVE was demented.'

'Did you hear that she was stalking Shelly?'

'Shut up! NO! But they're like "Insta-mum BFFs 4eva".'

'Yup. Appara that post Shell-Belle did a while ago about the troll was actually about PollysFewBits herself.'

'Juice.'

Ali slid lower down in her seat to hide from the other gals on the small plane chartered for W Y N D. She'd kept her hoodie up and glasses on since they'd embarked in Galway so she didn't have to chat and pose for selfies or, as it turned out, field questions about the latest Insta shitshow. Thankfully, at that moment the roar of the engines increased, preventing further gossip.

Ali turned her attention to the view from the tiny oval window to her right. The wing of the plane dipped and, through the low grey clouds, she got her first glimpse of Inis Brí. From this angle, it looked like an uninviting shard of rock rising from the Atlantic. Smoke billowed ominously from various parts of the island.

Must be the fire pits, thought Ali. At 4 p.m., their plane was one of the last to arrive on the island for the day. She searched the #WYND hashtag on Instagram to see how things were unfolding but the latest posts were hours old. Weird that nobody was updating. As the plane banked towards the island, Ali could see the strip of tarmac that constituted the runway. From up here, it looked to be the only road on the island, but that couldn't be right, could it? How would they have built the festival stages and accommodation without roads? As they flew lower, aiming for the runway, Ali could see bonfires on the beach and crowds dancing below.

Or were they waving? Ali pressed her face against the window, but the beach was already out of sight and the runway was rising to meet them.

Ali rubbed her belly. She'd been feeling crampy low in her abdomen on and off for a week, but the last time she was at the hospital, they'd said it was just Braxton Hicks, practice contractions that were common at her stage of pregnancy. They also said that first timers almost always went over their due date. *Thank God.* Ali was looking forward to slowing down for the next four weeks. With the show over and nearly all the baby prep done, she'd been toying with really just bedding in, starting from the beginning of *Law & Order: SVU* and doing the entire twenty-one seasons before the baby came. The thought of all that epic lying down time buoyed Ali as the plane bumped in to land. While she was still flying high from the rave reviews *My So-Called Best Life* had gotten, she was exhausted from the performance and the debacle with Polly. It had been a hectic few weeks. Offers from talent agents looking to represent her, offers from production companies wanting to adapt the show for TV and even a movie deal had all flooded in, but Ali was happy to wait.

She'd made a splash. She had a hit and had proved her worth to herself as much as anybody else. She had talent. She could make things happen. But all that could wait. The baby would be her main focus for at least the next six months to eighteen years. Things with Sam were still tenuous. The man could really hold a grudge. His continued standoffishness would be impressive if it wasn't so devastating. Ali kept thinking back to before the show when they'd been so close to getting their shit together. Yeah, the sex had been feral but even so, it was a reminder, however slapstick, of what she'd had with Sam. Of how close she'd come to getting it back. They were texting, of course, but each interaction was crushingly polite and it didn't feel like them anymore.

'Why are we just driving around?' brayed one of the girls who had been dishing on Polly at the back of the plane.

Ali sat up a little straighter. The girl was right. They seemed to be taxiing up and down the same barren stretch of tarmac. Weird.

'Excuse me, sir?' One of the group at the back broke off to approach the pilot, who was only separated from the rest of the plane by a beaded curtain. 'Excuse me, why are we just driving around?'

The pilot tried to ignore her, but she persisted.

'Excuse me? Hell-ooo? Hello? You can't just ignore me.'

Ali smirked to herself and leaned over to look out the window again. There was, she now saw, maybe two or three hundred revellers pressed against a chain-link fence running alongside the runway. So odd.

'Excuse me?' The girl was still pushing the pilot for an answer, despite his firm ignoring.

'Why are all those people out there?' Ali added.

'What people?'

Everyone peered out the right side of the plane to take in the crowd.

'Are they dancing?'

'I don't think so,' Ali said slowly. 'It looks like they're … struggling? Or being … held back?'

At last, the pilot spoke. 'Everyone get hold of your belongings. I'm coming to a stop and once I open the door, you'll have two to three minutes to disembark.'

'What the—?' Before Ali could finish her question, the plane door lowered down, doubling up as steps to the runway, and everyone around her immediately began piling out of the tiny cabin. Ali hung back to avoid getting squashed, but the pilot turned around and urged her off.

'I'm going, I'm going.' Ali shimmied through the aisle and down the steps, and was outside on the tarmac fixing her skirt when she realised the chain-link fencing had given way and a mob of people in fishnet body stockings and Native American headdresses were coming right towards her waving and yelling. The pilot yanked a lever and the cabin door closed once more. Ali backed away from the plane to avoid the onslaught of people, all of whom looked wild and desperate. One guy, wearing just leather lederhosen, tried to grab at the pilot's door but to no avail.

'Take us with you, you prick,' Lederhosen screamed. 'You can't leave us like this.'

The propellers began turning as more of the crowd started screaming and banging on the plane. Ali backed to the edge of the runway as the plane began to taxi and the crowd continued to try to thwart its takeoff.

'What is happening?' Ali asked, spotting a young guy crouched by the fence shaking.

'No one can leave,' he blurted, clawing at the ground between his feet. He peered up at her through bloodshot eyes. 'They have forsaken us,' he screamed, his pitch ascending just as the small plane took off at the other end of the island. Ali could see the mob watching, dejected.

'Can you stop screaming, please?' Ali sighed, pulling her phone out to WhatsApp any of the other influencers. Where was the transportation to the villas? Where were the villas? What was with these people? She recorded a voice note to the W Y N D influencers group chat:

'Heyyyy, I'm finally here! Just encountered some early casualties of what I can only assume is a bad batch – so everyone be warned.' She glanced back down at the boy who was silently rocking now, staring at his hands. Further along the runway the mob also seemed to have given up and was sitting down in a field by the tarmac. 'It looks like pills laced with maybe ket? I dunno. Anyway, let me know what the story is. I cannot wait to get into the hot tub and relax.'

She sent the message but could see it wasn't delivering.

'Signal's real bad on the island … it's been that way s'long as I've been here,' the boy whispered. 'That's how they'll break us, isolation, psychological warfare.'

'OK, well, best of luck with the K, don't forget to hydrate.' Ali, dragging her bag, made her way around the tattered chain-link fence.

Two men in high vis vests were heading down a dirt track about twenty feet away. 'Hey! HEY!' Ali called and hurried after them cradling her bump.

They glanced back at her and Ali slowed gratefully, but then the men, who seemed to be security, broke into a run, pegging it away from her.

'Fuck's sake,' Ali shouted, starting after them. 'Stop. Wait.'

The shorter guy glanced back again and Ali saw him catch his friend by the arm to slow him.

'Shit, dude, she's pregnant. We better stop,' Ali heard him say and they came to a halt.

'What's the deal?' Ali was winded by the time she caught up with them. 'Are you the transport team?'

At this, the short guy snorted, 'There's no "transport" on Inis Brí; there's barely food here.'

'But there's loads of good spots for selfies,' the taller guy added and they both cracked up.

'Don't forget to hashtag "W Y N D".' The short guy adopted the unmistakable Irish Insta voice. 'If there was any phone service.'

Ali took out her phone again to check on her voicenote – it still hadn't sent.

'Shit, do the phones not work?' Ali asked.

'Nothing works. Name a thing.' The short one was now clearly enjoying himself.

Ali opened her mouth to name something, but he cut across her. 'Doesn't work,' he blurted.

'Hot tubs, even?'

The two guys started laughing away again.

'Fuck you both.' Ali began storming up the dirt track to where she guessed the festival must be.

'Here, wait!' the tall guy called. 'Walk with us. I'll try to get someone with a wheelbarrow down here. The accom, if you'd call it that, is a fair walk away.' He pulled out a radio and spoke into it.

'To be honest, I've not much faith in the radio yokes either,' the other guy remarked. 'They look like Fisher-Price. This whole thing is a nightmare. I'm Liam, by the way, that's Paul.'

Ali was distracted by clouds of smoke rising ahead of them.

'What is this?'

'End of days,' Liam muttered.

'They're burning tents,' Paul supplied. 'The second they found out there was no oat milk or any other dairy-free milk substitute on the island, they lost their shit.'

Ali groaned as another cramp rippled across her belly. 'What do you mean "burning tents"?'

'Ah here, this could be our wheelbarrow now,' Paul interrupted as a cloud of dust rose up ahead. 'We'd better get you off your feet. How far along are you anyway? And why'd you come to a festival on an island when you're up the pole?'

'I'm thirty-six weeks. And I'm fine, just a bit achy but that's normal. I came to the festival because it's a wellness summit and I'm gonna be pampered for the weekend. Also, I'm making a paid appearance.'

'Shit.' Liam squinted at the dust cloud. 'That's not one of our guys.'

As the wheelbarrow drew near, they could see two wild-eyed Instahuns at the helm, pushing it through the dust and over rocks. It was filled with protein bars.

'Stop,' called Paul, stepping into their path.

To Ali's shock, the huns kept coming and mowed him right down.

'What the hell,' Ali shouted as Paul cried in agony from the ground. Liam managed to wrestle the women away from the wheelbarrow.

'She's preggers. We need this to transport her, ye demented loons,' Liam screamed. One of the huns pulled out a travel-sized Elnett and sprayed him in the face.

'Fuck you, these are the only gluten-free snacks on the whole pissing island!' The two women grabbed all the protein bars and stormed on towards the airstrip.

'I think my leg is broken,' Paul whimpered.

'My eyes! Oh my God, my eyes!' Liam staggered blindly and tripped over the wheelbarrow. 'Jesus!!!!' he screamed. 'My arm.'

Ali glared at the two of them. 'Right, into the wheelbarrow. We'd better get you to the first aid tent.'

'We are the first aid tent, luv,' Paul muttered. 'Although there was never a tent.'

'Please say you're joking.' Ali sighed.

❖

It was dark by the time Ali staggered into camp, pushing Paul in the wheelbarrow with Liam trudging alongside, holding his arm protectively.

She was wrecked. She must've walked two kilometres over uneven terrain pushing this deadweight in front of her. The trek had provided plenty of time for Paul and Liam to relate just how much W Y N D festival had descended into apocalyptic chaos in a mere six hours.

'Yer one Hazel was airlifted off the island about an hour after the first attendees began arriving. When it became clear that nothing the W Y N D promos had advertised was available on the island, people started going nuts. Lighting the relief tents on fire in protest when they discovered there were no villas and no luxury accommodation. Pretty stupid now, given no one'll have any shelter to sleep in tonight. No phone coverage meant everyone was trapped. Some people found Hazel's caravan and tipped it, but she'd already made off. And still, planes were landing and dropping off more and more people. And the pilots know it's a warzone down here but they're contracted by the festival and just wanna cash their cheque. We've been trying to raise the alarm with the Coast Guard but the range on the radios is about ten feet if the wind is with you.'

Ali couldn't believe it. Hazel's whole reputation was staked on this festival. How could she let it crash and burn like this?

'Great that all these fires are raging to light our way,' she huffed as they made their way to a large clearing. Just then, a feral hun rushed from the darkness and grabbed her wheelie bag from the wheelbarrow.

'Ah sorry, I should've mentioned the looters,' Paul winced.

Ali parked the wheelbarrow beside a hastily erected tent that seemed to be serving as an ad hoc catering solution. A young girl was rotating speared meat over a small fire and distributing Easy Singles on white bread with mayonnaise to the filthy, hollow-eyed hordes, their singed flower crowns and smeared glitter a sad mockery of the free-spirited Insta-mavens they had been just hours before.

'This is insane. All right, good luck, lads.' Ali bid them farewell and, exhausted, pushed through the crowds looking for somewhere to sit safely. *I just need to find one familiar face in this hellscape. Even Kate would do right now.* Ali could smell the meat and, even though she hadn't eaten since early that morning, it didn't appeal.

'Where did you get that lamb?' A shout cut through the darkness.

'I brought it with me.' Even from across the clearing, Ali could hear the girl's defensive tone.

'You did to feck,' the man erupted. 'I keep my sheep up in the back field and I'm short a lamb and now, here ye are, you Insta ingrates, with fresh lamb.'

Jaysus, they're butchering livestock! Ali shook her head. *They've barely been a day without food and they've gone full* Lord of the Flies.

She peered through the darkness to try to make out the farmer. Hazel had said the island was uninhabited so this guy must have got here on his own speed.

As she stood to see better, a pain deep inside gripped her and wrenched her back to the ground. 'Fuuu-uuuuck,' escaped from her mouth.

She moaned on all fours. *Shit, shit, shit.*

The pain at last receded and then ... nothing. *So weird.* She gingerly stood back up feeling more or less fine again. *Uh-oh.* She didn't even want to entertain the possibility that labour was starting. Her due date was four weeks away and all the midwives had said she could basically take it that she'd six weeks to go because she'd go over. She glanced at the chaos around her. If there was a worse place to give birth, she couldn't imagine it. To be on the safe side, she started the timer on her useless phone in case she got another bad pain – she couldn't bring herself to call it a contraction – and ploughed into the crowd looking for the farmer. She had to get off this godforsaken rock.

Just then she heard her name.

'Ali? Ali Jones?' Ali whipped around to see Blake Jordan in denim short shorts and a paisley shirt rushing out of the trees to her right with his hairless Sphynx cat, Julia Roberts, trotting daintily on a diamanté leash beside him.

'Blake.' She raised her hand and at that moment was crippled by another monstrous pain. 'Aaaaahhhhh.' She doubled over just as Blake reached out and caught her arms. She hung off him half crouching, half squatting. 'Fucking fuuuuuuck.'

'Eh, hun? Are you in—?'

'Noooooooo,' Ali cut across him trying to ride out the pain. 'I'm not, I'm not, I'm not.' She panted, which seemed to ease the twisting, knifing pain that was radiating from the top of her belly through the small of her back and down to her knees. 'It's. Just. Practice. Contractions.' It was getting hard to speak.

'Really?' Blake looked doubtful and disgusted in equal measure.

At last the violent pain seemed to ebb and Ali could straighten up a bit. She checked the time. Only six minutes since the previous one. She tried to shrug the thought away. *It's not happening now. It's not. No one's that unlucky, Ali. They said the practice pains could be bad.* She reset the timer again to be on the safe side.

'Ali? You dilating, hun?' Blake said with a smirk, echoing the night at the Glossies WildCard launch when this whole mess had begun.

'No.' Ali was firm. 'Definitely not.'

'Good, 'cos I'd say the only worse place to push out a baby would be the deck of the bloody *Titanic*.' He pursed his lips.

Ali opted to ignore that. She felt as if she'd just been returned to her body after that attack of agony. 'When did you arrive? What the hell happened? Did you see Hazel?'

'Oh no, she was long gone by the time we were abandoned here. Dead to me. Holistic Hoe, more like. Though, I suppose I don't have the full picture just yet. Word on the dusty track is that the Ezra guy totally screwed her. He was feeding her the same bullshit we all got about how amazing it was all looking and she just never bothered her bleached hole coming out and checking on progress. So, when she landed this morning it was the first time she'd seen this dumpster fire. Appara she did have a look around to see if it was salvageable. I met a girl earlier who said the Caffeine Colonics were the only thing available, but there was an early casualty there – let's just say running water is an ESSENTIAL component of that treatment and some poor bitch was juiced up but couldn't get a rinse for love nor money. Not pretty. If we all survive this, the coverage is going to be savage. I've been filming everything. I'm going to pitch it as a doc to RTÉ. I'm calling it *From WELL to HELL. And Back.*'

'Love it!' Ali leaned closer. 'Listen, I heard a farmer giving out about someone stealing a lamb from his land. Hazel always said Inis Brí was uninhabited, so he had to have come across by boat. I lost him in the crowd, but we have got to find him and convince him to get us out of here.'

'Thank Jaysus, culchie excellence will save us—'

'Blake?' Ali grabbed at him, the surging torment having come back. He took her arms again while also managing to hold her at bay. 'Blaaaaaake.' The noises coming out of her didn't sound like she was even making them. She could see Julia Roberts at their feet looking up at her perplexed. 'Blaaa … aaaa … keee, I feel. Like. My. Ass. Is. Gonna. Ex. Plode.'

'Ali??? Hun???' Blake sounded scared. 'These are Margiela, babes.' He lifted a distressed trainer gingerly. 'Can I just stand a little further back?'

'Noooooooooo,' Ali howled and dug her nails into the flesh of his arms.

'NAILS, Aliiiiiiiiiiii!!!' Blake howled with her just as Ali felt an unmistakable crack inside her followed by a gush of fluid. Blake managed to leap clear of the deluge, but Julia Roberts wasn't so lucky.

'OH my fucking gee, JULIA ROBERTS!' Blake wailed, scooping up the cat and just as quickly dropping her, as it hit him what she was drenched in.

'I'm so sorry,' Ali gasped. The pain had receded but was immediately replaced by abject terror. 'The baby is coming, Blake.' How could this be happening?

'Mother of God.' Blake made the sign of the cross. 'You and Julia Roberts stay here. I'm going to find someone. Cross your legs or something. Oh God.'

'Please don't leave me,' Ali pleaded, feeling the pressure building and radiating down to her knees again but he'd already hurried off. She got on the ground so she wouldn't fall over. 'I'm going to shit myself,' she whimpered to the cat.

She was far enough from the clearing that none of the festival goers were in danger of tripping over her but, if Blake didn't get back quick, she felt sure the baby would erupt out of its own accord. *I don't even have a blanket or anti-bac!* The pressure was insane, but she couldn't see what was going on back there. Had she already shit herself? Thank God it was dark. She started to cry between gasping breaths. It was so terrifyingly out of control. *Don't come, baby, don't come yet.* She tried to remember anything she'd ever gleaned from *One Born Every Minute*, then she thought of the YouTube tutorial Sam had downloaded and sent to her. *Please let me have saved it to the phone.*

She waited for the current swell of agony to subside and grabbed her phone. She found the video in her downloads. *Birth: Epic How To* was the title. It opened on a man.

'Welcome to our Epic How To for giving birth. Step 1: Go to a HOSPITAL.'

'Oh fuck youuuuuuuuu,' Ali screamed as another contraction took hold.

'If you are watching this while in labour, I cannot urge you enough to *go to a hospital.*'

Ali clenched and pounded her fists through the longest contraction so far. 'AaaAAAAAggghhhh. I need to push. What do I need to do when I wanna push?' she screamed at the phone.

Finally, the pain relented but Ali didn't think she could hold out much longer. *Fuck. Fuck. Fuck.*

'You can see her too, right? It looks like she's in labour.'

With the momentary reprieve between contractions, Ali noticed a small crowd gathered off to her right.

'Yeah, I see her,' whispered one of the crowd. 'I thought I was hallucinating from the Easy Singles – my system's not up to processed food. But she is there. Can you see the cat too?'

'Oh c'mon,' Ali hissed through clenched teeth, more to herself than anyone in particular. She didn't want anyone near her right now, except a doctor.

'Ali! Ali!' Blake hurried through the crowd, phone out and filming. 'I found Sean Óg – he's the farmer.'

'Oh thank God!' Ali cried as another contraction reared up. Now whatever else happened, here was an adult with some scrap of common sense. She dug once more into the earth and howled. The crowd to the right had started up a supportive chant of 'This pussy be yankin', this pussy be yankin'.' Which was weirdly working for Ali. She couldn't hold back now: the contraction seemed to have taken over and she found she was pushing whether she wanted to or not.

'Right, let's get her to one of the caravans – they're just through these trees,' Sean Óg instructed Blake. Between them they carried her, and Ali didn't even have the will to worry about what state she was in south of the equator. She was still in their arms when the next contraction hit. She squirmed and moaned but Blake and Sean Óg held fast. They hustled her through the narrow door of the caravan and set her on the floor of the living room area.

Blake ran to the door and screamed into the crowd, who'd jogged with them from the clearing, 'Anyone out there have towels, water, anti-bac gel, Jesus, anything clean?' he implored. 'Even a tarpaulin, bring it back here. We're havin' a baby.'

The crowd cheered, clearly into the biblical turn proceedings had taken.

'Oh yeah, for God's sake get the tarpaulin, protect this divine carpet,' Ali managed to scoff right before another wall of pain hit her. 'I have to puuuuuush.' She gave Sean Óg a pleading look.

'Yeah, we'll get you set, on all fours, good girl.' He patted her flank, then Ali saw him grab two ropes he had slung over his shoulder.

'What are they?' Blake had returned, camera out and capturing everything. Ali, meanwhile, was shoving her knickers off, relieved they were black. Small mercies.

'What? My calving ropes?' He held them up for inspection. A red rope and a blue rope with adjustable loops on the end. 'They're for pulling the calf out, by its legs, like.'

Ali couldn't even summon words by this point, so she reached up and grabbed one of Blake's arms and one of Sean Óg's and bore down as hard as she could. The contractions now seemed to be working with her. Building and receding like waves, each one crashed with the force she needed to push.

Suddenly she felt an unmistakable release and peered down past the bump and between her legs.

'Its head,' she screamed. 'Whaaaaa! It's turning. What the—? It's looking at me!'

Sean Óg started to rush to the back of her but Ali instinctively reached down, just as another contraction helped ease the rest of the baby out into her arms.

'Oh my God, wild. Ali, that was WILD.' Blake turned the camera to himself. 'What I've just experienced' – he was breathless – 'that was *the* most EXTRA thing I've ever seen.'

Ali had no idea what she was doing but she put the baby, who was turning from purple to livid red just like in *One Born Every Minute*, against her chest and wrapped them together in her hoody. Euphoric, she could barely grasp what had just happened. She felt as if she was off her face as she instructed Sean Óg to tie off the cord and cut it once it went white, with Blake filming and providing commentary all the way along.

'It looks like a unicorn's mickey.' Blake peered over Sean Óg's shoulder as he hacked at the umbilical cord with a Stanley knife.

Ali laughed dreamily. 'Just keep my nips out of shot, please.'

'Seriously.' Blake was blinking away tears of emotion. 'We could make a mint on this as a reality show, Ali!!! Three huns and a baby. This is a pilot no one could pass on. Sean Óg has real charisma and you've been doing very well of late,' he told Ali generously.

Sean Óg took off his cap and leaned down to scoop up the placenta. 'Is it a boy or is it a girl, then?' he asked, cradling the afterbirth tenderly.

Ali peered down at the impossibly tiny baby flopped on her breast.

She had a cap of dark hair like Sam's and she'd be called Millie for Miles, but Ali had brought her into the world with her own bare hands and she knew all they would ever need was each other.

Afterbirth
4 weeks later

The Big Short: How Bots and a group of digital anarchists calling themselves The EYES have caused chaos in the Influencer Economy

Shelly finally opened the article on the fifth or sixth time she was sent it. Amy had sent it, Hazel had sent it, Ali, Amanda. Even her dad had sent it from the other side of the bench they were both sitting on waiting for Shelly's name to be called.

'What do you think of that hacker crowd, then?' Jim shook his head while Shelly scrolled and Dash, her rosy new baby, sucked on the bottle she was managing to administer one-handed. It was Dan's first Friday taking Georgie to the apartment he was renting in Grand Canal, just south of the city centre, and they had both agreed it would be best for Georgie to go on her own for her first stay at Daddy's new home. Dash would go soon too but it was most important for Georgie to settle into the new arrangement before adding a baby to the mix.

The story had broken the previous week and Shelly had done her level best to avoid it. Instagram was reeling in the wake of an elaborate hack that had been years in the making. In a complex cyber heist, a small group of digital anarchists who go by the name of The EYES had infiltrated the company's systems and populated the app with bots. The fallout would be catastrophic to SHELLY. Amy predicted brands would be scrapping their influencer budgets and not renewing contracts as the picture came further into focus.

'A depressing end to a strange chapter in human evolution,' the article continued. 'Like Narcissus himself, we became enthralled by our own reflections, the influencers playing to an audience that potentially wasn't really there.'

Shelly glanced up to check that Dash was still sucking contentedly. Jim would take him when Shelly was called. Her dad was a real baby guy and it was lovely seeing him spend so much time with Dash.

'Users and brands alike have professed to feeling betrayed by the revelations. "I was broadcasting intimate moments 24/7 – was anyone even watching?" one influencer, who wished to remain anonymous, told the *Guardian*.

'Influencers and indeed the ordinary users are likely to struggle to find meaning, at least during this adjustment period,' advised psychologist Dr Meghan Bryce. 'Many have been essentially *performing* their lives for years and now, there is a danger of them becoming depressed or disillusioned.'

Shelly X'd out of the article to a voicenote from Hazel. She pressed Play and put the phone to her ear, careful not to disturb Dash.

'Shelly. How are you? It was lovely catching up last week. How's little Dash getting on? I'm just messaging to wish you luck with Polly's hearing. You know I'd be there with you, but the hacks would absolutely savage me. Also, some of the legal aspects of the W Y N D fiasco are unfortunately still far from resolved – motherfucking Consumer Rights people will dine out on this for ever, never mind all the civil suits. Anyway, good luck today. I know it's all been a bit mad with the Insta revelations but I'm proposing a little Insta-mum morning next weekend. For mums recovering from this Insta trauma. I think we need to all pull together. Eleven a.m. on Saturday, kiddies welcome. Maybe we can get them to show us how to monetise TikTok.' She laughed as the voicenote ended.

Shelly contemplated this oddly muted new Hazel. She sounded cowed by the events of the previous month. She'd been pilloried for the W Y N D debacle. Ezra had embezzled a frankly terrifying sum of money from her. He had funnelled every single ticket sale and brand endorsement fee into his own account and fled. Tens of thousands Hazel thought she'd been paying to contractors to create the festival were now bankrolling his exile. He had come so highly recommended, had shown her pictures updating her on how the build was coming and she'd never thought to question it or go and see for herself. Now her only source of income appeared to be completely collapsing. The only upside in all the mayhem for Hazel was that she'd managed to dodge being exposed by Jenny's *Under the Influence* podcast. Jenny had been heavily criticised for her coverage of Polly's breakdown and *Under the Influence* had disappeared from iTunes and Spotify. It was a small mercy but one Hazel was nonetheless grateful for. 'I couldn't take another scandal at this point,' she'd confided over coffee the week before. 'Not with my whole business imploding.'

Shelly, on the other hand, felt oddly relieved. She leaned down to brush her lips against Dash's velvety little cheek; she was shattered but free.

Free from the yoke of the phone, free from the anxiety over exposing her life and family, and free to make a fresh start. She was meeting a new agent after the hearing and, while she was nervous – the woman repped only the most respected talent in the country – she was determined to impress her. It was just a preliminary chat. Dash was still so tiny, she wouldn't be rushing back to auditions straight away, but she wanted to lay the groundwork. It was time to move on from *Durty Aul' Town* and push beyond her comfort zone. Ironically, it was Ali who had inspired her with *My So-Called Best Life*. Seeing her take that risk, be vulnerable and put something new into the world: that was something Shelly had once loved about acting before she'd begun going through the motions as Imelda and acting the part of herself 24/7.

'What time are we heading in to meet yer one?' Jim eased closer along the bench and took Dash, slinging him onto his shoulder for a bit of winding.

'Four p.m. in Brooks Hotel.' Shelly tidied away the baby paraphernalia so that she'd be ready for the call from the court clerk.

It was still impossible for her to see Polly as @_____. Even though it was a matter of public record now.

Shelly felt bad for Polly. At first, sure she'd been angry but that had rapidly given way to pity. To that end, she'd decided to attend the hearing and, should Polly be found guilty today, which seemed likely, Shelly would have the opportunity to deliver a victim impact statement. Obviously, she wouldn't be condoning Polly's actions – she'd endangered Georgie and terrorised Shelly – but she was sick more than malicious and Shelly wanted to try to appeal to the judge before he or she handed down their sentence. It wasn't strictly allowed for people to reference their own personal feelings towards a defendant in such a statement but, if Shelly could just get across that Polly needed compassion not punishment, then she'd be happy with that. Poor, poor Polly. From reading the online coverage of proceedings, it seemed her family hadn't attended court even once.

'Shelly Devine?' The clerk emerged from the throng of people milling in the hall. 'The defendant has been found guilty. Would you come this way for the reading of your statement?'

❖

'Honeys, I'm home!!!!' Liv's voice from the hall was jubilant. 'Every "i" is dotted,' she called as she navigated the hall's obstacle course of Millie's travel system, rubbish awaiting transportation to the bin and the unending laundry that migrated through the house, apparently of its own accord. 'Every reference is Harvard-approved, every image is credited, the bloody thesis is out of my life. Even if it is sham-fucking-bolic, I don't care. It's over.'

In the kitchen, Ali was in a state of exhaustion so acute that the sound of someone, even Liv, in a good mood was causing her actual physical pain.

Just. Be. Calm. She. Is. Just. Excited. She. Deserves. This. Ali held Millie – as she had for every second of this stupid fucking day so far – and jigged in time to each word as she thought it.

Liv came in pulling on the complicated stretchy sling that she'd completely gotten the hang of and Ali still couldn't be bothered with.

'How is my baby?' Liv cooed, hurrying over to take Millie and slip her into the cocoon of the sling.

'She's being a little cunt today.' Ali stormed back over to the onion she'd started trying to chop at exactly 10 a.m. that morning, more than eight hours earlier.

'Ah, Ali. Don't say that! She is just a baby – she can't help it. Leave that. Amy's on her way. She's gonna bring Thai. Please go lie down. Have a shower. Just give yourself a rest for a bit. I've got her.'

Ali threw the knife and the onion in the sink and stalked out of the room, down the hall to the shower.

Why does Liv have to be so nice all the time? Millie is objectively being a cunt today. And most bloody days. Just fucking agree with me. That's all I want.

She knew that she was being a brat and that Liv was not the person to take it out on but equally … *fuck EVERYTHING.*

She ran the overhead shower, stripped off her clothes and sat in the chilly bath underneath it. She watched blood snake towards the drain between her feet as the water pounded down on her from above.

When would the blood stop? It had been a month. When would any of this feel normal? Her body felt rearranged and her whole middle section was gelatinous while her tits grew and shrank with milk throughout the day. But it was the climate inside her head that was really disturbing. She'd known – or thought she'd known – that having the baby would be a headfuck, but nothing could've prepared her for the terrifying anxiety, random bouts of rage, glimmers of exquisite joy and bottomless sadness that took turns invading her day and night.

What is wrong with me? Calling Millie a cunt, what kind of a fuck up does that? She whimpered as tears poured down her face and pooled with the milk now streaming from her breasts. The boobs were very sensitive to Ali's emotions. It was yet more Motherland strangeness. Beneath the sound of the shower, she thought she could hear Millie crying, though she was plagued by the sound of baby cries, real or imagined, day and night. She reached up to turn off the shower and strained to hear.

Nothing.

Sighing, she'd pulled herself out of the bath onto the bathmat before she noticed she hadn't introduced so much as a drop of shampoo or soap into that bleak wash.

She slipped across the hall to her room, paranoid that Millie would smell her on the wind and start demanding another feed. It was seriously annoying being the food source for another person, like being hunted by a tiny, adorable cannibal in your own home.

She sat on the bed and tried to relax. This was her few minutes to herself. *I should sleep or tidy up. Do something*, she thought as she picked up her phone to scroll through pictures of Millie from earlier that day. She really was a divine baby, if a bit demanding – though if she was a total pushover, Ali supposed, that would be boring. It was mad: when she was home alone with the baby all day, all she wanted was for someone to come and take her away for a few minutes' reprieve. But in a very irritating catch-22, anytime anyone actually did, Ali wasn't at ease until she had her back in her arms.

The phone pinged. Mini.

Erasmus and I are going to stop in after the Arts Council meeting this evening. Liv said she'd include us for dinner. How are you doing since this morning? Any naps?

Mini and Erasmus. Ali shook her head, smiling slightly, pleased with the distraction – even one as bizarre as her mother and her assistant getting together. And Mini was clearly happy. Mini was also the only one with the tolerance for in-depth analysis of Millie's non-existent sleep patterns. She messaged without fail every morning to get a breakdown of the night before. It was extremely gratifying to report Millie's impervious-to-sleep ways even if Mini said little more than how difficult it was. You just needed someone to agree with you, Ali had realised. Someone to witness the struggle and say 'Yes, it's hard.' Ali texted back:

Great, see you then. PS What's a nap? FML 😁

Ali straggled around pulling clothes from various piles on the floor and Millie's bassinet, which mocked her from the corner, having been used exclusively for laundry-storage since the baby's arrival.

'She just doesn't power off, does she?' Sam had marvelled at about 1 a.m. the night before, as they paced between rooms handing the squalling baby back and forth. He was coming over at least five nights a week, sharing the night shift and then going home at stupid-o-clock to get ready for work. Ali didn't know *how* he was managing. And *he* wasn't flying into irrational strops and calling Millie a cunt. Then again, he wasn't being battered by hormonal storms on the daily. He was being himself, though keeping his distance, and Ali tried not to think too much about what was going to happen with them. Every now and then, it felt like old times between them. If they were laughing at something Millie did or if Ali caught him looking at her in a certain way, a tentative thrill of hope would swell inside her but then he'd return to his polite standoffishness and Ali'd slump, resigned to the fact that maybe some things just couldn't be salvaged. *And maybe I'm only in love with him right now because he's a source of reliable childcare*, she mused. *If Pol Pot was willing to share the nights, I'd probably start fancying him too.*

Crying had started up in the kitchen and Ali's boobs ached in response.

She put her still-wet hair in a towel and made her way back to the fray, glancing darkly at the room beside hers that they'd lovingly prepared for Millie before she arrived and disabused them of all their rosy notions about what exactly a newborn would tolerate when it came to sleeping arrangements.

Now, it was the room where Sam occasionally slept over though this was rare. Ali suspected it was at his therapist's advice – terrible when the boy you like starts 'working on themselves'. Ali sighed, entering the kitchen and rescuing Liv from the wailing Millie.

❖

Dinner cheered Ali up no end. She fed Millie while practically inhaling her green curry.

'It's mad how nihilistic you can get when you haven't eaten in a few hours,' she remarked.

'Oh yeah,' Erasmus responded vaguely and Mini, Liv and Amy looked over expectantly, but it appeared he was done talking. Stepping from the role of Mini's full-time assistant to part-time lover had done nothing for his confidence and he still seemed terrified of Mini and everything else in life. Liv was convinced they were a dom and a sub and loved speculating on who was which.

The sound of the front door and Sam bashing into every item between it and the kitchen distracted them all from Erasmus's awkward silence.

'Hey.' He waved and stooped to kiss Millie's head, then reversed rapidly, clearly remembering what she was currently suctioned to. He straightened up and gave Ali his patented cringey thumbs up. 'I'm just gonna do the bins.'

Ali returned his thumbs up and shook her head as he turned and threw himself into the changing of the bins.

'Do you want some dinner?' Ali asked, hyper-aware that the others were all holding their breath and watching the exchange with intense interest.

'Yep, whatever's going.' He bustled back out, heaving a black sack with him.

'Can you all please be normal?' Ali hissed, when the front banged behind him. 'I get it you're all rooting for us and that's nice but, look, he's made it clear, he wants boundaries. I'm respecting that. We're co-operating.'

'Ali's right.' Amy took charge. 'We're never gonna make this work without a proper strategy ...'

'Amy!' Ali laughed in spite of her irritation and exhaustion. 'Please stop engineering everything.'

'I'm sorry.' Amy held up her hands and forked some noodles into her mouth. 'Old habits,' she mumbled.

'So' – Mini turned to her – 'what is your plan now with the Instagram revelations, Amy?' Mini was interested in Amy – Mini had apparently told Erasmus if he wanted them to have a relationship, he would need to move on as her assistant. And he had gamely resigned and was on the hunt for another job.

'Well. I'm keeping an eye out for new opportunities and Liv and I are hoping to take a bit of a trip soon. I'm pretty much all wrapped up with Shelly – she's pivoting to serious actress mode, which is great. She had a meeting with an agent that went really well. She also spoke up for Polly this afternoon at the sentencing and it seems to have worked. Well, kind of. Shelly said the judge was annoyed about her trying to advocate for the defendant – appara it is *not* the done thing at all. But he did listen, and Polly got a four-year suspended sentence provided she complies with all the treatment they've ordered her to undergo.'

'Amazing.' Sam had caught the last bit as he came back in, grabbed a plate and began piling it with rice and curry. 'You'd think after everything she's put Shelly through, Shelly would want her punished.' He sat down beside Erasmus even though, Ali noted, it was much more of a squeeze by the wall and there was plenty of room beside her and Millie's boob buffet.

She looked down at her food sadly – bloody hormones – her recent pep suddenly drowned out once more by the reality of their situation. It wasn't all happy *Modern Family*. Liv and Ali would go off and leave her with the baby. Erasmus and Mini had their sub-dom play. Sam would get a girlfriend. And she'd be stuck here being tortured by this tiny human she made herself.

'Polly was sick. She was a victim of her disease,' Ali said, and she watched with horror as tears dropped to her plate. *Oh God, not more crying. It's just been a hard day. Ali, keep it together.*

On cue, Millie spluttered at her nipple and, when Ali sat her up – probably too quickly – she barfed all over Ali's chest.

'Oh, vom away, Millie,' Ali quipped. 'I only spend every waking *hour* producing it for you!'

Ali stood and waved off help from the others. She didn't want them to see her upset again.

'It's all cool.' She painted on a smile and hurried down to the bathroom to clean them both up. Afterwards she paced her room, jigging Millie to try to soothe her indignant shrieks but it was futile – she was into her nightly scream-a-thon now. From 8 p.m. to the early hours, it was like a wall of screaming with little to no let-up. Each day, Ali was convinced it couldn't be as bad as the night before and each evening Millie seemed determined to prove it could.

Ali'd spent many a night pacing and swaying and googling:

'Two-week-old won't stop crying …'

'Three-week-old won't stop crying …'

'Four-week-old won't stop crying …'

What was most unnerving to Ali – apart from the fact that the internet was apparently *useless* when it came to knowing how to stop a newborn crying – was the search bar offering its own suggestions like:

'Four-*month*-old won't stop crying …'

And

'Four*teen*-month-old won't stop crying …'

Christ, will there be no end? Ali felt like howling along with her baby.

❖

Evening bled into night and nothing seemed to console Millie. Mini and Erasmus had left soon after dinner and, although Liv had valiantly hovered at Ali's elbow making suggestions on how best to soothe Millie, Ali's obvious irritation eventually drove her away and she and Amy had retreated to bed.

Ali knew Liv meant well, but every time she tried to adjust Ali's winding position or suggest a different strategy, all Ali heard was how wrong she was getting it. Her only solace was that Liv was not lactating and, at least in that area, Ali wasn't a complete failure.

At 1 a.m. Sam appeared at the door and eased it closed behind him. Only then did Ali realise she still had her hair up in a towel since before dinner. *Oh well.* It was the least of it really. She was covered in breastmilk and baby vom and was pretty aware that her humongous sanitary towel reeked and needed changing. She was too wrung out to care at this point. The fucks she had left to give had long left the building by the fourth week of motherhood.

Without even a word exchanged, Sam and Ali did the baby handover and Ali waded next door to collapse for a few hours' oblivion on the bed Sam had just vacated. He always put her pillow on the bed for her before she went in. It had a *Jurassic Park* cover and smelled like her shampoo. And every time she swapped his back and buried her face in his smell. Exhausted tears leaked from her eyes and she didn't even really know why. She was just so tired. And afraid she was doing everything wrong. And tired of being afraid she was doing everything wrong.

At 4 a.m. her phone alarm buzzed, still in her hand, and she heaved herself up from what felt more like a coma than traditional sleep. She saw a WhatsApp from Sam:

Please sleep more if you can. I can give her a bottle. You need the rest. We're fine.

God love him, they did not *sound* fine. Through the wall, Ali could hear the baby's rhythmic cries, which sounded oddly like grinding machinery. Anyway, even if she could go back to sleep, her boobs wouldn't have it. Her tee shirt was soaked and her chest throbbed.

Why does no one talk about how moist motherhood is? She ducked into the bathroom to pee and caught herself feeling actual nostalgia for a time – any time! – when she was just not moist. Not even happy or warm or comfortable. Just not covered in fluids. It was such a simple longing …

She changed the sanitary pad but couldn't source a dry tee shirt. What was the point anyway? She'd just be moist again after the feed, when Millie would presumably hurl the whole thing back up on her. The fecking waste of breastmilk killed Ali more than anything.

She pushed the bedroom door open to find Sam trapped in an elaborate sway that seemed to involve some kind of full body figure-of-eight motion.

'It's sort of working.' He grinned over at her. The sky outside was beginning to lighten and Ali caught herself thinking she'd never forget him there like that, doing middle-of-the-night cardio to appease their baby.

'How do babies get us locked into these annoying rocking scenarios?' Ali mused as she settled herself on the bed and accepted the proffered Millie, who clamped immediately to her left boob.

'They're conniving,' Sam replied plainly, sitting on the bed.

Ali snorted. 'Yep.'

It was the end of his shift. Usually he went back to his house at this point. He was staring at Millie gorging away.

'Does it feel crazy?'

'No.' Ali thought for a minute. 'Or not the way you think it would. It feels like relief – a bit like a sneeze.'

'It's so mad that you made her and now you feed her. It's amazing.' He shook his head and Ali felt a twinge of panic that he was about to get up and leave.

'Well, it's amazing for fleeting moments,' Ali agreed. 'But she was being a total cunt all day today TBH.'

'Oh my God, I *know*. What is with that?!!?' He mugged as if they were having a bitching session about some annoying mutual in the group chat and Ali, relieved, burst out laughing.

'Like you couldn't have a better life, you little ingrate,' he jokingly admonished Millie.

'Yeah.' Ali grinned at the baby. 'Seriously, what problems could you possibly have?'

At this, Millie paused in her feed and seemed to regard them both warily. Her little knees drew up and her face scrunched, preparing to cry.

'Ah, ah, nope.' Sam leaned over her. 'None of that now. You stop being a lil dose to my ...' He trailed off. The awkward silence spoke volumes, thought Ali; they still didn't know what they were to each other.

'His baby mama,' Ali told the baby to save them both the angst.

'You're not my baby mama, Ali,' Sam said quietly. He was still very close to her.

Ali barely risked breathing in case the moment would come apart and they'd never be this close again.

Millie, of course, was only momentarily silenced by Sam's warning and now let out a piercing squall, startling Ali. She put the baby on her shoulder and began patting her.

'You're my Benson, Ali,' said Sam over the screaming, brushing her hair back from her face.

'So… does that make you Stabler in this analogy?' Ali asked. ''Cos if you are, I'm not sure it works … you know they never actually—'

'Ali, shut up, please.' Sam grinned. And then they were kissing as Millie howled indignantly between them.

Acknowledgements

To the readers: every single person who read *Filter This* and tweeted and shared and sent me such wonderful messages about Ali and Shelly. Your messages were like life support while writing *Unfiltered*, even if I did feel a little under pressure to deliver lol.

To the listeners: everyone who tunes into *The Creep Dive*, *Mother of Pod* and *The Vulture Club*, we have the best fun making these shows and it's a pleasure to entertain a brilliant hive such as yourselves!

To the ones who make it all possible: my wonderful editor Ciara Doorley, you are the best! Thank you so much for making my dream job a reality and my work infinitely better – we'll always have the Eamons! Joanna Smyth, Elaine Egan and everyone else at Hachette Books Ireland who help bring books into the world. My agent Tanera Simon at Darly Anderson for patient guidance and invaluable wisdom.

To the cheerleaders and collaborators, friends and faves, in no particular order: Cassie Delaney, Jen O'Dwyer, Liadán Hynes, Louise McSharry, Emer McLysaght. The Rogues – Aisling Keenan, Sarah Griffin, Louise Bruton, Fiona Hyde, Fionnuala Jones, Nadine Reid and Taryn deVere. Ellen Coyne, Lisa Coen, Sarah Davis-Goff, Soobie Lynch, Esther O'Moore Donoghue, Pauline Bewick, Poppy Melia, Siobhan Cleary, Joe Dowling, Brendan O'Connor, Gemma Fullam, Jane Doran, Emily Hourican, Teresa Daly, Paola Felix, Yvonne Hogan, Liz Kearney and Marian Keyes.